The Divine Unleashed
By
Allen J Johnston

Cassandra,

I would love to know what your favorite scene is. Feel free to let me know on Facebook,

Allen Johnsto

Cover art by: Amber Johnston
Editor: Ken Poff
Editor: Holly Schaffer

Acknowledgment

I am blessed to have the privilege of calling Mike Persons my friend. He is one of the good people that walk amongst us. He has been with me on this journey for many years and I am certain he will be there for quite some time to come. I cannot express my thanks enough. I would also like to say thanks to Branden, my first son, Cole, my second and Blake, my third for making life so fun. And what author would even be an author without his amazing readers. Thanks to all you who hold this book in your hands and lose yourself in my world.

CH1

Kade closes his eyes and his heart starts to pound as his memory shows him the massive hand of the giant Alluvium reaching out for them as they race off the edge of the cliff. He takes a sharp inhalation as his eyes shoot open just as the hand was closing on him. It was so close it could have gone either way, but they were safe...for now.

He glances over his shoulder in the direction of the cliff and takes a deep breath, attempting to settle his nerves and slow his racing heart. His muscles ached furiously from use. Even with his extra strength, it was a challenge to stay on the dragon as it dodged and weaved in and out of the Alluvium as they filled the fields. He knew he was going to be sore all over when they finally decided to land but better this than lying dead in the field.

"We need to go to the cave you spoke of," Doren said, startling Kade out of his own thoughts.

"Rayden, can you get us back to the spiders?" Kade asked. The dragon responded in the affirmative through the mental link. "Then take us there," the apprentice said out loud. The dragon banked gently and headed toward their next destination. The wind whistled by calmly. It was a welcome change as they glided smoothly on the back of Rayden while catching wind currents.

Kade was at war with himself. One part of him desperately wanted to bring Morg to justice while the second part wanted nothing more than to exact revenge. He was not sure which motivation was more dominant, and he was starting to care less and less about what that meant. He knew that in the end, he wanted the man to suffer horribly. Kade wanted to crush the life out of him just as the evil Chosen had tried to do to him when they were in Doren's study. He wanted to see the fear in the man's eyes as his time on this world came to a painful end. He did not care if it was wrong or right, he wanted it.

"Kade?" Darcienna asked, concern thick in her voice as she felt the muscles in his shoulders and arms bunching and relaxing over and over.

The Apprentice Chosen took a deep breath and let it out. He unclenched his fists and relaxed the muscles along his jaw. He was not aware how tense he had been until the sweet sound of Darcienna's voice broke through to bring him back from his own torment. He hated feeling this way but something in him was changing. He wanted to call on every ounce of Divine Power he could muster and crush that evil man. Right or wrong did not matter.

"Kade?" Darcienna asked again, feeling him tensing all over, once more.

The Apprentice Chosen felt as if he wanted to roll his head back and scream at the sky. He hated that he felt like this but he could not stop seeing Darcienna hanging in the air. He could almost see her dying as he recalled the way the Divine Lightning ricocheted off Morg's shield. How he recognized that Darcienna hung in the air between himself and Morg was beyond his understanding. He felt a momentary flush run through him as the realization that that situation could have easily ended with her dying because of his rage. Again, he unclenched his fist, took a deep breath and let it out while forcing his muscles to relax. Darcienna reached around him and squeezed, attempting to bring him some comfort. Kade closed his eyes and let himself melt into those loving arms as he forced himself to calm his breathing. He opened his eyes and surveyed the ground as they flowed effortlessly along. Kade could hear the concern in her voice but he did not respond.

The more he thought on their situation, the more he began to dread what was in their future. As much as he wanted to whisk her away to safety, he was certain his path to safety was first going to lead him directly into extreme danger. Kade glanced back at the overweight man riding uncomfortably behind the wing and knew that this Master Chosen was only going to be child's play for Morg. He wished desperately that Zayle was with them. He would know what to do.

Kade turned back around and shook his head as his thoughts continued on. Darcienna rubbed his arm to help sooth him. It did help calm him… slightly…but his mind could not help recalling that evil trick that almost ended with Darcienna dead at his hand. He clenched his jaw in anger and felt as if he wanted to scream again but took another deep breath and let it out.

"Kade," Darcienna said in a smooth, even tone, "when you were growing up, what did you like to do for fun?"

"For fun?" Kade asked as he turned to look at her, shocked that she would ask this out of nowhere. He shook his head and turned back around as he thought back on his childhood. After several moments of consideration, he could not help but to chuckle as one memory came to mind.

"Well, I recall finding this spider that had to be as big as my hand. It was dead so I took it into the house and decided to have some fun with it," Kade said as he let out a chuckle. He opened his mouth to continue and let out another laugh as the memory sharpened in his mind. Darcienna smiled to herself as she listened eagerly. "I tied a black thread to it and put it across the room where my mother sat in her favorite chair. Then, I slowly pulled it across the room." Kade let out another chuckle.

"That is mean," Darcienna said but she smirked and did her best to keep from laughing. "So, what did your mother do?" she asked, genuinely being drawn into the story.

"She screamed," Kade said as he chuckled at the memory once more. "Father jumped up from his chair and tried to swat it with something, but of course, that only caused it to jump, which caused him to scream. Seeing my dad scream was almost better than seeing my mother's reaction," Kade said as he turned to look Darcienna in the eye. She could not help but to give a little chuckle as she covered her mouth in an attempt to stifle her laugh. How could she chastise him if she laughed at the story? Kade grinned childishly as he smiled at her attempt to hide her mirth. Darcienna dropped her hand and grinned while shaking her head in a way that said, "There is something wrong with you," but the smile never left her eyes. Kade could not help but to give her a laugh at that. It reminded him of the times he and Darcienna played their games. He recalled the lake and grinned even more.

Darcienna smiled to herself as she felt the tension in his muscles slowly melt away. Yes, he needed her more than he realized, more than he would ever know. He was a man. How could he ever know what was best for himself?

Kade turned around as his mind pictured the first time he looked into those beautiful, blue eyes. He took a deep breath right then just as he had done the first time he saw her. He smiled at the memory and flitted to the next memory of her holding his clothes playfully at the edge of the hot spring. Next, he visualized her lying

4

next to him in their make-shift bed in the spider's home. He closed his eyes as he recalled how sweet and innocent she looked. He turned around to look at her again to compare the memory of her sleeping self with her waking self. Kade did not realize that his mood had shifted dramatically. The world did not seem that ugly a place anymore.

"What?" she asked suspiciously as she saw his mind working.

"I was just thinking," Kade said as he faced forward once more. "Just recalling something," was all he would say. Darcienna narrowed her eyes as she studied the back of his head, suspicious and curious all at the same time. Kade let it go at that and truly felt that the world could be a wonderful place. With Darcienna's arms wrapped around his waist, how could it not be? He let his left hand settle on her arm as he gripped Rayden's ridges with his other.

Kade recalled the momentary fall off the cliff and his hands instinctually gripped a little tighter. He glanced back, checking to see if he could still see the cliff, but it was far behind. Kade felt the muscles in his back and shoulder unwind as he leaned back into Darcienna's embrace just a little more.

All the riders fell into their own thoughts. Each one appreciated the opportunity to relax and recover. Kade felt his heart slowly return to normal. He looked down at the ground and appreciated the peacefulness of it. The only sounds he heard were that of Rayden's occasional grunt as he pumped his wings and the wind as it whistled by. Kade closed his eyes and breathed deep for several long moments as his mind continued to slow. Fatigue started to weigh on him as he felt his body relax more and more. Darcienna leaned forward and whispered into his ear. He quickly spun and locked accusing eyes with Doren. Kade reached back and untied the books from the dragon's wings. Without an ounce of respect an apprentice would show a master, he roughly yanked the sack from Doren's grasp. Master Chosen or not, this was one line that was not to be crossed. Doren shrugged easily and looked away.

It was what they did. They coveted knowledge any way they could.

Kade did not want to think what would have happened if Doren had actually slipped his hand into the sack and caused one of the books to open slightly. He shivered as he thought about the demon on the cover in the circle. *Would it stop with Doren or would it have continued until we were all dead?* Kade wondered. His grip on the sack tightened at the thought. One thing was certain; he never wanted to find out.

Kade tied the rope around his waist and let the sack hang off his side. It was uncomfortable and caused him to shift more to the other side to compensate for the weight, but it was better than leaving it for Doren to rifle through. Kade turned his attention to his winged friend as the dragon carried them away to safety.

"You did well, Rayden. You saved us," Kade said as he patted the dragon affectionately on the shoulder, shoving the thought of the books right out of his head. Kade sensed the dragon's weary response through the link. Rayden was exhausted, but he still basked in the praise. For a moment, Kade wondered if the dragon could become so tired that his wings would just fold up, but then in the next instant, he was certain that the dragon would know to land. *It's not every day that a dragon falls from the sky. For that matter,"* Kade pondered as he chuckled, *" it's not any day that a dragon falls from the sky,* he thought to himself in amusement.

Kade closed his eyes, and the image of Zayle floated before him. He shuddered as he thought about the cave. He almost flinched, surprised that this is where his mind was going. Taking a deep breath, he steeled himself for what was to come. He kept his eyes closed as he relaxed, leaning back into Darcienna's embrace once more. Peace enveloped him in those arms and he welcomed it eagerly. The image of Zayle faded to be replaced by Darcienna. A slight smile worked at the edges of his mouth as his mind imagined being with her in other ways. He sank into those visions and let them take him away. It was not long before he was breathing

6

deeply. The only thing keeping him from plummeting to his death was the woman behind him, who would be there for him, even when he did not realize it.

Kade jerked awake as he felt himself slipping off the dragon. Every muscle went rock hard as he gasped and felt a hot flash race through is body at the thought of almost falling to his death. He looked down and saw patches of ground slide by between the clouds. His stomach lurched at the thought of that long fall. He shook his head to wake himself.

"You okay?" Darcienna asked, still gripping him tightly.

"Just finding it difficult to stay awake," Kade said as he rubbed his eyes. Darcienna's musical voice drifted to him in the form of her sweet laugh. "What?" he asked as he looked over his shoulder at her.

"You have been asleep for quite some time," Darcienna said with a smile. Kade shivered as he looked down once more. It was a long fall. His stomach clenched at the thought. He reached down and put his hand on her arm, certain she was the only reason he had not already hit the ground. The security of that embrace was calming.

"Thanks," Kade said as he squeezed her arm.

"Someone has to keep you safe," Darcienna teased. Kade laughed, but one glance down kept the laugh short.

He tilted his head to the side and then shielded his eyes with his hand to block out the sun. He peered hard ahead and then nodded. He was thinking of the bed in the spider's tree and felt himself craving more sleep. His back was cramping and his bottom was so sore he was sure he had bruises from his waist to his knees.

"Kade, we need to find a place to rest and find nourishment," Doren said.

"I'm sure we are close," Kade called back. He could hear the discomfort in the master's voice, also. Yes, they were going to have to find a place to stop.

Just as Kade was considering where he wanted to land, the

dragon started a gradual descent. Kade could see the mountain rising well above the clouds as they closed in on it and smiled to himself in relief. He peered hard at the ground, trying to make out the tunnel. Still too far away, he sat back and scanned the area for danger. Nothing moved. The closer he got to the ground, the more he tensed, dreading what he knew he must do.

Maybe I can show Doren to the arch and be done with all this, Kade thought, trying to convince himself that his involvement was going to be minimal. He pressed his lips tightly together as the feeling in his gut said otherwise. Well, until he learned otherwise, he was going to plan for a short stay and then return to his parents' place for some much deserved rest.

The dragon was soon gliding toward the ground, and Kade could feel waves of exhaustion coming off his winged friend. For a moment, he was afraid the dragon might just hit the ground and crash to a stop…if he was able to make it that far. Darcienna stretched, as the ground came up at them. The dragon leaned back and flapped hard several times as it touched down, trying to be gentle. Its wings fell to the ground and it collapsed, breathing heavily. Doren lurched sideways and barely hung onto the dragon's wing-joints. Kade and Darcienna surged forward as their momentum almost pitched them over the dragon's head. Kade pushed back and both he and the beautiful, blue-eyed rider righted themselves.

Kade tried to swing his leg over the dragon's neck, but his muscles protested painfully. He gritted his teeth, and on the next attempt, swung his leg hard. He flipped over onto his stomach and slid down. He landed, and after almost falling, stumbled around while pounding on his legs to get the circulation back in them. Doren gracefully worked his way down the tail of the dragon and stopped, surveying the area. Kade saw what looked like suspicion in the master's eye, but after glancing around himself, he dismissed any concerns. Darcienna leaned forward and swung her leg behind herself, then turned and slid down into Kade's waiting arms. She arched her back, stretching and rubbed her back side.

Darcienna stopped and slowly turned while scanning the area. Kade watched her, and as she completed the circle, coming around to face him, her eyes were glowing softly. He tried to muster the energy to care and almost failed. He took a deep breath and let it out, feeling his mind become a little more alert. He could swear that her eyes were permanently glowing anymore. With a sigh, he warned the dragon of the possibility of danger. The dragon drew in its wings, scraping them along the ground instead of curling them in and wearily lumbered to its feet. It sniffed the air several times. Kade could feel confusion through the link. It definitely smelled something, but it was a familiar scent that was not associated with danger.

Kade walked around the dragon, watching the cave closely. Nothing moved. He turned and scanned the trees carefully. Something about them was not quite right. Kade squinted and tried to focus, but the sun was making it hard to see.

"Kade," Darcienna said slowly. "It's too quiet, and something is definitely wrong."

It was as if Darcienna's words caused the area to explode in a frenzy of activity. Spiders dropped from the trees and charged out from everywhere. There were hundreds. They poured out of the cave in droves. Kade spun through the moves for the Fire Calling and had it held high, ready to let fly when it occurred to him that it was spiders he was seeing. They rushed him and he welcomed them as the fire evaporated.

"Kade," Darcienna said, but he did not look at her as the spiders came at them. Had he spared her so much as a glance, he would have seen that her eyes were glowing and getting brighter by the moment.

"I see," Kade said as he stepped up to greet his allies.

"Kade?" Doren asked in a firm, critical voice.

"They are our friends," Kade said as the spiders closed in on them.

9

"Kade!" Darcienna yelled as the first of the spiders reached them, her hands raised in indecision. Her eyes flared brightly.

Kade's belief that he was being greeted by allies quickly turned into shock and disbelief as he was violently driven to the ground. He struggled to catch his breath, the wind being knocked out of him. The dragon leapt to its feet and roared in confusion. It backed up a step as it readied itself to launch into the attackers that were holding Kade pinned to the ground. Doren had a sparking energy dancing between his fingers and was on the verge of attacking.

"No! Do not hurt the spiders. There has to be a reason for this. Doren, don't!" Kade yelled while making eye contact with the Master Chosen. Doren clenched his jaw and let the spark flash out of existence. The spiders quickly overwhelmed the Master Chosen and drove him to the ground.

"Apprentice, you had better be right," Doren hissed, seething. Kade rankled at the way Doren used the title but that was the least of his concerns at the moment.

Rayden was swinging his head back and forth, roaring over the buzz. As weary as he was, the dragon was not too weary to come to Kade's aid. Rayden was readying himself for full-fledged battle. He inhaled deeply, ready to burn them to dust. Allies or not, anything that attacked his Chosen was not going to live long.

"Rayden, stand down!" Kade yelled. "Rayden, do not hurt them!"

The dragon puffed up and let loose with a roar that shook the ground as it threw its head forward, bellowing its rage. Kade's ears rang but the spiders still held. They were no longer attempting to attack the dragon, but they were not backing off, either. Rayden charged the spiders that had Kade pinned.

"NO!" Kade yelled. The dragon threw his head wildly, fighting the urge to rend the attackers. Kade could feel the link explode with the dragon's desire to tear these creatures to pieces.

Darcienna turned to rush to Kade's aid, her hands extended,

ready to call up her shield, but with the spiders holding Kade, it would only trap him in with his attacker. Unfortunately, as she ran, she did not see the spider charging off her right side. Kade was certain it was not planning on just restraining her, but instead, was coming in for the kill. Its fangs were extended as it scurried forward, focused on its victim. Kade struggled as he flexed his muscles, trying to gain leverage. Regretfully, he knew he was going to have to hurt the spiders as they were not going to let him up willingly. Kade gritted his teeth, ready to use his extra strength to do what it took to save the woman racing to save him.

Just as he was readying his muscled to go into action, he saw a flash of black that charged in and collided with the spider violently. The black mass had thick, plush fur that flowed in the wind. It was larger than the attacking spider by almost twice. The two spiders rolled end over end with the larger, black spider pinning the smaller one roughly. The black spider hissed violently at the one on the bottom, buzzing several quick, strong words as it pressed down, making it clear who was in charge. The pinned spider went limp and slowly turned its head to look at the Apprentice Chosen. Kade smiled as Crayken got up and spun toward the spiders that still held his arms. With the full command of a king filled with rage, Crayken marched at them. They shrank at his presence as he stalked up to them and glared hard. He buzzed angrily and they fell away as if struck. Kade was still very confused as to what was going on, but he very much enjoyed seeing the king show them who was in charge and who it was that they had just attacked.

"Kade," Darcienna said, moving next to him. "Why would they attack us? Did they forget us that quickly?"

"I am not certain, but I am betting there is a good explanation for all this, and we are going to get that very soon, I am sure," Kade said as he spared a glance at Doren. The Master Chosen stared in awe as Kade stood tall and proud.

The regal, black spider presented an impressive image as he stalked toward the herd of spiders surrounding them. Kade could feel the fury coming off the king as he marched back and forth buzzing angrily. As if choreographed, all the spiders flinched and then turned to stare at Kade. The king stood silently, letting his words sink in. They started dropping to their knees and put their heads against the dirt.

"What was that all about?" Darcienna asked as she stalked up to the king. "I thought you were our friends, but as soon as we come back, the clutch attacks us?" She started to get worked up. The king tried to speak but Darcienna was exhausted, sore and too angry to think calmly.

"Darcienna," Kade said as he put a calming hand on her arm. "Let the king speak. I am sure there is a good reason," Kade said confidently as he turned toward Crayken, eager to hear the explanation.

"There is," a familiar voice said as the most majestic, beautiful white spider flowed out of the crowd. "These spiders are from another clutch and did not recognize you. They were protecting the cave from intruders for you. We did not expect you back so soon," she said as she glided up to stand directly in front of him.

"We did not expect to be back so soon, either," Kade responded as he breathed a sigh of relief. He smiled and stepped forward while placing his hand on her shoulder. She returned the gesture. Several spiders gave out what could only be called a gasp. Kade ignored the reactions as he continued with the conversation. "We ran into Morg," Kade said and then seemed to remember Doren. "Forgive my manners," Kade said as he turned toward the Master Chosen. "This is the Master Chosen, Doren. Master Doren, meet the king, Crayken, and the queen, Rakna."

"I have heard many good things about you," Doren said, matching their poise with his own.

"It is our honor to have another Chosen with us," Rakna said with a slight inclination of her head.

"The honor is mine," Doren said with a slight bow as he

12

cocked an eyebrow at Kade. He inclined his head to the queen and backed away to turn and stand next to Kade. "Chosen?" Kade let the question go without answer. Technically, he was an Apprentice Chosen. For one to have the title of Chosen, they had to hold the rank of Adept or Master. Doren sighed. Kade knew he was going to hear about this later.

Kade could see an obvious problem brewing. He was not certain he was going to be able to show the Master Chosen the respect he demanded if his condescending tone continued. He was not very confident that things were going to go as smoothly as he hoped. He mentally sighed and refocused on the royal couple.

The queen turned to approach the king when one of the spiders buzzed quietly. Rakna froze, as did Crayken. They looked at each other and then back to Kade. Based on the royal couple's reaction, he was certain that the words were not kind. The queen's anger flared as her composure slipped slightly. She turned on the spider and buzzed firmly.

"If he chose to, he could have destroyed you in the blink of an eye!" the white spider said firmly in her language. The queen buzzed several more times as Kade stepped up to stand next to her. Rakna paused to glance at him.

"I would like to speak to the spider, if that comment was directed at me," Kade said as he turned his gaze on the offender. Rakna hesitated. "Would Crayken have you speak for him?" Kade asked while lifting his chin slightly. "If the spiders are to respect me, then I must give them a reason to." Rakna glanced at the king. He nodded one time but did not take his eyes off the spider.

"As you wish," Rakna hissed.

"Please translate for me," Kade said as his eyes locked on the new spider.

"I shall," Rakna said as she turned to face the spider, fury rippling through her.

"What was said?" Kade asked, leveling his gaze at the offender.

13

"He said he finds it hard to accept that you are the one who conquered the leader of the Morphites. He says they were able to overcome you without much effort," Crayken said.

Kade nodded his head slightly as he considered the situation. He took a breath and tilted his head back in confidence. He looked over the crowd slowly, making sure he had all the spiders' attention. Everyone was locked onto him. No one moved. The shuffling died down and hundreds of spiders watched closely, for what, they did not know, but there was an intensity in the air as all waited.

"Kade, what is going on?" Darcienna asked in frustration.

"The spider doubts our abilities. He does not believe we killed the black leader. I am going to...show him that we do, indeed, have the power to accomplish such a feat," Kade said as he smiled mischievously. He felt the swirl of power start to fill him. The block slid away and his head spun from the Divine that raced through him, eager to be let loose. Kade had to focus as the Divine threatened to overwhelm him but it only took a moment and his thoughts were his once again. He smiled as the raging torrent of power was now at his command. *So they doubt me?* Kade thought as his breathing deepened and his pulse quickened.

Doren's eyes widened as he could easily sense the Divine crashing through the Apprentice Chosen. He studied the young man, waiting. A hunger grew in him as he watched Kade fill with power.

"I hope you know what you are doing," Darcienna said, but there was a glint in her eye.

"Trust me. They will not soon forget us," Kade said with a snarl.

The queen followed Kade as he walked over to stand directly in front of the spider. He looked down at his victim and tried to imagine how the king would deal with this. It did not take long for Kade to know how he wanted to make his point.

"So, you question my abilities?" Kade asked dangerously. Even had Rakna not translated, he was certain the spider would

14

have caught his tone.

"We saw nothing for us to respect. We took you easily," the spider said, fidgeting slightly.

"Then you would have preferred me to do this," Kade said as his arms became a flurry of motions.

The Lightning Calling exploded from his hand, racing over the ground, leaving a blackened trail to crash loudly into a nearby tree. The explosion shook the ground and the spider screamed in terror. The tree splintered, sending limbs, leaves and twigs high into the air to shower down around the spiders. The tree fell with a crash. Kade quickly spun into the moves for the Divine Fire Calling, creating as large a fire as possible and unleashed it on the fallen tree. It was engulfed in a blue flame that reached high into the air. Kade caught a look from Doren and was certain it was approval, but it was also something else. Hunger? The look was gone instantly. The spiders wailed in horror. The spider facing Kade cringed in horror and started to back away.

"And do not forget the dragon," Kade said as he indicated Rayden. The dragon caught the mental request from Kade and roared loud enough to be heard for miles. It took another deep breath and then while sweeping its head back and forth, marched forward, bellowing its rage at the spiders. They shook in sheer terror. Rayden inhaled deeply and then in a dramatic show, unleashed his dragon's breath on the tree. The heat had the spiders retreating to a safe distance, or it may have been the fear that almost had them running for their lives. The tree would be nothing but a pile of ash when it was done burning. Rayden stalked around the clutch of spiders as if he were hunting prey. His muscles were flexing as he slunk like a stealthy cat circling a helpless victim. He moved smoothly over the ground in a half crouch as he flanked the spiders, his head swinging back and forth as if trying to decide which one should be his next target.

Kade stalked the offending spider, matching its pace, keeping just inches between it and himself. "He could have killed half of you without effort. All I needed do was give him permission," Kade said and then he paused, waiting for the full effect to hit them. "Do you really believe that I could not defend myself," he said as he turned to look to the side as if the spider directly in front of him was of no consequence, "or do you understand that it is more accurate to say that...I showed you mercy?" he finished as he slowly turned back to glare dangerously deep into the spider's eyes.

Kade knew, after watching the queen when they first met, that this was their way. If he wanted their respect, he knew he had to demand it along with earn it. He stared daggers at the spider. It started to wail.

"Understand that I will not tolerate this ever again," Kade growled, imagining that this was exactly what the queen had said to the spider she had pinned during their first meeting.

"Chosen, please forgive me," Rakna translated. The spider wailed and Kade knew it wanted to be anywhere but under his glare. "I meant no disrespect," the spider babbled quickly as it proffered itself before Kade and begged for forgiveness. Rakna looked at Kade for a response.

"I am certain he will not make this mistake again," Kade said. He looked at the spider queen and gave one slight nod.

Kade, again, thought back on how Rakna had addressed the spiders when they had first met and followed suit once more. He slowly stood and stalked among the clutch with the queen in tow. Any spider that appeared to challenge Kade got a glare that sent it to its knees.

"I am Kade, second in line after Crayken," Kade bellowed, making eye contact with each spider, challenging any to speak out. "You will show me the respect due as second in line and as the vanquisher of the black leader," he finished, moving to stand next to the royal couple.

"Your words are wise, Kade." Crayken said. Kade could sense appreciation in the king's tone.

"Are you sure you are not royalty born?" the queen asked.

"I'll take that as a compliment," Kade said as he felt the weariness creeping in on him once more. "We must talk. I have news that I must share with you," Kade said to the royal couple.

"Let us return to the great hall. We shall feed and then we can talk," Crayken said.

"And maybe some rest," Kade added.

"That was incredible," Darcienna said as she wrapped her hands around his arm while they walked.

"When you said they treated you like a king, I did not know you meant they treated you *as* a king," Doren said, impressed. Before they could take even one step, the Master Chosen continued to speak. It was clearly a tone that indicated that the Apprentice Chosen was to give the Master Chosen his full attention. "Kade," Doren said, as he moved to stand face to face with the Apprentice Chosen with all the confidence of a master taking charge. "I would prefer if we were to see this doorway," he said as he cast a glance around.

Kade's eyes turned toward the cave. Doren saw where Kade's eyes had gone and he quickly cast his eyes in that direction, too. Kade felt weary beyond words but he was not going to be able to disengage himself from this tangled mess of danger until the Chosen was shown to the infamous doorway to the dead. Kade looked at Darcienna who waved an agitated hand in the air as if to say, "Whatever."

The king and queen both watched Kade for his decision. Doren was becoming increasingly irritated at the delay. When he realized that his decree was not followed immediately but was still waiting for the approval of the Apprentice Chosen, he started to lose his patience. His eyes went from the king to the queen and then slid to Kade, who was watching him. Kade quickly spared a glance for the king and queen. If he did not do something quickly, Doren's anger would soon turn into rage. A Master Chosen was not used to being put off.

"The Master Doren needs to see the arch," Kade said as he avoided catching Doren's eye. He was not sure how he should handle the displeasure he knew was still there. Kade could feel the pompous man's eyes boring into him. He felt his own irritation start to rise when Darcienna wrapped her hands around his arm and gently lead him toward the tunnel.

"This way," Darcienna said sweetly over her shoulder.

"I shall come along, also," Crayken added ominously. Kade spared a glance for the king but Crayken did not add anymore so Kade let it go.

Kade gave Crayken a smile and a nod of his head and then continued toward the cave. He shuddered as the memories of his last visit to the arch sprang into his mind as if he were here just minutes before. The smell of old, leather books came to him as if he were sitting in his master's den. He felt the swirl of emotions begin to build. He closed his eyes and the face in the dark formed once again. He could not help but feel for the presence of his master.

Would Zayle attempt to contact me again? Kade asked himself. He forced his emotions to calm as he entered the cave. He glanced over to see the Master Chosen studying him closely. Most people would look away or make a gesture to smooth over the awkwardness of the moment but not Doren. He would look away when he was ready and he was not about to apologize for any odd behavior. He was the master. He was the one that was to be deferred to…or so he believed. Kade ground his teeth together in agitation as he attempted to control his ire.

"Kade," Darcienna said, mirroring his own irritation but attempting to disarm the explosion that was just on the horizon, "we will be needing some light."

She was quickly coming to the conclusion that she cared very little for this arrogant, rotund man. He may be a Master Chosen, but he was not *her* master. She glanced at Kade and knew she had to keep her own temper under control for his sake. She may not be subject to Doren's whims but she was unsure how much Kade would be. She took in a deep breath and let it out in a sigh. Kade gave her a questioning look but she waved away his concern. Nothing she said was going to make any of this any better. As a matter of fact, she was sure it would only fuel Kade's anger to know that she was feeling the same way.

"You are correct," Kade said as he disengaged her hands from his arm. He felt a momentary regret at the absence of those soft, gentle hands as they slipped from his arm. Without a thought, he started to perform the Fire Calling and then stopped. No need for protection. It was obvious that there was no danger. The spiders had control of the cave and Kade doubted that anything was coming through the gate so he decided on the simple Illumination Calling. He grinned slightly to himself as he raised his hands, as if to light the way for Doren, and called on light…maybe a little too much light. Darcienna had her hands wrapped around his arm once again but this time she was squeezing in disapproval. Kade gave her what was supposed to be an innocent look but she only glared back until the light lessened. The Apprentice Chosen glanced at Doren and found the Master Chosen studying the light with his eyes narrowed as his mind worked.

He is trying to figure out what I did to call on the light, Kade thought in surprise. Doren had his left hand hanging at his side as he focused on the light coming from the apprentice. His fingers formed the shape of a bowl just like Kade's. *Is he actually going to attempt to make light?* Kade asked himself incredulously. He watched Doren, his curiosity growing as he waited. Kade felt Doren draw in the Divine as he studied the apprentice's hand. Kade focused to make sure he gave nothing away. The Master Chosen should have clearly known that it was not okay to attempt to learn a calling without being taught. But, the simple calling was too tempting for the man to pass on trying. There was one small exception that all Chosen allowed when trying to learn a calling without a book or being taught. It was called, The Taking in Plain

19

Sight. Kade waited, almost eager to see the Master Chosen attempt the calling without learning it the proper way. Doren half raised his hand as he studied the light. Kade forgot everything else in the world as he focused on Doren.

This was important because even a simple calling could cause issue for those around the caster. But, Kade knew that Doren was trying to cast this calling without performing any moves at all. This should make it virtually harmless. At least, that was what Kade was hoping. A type of thrill went through him as he waited. It was something the Chosen did. When one Chosen thought he had learned the secret of another without being taught…well…it was like a type of game. It was a game that all Chosen desperately wanted to win. If a Chosen could learn a calling without being taught, it was like winning that game. It was rare but it did happen once in a great while, and of course, it was with the simplest of callings that were attempted. No matter how small the new skill that was procured, it was still one more calling than was known before. Both men knew the game and the challenge was on. Kade could not help but to grin as Doren focused hard and raised his hand. The Apprentice Chosen thought he was going to see sweat start to appear on the man's forehead with how intent he was. The Master Chosen was determined, as all Chosen were when taking this challenge.

Give it your best, Kade thought in amusement. *Trying to learn without a book or being taught is almost impossible.*

Doren filled himself with the Divine and looked at his hand, waiting for light to shoot forth. His fingers formed the shape of a bowl, but still, nothing. He even flexed his fingers as if turning them into claws, and yet, darkness. He even jabbed his hand out as if to shake the light from his palm. Still, nothing. Doren returned his gaze to Kade's outstretched hand and studied it hard. His eyes lost focus as he tried to recall anything he was missing. Kade waited, excitement flowing through him.

"Kade…," Darcienna started to say but he quickly shushed

her without taking his eyes of Doren. She folded her arms in frustration but did not say another word. She could see something was happening, even if she could not understand what. The royal couple waited, knowing that this had to be something important. For the two Chosen, it was.

A simple calling such as this was still beyond the reach of even a master if the Chosen did not know the moves involved...even if they appeared simple, as this one was. No Chosen, Master or Apprentice, ever tried to emulate a calling without being taught or learning it from a book, except with the Taking in Plain Sight. It was normally just too dangerous to try to replicate. One wrong hand gesture and everything could go horribly wrong. Even a simple calling like this could cause something undesirable like making your hair fall out. Generally, the fewer the moves, the less dangerous the consequences, but still, who would want to go through life with no hair on their body?

After just a moment, Doren took a deep breath and let it out, completely giving up. He shrugged his shoulders, and with that, it was over. As much as he wanted to know how this was done, he knew that Chosen did not share callings on a whim...even an Apprentice Chosen. It was just the way of things.

Kade let slip a slight grin as he caught the look in Darcienna's eyes. He held his hand closer to her to make his point... the point that this was the prize. He let the light disappear and dropped his hand. Darcienna was none the wiser with his explanation. Doren turned to watch and Kade knew the man was watching him like a hawk once again. It might be a simple calling, but if Doren's only ability to create light was from the sparks dancing on his fingers, a calling like this could be invaluable. *Every calling was critical, even the simple ones*, Kade thought to himself. His eyes came open wide at his own thoughts. He recalled there was a time when he dismissed simple callings as if they were worthless, but now, he felt himself starting to covet even ones such as this. He wished he would have been wise enough to understand

21

what his teacher was always trying to get him to realize. But, every time Zayle tried, Kade just would not hear or internalize what the Master Chosen was trying to get his apprentice to learn.

Kade let his hands fall to his side as he turned slightly away from the Master Chosen as if not paying attention. But, Kade was quickly becoming very versed in this game. The way he positioned his body was no mistake. His right hand hung just barely out of Doren's view so his fingers could not be seen.

"Apprentice, we should be moving on," Doren said. He finished and was almost not breathing as he watched closely.

Kade feigned indifference and brought up his hand and the light shone forth. Doren's eyes came open and then his face scrunched up in anger. His lips pressed together tightly as he studied the outstretched hand. He could see nothing new that he did not see the first time. He locked eyes with Kade and anger flared for just a moment and then faded.

What he was not seeing was that Kade had his fingers together as if to pinch something and the only move was spreading them apart into the shape of a bowl. To Doren, there appeared to be no move at all because it seemed to be a natural motion of raising the arm, and Kade knew this. Zayle had played this very game with Kade while teaching him how Chosen attempt to take callings from each other. It was absolutely the only time it was sanctioned for a Chosen to take a calling from another Chosen without permission. Zayle had used this very calling as a way of demonstrating that even the trained eye can miss the obvious. But, to be fair, Doren could not see that Kade had drawn his finger apart while they were barely hidden by his leg. If there was one Chosen that might spot the move needed for this calling, Doren would be it, but even in the open, Kade was betting that the man would have missed the move.

The king and queen waited patiently for Kade to lead them down the tunnel. It was not lost on them that there was something going on between the Master Chosen and the Apprentice Chosen. They did not live a life at the head of a society without seeing the subtle indications of trouble between positions of power and there was clearly plenty of power to be had between the two men leading them.

Doren, again, shrugged his shoulder in resignation and turned, waiting for Kade to lead the way. Darcienna put a hand on Kade's arm and caught his eye as she turned her head slightly as if to ask, "What was that." Kade grinned and mouthed, "I will explain later," as he started walking. She eyed him wearily but he mouthed again, "Later." She reluctantly gave up, even though her curiosity was fueled into a blaze. The ways of the Chosen intrigued her and something important had just happened. She would not forget to ask, even though she was sure he would forget to explain.

Kade headed for the tunnel and held his hand up for the light to lead the way. Darcienna stayed close at his side while Doren eagerly searched the darkness for the famed doorway to the dead. It did not surprise Kade that Doren so quickly dismissed the loss of their contest. With the doorway to the dead just within reach, he was surprised Doren had even considered wasting time trying to take a calling. Kade glanced over and saw that look in the man's eyes…that look of hunger. Kade started to get an uncomfortable feeling in his gut as he watched the Master Chosen. The words of warning from his master came back to him and he reminded himself to be cautious of all Chosen once more.

"How far?" Doren asked as his eyes peered hard into the darkness. He did not even spare a glance for Kade as he waited for the answer.

"It is just a little ways yet but we must go slowly. You would not want to walk into that thing," Kade said as he recalled the black wisp that had shot out at the queen.

"I shall be safe enough," the arrogant Chosen responded. For just a fraction of a moment, Kade envisioned himself giving Doren a little push when they arrived at the arch and then instantly was shocked at his own thoughts. He shook his head and reminded himself that Doren was one of the good guys and his thoughts were…wrong.

"Of course," Kade said.

"I am sensing something very powerful. The arch must be close?" Doren asked.

"Yes," Rakna said.

Kade and Darcienna looked at each other with questioning glances. Kade shrugged his shoulders to indicate he was just as confused as she was and then turned to Doren for an explanation. The Master Chosen noticed the look and explained.

"It is my gift from the Divine," Doren said simply. "Not as impressive as others, but it has come in handy at times."

"What exactly is your gift?" Darcienna asked.

"Anytime there is power in use, I can sense it. It does not matter if it is Nature's Gift," Doren said as he indicated Darcienna, "or the Divine Power," he said simply. Doren noticed the disappointed look on Kade's face and smiled. "Try to sneak up on me with that Transparency Calling," he said as he lifted his chin slightly. Understanding hit Kade and he nodded once in understanding. No gift should be dismissed as useless, he realized.

Doren turned back to look down the tunnel and continued talking. "I don't know what powers this gateway, but I can tell you it is incredibly strong. I have never felt such power in all my years," Doren said as he held out a hand in front of himself.

The group walked quietly down the well lit tunnel. The king and queen glided along silently. Kade even looked back a time or two just to make sure the royal couple was still with them. He could tell that Crayken was on edge as they descended deeper into the tunnel. He made a mental note to ask what had the king so concerned.

The air became thick with an earthy smell. Kade recalled how it made him feel the first time he was here. It reminded him of the presence that kept trying to make contact with him. His mind, again, felt for the invader but there was nothing. *Wait,* he thought to himself. *Zayle is not an invader,* he corrected himself, feeling as if

24

he were dishonoring his mentor. Even though he was specifically talking about the entity that had tried to take him over, he still felt he should clarify what he meant, even though it was just in his own mind. *No, you were not an invader,* Kade thought as though Zayle may be able to sense his mind and make contact again. But still, there was nothing.

Kade was in his own mind as they walked when, suddenly, Darcienna pulled him to a stop. His eyes focused on the darkness that was not more than two strides in front of him. He reminded himself to pay closer attention as he was certain he would have walked right through the arch to his demise. With a tight lipped smile, he turned and thanked Darcienna with a nod of his head. Doren, on the other hand, had not been daydreaming. He was inspecting the darkness like a child inspects a wrapped present. Kade was not sure if he liked sharing this with the Master Chosen, but he really had no choice. At least, that is what he told himself now that he had lead Doren here.

"This is it," the Master Chosen said, unable to hide his excitement. "This is it."

Kade stood back as he watched the Master Chosen study the arch. He waited. Maybe, just maybe, Doren could reveal something that he would find useful. He had his doubts but he could still hope.

Doren's eyes broke from the arch and quickly started scanning the walls. It was not long before he found what he was looking for. Kade turned to see the drawings standing out as if the wall had been cleaned. He spared a glance for the king, certain that it was the spiders that had cleared away the dirt. Crayken still appeared to be…tense was the best way Kade thought to put it. He considered questioning the king when Doren ordered him over to the side of the tunnel where the images were. Kade quickly complied and something in him despised how he scampered to the Master Chosen's command without hesitation.

"This is what you were talking about?" Doren asked, but it

sounded more like a comment.

"It is," Kade said as he studied the drawing.

Doren ran his fingers along the image of the man floating through the air. He studied each and every mark on the wall until his mind had absorbed every little detail. It was clear to Kade that the Master Chosen was not going to be denied any knowledge that he may gain from what this tunnel had to offer. It even became clearer when Doren quickly marched toward the doorway to the dead. Kade gasped as it appeared that Doren might actually march right through the arch into the darkness. The Apprentice Chosen was absolutely certain beyond a shadow of a doubt that Doren was on the verge of charging off to his death. However, just as he got close to the doorway, he shocked Kade with what he did next.

"Keep watch over me," Doren commanded as he quickly dropped to the ground and prepared his calling.

"Master?" Kade asked, concern thick in his voice. "What are you planning?"

"Just keep watch over my body," Doren commanded firmly, irritation showing due to being delayed and closed his eyes.

"You know the Drift Calling?" Kade asked, still unsure about this plan. It was rash at best. Even he, an Apprentice Chosen, could see that.

"There are some callings that almost all of us Chosen know. Now, stop babbling and let me focus," Doren barked and that was that.

Kade got a sick feeling in his stomach as he felt the Divine growing in the old man. He watched for any sign that the Master Chosen was leaving his body, but of course, there was none. There never was. Even when Zayle used to demonstrate, the Apprentice Chosen would try to catch some glimpse of a haze or silhouette but nothing was ever discernable. Kade scanned the few members of their party that were watching intently. He was about to look back at Doren when the king drew his attention. Crayken was highly agitated as he watched Doren closely. It was almost as if the king were flexing, ready for battle. Kade could not contain himself any longer.

"Crayken?" Kade asked as he tried to draw the king's attention, but the majestic, black spider was too focused on the man lying on the floor. "Crayken?" Kade asked again, a knot building in his stomach. The queen mirrored the kings stance as they both focused on the body. Kade turned as if to consult Darcienna and saw her eyes steadily glowing more and more by the moment. It was as if the danger was slowly creeping toward them. Kade's frustration grew. He could not shake the feeling that he was an outsider, not privy to what was going on. He wished he would have questioned the king before now, but there was no getting his attention. Something was wrong and Darcienna's eyes were the proof.

Kade readied himself for this unseen danger that stalked them. He cast a quick glance at Darcienna, and before he could ask what the danger was, she spun to face the arch. Everything was deathly quiet. Kade could feel his heart pounding like mad in his chest as he struggled to understand. The royal couple stood as if statues, and Darcienna appeared to be holding her breath. For a moment he wondered if she could hear his heart pounding on the inside of his ribcage.

Blood and ash! I wish someone would tell me what the ever lovin Divine is going on! Kade thought as the quiet hung in the air. Not a person or spider moved as they waited for the danger that everyone but him seemed aware of.

Rakna and Crayken both crouched lower to the ground as if ready to pounce. Darcienna clenched her hands into fists and then relaxed in an attempt to control the fear that threatened to consume her as her eyes began to blaze. Kade had had enough. He knew he may anger the Master Chosen but it was better than letting him lay on the ground while the danger arrived to ravage the prone body. He knelt down next to the Master Chosen and reached out to touch him on the shoulder. Just as his hand made contact, Doren's body clenched hard as though a charge had gone through it, causing every muscle to contract.

Kade shot back and stood but lost his balance and fell only to scramble back to his feet. His heart pounded so hard he could feel it hammering at his chest as if it were trying to break free. Doren arched his back hard as his fingers turned into claws that raked the ground. He drew in a deep breath until he could draw in no more air and then his eyes flew open, but there was nothing of their normal color. They were milky white. At the same moment his eyes went wide, he let out a scream that shook Kade right down to his soul. Darcienna's eyes flared and the king and queen pounced.

Rayden roared his battle cry as the link between him and Kade came to life. The Apprentice Chosen did not have the luxury of trying to explain to the dragon what was going on so he did his best to reassure his friend he was safe and then returned to trying to deal with this current dilemma. Rayden roared once more, sending an echo down the tunnel. Kade could only hope that the dragon would not get itself stuck by trying to claw its way in. He put Rayden completely out of his mind and forced himself to focus. He needed to figure this out but the enemy here was his ally. How was he to defeat this?

Kade was stunned and at a loss as of what to do. He had the Blue Flame of the Divine dancing high off his hands, but what could he do with it? Doren was the source of the danger. He could not kill the Master Chosen.

Rakna and Crayken struggled with Doren, dragging him away from the arch as they tried to work their web. Doren got his hands on one of the spider's legs and Kade heard a loud crack as the leg broke under that grasp. Kade let the flame die away as he leapt to assist but the room fell into darkness. He quickly called up the Divine Light and heard another loud crack as the king cried out. That was enough for Doren to break free and bound to his feet. He turned as an evil grin spread across his face and then raced for the exit. He did not get more than two steps before the king and queen were on him again. Doren was once again reaching for any leg he could get his hands on but this time Kade sprang into action. Just as the Master Chosen was reaching for one of the queen's hind legs, Kade grabbed him by the wrist and twisted, not caring if he broke bones. Doren could be healed after he was subdued.

"Use your web," Kade cried out but the king and queen were already doing just that.

Doren let out that inhuman scream once again, causing Kade to cringe. The Master Chosen's skin was so pale it was almost white. His eyes were sunken into his head making it almost appear that his face was that of a skull. What looked back at him with pure hatred was not the man he knew. The Apprentice Chosen took an involuntary step back as he held the creatures gaze.

Kade quickly moved over to the queen's injured leg and performed the healing calling. Next, he rushed to the king and fixed that injury, also. Both spiders flexed their legs, testing the healing. Kade returned to stand in front of the trussed up man lying on the ground. Evil Doren struggled furiously with his bonds but the spider webbing was stronger than steel. He was not getting loose until the spiders allowed it.

"You knew," Kade said accusingly to the royal couple. "Why did you not say something sooner?" the apprentice demanded.

"We believed that Doren might have known what he was doing. We hoped we were wrong about there being a danger beyond what we have already seen. We know now that we were wrong. We meant no disrespect but we did not want to offend the Master Chosen by questioning him. He is a Chosen," Crayken said humbly. Kade was considering letting the matter drop when something occurred to him that he should have realized much sooner.

"How did you know?"

"One of our own got too close to the arch and something

came through. We had no choice but to end its life," the king said as he indicated a spot on the ground next to the wall. Kade looked closely, and for the first time, noticed that there appeared to be a crimson stain in the sand. It was clear that this was a painful issue for the royal couple. They looked at one another and then back to him. Kade felt his anger quickly fade. The spiders had trusted him and Doren because they were Chosen. It was he and the master that had failed the spiders. He felt responsible for the death. The guilt of putting the king and queen in a position of having to kill one of their own made Kade feel… well, there were no words to convey how he felt.

"I am sorry you had to do that. We are still learning about the arch," Kade said. It was the best he could think to say, and yet, it was dismal even in his ears.

"We understand," Rakna said. "We should have been more cautious. After the first time coming here, we should have known, but one of the spiders was curious and got too close to the arch," Crayken said.

"Drak turned wild and attacked everything and everyone. We could not contain him so we had to end his life. It was as if whatever had invaded his body was exacting revenge on the living for a torment that could not be understood," the queen said as she spared a glance for the king and then continued. "One thing is certain. That thing was definitely evil and it could not be left to exist in this world."

When she finished speaking, both her and the king looked down at the man lying in webbing. Kade felt a knot growing in his stomach. He turned to face Darcienna, who was standing quietly with her eyes glowing softly. They were far from normal but they were not even close to the level of intensity they had been moments before.

"Are you able to help?" Kade asked, dreading that this thing may be too strong to remove.

"I can only try," Darcienna said as she looked the creature in the eyes. It flinched at what it saw and even tried to scoot away. The seething anger slowly faded to be replaced with panic and soon turned into terror as Darcienna reached out a hand toward it.

"It would seem that the creature sees something in her worth avoiding. This is a good thing," Crayken said confidently.

Darcienna gave a half grin as she closed the distance with the cowering figure. The evil entity tried to look for some way out of its impending doom, but with the two large spiders holding it in place and the webbing keeping it secure, it was obvious that it was going to be at Darcienna's mercy any moment. Just as she was about to touch the foul creature, the look in its eye changed. Her eyes blazed instantly but it was too late. She was committed. The instant she made contact, she threw her head back and screamed but did not let go. Her grip turned to iron as her knuckles turned white. She could not let go if she wanted. Kade took this all in and readied to pull them apart. Darcienna ground her teeth in determination as she struggled to purge the evil from Doren. The Master Chosen's eyes began to show the true color of brownish green. Kade felt hope until he looked into Darcienna's eyes. They were starting to turn milky white.

"It is trying to jump into her!" Kade screamed as he leapt for her. Rakna quickly intercepted Kade and held him fast. "I must get to her," Kade said forcefully. "She needs me!"

CH2

"She must fight this battle, Chosen. She is the only one. If she loses here, we will never be able to purge this creature unless you know a calling that will accomplish this," she said as she waited for him to respond. After a moment of silence, she continued. "Then we must let her do what she must. Have faith, Chosen. She is strong. Watch," the queen said as she drew his attention back to the struggling Essence Guardian. It was obvious the queen had more faith than he.

Kade quickly turned to watch the battle. Again, he felt helpless. The amount of raw Divine Power he was able to call on and it was all useless. He ground his teeth and indicated to the queen with a tap on her leg that he was ok. She let her grip go and he stepped closer to Darcienna.

"Chosen, I would not get too close," Crayken warned. It was good advice.

As Kade watched, her eyes faded from the milky white to the brilliant blue and then back again as the internal struggle was fought. The creature waged war on her but she stood her ground and waged war right back. Her jaws were slammed shut in such intense concentration that Kade feared she may crack a tooth. Her lips were slowly pulling back as she struggled to win this contest of wills. She balled her fists tightly as a growl started to escape from her lips. Was that her voice or the creature's? Her eyes struggled to hold either color as both combatants fought for victory.

"Darcienna," Kade said, fearing he was starting to see the milky white more often. That was all she needed. Something in her must have heard his voice. If she lost this battle, she would lose him and that was just not going to be acceptable. With that, she took a deep breath and clenched every muscle in her body as she threw every bit of sheer will power into destroying this internal enemy. Darcienna's face turned crimson from the effort. The creature screamed as it struggled but only Darcienna could hear its torment. With one last final burst of strength, the creature was violently ejected from her body and the bright blue eyes blazed for all to see. A piercing wail echoed up and down the tunnel at the same moment she fell to her knees, gasping for breath. She was on all fours, her arms shaking as she focused not to fall on her face. Kade feared she was about ready to collapse so he quickly dropped down and held her just like the day back in the clearing where they met. She eagerly accepted his embrace and her muscles turned to water as she fought to get her breathing to slow. Her heart was still racing as she slumped even more into his arms.

"You did well, young one," Rakna said in a soothing voice.

"It would appear that I was a little hasty in my desire to…learn what we could in our efforts to fight Morg," Doren said weakly as he sat up and looked at Kade and Darcienna. His eyes struggled to focus and his head threatened to fall back to his chest.

"Are you well?" Rakna asked with concern.

Kade did not feel the same compassion the queen was

showing. Darcienna could have been lost. And for what? Kade was not completely convinced it was to find a way to fight Morg, but he could not prove otherwise. Doren's motives would only be known to the Master Chosen, but it warranted keeping in mind. With that, Kade let it go.

"It would appear that only the Ancients and their ancestors are able to pass through," Doren said as he climbed to his feet. His portly stomach caused him to lose his balance momentarily before he was able to right himself. He dusted himself off and then cast a glance at Kade.

"You…tried to pass through?" the apprentice asked incredulously.

"I was hoping to make contact with the Ancients," he said casually, completely dismissing Kade's concern. "When I tried to pass, I was met with resistance. But, that is not all. As soon as I touched that veil, it set off a call. That thing attacked me before I knew what was happening. The more I think on it," Doren said in that superior way of talking that only he had mastered, "it was like being stuck in a web. I am not sure I could have returned to my body if it were not for that creature."

"I think it is time we leave if you have seen enough, Master Doren," Crayken said.

"I would agree," the queen added.

"Darcienna?" Kade asked, checking to see if she had recovered enough to walk.

"I am ok," she said as she pushed him away gently by placing a hand on his chest and then taking his offered hand as he stood.

Kade cast another glance at Doren and did his best to hide his disapproval. After all, an Apprentice Chosen has no place judging a master. They did what they did for their own reasons and that was that.

The color started to return to Doren's cheeks as he walked up the tunnel. He cast several glances over his shoulder at the arch

34

as it disappeared in the darkness. His mind worked as if trying to figure something out. His eyes were distant as his thoughts worked their way round and round his head. He looked back one last time and then seemed to dismiss any remaining consideration of the doorway to the dead.

By the time they reached the entrance, Darcienna was almost back to her normal self and Doran looked just as he had prior to entering the cave. There was no sign that just mere moments before, the Master Chosen had almost lost himself to another entity entirely. Kade dismissed the notion as he entered the light of day. He did not realize how much he disliked being in that cave until he was outside of it.

Rayden was eagerly waiting for his companion to emerge. Even exhausted, he had found the energy to be prepared for battle. He shoved his muzzle into Kade's face as he rapidly inhaled the Apprentice Chosen's scent, ensuring that he was unharmed. Kade held his breath, waiting for the dragon to finish. After several long moments, it seemed to relax and its wings settled back to its body. A moment later and the dragon was lying down. It dropped its head onto its front legs and was fading quickly. It was obviously still exhausted from the long flight and desperately needed rest. Kade smiled as he watched the dragon's eyes start to glaze over as he watched. It would not be long before Rayden let his eyes close and then he would be out.

Doren's gaze turned on the tree and he walked over to stand next to it, or as close as he could, seeing that it was still putting off a considerable amount of heat. A smile spread across his face as he nodded in what appeared to be approval. Kade felt himself being affected by the unspoken praise from the Master Chosen. A part of him hated caring what Doren thought. A part of him was still firmly entrenched in the apprentice mindset. He knew he was not going to get out of that anytime soon. Ten years of carrying buckets of water and meditating for hours on end did that to a person.

"I must admit that I did not expect that," Doren said as he

indicated the tree. "Nor that," the Master Chosen said as he indicated the spiders, meaning Kade's interaction with the clutch. It was not lost on any what Doren meant.

"He is the third most powerful among us. The other kings and queens have agreed to unite under our clutch because we were the ones to vanquish the leader of the Morphites. That would mean following Kade, also," Crayken hissed

"I was very impressed with the way you handled that. You displayed the ability and thought of a master," Doren said as he studied Kade. "And, you are only an apprentice?" Doren asked as he cocked an eyebrow.

"Only an apprentice," Kade said, showing no outwardly sign of the slight he felt at the way Doren used the word apprentice. The way Doren used the word made it sound as if it could mean any form of life that was not considered sentient. He knew what was said should be a compliment, but when Doren used the word the way he had, it was as though he were speaking of a lower life form.

"Interesting," Doren said, his brow still raised. "Zayle must have high standards for his apprentices for you to still hold that position after what I have seen. I would think you easily an Adept," he said. He nodded his head as if to confirm to himself that his judgment was correct.

As much as he did not want to allow Doren to have an effect on him, Kade could not help but to beam at the thought of reaching the rank of Adept. He had been apprentice for ten years. He was starting to believe he would never achieve another rank ever, but now…a Master Chosen was judging him to be ready for the next level.

"You are able to raise me up?" Kade asked, trying to hide his excitement.

"I am a Master Chosen," Doren said as if that was all that was needed to be said.

"I meant no offence," Kade said a bit hesitantly. "I did not expect…to be honest, I did not even give it any thought."

"You have lost your master and I have lost my apprentice. It is within my purview to grant this, as I see fit," Doren said with patience. Kade could still sense the master apprentice relationship. He was not sure if this worked for him, but it would not hurt to give it some consideration. Doren's keen eye picked up on Kade's indecision, and he continued. "You do want to continue to learn, do you not? And, I am certain Zayle would not want you to stop until you have mastered the ways of the Divine," he said. Kade noticed that the Master Chosen had been looking at something by the dragon as he spoke. Kade casually glanced over and saw the sack of books. He mentally sighed and walked over to retrieve the tomes of knowledge.

"Yes, I do believe Zayle would want me to continue my studies," Kade said, tightening his grip on the sack.

"Then you shall finish your studies under me. I am sure you will easily prove, in a very short time, that you deserve the rank of Adept," Doren said, watching Kade for a response.

"Master Chosen Doren, I am honored. Thank you," Kade said, sensing that Doren had two motives for his offer, and the sack in his hand was one of them. Kade suspected that the other motive was that Doren was used to having an apprentice to work with, and he truly did love to teach...or was it that he liked to hear himself talk? *Possibly both*, Kade thought. Maybe, Doren found meaning in teaching. There was a genuine offer for him to continue to learn, and yet, he gripped the sack tightly, hesitant to accept the title of Doren's apprentice.

"Kade," Darcienna said as she laid her hand on his arm. "They are waiting on us," she said as she indicated the spiders.

"Then we should be going," Kade said. He glanced at the dragon but quickly decided against riding. Besides, Rayden was lying on the ground and his eyes were shut tight. "I think it would do us well to walk so we can work out the stiffness."

"I approve," Doren said. Kade cringed. *Approved?* It was not to say he agreed but to actually give his approval as if Kade had asked permission. The apprentice took a deep breath and exhaled, doing his best to let it go.

"What is expected of an Adept?" Kade asked, filling the time, thinking this felt like a betrayal to Zayle. It felt…wrong. Zayle was his master. Doren was not Zayle.

"You would no longer be under the close supervision of a Master Chosen. You would be given tasks occasionally to continue to hone your abilities. You would venture out into the world to ply your skill. If you were to need assistance, you would come to me," Doren said casually as he walked.

Kade was surprised and relieved more than he could say. He was certain that returning to the status of an apprentice under a Chosen Master would have virtually been impossible. *At least, with this master*, Kade thought. He breathed such a sigh of relief that Doren turned to regard him, misunderstanding the exhaled breath.

"Kade, you cannot continue to hide behind a Master's robes," Doren said, believing Kade frustrated. "You must work toward the rank of master."

"I understand, Master Doren," Kade said and quickly turned to survey the land to hide his true feelings.

"I will continue to teach you, but your training must come from life. When you need me, I will be here," Doren said with finality.

"You are wise and I shall do my best," Kade said as he gave Darcienna a glance. She returned a sly look and it almost appeared as if she was on the verge of laughing. Kade was aghast. She was actually enjoying his torment. He glared at her with a tight lipped expression, but this only served to make it worse as she covered her mouth with the back of her hand to hide her mirth. Kade sighed again.

"Your mastery of the Lightning Calling was very impressive. How long did you study that calling?" Doren asked casually, walking a bit more easily as his muscles worked out the kinks.

"A day," Kade said as he was watching the king and queen

talk amongst themselves.

"I mean…how long did you study it before you mastered it?" Doren said as he watched Kade, trying to be patient while repeating what should have been an easy question to comprehend.

"I learned this calling in one day," Kade said casually as he glanced at Doren and then looked back at the spiders.

Kade did not see the look of disbelief on the Master's face as Doren came to a stop. Kade glanced over and ground to a halt when he noticed Doren was no longer with him. He turned and saw the man standing there with his mouth hanging open as if trying to formulate words.

"Master?" Kade asked in confusion.

"It's true," Doren said, his eyes distant as his mind worked rapidly. His eyes focused when he realized Kade was watching him. His composure returned instantly and Kade would have never known the level of the man's shock had he not just seen it with his own eyes. "Zayle said you held the key to our salvation," Doren said as he looked at Kade as if seeing him for the first time. "Zayle was able to…teach you that complex a calling in a day?" Doren asked, but his tone gave away his disbelief. Kade sighed.

"Zayle was…" Kade started to say and then stopped.

"Zayle was what?" Doren asked as he stared deep into Kade's eyes, as if trying to detect deception.

"Zayle had been killed by that time. I found the book and learned it on my own," Kade said, firmly vowing to keep the despair from surfacing at the loss of his cherished master.

"Who taught you the Calling?" Doren asked suspiciously, not believing what he was hearing. Or, maybe it was that he did not hear the response.

"I did. I learned it on my own," Kade said.

How much more clear can I make it? Kade thought as he watched the Master Chosen. Kade could see that Doren was like a volcano getting ready to erupt and flinched.

"Kade!" Doren exploded. It reminded him of how his

master, Zayle, used to react when he had made a mistake that was life threatening. "That was foolish! Foolish beyond words!" Doren exclaimed, anger reddening his face. "You could have easily destroyed yourself! You are too important to take irresponsible risks like that!"

Kade sensed that Doren was not just angry at him for putting his life in danger, but for something else, also. He recalled the cabin he had lived in for most of his life and could not help but to agree. It was foolish. Was he ready for so much power and responsibility? What was past is past and cannot be changed now.

No reason to dwell on it, he told himself, but he was not able to shake it off.

Doren clenched his fists in anger as his mouth worked. Kade was certain that if any sound accompanied those unspoken words, they would be harsh words indeed. He could not bring himself to speak as he tried to comprehend all that was happening. Doren began to walk again as his mouth twisted without saying the words that formed on his lips.

As they walked, neither said anything for quite some time. Kade avoided looking at Doren, sure he would see a scalding glare. *It must be a requirement for Masters to know how to scold,* Kade thought as he recalled how proficient Zayle was at it, also. Kade did not speak and dearly hoped that Doren would let the silence stand. He was relieved beyond words that the Master Chosen decided to stay quiet. As time passed, Doren softened, and inevitably, started to talk once again.

"Zayle used to have an extensive library," Doren said in as relaxed a tone as he could muster. Kade was not sure if it was a question or a statement so he continued on in silence. "Those books are still kept safe, I take it?" Kade cringed and came to a stop. "Apprentice?" Doren asked in an ominous tone. Kade forced himself to meet Doren's gaze, which was quickly turning into another glare. He looked down and did his best not to shuffle.

"With the exception of these," Kade said as he hefted the

sack slightly, "they did not survive." He knew where this was going. He waited for the next heated question. The silence drew on and he worked up the courage to glance at Doren. The Master Chosen was so pale that he was on the verge of having no color at all. For the second time, he was doing a better job of looking deader now than when he was back in his hidden study. Kade wondered if the Master was going to get sick. Darcienna squeezed Kade's arm in support.

"How?" Doren managed in a whisper. Kade could have sworn that someone had just told the man that his entire family had just been slaughtered. The Apprentice Chosen closed his eyes, knowing he was going to get a tongue lashing that was going to rival any he had ever gotten from Zayle. For a moment, he thought he might prefer to be Morg's prisoner again over this.

"From the fire," Kade said, taking in a steadying breath, still not moving.

"Fire?" Doren asked, gaining strength by the moment.

"The one I started with the Lightning Calling," Kade said. He had to fight the instinct to flinch.

"Blood and ashes and all that is Holy with the Divine!" Doren swore. "It is a miracle you are even alive! Practicing callings that you know nothing about, destroying decades of knowledge in one foolish move!" he roared while throwing his hands up dramatically. "How...are...you...even...alive?" Doren screamed. This was all Darcienna could take. She rounded on Doren like gale force winds full of fury and growing stronger by the second. Kade moved back, not daring to get in her way. If Doren's eyes could glow to warn of danger, they would have been blazing fiercely.

"How dare you judge him!" Darcienna unleashed. "He has bested Morg three times while you have done what? Hid in your cellar, hoping your trap worked?" she challenged as she poked him hard in the chest. He flinched and took a step back. Darcienna pursued him like a predator stalking its prey. "And might I point out that your trap failed miserably!" she exclaimed so vehemently that several of the spiders scurried away. "And where would you be if not for him?" she asked, stabbing a finger at Kade with such force that Doren cringed despite trying to hold the air of a Master Chosen. He opened his mouth to speak, trying to regain control, but she attacked, holding nothing back. Kade winced, actually feeling sorry for the Master. "You need him! I would suggest you start showing the wisdom you claim to possess, or so help me by Nature's Gift, I will feed you to the dragon!" Darcienna vowed, red faced, as she poked him one more time so hard he was sure to have a bruise for a week. He tried to hide his discomfort but failed miserably as he swallowed hard. Darcienna huffed and spun on her heels, walking back to stand next to Kade, clenching her fists hard.

"I may have been a bit hard on you," Doren said to Kade. Darcienna's head whipped around to glare at him. Doren swallowed again. "I was a touch too hard on you," he corrected while holding his head up to regain some composure. "I am sure it would be best if we all put this to rest, for now, and talk later," he said, sparing a glance for her. She huffed again and turned away.

Kade did his best to not look at either of them. Darcienna was giving off waves of anger while Doren was unreadable. Kade started to walk again and pulled Darcienna along. He gave her a look that said, "Enough" and she softened…but only a little.

"Your Mordra returned several hours ago," Rakna said. "It is why we are here. When you did not arrive shortly after, we were afraid you were coming straight to the caves so we came as quickly as possible. We were afraid we were going to be one clutch less if we did not get here to save them."

"A Mordra! You have a Mordra?" Doren asked incredulously, completely forgetting about being humble. "By the great Divine, you never cease to amaze me! How did you come to be in possession of a Mordra? First a dragon, which has not been heard of since the Ancients, and now a Mordra?" He shook his head in disbelief while glancing at Darcienna, checking to see if she was going to react to his outburst. "You did not tell me of this," he said with just a little more control.

"I did not think it was important. It is just an animal that seems to be attached to my books," Kade said as he hefted the sack again.

"Just an animal?" Doren asked again, shocked at what he was hearing. "They are rarer than your dragon," he said, shaking his head. "You have no idea." Kade was not sure if that was an insult or an honest observation.

"I don't understand," Kade said, glancing at the Master Chosen. Doren took a breath and readied himself to switch into lecture mode. The anger that Doren had been so completely filled with just a few short moments before was nowhere to be seen. Hearing of the Mordra really had Doren's interest.

"There are many guesses as to what it is. But, one thing is certain; it is definitely connected to the Divine. I am not sure if it is part of the Divine or if it is just allied with the Divine, but nevertheless, it senses the Divine. It most likely sensed your use of the power. And I am certain, knowing Zayle and how protective he was of his books, it sensed the protective callings placed on them," Doren said, nodding toward the sack in Kade's white-knuckled grip.

Doren waited a moment, watching closely for Kade to either confirm or deny what he had just said. Kade opened his mouth to speak when Darcienna squeezed his arm tightly, her nails digging in. He turned toward her, and for a moment thought her eyes were just ever-so-slightly glowing. But then again, it could be just the way the sun was hitting them. Kade turned back to Doren without saying a word, waiting for the Master to continue. Doren sighed and started talking again.

"It is said that they appear and disappear without notice, but once attached to someone, they affect that person's life in profound ways. It is interesting, really. It is as if they see how events are unfolding and affect them with just the slightest interaction that causes the greatest change. For example," Doren said, clearly in his element as a teacher, "you may be in a mortal struggle for your life. The Mordra may walk by, distracting your opponent at a crucial moment, turning the battle in your favor and garnering you victory. They do not stay involved, but what little they do, brings about great change," Doren said as he looked to ensure his student was absorbing what was being taught.

Kade nodded his head as he thought back on the first time he had seen the Mordra. It had taken the books. So that part made sense. Doren watched silently, allowing Kade to assimilate the information. Kade thought about how the Mordra had bitten Morg when the evil Chosen was about to deliver a killing blow. It had been no more than seconds and the creature was gone. It did turn the tide of battle. He recalled how it led Dran to the dungeon and he smiled, recalling the dagger flying out of nowhere to topple Manboy. He nodded his head and turned back to look at Doren. The Master Chosen smiled and nodded once, seeing that his pupil was ready for him to continue.

"I have never seen a Mordra. I look forward to it," Doren said, picking up the pace. "It is believed that the Ancients created the creature as a pet, if you can believe that," Doren said as he let out a chuckle.

"That is all very interesting, but...how did it know to come here?" Kade asked as he turned toward Doren.

"This is all conjecture, mind you, but there is much to support what I say," Doren said, scratching his chin with his thumb and index finger as he narrowed his eyes while thinking. "They are a mystery. They will stay attached to you for as long as you want. They know where you are at all times, and some of the Ancients even believed that they know where you will be at any time. That would explain how it got here ahead of you," he said, nodding his head as if deciding what he had just said made sense.

"That does seem to fit," Kade said as he surveyed the land casually.

"It was also said that any Chosen that had a Mordra was

blessed by the Divine. I, myself, searched for one for a decade. I gave up, thinking they were extinct," Doren said.

Kade sensed the Master Chosen's eagerness to see this creature grow by the moment. He turned and regarded Doren closely. The Master Chosen smiled easily under Kade's watchful gaze, but Kade was sure he saw hunger. Yes, there was definitely a hunger there. After a moment, Kade decided hunger was not a strong enough word.

"So, only a Chosen can have one of these?" Kade asked.

"Or one that is very strong in the Divine," Doren answered. "It's as if it can see you because of your connection to the Divine."

"But, it can still see others like, say, Darcienna?" Kade asked.

"Oh its eyes are very acute. I think a better way to explain this is to say that they see you and me in color, and they see everything else in black and white," Doren said. "From what I have read, they are part Divine and part normal, as far as I can tell."

"Kade, I think maybe we should call your dragon," Darcienna said as she looked back to see Rayden's form still by the cave. Kade opened himself up to his friend and smiled. The fierce creature was deeply asleep.

"I would agree," Kade said, testing his muscles. They were still sore, but they did feel better. He opened his mind up to Rayden fully and called to him. There was no response. Kade tried again, but again, there was nothing. "He is really out," Kade said as he came to a stop and stared at the still form off in the distance.

"Kade, it will take us a day or more if we must walk," Darcienna said.

"I know. I have an idea," Kade said with a mischievous grin. He closed his eyes and smiled even wider. After just a few moments, Kade let out a laugh. Darcienna was about to ask what he found amusing when she saw the dragon's head shoot up. It leapt to its feet and spun around as if trying to locate something. It stopped, looked in their direction and then charged. Rayden took two great strides and then leapt into the air, its wings beating furiously as it picked up speed. It spread its wings out wide, gliding directly at them. Darcienna looked at him as if to ask, "What did you do?"

"Oh, I sent it the image of a big, juicy piece of hot meat," Kade said and laughed again as the dragon landed, sending a cloud of dust into the air. It did not slow much as it continued toward the group, and at the last moment, skidded to a stop as it tossed its head a few times in anticipation.

Doren watched closely, concerned that the dragon might run him over. It stopped and towered over the Master Chosen while looking at Kade. The Apprentice Chosen took several steps back as did Darcienna. Doren turned to look at Kade and flinched as something wet hit him on the head. Doren reached up and ran his hand through his hair. He pulled his hand away full of slime and scowled. Kade laughed even more.

"Kade," Darcienna said, scolding him, but even she was fighting a grin. Doren glared at Kade through his brow, marched over to a patch of grass and wiped his hands. "You really must curb that sense of humor," she chided.

"I know," Kade said as he regarded the dragon. "Ready to eat?" Kade asked Rayden. The dragon shuffled from foot to foot, eager for its meal.

Kade removed Darcienna's hand from his arm and stepped back, preparing himself for the calling. He closed his eyes to relax his mind so as to focus better. He called the first piece of meat into existence and tossed it high into the air. Rayden lashed out, and with a crash of teeth, snapped up the meat and swallowed without even chewing. Doren visibly jumped. After a moment, he turned and studied Kade closely with suspicion in his eyes. It was all Kade could do not to grin.

"Stop," Darcienna whispered, her teeth clenched together and her lips the only thing moving. He shrugged easily but Darcienna could see the laughter dancing in his eyes.

He closed his eyes and forced his mind to focus. It was no

easy task, but soon, his mind was clear and he went through the motions again. He made the usual ten pieces of meat and then continued to make an extra five. The dragon eagerly snapped up every piece. Rayden appeared to recuperate with every tasty morsel he inhaled. While cooking, Kade felt his stomach growl and decided a few extra pieces would do well for him and Darcienna. He made the first piece for her and then made a piece for himself. He was looking forward to taking his first big bite when Darcienna elbowed him in the ribs. He went to take a small bite and she elbowed him again. Kade looked at her in exasperation. Her eyes flitted to the Master Chosen and back to him again. Kade slowly turned to see the master watching them closely. The hunger was apparent in his eyes.

"Kade," Darcienna said as she motioned him toward Doren. "I don't think he can make any," she said as she glanced past the apprentice.

"Oh," Kade said, surprised. He proffered the meat to Doren who quickly accepted. "You can't call food?" Kade asked the Master Chosen.

"Zayle guarded his secrets more closely than a mother bear does her cubs," Doren said with deep scorn in his voice. Kade looked back at his sack of books and vowed to himself not to let them out of his sight.

For all his failings, Kade did enjoy seeing Doren savor the taste of his food. The group ate in silence with Darcienna only glaring at Kade one time for his eating habits. They finished their meals and then climbed onto the dragon. It kept its wings in and chose a relaxed comfortable stride. They all sat in silence, enjoying full bellies as the land smoothly flowed by. It was not long before they were stopping in front of the tree that housed the Great Hall.

"Show me to the Mordra, please," Kade said.

"This way," Rakna said as she led them through the tree and to the room at the end of the hall.

Kade smiled, recognizing the room immediately. It was the

room he and Darcienna had previously slept. He reached for the block of wood that was used for a handle. There was no locking mechanism and the hinge was a leather type material. It was a basic door but that was more than enough for Kade. He pushed it open, and there, on the bed, was Chance. Doren all but shoved by to get into the room. Kade glanced sidelong at the Master Chosen and then placed the sack of books on the end of the makeshift mattress.

"My friend," Kade said as he reached out to the silky creature. It nuzzled his hand affectionately and then uncurled around its prize. Kade stared in awe. There, lying on the bed, being guarded protectively by Chance, was the small, black book.

"Kade!" Darcienna said in shock.

"I see," Kade said as he gently picked up the book and turned it over in his hands. "Well, aren't you a resourceful one," he said as he let the creature nuzzle his hand again. It allowed him to pet it affectionately for a few moments, and then its nose started to work rapidly as it took in the scent of the previously handled food excitedly. "You and the dragon," Kade said as he chuckled.

"Are we to never be without that cursed book?" Darcienna added in exasperation. Kade gave her a reproving look and then turned back to his silky, black friend.

"Amazing!" Doren said, wide-eyed in wonder. There was a hunger in those eyes that ran deep. Kade and Darcienna exchanged a knowing glance.

Doren looked on in awe. He moved next to the bed as he studied the creature. Chance turned his head this way and that way and then seemed to tense ever so slightly. With his hackles up, he slunk over to the sack of books and curled around it protectively. Doren reached a hand out to the Mordra and it bristled. The closer Doren got, the more Chance appeared to be tensing.

"Doren," Darcienna said while gently laying a hand on his arm. "I don't think that would be wise," she said as she watched the creature's lips start to twitch.

"Maybe when it gets to know me better," Doren said and

regretfully let his arm fall to his side.

"Maybe," Kade said, but deep down he was fairly certain that the Mordra was never going to let the Master Chosen get too close. Kade was also very certain that the silky, black creature was never going to let Doren anywhere near the sack of books, with how protective it was being of them.

"We took the liberty of making you and your lady some clothes out of a special material. We produce this naturally. I think you will approve of the colors we chose. We used the most vibrant greens for the lady and the deepest blues for you, Kade. We thought you may need it someday, and it appears that we were correct," Crayken said as he eyed their outfits. "There is a tunnel at the back of the great hall that leads to an underground spring. It is cold, but it should do for a place for you to bathe," the king said as he looked at the three of them.

"I am in no need of cleaning," Doren said as he bowed slightly. "Thank you for the offer."

"Then you may join me while Kade and Darcienna wash," Crayken said. "The queen will show you to the spring. I will have your clothes brought to you," the king said to Kade and Darcienna.

"Thank you," Kade said as he scrutinized his outfit he was wearing. He was not sure of the new clothes as he was very comfortable in the ones he was wearing, but they did appear to be very nice. Darcienna saw how he was eyeing his outfit and gave him a stern look. "I know," he said, accepting that he needed to change after the bath.

Kade turned his attention back to his Mordra and stroked the animal affectionately. Chance let out a deep, rumbling purr. The creature got up from the books and sat back on its haunches while looking at him expectantly. Its paws were together as if praying. Kade easily recognized this by now and chuckled. He gladly called a piece of fresh meat into existence and handed it to Chance, who eagerly took it into his paws and pulled it to himself protectively. After surveying the room to make sure no one was going to take away its prize, Chance settled down and starting chewing hungrily.

Kade opened the sack and gently rolled the sides down until the stack of books were exposed. Doren was watching intently while trying to appear to be uninterested. Kade put himself between the bag and Doren as he worked at the bindings. He loosened the strap and slid the black book into place on the top of the pile and then cinched them tightly again. Chance glanced at the sack, then to everyone in the room and then back to the sack. Content that everything was as it should be, he continued to happily chew on his food.

Crayken exited the room and Doren reluctantly followed. Kade was relieved and a little surprised at how uncomfortable he had been until the Master Chosen was no longer present. He shook off the unease and smiled at Chance, appreciating his friend's protective nature with his books.

"This way," Rakna said as she left the room and waited for them in the hall.

Darcienna glanced at the books and then back to Kade. He could see the concern on her face. Kade glanced at Doren as he and the king were almost out of sight and then back to the Mordra while smiling.

"They are safe," Kade said as he patted the Mordra on the head. He felt sorry for the fool who would try to touch those books with this thing around. Kade started to reach for the new clothes when the queen spoke.

"They will be brought to you." Kade shrugged his shoulders and left the clothes where they lay.

Without another word, they turned and walked out the door. They worked their way through the tree to the exit and over to the other massive tree that housed the Great Hall. The queen led them down the stairs and through the expansive Great Hall to a tunnel at the back. The queen continued until they had walked almost two hundred feet down the tunnel. They were standing in front of a pool of water that was crystal clear. It was only ten feet wide in all directions. Kade could see the bottom as though the water was not even there. The slight ripple on the surface as water churned in was the only evidence that there was any water there at all. A soft light coming from luminescent algae hanging on the walls and ceiling helped light the area. Kade moved over to the wall to examine the light-giving substance. He reached out a hand and brushed the algae lightly. It flared brightly for a moment and then faded out completely.

"I'm sorry. I did not realize," Kade said as he pulled his hands back, afraid that he may have committed a grave error.

"They are very fragile," Rakna said as she surveyed the dead plant. "It will be replaced," she said as she pulled it from the wall and moved over to the water. "It makes for a great cleaner, also," the white queen said as she handed it to him. He gently took the proffered algae and noticed how slick it felt. It was almost slimy, making him want to drop it and wipe his hands on his pants.

"It does not feel," Rakna said, noticing how gently he was handling the plant. "Think of it as grass. It is there for us to use. Your clothes will be here shortly," she added as she settled down a little ways from the pool of water.

Kade hesitated, watching the queen fold her legs under herself as she prepared to wait. He glanced at Darcienna, who was also watching him. It occurred to him that none of the spiders wore anything at all. Clothing was strictly something used by people. He looked back to Darcienna and noticed a slight grin creeping across her face.

Okay, he thought to himself and decided to call her bluff. He undid his shirt while she watched. Her face became one of suspicion. He reached for his pants and smiled. Her eyes came open wide and her cheeks colored a deep red. As he undid the strap that served as a belt, she quickly faced away. He smiled to himself as the rest of his clothes hit the ground. He turned and walked into the spring. The water sent shockwaves of cold through his body. He shivered hard.

51

"Holy Divine this is cold," Kade said as he quickly waded deeper and dunked his head.

Kade recalled the cold lake the previous day and knew if he went too slowly, he would take all day getting in. He held his right hand out of the water as he gripped the algae tightly. With his head still under, he vigorously scrubbed his hair with his left hand, shaking lose any dirt. After surfacing and gasping for breath because of the cold, he then rubbed the algae through his hair. He still felt odd about using something that appeared to have been alive just moments before, but it did seem to lather. He scrubbed eagerly and then dunked his head back under the surface. The dirt drifted away. The water clouded momentarily and then cleared as the underground spring continued to bubble in, cycling out the old water.

Several spiders skittered in and dropped their newly made clothes onto the ground. Darcienna got up from next to the queen and hefted one of the outfits. It was surprisingly light. She was not quite certain she wanted to wear something so fragile, though. She tried to put a small tear in it but it held strong. She pulled, using more of her strength, and still, it gave no sign of ripping. Next, she gripped it in both hands and put all her might into it. There was not even the slightest bit of damage. She nodded her approval and turned to see Kade watching.

"It is quite amazing," Darcienna said as she held the clothes out for him to see.

"They appear to be durable," Kade said skeptically as he shook the excess water from his hair and prepared to exit the frigid water.

Darcienna was flipping through the clothes when she came across what passed for towels. She brought one to the edge of the water, dropped it on the ground and turned to walk away but hesitated as a smudge of dirt on his forehead caught her attention. She got down on her knees and motioned for Kade to move closer.

"Almost," Darcienna said as she reached out and scrubbed

his forehead with her bare hand. Kade enjoyed her touch and even found it a little arousing. Her full lips were slightly parted as she focused on her task. He could not help but to stare as she ran her tongue just behind her teeth. He leaned closer, feeling an attraction building. His body urged him on as his pulse quickened. His breathing became deep as he moved even closer yet. He looked into her eyes as the distance between them shrank little by little. She leaned forward to inspect her work as she concentrated on removing the dirt. He felt the soft caress of her breath on his face and inhaled. His body started to react as thoughts of her in his arms drifted through his mind. He ached to embrace her firmly and pull her into a kiss. He moved closer to those lips that beckoned him, yearning to feel them against his. She leaned down just a little more and then locked eyes with him. Her hand stopped on his forehead as he moved slowly toward her. Kade felt his heart pounding hard. She closed her eyes, and her lips parted ever so slightly as she ran her tongue along them, preparing for the kiss that was just a hairs-breath away. He felt just the lightest brush of her lips on his when a voice exploded in his mind, causing him to flinch back.

The king is ready for us at the royal table, Rakna thought to him. Darcienna's eyes flew open, and she looked at him in confusion. Kade's mind scrambled, trying to find the words to salvage this, but it was too late. She quickly got to her feet and stalked away.

"It's not what you…," Kade was trying to say, but she had no interest in hearing what he had to say. "Blood and Ash!" Kade swore.

"You may get out anytime," Darcienna said from next to the queen, tightness in her voice.

Kade reached for the towel and covered himself as he exited the water. He dried off and then wrapped the towel around his waist. He walked over to her, put his hand on her shoulder and turned her around. She ducked out from under his arm and smiled but the smile did not make it to her eyes.

"Darcienna," Kade said, but look in her eye said she was done listening. "Your turn," he said, thoroughly frustrated.

Kade kept his back to Darcienna as she disrobed and stepped into the water. He could tell that she had entered the frigid pool by the way she inhaled a hiss through her clenched teeth. He fought the urge to turn and stood facing the queen.

"I am going to get dressed," Kade said over his shoulder.

"Your clothes are the ones on the bottom," Darcienna said through chattering teeth.

"Thanks," Kade called back as he bent and picked up the neatly folded pile. He vowed that if he was able to get his hands on fate right then, he would have throttled her.

Kade walked around the corner, out of sight of the pool and let the towel fall. The air felt good on his skin as he dried. He shook out the clothes and surveyed them as they hung from his hands. They were light, but not too light, nor were they too thin. He rubbed them between his fingers and nodded, pleased with the feel. He pulled the pants on and then pulled the top on. It was snug around his shoulders but widened as it moved down his arm. They stopped at his wrist and hang down almost a foot. He could hide a loaf of bread in those sleeves. The pants were the same. He waved his arms around and smiled at the affect. The sleeves flowed smoothly through the air. It reminded him of the king and queen's fur. He walked up and down the tunnel, marveling at how comfortable the outfit felt.

"These move pretty good," Kade said as he walked back into the open room. Darcienna held a towel up to herself and waited for him to notice. His eyes took in what was going on, and without slowing, immediately turned and walked back out.

"Sorry," Kade called over his shoulder as he walked down the tunnel.

"Give me a minute," Darcienna called back but her tone was still unfriendly. There was definitely still ice there and it had nothing to do with the cold spring.

"Just call out when you are done," Kade yelled back. "The queen says they are waiting for us."

"You may come back in," Darcienna called out. "She said nothing of the kind," she added as she glanced at the queen.

"She said it here," Kade said as he walked around the corner and tapped his head. She looked at him, studying him closely to see if he were playing games with her. Kade did not see the suspicious look in her eyes or he may have realized that she was more confused after the explanation. He turned to go and then stopped with his back to her. Darcienna started to walk past him, but before she could take two steps, he grabbed her by the arm, spun her around, wrapped an arm around her waist and pulled her into a deep embrace. Darcienna put both her hands on his shoulders, ready to push him away, but the moment his lips touched hers, every last little bit of strength in her body evaporated. Her lips molded to his and she melted into his arms. Her right hand slipped over his shoulder to mix with the hair at the back of his head. After several long seconds, he let her go and confidently turned to walk up the tunnel.

Darcienna was stunned to the very core of her being. No calling or Nature's gift could have affected her as profoundly as that kiss. She fought to regain her breathing as her hand drifted up to her mouth. She could still taste his kiss on her lips. The queen stood by, watching curiously.

"Forgive me but I must ask. Is that normal for a man to...do that to his mate?" Rakna asked curiously. It took a long moment for Darcienna to realize that the queen was addressing her and even longer for her to formulate an intelligent response.

"It is," Darcienna said. That was the best she could do while her mind grappled with what had just happened.

Kade worked his way back to the Great Hall. It was filled with spiders from wall to wall. There were spiders in every doorway. They were on the walls and some even hung on the ceiling. Some had different markings on their body but they were all of the same shape and size. Doren and the king were by the throne, talking. Kade started toward the king, and the spiders parted easily for him. He walked up the steps and stopped in front of Crayken.

"Many leaders from the other clutches will be here. They all want to hear what you have to say," Crayken said as he turned to lead them to a table that sat behind the thrones.

Kade bent his arm at the elbow while holding his hand over his midsection. Darcienna reached through to wrap her hand around his forearm as she was becoming accustomed to. He smiled ever so slightly as he followed the royal couple to the table. Rakna indicated for Darcienna to take her place at her side. Kade surveyed the spiders already sitting and wondered what was to be expected of him.

He glanced at Doren, ready to ask a question, but before he could speak, he noticed a scratch on the master's wrist. Doren pulled his sleeve a bit lower. Kade narrowed his eyes as he fixed Doren with a glare. The master appeared not to notice Kade's accusing look as he walked gracefully toward the table. Kade, begrudgingly, let it go…for now. Turning, he glanced at Darcienna on the other side of the table. He was not sure where he should sit, but he was certain that there was going to be some order to bestow honor based on rank.

"Kade," Crayken said as he indicated the seat directly to his left at the head of the table.

"Darcienna," the white queen said, indicating the seat next to her. Kade and Darcienna gave each other a glance and then took their seats. Nothing was said to Doren so Kade motioned for the Master Chosen to sit on his left. Doren hesitated. Kade indicated more firmly and Doren sat. The rest of the spiders then took their seats. When everyone was settled, Crayken rose and addressed the congregation.

"This is the one I spoke of. This is the mighty Kade, slayer of the black plague and savior of our kind; the wielder of the Divine and rider of dragons!" Crayken said dramatically as he looked each and every one of them in the eye. He had the desired effect as all eyes turned to regard Kade closely. Most nodded their head in approval while others just stared. "He fights for our kind and all sentient beings. He is our best hope to rid this land of an evil one named Morg."

"And you would have us join this fight?" a king with gray climbing up his legs asked.

"I would," Crayken said evenly but firmly.

"If this Morg is as powerful as you would have us believe, could he not destroy us easily?" another ageing spider asked.

"That is why we ally with him," Crayken said as he indicated Kade. "If we don't work with this Chosen to stop Morg, then sooner or later, when Morg turns on us, we will have no hope of surviving. We must stand with him now!" Crayken said as he put his front legs on the table and leaned toward the spider for emphasis.

One of the spiders buzzed rapidly to Crayken. It was large and black just like Crayken with the exception of a crimson shaped diamond on its chest. Kade glanced at the white diamond shape on Crayken's chest and wondered if there was a connection. Crayken buzzed back angrily while gesturing to Kade. Darcienna glanced at Kade and then back to Red Diamond.

"We will speak so all can understand," Crayken hissed. The angry spider took a breath and repeated his words for all to hear.

"What will keep Morg from tracking him here?" Red Diamond hissed. "I have heard of this Morg. It is known that he can track those that practice the ways of the Divine. So I ask again," the spider said as he stood challengingly, "what keeps him from coming here at this very moment?" the old king asked in an almost accusing tone.

"I have this," Kade said as he produced the amulet. "It keeps me hidden."

"That is all very well and good for you, but is he not versed in the ways of the Divine?" the spider king asked as he violently jabbed a leg in Doren's direction.

Kade froze. The thought had not occurred to him that Morg might, indeed, track them through Doren. He recalled how the Master Chosen had used the Divine to ready himself for battle against the spiders and felt panic well up in him. Red Diamond was right.

"It is not just an amulet that protects the user but an amulet that protects an area," Doren said smoothly and confidently.

In a flash, it made complete sense. How else would Morg have not found Zayle all these years? He relaxed and hoped his fear had not shown on his face. The old spider seemed mollified with this.

"We must be wise in our approach," Red Diamond said. "We will, most assuredly, have one chance at this. I am certain that when Morg knows we stand against him in force, he will do everything in his power to destroy every last living spider," the old king said loudly and then pounded the table for effect.

"You have vowed to follow," Crayken reminded him firmly.

"Aye, I have, but only because I believe I have no other choice," the spider said. "I hope that our decisions here today do not prove to be fatal to our race," the old king added with a considerable amount of doubt. His statement hit home and the mood became deadly serious. Kade's head spun at the thought of a civilization coming to an end because of him.

"We have fought against the black creatures for centuries," Crayken said and then paused dramatically to make his point. "He wiped them out in one day!" Crayken roared as he leapt up onto the table. "Completely eradicated them!" the king yelled. All eyes were fixed on him. Almost all of the spiders were nodding in approval, but Red Diamond still held his ground.

"I will give him credit for accomplishing such a feat, but Morg is a force of power that is well beyond that of the Morphites," Red Diamond said as he turned his gaze on Kade challengingly.

Maybe a demonstration, the queen said in his mind. Kade was so focused on the old king that he visibly flinched. The old spiders eyes widened slightly as he misunderstood, believing he had offended Kade. In a rush, everything about the way these spiders ruled made sense. It was obvious. Even these kings and queens needed a reason to trust someone if they were to follow them. Talk was all well and good, but a display of power is what made them believe. For the third time, he recalled how the queen had done this on their first meeting. He recalled how he and the king had done this just today with the spiders by the cave and now…it was his turn again.

"Do I appear weak to you?" Kade asked dangerously. The king and queen exchanged quick glances and then Crayken slowly moved toward his chair. Crayken lowered himself off the table and into his seat, making sure not to draw attention, ensuring that all eyes were watching Kade. "Do you need a demonstration?" Kade hissed. "Then I shall give you one," Kade yelled as he threw his hand dramatically into the air. Light exploded to fill the room. It was blinding and every spider cringed. As Kade suspected from their first meeting, they had a fear of this light. Kade was also surprised as even Doren shrieked.

The Apprentice Chosen leapt onto the table as Crayken had done. He let the light fade…but only enough for the spider to be able to look upon him. He glared at the old king. The spider was visibly shaken and flinched when he saw that Kade was now on the table, but he still met the apprentice stare for stare. This aged king did not get to be this old by folding at the first sign of power. Kade's respect grew.

"That is just the start," Kade said and then flew into a flurry of moves.

The new clothes flowed, reminding him of the way the king and queen's fur moved with the wind. A part of him knew the design of the clothes was no random act. The display was impressive. The Blue Flame of the Divine sprang into life. Kade held his hand high and drew the Divine Power into it as he spoke.

"My abilities are no trivial matter," Kade said as he stalked around the table. The flame grew larger as it danced several feet off his hands. Doren stared wide-eyed. "There is a reason Morg fears me," he said as he jumped down from the table and drew in so much of the Divine it appeared his entire body was on fire. Unknown to Kade, his block was completely gone as the Divine bent to his will. "He has good reason to fear me!" he said again, raising his voice as he threw his arms out to his sides. Kade appeared to be an inferno of blue fire as the flames engulfed his entire body. The kings and queens shrank back in fear. The block was gone and the Divine was raging through him like the fiercest of storms. Doren continued to stare in awe.

Chosen, Kade heard in his mind. *Chosen, you have made your point*, Rakna said. There was something in her tone that said he may have gone too far. He realized the queen was correct. He could not have them see him as a power to be feared as they did Morg. He needed them to respect him, not fear him.

"But, even you cannot deny that he holds immense power while he holds the staff," the old king said, all the fire gone from his voice and it was all he could do not to cringe before Kade. *How did they know of the staff?* Kade asked himself. A quick glance at Doren then Crayken and his question was answered.

Kade stood still, all eyes on him. Were they looking at him in fear? Did they see him as they might see Morg? He had to get this back under control or he would lose before he even began. With considerable effort, he stemmed the tide raging through him and brought it to a mild flow. The flames receded and shrank to just his hands.

"It is true that he wields great power while holding the staff," Kade said as he did his best to hide his near loss of control of such power. "But, he is one man while we are many. He was beaten before, and he can be beaten again," Kade said as he looked around the table, his heart pumping strongly but slowly coming back under control. He was, again, met with more approving nods. Crayken stood up and all eyes swung toward him. Kade knew to let the Divine extinguish as he worked his way back to his seat. It was Crayken's turn. Kade could see that the synergy between them was affective.

"Many of us would prefer to live in peace, but peace is not possible while this evil walks our land," Crayken said.

"What of this cave? How are we to hold this, and why does it matter?" Red Diamond asked, recovering a small amount of his confidence. Kade was grateful that he had not broken the king's spirit.

"We know this tunnel houses a link to the land of the dead. Morg wants it to increase his power. There is knowledge that he seeks. We must not allow him this knowledge, or he will become too powerful," Crayken said, making a point to emphasize every word.

"As of this moment, Morg still seeks the cave. If we are careful, he will never learn of its existence," Kade said. "Morg is not even aware of what is in the cave, but it will not take him long to figure it out once he finds it," he added firmly. "The time is near for the coming battle. We fight together as a clutch," Kade said as he hit the table, "or we fall as individuals," he finished and eased back in his chair.

"I can see why you have so much faith in this one," Red Diamond said to Crayken.

"When you see him in action, you will have as much faith as I and then some," Crayken said with a knowing grin.

Kade only hoped he could live up to their expectations. This was an entire civilization betting everything on him. They were risking their very existence for his cause. He looked over at Doren and saw that the Master Chosen had a look on his face as if he was seeing Kade for the first time.

"Then it is settled," the white queen said as she smoothly rose from her seat. "For now, we dine."

"We meet in one hour to plan," Crayken said. The kings and queens rose and dispersed to their clutches. When all the spiders had left the table, Crayken turned toward Kade. "Is there more we should know? It would seem that our task is a difficult one with the limited knowledge we poses."

Kade was about to shake his head when Doren sighed loudly. All eyes turned on him. Kade got a sick feeling he was not going to like what Doren was about to say. Darcienna turned to look at Kade with a question in her eyes. Kade could only shrug and turned back toward Doren, waiting, but his patience was slipping. As he studied the Master Chosen, he was more certain by the moment that he was not going to like what was about to be said. It vaguely reminded him of another situation but he forced his mind to focus as his look was most certainly turning into an accusing glare that even Doren could see. The more the Apprentice Chosen considered the situation, the more certain he was that the man was not as forthcoming previously as he should have been. The Master Chosen took another deep breath as he drove right to the point.

"We must go back to the arch," Doren said and then locked eyes with Kade.

Darcienna's eyes went wide and Kade followed suit. His mind started to spin as he looked into Doren's eyes. He felt a sense of panic, and he did not even know why, yet, but he feared he was about to learn.

"We must return to the arch," Doren repeated, still not taking his eyes off Kade. Darcienna felt anger growing in her.

"We just left there. Why would we need to go back?" Darcienna asked heatedly. She saw the way Doren kept his gaze on Kade and worry flooded through her. Anger mixed with concern made her want to walk right up and punch the smug, pompous, overweight man squarely in the nose. He had kept something from them that they should have known about. "Out with it. Out with all of it!" she said with her hands planted firmly on her hips. Doren sighed, as if bored, and looked at her as if regarding a child. Kade could see her flex her hands into a fist and was certain she was about to climb over the table to give this arrogant man the clubbing of his life.

"It is very important. We may have allies in the land of the dead that might be able to help us," Doren said almost casually. Kade felt himself start to mirror Darcienna's thoughts. Doren had kept something from them and was acting as if it was just a minor slip of the mind. Nothing with this man was accidental when it came to power of any kind.

But, what would he want to keep from us? Kade wondered as he began to glare more without realizing it.

"The apprentice," Doren said, seeing the glare and making a point, "may be the key to us receiving knowledge that may bring us victory. If he can communicate with the Ancients, he may be able to learn of a way to overcome the might of the staff," Doren said as he shifted his gaze to the king and queen.

Now it made complete sense to Kade. He recalled how he had explained the ways of the Chosen to Darcienna while on the beach and this was a perfect example of it. Doren wanted to communicate with the Ancients and gain knowledge or power for himself. And in the way of the Chosen, he did not want to share. But this was different. The lives of everyone depended on the Chosen working together. Kade ground his teeth in frustration.

"Why did you not share this with us when we were at the arch?" Darcienna growled. Kade looked at Darcienna and gave a slight shake of his head. She went wide-eyed, stunned that he was telling her to stand down.

"He was still recovering from that creature that tried to take him over. Would you not want to leave if you just had barely survived being consumed by that thing?" Kade asked but he gave another slight shake of his head. Darcienna closed her mouth and her lips made a thin line as she clenched her jaw in exasperation. He would explain later. Right now he could not afford to have the king and queen distrust Doren or they might start to see all Chosen in a bad way.

"So, what the queen has said is true?" Crayken asked. "You can, indeed, speak with the dead?"

"That is the theory," Doren said. Kade cast a glance at Darcienna. The worry that flashed through her eyes was impossible to miss. He recalled his talk with Morg and knew it was inevitable that he was going to make another trip to the arch. "We may be able to learn something about the staff," Doren said. Kade tried to put on a brave face, but after recalling his last encounter with the arch and Doren's encounter today, he was far from eager to try anything with the doorway to the dead. His stomach was in knots just thinking about it.

"When do you plan on making this journey?" Crayken asked.

"I fear that we should go as soon as possible," Doren was saying, but Darcienna quickly cut him off.

"After he has had some rest," she said firmly, allowing no room for argument. She glared daggers at Doren. The Master Chosen shrugged his shoulders as if it mattered nothing at all to him. It was almost as if he was giving them permission for the delay with the way he waived them away.

"After I have had some rest," Kade said, not caring to even try to argue with her. He was quickly learning that when she was firm in her resolve, it would be easier to move a mountain than to change her mind. He was also very grateful for the delay.

"She is wise," Crayken said. "You should always listen to your promised one," he said as he turned to look at Rakna.

"I will lead you to your chamber," Rakna said to the young apprentice and then turned to face Doren. "We have room for you, also," she told him.

"Your offer is generous, but for now, I would speak with the king. We need to plan while Kade rests," Doren said with a slight bow.

"As you wish," Rakna said and turned to go.

64

"Please convey my apologies to the clutch for not staying," Kade said to the king and proceeded to follow the queen. He took several steps after Rakna and then stopped, turning back to Crayken. "If I may have the company of the queen on my journey to the cave, it would be much appreciated. I will need to communicate with the other spiders."

"If that is her desire, then let it be so," Crayken responded.

"His request has merit, my king. I shall accompany him when he wakes," Rakna said and then turned to lead them to their room. She stopped in front of their chamber, and with a curt bow, excused herself.

Kade could feel his eyelids already growing heavy. As he walked through the door, he glanced around for the sack containing the books. The bed was empty. Kade felt his pulse start to pick up as he recalled the scratch on Doren's wrist. He walked around the bed and saw Chance curled protectively around the sack. The Mordra glanced up once, unconcerned, and then laid its head back down, its eyes already closing. Relieved more than he could say, Kade let himself fall onto the bed, deeply grateful for Darcienna's persistence on his behalf.

Kade and Darcienna talked for almost an hour about the day's events as he fought off sleep. Darcienna was full of praise for his prowess, complimenting him with how he had spoken to the kings. Kade soaked up her words and felt himself open up more and more at her prompting. She loved to listen to him speak, and anything she could do to get him to talk was fine by her.

The activity in the great tree slowed and quiet descended. Kade felt himself fading fast as his mind unwound. It would not be long before his words came in slurs as he struggled to stay awake. He stopped fighting his exhaustion and let his eyes close as he listened to Darcienna's musical voice drift through his mind.

"Thank you," Kade said, his words almost indistinguishable. He smiled as his mind began to paint images of her.

Darcienna snuggled next to him. She laid her head on his

chest and looked up at him as his breathing became deeper by the moment. She started to move away when his breath caught in his throat. Without realizing what he was doing, he reached up, put an arm around her shoulder and held her tightly. She stopped moving, and the deep breathing returned. They stayed like that for hours without moving. That was just fine with Darcienna as she drifted off, enjoying having his arms around her. If she only knew what the day was to bring, she would have found sleep almost impossible.

CH3

Kade awoke to find the place dead quiet. He unwrapped his arms from around Darcienna and rolled to the edge of the bed. He swung his legs down and stood, stretching. He walked over to the slit in the wall and peered out. It was pitch black, and the sounds of night drifted in through the window.

"How did you sleep?" Darcienna asked, startling Kade.

"I thought you were still out," Kade said, his hand over his heart.

"I was until you got up," Darcienna said as she sprawled over the entire bed and stretched. "What are you planning?" she asked, certain she was not going to approve of the answer.

"I should get this over with," Kade said as he turned to look out the slit. Darcienna did not have to ask to understand what he was talking about. It was clear that the dreaded arch deep in the tunnel was on both their minds.

"Kade, are you sure this is the best way?" she asked, her voice heavy with concern. She sat up and tilted her head slightly as she waited for him to answer. He turned to look at her but her eyes were closed as she clenched her fists in the soft fabric on the bed. She swallowed hard and Kade knew she was reliving the battle with the unknown creature. He slowly sat on the bed and put a gentle hand on her arm. Her eyes came open and she breathed deeply, holding it for several long seconds, and then let it out as if to expel the stress and frustration from her body. Or, maybe a symbolic exorcism of the evil being that had tried to possess her. Kade smiled at her, trying to soothe her fears. She relaxed as she saw the way he was looking at her and even found it...alluring. He made her feel safe, even in the thickest parts of battle or the most dangerous of situations. She cleared her head of the terrible memory and looked at him, waiting for him to answer.

"No, but what other options do we have?" Kade asked. He watched her closely. He was hoping that she would say not to go and offer a better idea or that he should come up with a different plan, but she was silent. She was not going to offer a better way. She was not going to offer any way. As a matter of fact, he realized she was not even going to put up any more resistance at all. She knew this was what he had to do. Realizing that his path, once again, was laid out for him, he took a deep breath and then reached out to the dragon.

Rayden, we must go to the cave, Kade sent. At first, there was nothing, but with a little prompting, the dragon's weary thoughts came back to him. Kade heard movement outside the window and turned to see a huge, half-lidded, golden eye peering back. "Rayden is ready," Kade said as he mentally prepared himself for the task.

"Just promise me you will be careful," Darcienna said as she grabbed him by the arm and turned him toward her. She needed him to look her in the eye while making this promise. She had to know he would take this vow to heart and not just say it to placate her. Kade felt her pulse through her grip and knew this was difficult for her.

"I will be as safe as I can," Kade said. Darcienna did not

68

like the response, but it was the best she was going to get. He gently removed her hand from his arm and then turned and walked from the room with Darcienna close behind.

Kade worked his way down to the exit and was met by his faithful companion. Rayden nudged him a few times but Kade's mind was on his task. He scratched his friend on the side of the jaw as they walked but his eyes focused on the tree that housed the Great Hall. Kade patted the dragon on the side and mentally asked it to wait patiently for him to return.

Kade walked through the entrance and down the wide set of stairs carved out of the earth. He stepped into the massive chamber and took the time to survey the room. The Great Hall was completely deserted with the exception of the beautiful white queen and the majestic, black king, pouring over a map of the area. There were a few guards sitting at a table, talking quietly. The queen noticed Kade and motioned for the king to turn around.

"Am I to understand that you are to leave at this early hour?" Crayken asked, surprised and concerned.

"I would only be delaying the inevitable," Kade responded. "Besides, the sun rises soon."

Rakna called to the two guards, who promptly leapt up and came to her. She buzzed instructions to them and turned back to Kade. The king reached up and placed a leg on Kade's shoulder.

"Be safe, and may the Divine watch over you," Crayken said with worry. He tried to hide his concern, but it was plain for Kade to see. "Look after my queen," the king added and then turned to Rakna. "Keep him safe, my love. Our survival depends on it."

"I will," Kade said as he returned the gesture.

"He is capable, but I shall do what is within my power, my king," Rakna said.

"This is a very early hour, Kade," Doren said as he entered the Great Hall. His eyes shown of someone who had just awoke from a sleep they preferred desperately to still be enjoying.

"I would understand if you preferred to stay, Master Doren,"

Kade said, wondering how the Master Chosen knew to come to the Great Hall. It had to be a calling that he was not aware of. Maybe a calling placed on his door that would alert the Master Chosen of its use. Kade had a feeling he would never know. Doren was a master and had to have his share of callings.

"You are going to the cave?" Doren asked.

"Yes," Kade responded. He realized he should have known that Doren would not dare stay if there was a chance that Kade could learn something new.

"Then we should depart," Doren declared as if the decision were his. Kade wished dearly that the man was staying behind, but he had no way to compel the Master Chosen to stay. And, he was certain that Doren was not going to let Kade access the doorway to the dead without being there.

Without any more delay, they said their goodbyes and exited the tree. Rayden was waiting patiently by the entrance. They mounted and readied to go. The dragon turned and headed off at a run but did not leap into the air as Kade expected. He questioned the dragon and received a reply just as Darcienna was speaking.

"We are not flying?" she asked, still holding tightly. Doren was leaning around Kade, apparently ready to ask the same question. He was watching the apprentice closely, waiting for the response.

"Rayden prefers not to fly at night. As best as I can tell, dragons don't like being in the air when it is dark," Kade responded. Darcienna said no more, and Doren leaned back into place so Kade let the subject drop. The flight may have been much quicker and smoother than running, but this was far better than walking.

Kade's mind could not help but to see Zayle coming through the dark and wondered if he was going to see it this time, also. Would his cherished master make his presence known once more? If Zale was not there to meet him, would he be able to find his teacher when he crossed through the arch? He tried to ignore the possibility of running into one of those evil creatures, but the worry

70

was getting stronger the closer they got to their destination.

It was not long before the dragon lumbered to a stop outside the cave. Kade swung a leg over and leapt to the ground gracefully. He turned deftly to reach out for Darcienna as she slid down the dragon's side and into his arms. He smiled as he looked into her eyes and considered pulling her into an embrace, but Doren grunted, drawing their attention. The two slowly untangled and stepped back.

"Kade, please lead the way to the arch," Doren said with a touch of impatience.

Darcienna gave the Master Chosen a glare but Doren gave no indication of noticing. Kade turned and led them into the cave. There were approximately ten spiders that leapt up, ready to attack. The queen buzzed at them and they immediately knelt down, putting their heads to the ground. Kade walked to the entrance of the tunnel and brought the Divine Fire to life. Doren glanced at the fire and then to Kade as if to ask, "Is that needed?" Kade realized that the Master Chosen was expecting him to call on the light, hoping to catch what he was missing. He was determined to catch Kade using the Illumination Calling and steal the secret. The apprentice realized that had he chosen to call on light, the master may have figured out the move. He affirmed to himself that he needed to be more cautious.

"If Morg is searching for the doorway, I would prefer to be prepared," Kade said, wondering if he was being over cautious. Doren nodded and raised his hands. After several elaborate gestures, there was a bright, blue spark jumping from finger to finger. It reminded Kade of the spark that protected the black book. It did not provide the light that the Divine Fire did, but Kade was certain that Doren did not call on it for its light giving ability. Kade found himself studying Doren's gestures. The Master Chosen had a look in his eye that was pure amusement. Kade colored slightly as he caught Doren's eye and turned away. He was not about to play the game with a Master. It was sure to get him killed. Kade started walking without looking back. Something told him that if he checked, Doren would still be standing there, holding his hands out with the spark dancing from finger to finger as if tempting the apprentice to try. Kade knew better. He was certain beyond a shadow of a doubt that he could not cast that calling without being taught, and yet, he had to admit to himself that he was tempted. He relaxed his shoulders and marched on. The master shrugged his shoulders, even though Kade could not see and quickly caught up to walk side by side with the apprentice.

Darcienna walked along Kade's right while Doren walked on his left. The queen walked next to Darcienna as they worked their way down the tunnel. Each was studying the darkness intently until Kade broke the silence.

"Here," Kade said as he came to a stop several paces from the arch and reached out to keep Darcienna from walking further. The queen moved a little closer to Darcienna's side while eyeing the arch with clear distaste. Doren edged forward slowly and then drew back to stand next to Kade. He turned to look at the apprentice. Kade walked over to stand next to the drawings on the wall.

"I am eager to see if this will work," Doren said with excitement at the thought of contact with an Ancient, even if it had to be through an apprentice. The Master Chosen also studied the wall with the images drawn on it. "The calling is so simple, and yet, you are the only one who can use it," Doren said as he glanced at Kade and then back to the drawings. He recalled his previous attempt and had no urge to try again.

Kade looked at the blackness and shivered. *Am I really going to voluntarily enter the land of the dead?* he asked himself and felt a sliver of fear work its way into his heart. He did his best to keep a brave face for Darcienna, but something told him that he was not fooling her.

He recalled, too vividly, the entity that attempted to take him over, not to mention the one that almost took Doren and then Darcienna. He knew he had come too far to turn back now, but it did not make it any easier. He mentally prepared himself for what was to come as he stepped up to the wall, making sure he understood all he needed to know. Doren watched him, his excitement continuing to grow. The thought of new knowledge made the man act as a kid might when receiving a brand new toy.

"Are you ready?" the Master Chosen asked. It was not necessarily to ensure Kade was prepared as it was more a push to continue.

Kade did not answer the question. He turned toward Darcienna and tried to find the words he wanted to say. There was so much he wanted to tell her, and yet, he could not find the right way to say it. She tried to smile reassuringly but her mouth twisted into deep concern as her brow knitted together. He wished he had made her stay back at the tree, but he knew that short of tying her up, she would not have accepted being left behind.

"Okay," Kade said as he glanced at the wall one last time. "I am only delaying. I am ready," he said, avoiding Darcienna's eyes.

The rest of the group moved back to give him room. Kade let his Divine Fire fade as he looked at the ground for a spot where he could lay. With only Doren's spark to give light, Kade could barely make out the floor. It was eerie and did not inspire confidence. The queen's eyes glowed as they reflected the faint, blue spark, adding to the ominous scene. Darcienna's eyes did not help, either. The knot in Kade's stomach tightened. He wished the room could be well lit, but he was the only one able to do that and he was not willing to teach Doren the calling. He realized he was truly becoming a Chosen when he decided to deal with this extreme discomfort just to keep a secret.

After stalling for just a few more seconds, he laid down and closed his eyes. It took a while of deep breathing for his mind and body to relax. With Doren hovering over him, it was even more difficult, but in time, he was able to get his discomfort under control. He brought the Divine through him like a lazy river. His awareness slid out and floated toward the ceiling.

Kade drifted down and stopped in front of Darcienna. He gently leaned forward and kissed her on the lips. She blinked once and raised her hand, placing her fingers lightly on her lips. She slowly lowered her eyes to look at Kade's body.

Turning toward the gate, Kade froze. There were several people standing there on the other side of the arch, watching him. His heart, if he could call it that in this form, skipped a beat. They looked as solid as the group he was with. It was the figure in the middle that he locked eyes with. Kade drifted down to stand firmly on the ground.

"I see you have mastered the Drift Calling," Zayle said with praise.

"I should have tried harder," Kade said, feeling a swirl of emotions.

"Do not dwell on what has passed unless it helps you in the present or future," Zayle said wisely. "Tell us what has transpired since my passing."

"There is so much, Master. I don't know where to start," Kade said.

"Tell us what you believe to be relevant," the man to Zayle's right said. He was tall and looked like a warrior. He had broad shoulders and a thick chest. The look in his eye said he meant business but it also showed deep wisdom. The person who tried to pull one over on this Ancient Chosen was going to learn a hard lesson.

"This is Talos," Zayle said with a casual indication of an open hand. Kade gave a nod at the solid looking man and then returned his eyes to his teacher.

"I have been in contact with Morg several times. He almost killed me twice," Kade said, cringing at the memory.

"We are aware. You almost crossed," the other man said. He was not even half the bulk of Talos but there was an air of confidence that said he was as deadly as they come. Kade expected to hear the voice of an old, frail man, but instead, there was power when he spoke. Kade was certain that he would be a much better match for Morg than Doren. The confidence and sheer force of will with this Ancient was palpable. Kade cast a glance at Doren for just a moment. Having the Master Chosen to assist with this fight against Morg was better than nothing but having one of these men at his side would have been more than he could hope for. He faced the three figures once again.

"This is Lokk," Zayle said with another open handed gesture. The man gave a friendly smile but his eyes were solid steel. Something told Kade that of the two Ancients, this one was dangerous beyond understanding. And yet, he gave Kade a nod as if meeting another full-fledged Chosen. The apprentice could not help but to swell at the show of respect.

"Morg needs you so he can reach the Ancients," Zayle said as he indicated the men standing at his sides. He saw the confused look on Kade's face and gave a nod of his head as he spoke. "I assure you, they are the Ancients. They may not look thousands of years old, but I promise you that they are the wise ones from long ago." This seemed to satisfy Kade so Zayle continued. "We must know if Morg has knowledge of this arch."

"No, he is still searching for it," Kade said. The two ancients relaxed visibly.

"How do we stop him while he has that bloody staff?" Kade asked as his mind recalled the brutal beating he had taken from the ornately carved piece of wood. Morg seemed invincible while in possession of that all too powerful weapon. "Blood and Ash! He is unbeatable with that thing!" Kade swore and instantly cringed at the use of such harsh language in his master's presence, not to mention the Ancients. The taller one seemed amused by Kade's outburst and cast a quick sidelong glance at Lokk. It was almost a look of approval but Kade did not watch him long enough to decide. Zayle started to speak once more. Kade missed the slight nod of the man's head.

"You have no choice but to take it from him," Zayle said,

ignoring the profanity.

Kade's eyes went wide. He felt panic well up in him at the thought of being paralyzed again. To be made a puppet while he was forced to watch the evil Chosen do as he wished scared him to the bone. Kade could not imagine the torment he would feel if he were made to watch while Morg tortured Darcienna? This was not the solution he was hoping for. This was not what he expected from the wise and powerful Ancients. The man on Zayle's right saw Kade's frustration and stepped forward. His voice was deep and resonated with confidence and command. Kade would have thought him a general in an army getting ready to lead the charge.

"As daunting a task as this may sound, the Divine Power is only as wise as the man using it. Yes, the staff is powerful, but do not forget that he who depends solely on the Divine, has weaknesses that may be exploited," the Ancient said. He watched Kade calmly as he waited for the apprentice to fully comprehend what was just said. "And, you have abilities which are not to be taken lightly," Talos said with a grin. There was a glint in his eye as he studied the Apprentice Chosen. "You have power beyond what you are aware of, Chosen," the Ancient said, adding the last part as a title of respect. Kade beamed at that.

"He sounds like you," Kade said to Zayle as he pondered the wise one's words.

"That is a great compliment," Zayle responded while giving a nod of his head.

"Master, I have so many questions I must ask. I have some that are of a more personal nature," Kade said hesitantly.

"You may ask," Zayle prompted. Talos gave a great heave of his chest and stepped back, allowing the young man a chance to speak his mind with his teacher.

"Master...it may sound foolish, but Doren has said he is prepared to take over my training," Kade said as he glanced at the Master Chosen still standing over his body.

Kade turned back to Zayle and opened his mouth to continue

but stood there without saying a word. He knew he should be using this time to find the answers needed to defeat Morg, but coming face to face with his grandfather gave him the opportunity to address an issue that he was struggling with. His heart ached. He glanced at the Ancients, but neither had judgment of any sort in their eyes. It was more infinite patience than anything.

"Continue to use the Divine, and practice your skills anyway you must. Learn what you can from Doren, but be careful not to trust him too much. He can be a formidable ally and an excellent teacher, but his thirst for knowledge is unquenchable. He craves power more than any other of our kind. Be cautious while walking that path," Zayle said. Before Kade could continue, the Master Chosen held up his hand. "We will have much time in the future to talk," Zayle said as he gave one of his rare, reassuring smiles. Kade yearned to reach out for his grandfather but that was not Zayle's way. It was clear that this talk needed to be about the current crises. Kade brushed aside his feeling and focused on the task at hand.

"How does the staff work?" Kade asked, desperately hoping to find a weakness. He was certain that this line of questioning was not going to give him a way of taking the staff from Morg, but he still thought it best to know the weapon as best he could before trying to acquire it. Before Kade could say much more, Lokk, confidently, but calmly, took two steps forward without taking his eyes off the young apprentice. Kade fought the urge to step backward. He was grateful that this man was his ally. Lokk stopped next to Zayle as he cocked his head as if assessing the young man. After a moment, he came to a decision and spoke.

"The staff embodies the movements needed to mold the Divine. Each calling has a symbol that represents it. The callings that the staff is imbued with are the callings the Chosen can perform. No more and no less. If the calling requires words to be spoken, then they must be spoken. There might be callings on the staff that Morg may not be aware of," the thinner Ancient said thoughtfully. "Morg has become dependent on the staff for his power. Remove the staff and he will be virtually helpless," he said in conclusion and stepped back.

"What would happen if Morg was to find this place? Why is it so important to him?" Kade asked.

"We have several guesses as to what he plans," Talos said. "If he destroys the calling set within the arch, he may set loose upon the world an evil of such proportions that it will never recover. If the evil on this side gets through, there will be such suffering that even death will not be an escape," he said with a seriousness that made Kade shiver. "It is not the arch that is important but the calling held within the arch. It is complicated. By destroying the calling, he will tear a hole in the veil that separates the living from the dead. But, if the arch is destroyed, the calling will just dissipate and there will be no way to cross from one side to the other. Unfortunately, there will be no way for us to communicate, either." Zayle's eyes went distant as he contemplated the Ancient's words. Kade watched his teacher for just a moment before continuing on.

"Does he have the power to destroy the arch or the calling?" Kade asked.

"He does, but he does not know it, yet," the Ancient said cryptically.

"How could he have the power to destroy the gate but not know it?" Kade asked, pressing for the answer he knew they were hesitant to give. The Ancients looked at each other and then to Zayle.

"Zayle?" Kade asked. The Master Chosen sighed and reached out to put his hand on Kade's shoulder. The apprentice was so stunned at the physical connection that his knees almost gave out. He did not expect to feel that touch, but more importantly, his teacher rarely showed affection with him in this way. It was his grandfather he was seeing now.

"Be very careful, Kade. Morg still believes he can use you to communicate with the dead. He believes he can gain the knowledge he needs through you," Zayle said.

"I will not tell him anything!" Kade said vehemently. He was certain that nothing could be truer than what he had just vowed.

"No?" Zayle asked as his gaze fell on the beautiful, blue-eyed blonde kneeling over his body. Kade turned and saw what his master was looking at and faltered. "Even if her life hangs in the balance?" Zayle asked, nodding toward Darcienna with a raised brow as he studied Kade's face closely. The apprentice opened his mouth but no words came out. He felt an invisible hand squeezing his heart. A knot the size of his fist grew in his stomach and he realized in horror that the vow he had just spoken may, indeed, be difficult to keep. He did not believe he would bend to Morg's will, but he could not say how he would react if her life were to be threatened. Zayle saw the look in his grandson's eyes and nodded in the wise way he always did when he was able to teach a new lesson. "We all have our weaknesses. Be careful, Grandson. Be careful."

"I will, Master," Kade said. He did not know what he would do if her life were threatened, but he could no longer repeat the vow he had just given. He was certain that Zayle, along with the Ancients, saw right through him as his mind struggled with how he might respond if it came to her life or the information from the Ancients.

"There is no shame in love, young one," Talos said in his deep voice. If you could so easily stand your ground, you would not be worthy of her love. You are a good man. We can see that," the Ancient said with a knowing look. Kade felt like an infant in the presence of greatness.

"There is another here that has joined our fight thanks to you, my apprentice," Zayle said as he smiled.

Kade looked past his teacher, and there stood a woman, where a moment before, there had been no one. His eyes widened in awe as he looked upon her face. Kade quickly glanced over his shoulder at Darcienna and then back to the old woman. She locked eyes with him, gave a smile and nodded once. He looked back at

Darcienna, eager to give her the news.

"Jorell has joined our cause thanks to you. She has Nature's Gift with her. She is the first of her kind to bring her gifts when crossing over. This is important, Kade. Know this and remember it. If her kind must pass, you can help them," Zayle said. "There is more that you must know," he said, becoming deadly serious.

"There is a book with many very powerful callings in it that belongs with the staff," the larger of the two ancients said in a very deadly tone. He was all business now. "It is a book that explains all the callings that the staff is empowered with. One of the callings is very complex and takes forty one moves to perform. That is the one we used to create this arch. With the help of the staff, it was possible to accomplish this. There is also another calling that is equally as complex that could be used to destroy the arch. The book was split into four separate books. It is important that the books not fall into Morg's hands. It may even be best if they are destroyed."

"Four?" Kade asked.

"There was only one, but it was split into several smaller books. The information can only be attained when all four books are put together," the smaller of the two Ancients said.

"Where are these books? How do I find them?" Kade asked.

"To the one who finds them, they will appear to be blank. The cover will be made of a metal-like substance," the large Ancient said.

"Maybe that is what Morg is after. Maybe that is why he wants to use me to access this gate," Kade said. The Ancients looked at each other and then back to him. Kade got the feeling that he was missing something but decided to come back to it later. "I want to know more about the books. Where can I find them?"

"You have already found one," Zayle said as he watched his apprentice. Kade shook his head in confusion and then his eyes came open wide as he recalled seeing a book that fit the description. It was in the sack being guarded by the Mordra. "Yes, you have one of them," he said, seeing the look on Kade's face. "I have been trying to locate the other books my entire life. I know they need to be found, but I was not able to locate more than one of them. The other three are scattered far and wide. Find them."

"Where can I find them?" Kade asked, sensing he was being forced to walk further down this path than he was hoping.

"I can only tell you that in one of my visions, I saw a landscape of crystal trees. The area was of the purest white. The sky was blue without a cloud in the sky. I only saw this briefly but it was enough to tell me that one of the books can be located once the crystal trees are found. I have no more about the books," Zayle said with a slight shrug of his shoulder.

"Why can't I just destroy the book I have and be done with it," Kade said, but he feared it was not going to be that easy or Zayle would have already done it.

"If only it were possible," Zayle said sadly as he shook his head. "The books are indestructible until they are rejoined. Once all of the books are put together, then and only then can it be destroyed."

"If Morg does not have me or the books, then you are safe, correct?" Kade asked.

"Yes and no. While we are not in danger directly, he could destroy the arch and we would no longer be able to communicate. It is critical that the arch stay safe," the thinner Ancient said. There was definitely an intensity to his words.

"Then we must stop him before he learns of this doorway," Kade said resolutely.

Before the conversation could continue, Zayle and the other three looked to their left. The imposing one became deadly serious as he turned to face whatever had gotten their attention. He scowled at something Kade could not see. Jorell took a step away to give him room and then the man flew into a series of elaborate moves that ended with him holding his hands in front of his chest, one facing down and the other facing up. There was a glowing orb the size of a man's head pulsing between his hands. Kade had the urge to lean forward as though looking out a window to see what had them on edge but that meant entering the world of the dead and he was not about to do that. The other Ancient slightly turned but it was clear that all expected the man holding the pulsing ball to easily dispatch what had their attention. The formidable Chosen pulled his lips back as if in deep disgust and then lunged forward, letting loose this unknown weapon. There was a screech that reminded Kade of the one he had heard the previous day. He shivered. The Tall man sneered in contempt as he took a breath and let it out again. He returned to the calm, powerful Ancient once more.

Yes, Kade was certain that this Master Chosen would be a match for Morg. Jorell cast a glance around to ensure they were no longer being threatened. Zayle never appeared to be concerned as his fingers were still interlaced in front of himself where they had been the entire time. Lokk had barely turned as he watched.

"There is great danger here that must stay here," Zayle said as he watched Kade's reaction. "I wish I could say that all who use the Divine are of a pure heart, but alas, they are not." Kade got the feeling that Zayle was on the verge of looking at Doren but kept his eyes where they were. "They sense your life force and hunger for it. It is the promise to return to the world of the living. If they can enter a person, they can walk the land of man once again."

With a sinking heart, Kade realized he was far from done with this danger. He recalled his flight on the dragon and how he desperately wanted to just drop Doren off and then be on his way. He felt like a fool for believing he had a choice. Not only did he need to deal with Morg and the staff but he was expected to search for these metal books, also. With regret, he knew he was only trying to convince himself he was in charge of his destiny. The more he thought about it, the more he realized that the decision to go after Morg had been made when he was on fire with the Blue Flame of the Divine as he worked at convincing the kings and queens to join this war. The decision to go even beyond that was not his to be made, either. It was appearing more and more obvious that he had virtually no say in where his life was supposed to be heading. It was decided. All of it was decided and he was powerless to change it. He was in this until the end. The imposing Ancient must have seen the thoughts running through Kade's mind.

"It is the way of the Divine, young one. We are given great power and we must use that power to ensure that those that would threaten the good in life are kept in check. You would not expect to be one of the Divine's Chosen only to waste away on a farm, would you?" the man said with a half smile. Kade could not say why but what the man said helped. Talos saw the change in Kade's eyes and gave a broad smile. "Just because the Divine gives us a path to walk, all of us, does not mean we cannot still live a life that we find acceptable," he said as he cast a glance at the beautiful blue-eyed woman staring down at the body of the apprentice. Kade caught the man's eye and grinned like a boy. "That is more like it," he said, crossing his arms over his broad chest and adding a nod of his head.

"Thanks," Kade said, feeling a relief wash over him. The Ancient was right. With a nod of his head to indicate he understood, he returned to the more pressing concern of Morg. "When must I leave?"

"You have some time, Kade, but not much. A days rest may do you well," Zayle said.

The teacher looked upon his student with pride. A smile crept across his face, which was another odd thing for Kade to see. Jorell came to stand next to Zayle as she looked past Kade to gaze fondly at her student. She clearly had a soft spot for Darcienna as her eyes took on a loving look that was impossible to miss. She put her open hand up to her mouth in a way that gave Kade the impression that the gesture was a subconscious habit.

"You love her, don't you?" Jorell asked through her fingers as her eyes locked with his. Kade was certain that she already knew the answer, but how? He just stared. "It was obvious from the moment you arrived at the arch. Take care of her and she will always take care of you."

"I will," Kade said, all pretense of trying to hide his feelings falling away.

"You have accomplished much since my passing, Kade," Zayle said. Deep in his heart, the apprentice could feel the love his grandfather had for him. He could also see regret in the man's eyes. He, too, regretted that their relationship had only been one of master and student, but Kade understood why. "How were you able to do so much with what meager callings you had?" Zayle asked.

"I learned a few more when I found your books."

"You…learned more callings?" Zayle asked cautiously as he narrowed his eyes.

"The Lightning Calling," Kade said, proud of himself at first until he recalled that he had destroyed the cabin with his newfound skill. Zayle's eyes went wide.

"The Lightning…how?" Zayle asked as he glanced at Doren. "I was not going to teach that one to you for another year because you were struggling with the lesser callings. You barely became proficient in the Divine Fire Calling with its six moves," Zayle said in disbelief.

"I practiced for a whole day until I had it," Kade said, smiling lightly, dreading telling Zayle of the doom that befell their home.

"In a day? Just one day?" Zayle asked incredulously. He looked down at the ground as if to find what he was seeking while he considered what Kade had just told him. "That's amazing. And you did not hurt yourself?" Zayle asked as he quickly looked Kade over.

"Well…actually…I almost killed myself with the calling," Kade said as he shuffled his feet a bit. "I burned the cabin down by accident. If the dragon wasn't there to pull me out of the fire, I would be with you now."

"Kade!" Zayle said, reverting back to his prior self as the teacher. "You must be more careful! That calling could have…," Zayle was beginning to yell when he stopped. He took a deep breath and his face softened considerably. "Grandson, please be careful," he said with such emotion that Kade felt his heart ache. Zayle stepped forward through the gate, reached a hand behind Kade's neck and pulled him into a hug. "I love you Grandson. I have faith in you." For a moment, Kade thought there was more to his comment but brushed it off as his grandfather's loving arms wrapped around him.

Kade felt the flood gates of his heart open wide. The pain he had been trying to hide hit him like a tidal wave. For the first time that he could recall, he felt like a boy in the arms of a loving parent. The tears flowed freely as he hugged his grandfather for the first time in his life. There was no longer Zayle the Master but Zayle the father of his mother. After a short while, Kade felt a relief so profound that it left him speechless. A weight lifted off him that he had not realized was there until that very moment.

"I am very happy to see you again, Master. I thought you were gone forever," Kade said as Zayle stepped back.

"Grandfather," Zayle corrected.

"Grandfather," Kade said, wiping away a tear, liking very much how that sounded.

"It is also good to see you, my apprentice," Zayle said with a smile as he emphasized the word, "My", sparing a glance at Doren.

"Grandson," Kade corrected with a grin. Zayle laughed as he grinned back at the boy who had grown into a man. Kade had not missed the point Zayle was making. He glanced back over his shoulder at Doren and then smiled even wider at his grandfather.

"And I hated that cabin," Zayle said with a shake of his head. "It was like a prison. The only reason I was there was to keep you safe. I miss your mother and father, but it had to be. I am sure you understand now."

"I do," Kade said, comprehending fully what his grandfather had sacrificed for him all these years. Zayle paused as his eyes widened.

"Did you say…you were saved by the dragon?" Zayle asked,

unbelieving.

"Yes," Kade said with a grin that went from ear to ear. The look on his grandfather's face was priceless. "It has been critical in helping me survive. Without Rayden, I would not be here," he said with pride.

"So this dragon, it has stayed with you? The very dragon that carried us?"

"Yes. Rayden is just outside the cave," Kade said, enjoying the reaction he was seeing. He grinned even more as he readied his next piece of news. "Chance is also back at the tree."

"Chance?" Zayle asked, knowing that Kade was going somewhere with this.

"Oh, my Mordra," Kade said, feigning disinterest. The shorter of the two Ancients became alert at the news. Kade waited for him to add something as he appeared to be on the verge of speaking but then he relaxed without saying a word. The look on Zayle's face was worth all the years of wood splitting and working in the garden. Kade laughed openly.

"You never cease to amaze me, Grandson," Zayle said in awe. You must tell me this tale when we have time. You are aware how rare those are?" Zayle asked as he, again, glanced at Doren. He grinned, knowing full well of Doren's search for the infamous creature. Before Kade could answer the question, his eyes widened as he looked at the gate and then to his grandfather.

"You can pass through the arch?" Kade asked, excited at the possibilities.

"It is hard for us. We can pass for short times only. If I stay out too long, I risk the chance of dying the final death."

"What exactly does that mean?" Kade asked.

"My awareness would fade and I would cease to exist anywhere," Zayle said in all seriousness.

"Then I will let you go back through," Kade said as he retreated from his grandfather.

Zayle hugged his grandson one more time, holding him for

86

several long seconds before releasing him. As Zayle backed up, he let his hands fall on Kade's forearms and squeezed one last time before stepping through the arch. Kade was surprised to feel a touch of sadness as his grandfather looked at him from the other side.

"You should be on your way," Zayle said.

"I expected to cross over" Kade commented as he looked up at the arch.

"NO!" Zayle said with such force that Kade took a step back. Zayle took a breath, and continued on more calmly. "Only in the most dire of circumstances are you to ever cross this arch. There is danger on this side beyond your understanding. No. We will always speak like this," Zayle said as he softened.

"I understand," Kade said, surprised at the sudden outburst and relieved at the same time. As he was about to turn, he recalled something else that he believed his grandfather would appreciate hearing. He smiled, eager to see his master's reaction. "I thought you would like to know that I slayed the giant that killed you," Kade said proudly.

"You did?" Zayle asked and then glanced at the Ancients. Talos gave a slight grin and a barely perceptible nod of his head to Lokk. Kade was certain that he was the topic of those unspoken words but decided he did not have time to learn what had passed between the two. "Please, do tell," Zayle said, again, amazed.

"I used the Lightning Calling, and I had the help of the dragon. He almost had us, though. It could have gone either way, but in the end, there was a lot of food for the animals. They should be happy for weeks, or until the meat rots," Kade said with a smile.

"Your gift makes you a formidable opponent indeed. It will be Morg's undoing if he thinks you an unworthy adversary. This may be to your advantage," Talos said. Out of the four people standing on the other side of the veil, Talos was definitely one that saw the strengths and weaknesses of any battle.

"You have done well," Zayle said, shaking his head in

disbelief.

"Kade, we need to return to the Great Hall!" the queen hissed urgently to the body lying on the ground. "The king says there is danger!" She jumped to her feet.

"Grandfather, I am needed back at the spider's tree, but before I go, I must ask. When you said you had faith in me, were you talking about defeating Morg? Or...was there more?" Lokk made a slight gesture with his hand just as Zayle opened his mouth to answer. Everyone faded from view.

Just as well, Kade thought as he quickly turned away from the arch.

He willed himself back to his body, ready to confront the danger that threatened his clutch. When he sat up, Darcienna jumped. He was eager to tell her of Jorell, but now was not the right time; not when they had to rush off to face danger. He leapt to his feet.

Doren was beside himself, eager to hear everything Kade had to say. He desperately wanted to stop Kade in his tracks and make him spill everything he had learned. It was almost agony for him to wait even one more second for the apprentice's report. Doren knew the young man was gone too long for something not to have happened. And with the lack of any presence trying to take over his body, the Master Chosen was certain that Kade had found what he was seeking.

"Hurry, Kade, hurry!" Rakna urged as she raced up the tunnel.

Doren's face screwed into a scowl of frustration as he looked after the small group that was quickly racing up the tunnel. With a last glance at the arch, he ran after the group. It might be a small delay, but in the end, he would have his apprentice telling every little detail of this small adventure. And with that, he forced the agony of the wait out of his mind and picked up the pace.

CH4

"Rakna," Kade said, feeling his pulse quicken. "What is the danger?"

"I am not sure. What the king is saying is not making sense," the queen hissed as she worked her way up the tunnel. "He talks of many different creatures and then speaks of only one. It is confusing, Chosen," Rakna said.

"Kade," Doren said. "Be ready for anything. If Morg has found us…." He left the rest unspoken. They were all aware that this would be a crushing blow if the evil Chosen were to find them before they had a chance to prepare. Kade felt his heart skip a beat at the thought. He felt as if his chest were being constricted and cringed. It was something he desperately hoped never to feel again. He steeled his will and continued on. This type of fear was going to do him no good, and besides, it was Morg who was going to suffer, not him.

"Then we should pray to the Divine that this is not the case,"

Kade said as he rushed up the tunnel, eager to meet the challenge.

"Kade, I am not sensing danger," Darcienna said as if trying to listen to a far off voice.

"Not here," Kade said.

"I understand," Darcienna said, annoyed that he was treating her like a child that needed something explained. "But, if we were heading into danger, which we would be, I would get something. But...I can't really say. It...does have potential," she said as she cocked her head to the side.

Kade studied her as they hurried toward the exit. He watched her closely, waiting for her to decide what she was sensing. He had come to know deep in his heart that when she said there was danger, there was danger. So, why would the king warn of danger if Darcienna did not sense any?

This was not making sense, Kade thought. Her eyes did indicate something. For just a moment, they appeared to lighten a shade. He was surprised to see that she was no longer listening for that far off voice, but was instead, staring at him. He was studying her so closely that he missed the change.

"Let me know if you can make anything of it," Kade said as he looked away.

"I am not sure if it is going to change. I think it is going to depend on you. I cannot explain why but...I think you are the key," Darcienna said as she spared a glance for the queen. Rakna was listening closely.

"I would not be surprised if it were dependent on Kade. He will, of course, deal with this danger," Rakna said in complete confidence. It was not what Darcienna meant, but the end result was still the same. Kade glanced at Doren and wondered if the Master Chosen took offence at the unintended slight. Rakna may have great respect for Doren, as he is a Master Chosen, but it was Kade that she expected to deal with this. After all, she did witness him dispatch their lifelong foes. Surprising to Kade, Doren was looking right at him. Kade brushed off the awkwardness and refocused his attention on the queen.

It was obvious that Rakna had no doubt that Kade could conquer anything that threatened them. *If only she had seen how Morg had made a puppet out of me,* he thought. *How would she look at me then?* he asked himself. He hoped the day never came. The shame of letting down so many, who looked upon him as their hero, would be crushing, not to mention that an entire civilization might fall because of him. He felt a weight that was almost too much to bear. *How did I get into a position where so many depended on me?* he pondered again as he exited the tunnel into the cave. He shook his head, trying to dispel the thought.

"Kade," Darcienna said, seeing a frown cross his face. "What is it?"

"Nothing," he said as he reached out with his mind. "Nothing I can change now," he added as he took a deep breath and let it out.

Rayden, we need to go. There is danger back at the tree. Come to the cave, Kade sent. There was a tremendous roar off in the distance. Kade wondered, for just a moment, if Rayden had a personal challenge for himself to make his latest roar louder than the previous one. The echo that came off the mountains was impressive.

"You have requested your dragon's return?" Doren asked as they exited the cave. The sun was just cresting the horizon and light was starting to spread across the land.

"I have, and he says he is on his way," Kade responded.

"Kade," the queen hissed cautiously. "The king indicates that things are under control, but your presence is still requested."

"Thank you, Rakna," Kade said, relieved.

The next roar came from directly over them. Kade flinched hard as did the rest of the group. He was not yet used to Rayden flying and was watching the horizon for the dragon instead of the air. The two guard spiders scrambled in opposite directions until they got themselves under control. The instinctual fear that

91

assaulted them was too much for them to overcome. Even Rakna appeared to have been shaken, but she held her ground.

Kade looked up and saw the dragon diving straight for them only to bank away hard at the very last second. The group felt the woosh of air. Rayden swerved and swooped in low to glide just above the ground as he flew away from the group. His legs were tucked back, making him streamlined, but if he chose, he could have touched the ground, he was so close. He flipped his tail back and forth to slow his flight. When he had lost enough speed, he banked hard and turned directly for them. He was headed toward the group when he pulled up sharply while swinging his feet forward and pumping his wings, sending a dust storm high into the air. Kade could have sworn the dragon beat its wings a few more times than was needed before finally folding them in. Doren glared at Kade as he waved the dust out of his face.

"Yes," Kade said, as he felt the link come alive. "We are impressed." He brushed the dust off his new clothes. The dragon enjoyed this display of prowess. "Now, if you are done showing off, we must return to the Great Hall."

"Yes," Doren scoffed. "Quite an entrance," he said as he straightened his cloak. "What happened to him not liking flying at night?" Doren asked, clearly very displeased.

"Well, don't be too hard on him," Darcienna said as she patted the dragon on the muzzle. "The sun is up. Besides, he just recently started flying again and wants to show off a little," she said and then addressed the dragon. "But, we are in a hurry so maybe a little less playing around," she scolded. Rayden tilted his head back and forth as he studied her.

"We must go," Kade said as he indicated for Rayden to kneel. "Keep the wings in. There are too many for us to chance flying."

Rayden gave a huff and knelt down. Kade swung Darcienna up deftly and then grabbed Doren. Just before boosting the Master Chosen up, Doren gripped his hand and stopped him.

"Gentle, Apprentice, gentle. I am not as young as I used to be. Now would not be the time to nurse a broken rib back to health if I were to be crushed under that grip of yours or fly clean over the dragon's back," Doren said as he put his hands on the side of the dragon.

"I will remember that," Kade said as he eased his grasp a little.

Kade was as gentle as he could be while boosting Doren's massive bulk onto the dragon's back. The Master Chosen reached forward and grabbed the wing joints, holding on tightly. Kade turned, and with the skill of an acrobat, bounded off the dragon's knee to land just in front of Darcienna. He laughed as Rayden shivered. It was a sure sign that the spiders had climbed on and were situating themselves.

"Yes, they are spiders, but you will need to learn to accept it," Kade said. And yet, he did find it amusing. *Serves the dragon right,* Kade thought as he brushed off more dust from his clothes.

"Still does not like the idea of spiders?" Darcienna asked.

"No, and I don't think he ever will," Kade responded.

We are ready, Kade heard in his head. He patted Darcienna's hands that were firmly in place around his waist where they belonged. He was not sure what he enjoyed more; the riding of a dragon or having her wrap her arms around him. Kade was certain she did it to hold on, but no matter the reason, he enjoyed it.

"Okay, Rayden. Anytime you are ready. Go easy so we don't lose anyone," Kade said as he gripped the ridges tightly. He might have asked the dragon to take it easy, but he was learning quickly that it was no guarantee that Rayden was going to heed his request.

Kade was pleasantly surprised at the careful ease with which the dragon picked up speed. They continued on in a relatively smooth pace and were back at the Great Hall in no time at all. Kade was lowering himself down when he heard an ear-splitting screech that made his hair stand on end. His heart jumped, and he threw a quick glance at Darcienna. Her eyes were only glowing faintly. With a screech like that, he expected them to be blazing, but no matter, even a faint glow was worthy of caution.

"Let's go," Kade prompted, eager to get inside. Darcienna slid down and landed in his arms.

"Careful, Apprentice. You do not know what the danger is and we cannot afford for you to be lost to us." Doren said. Kade felt his ire grow at being treated like a simpleton. He was still an apprentice, but the way Doren used his title was grating on him. Kade thought that the Master Chosen could have easily replaced the word apprentice with the word child and it would still sound the same. But, something told Kade that Doren wanted him to survive for his own reasons. That hunger was back in the man's eyes. Kade decided he did not like seeing that look but quickly put it aside to deal with the current dilemma.

"I will be as careful as I need," Kade said. Darcienna shot him a look and Kade quickly changed his tune, adding, "Master Doren," in a more civil tone. Kade glanced over at her to see if this met with her approval. She nodded with a slight grin. He rolled his eyes and headed for the entrance.

"Since when do you care how I interact with him?" Kade grumbled.

"It reflects badly on you. There are other eyes," Darcienna added with a very slight nod of her head in the queen's direction. Kade instantly saw her wisdom, and with a slight smile, nodded his thanks to her.

The queen went in with the two guards trailing close behind. Kade was next with Darcienna in lockstep. Doren brought up the rear. It was obvious that the Master Chosen was in no hurry to discover what this was all about. Or, maybe he did not believe there was much danger to face. Either way, Kade was going to find out soon enough.

"What is all the excitement about?" Kade asked as he pushed his way through the crowd. As soon as the spiders saw

Rakna and Kade, they fell all over themselves to get out of the way.

"We found an imposter among us," Crayken said imperiously. He pointed to a crevice in the wall behind the great table.

Kade spared a glance for Darcienna. He was about to look away when he froze. Her eyes were softly pulsing. The glow would come and go ever so slowly, as if it could not decide.

Either there was danger or there was not, Kade thought in frustration. This was no help. Another mystery he needed to figure out on his own. *Why does everything need to be so complicated?* he thought in frustration.

"How is a spider an imposter? Are there spiders that are not allowed in the clutch?" Kade asked as he stood several feet away from the crevice.

The opening was just large enough for a man to enter. It closed in on itself after approximately ten feet. Kade was about to look away when he caught sight of a pair of eerie, red eyes peering out at him. They were locked onto him; him and no one else. It felt strange and unnerving, but at the same time, there was something familiar about those eyes. He could not place it, but something in the back of his mind was nagging at him. He reached up and grabbed the amulet, but he already knew what to expect. It was neither warm nor cold.

"Kade," Darcienna said cautiously as she squeezed his arm. He gripped her hand in reassurance and then gently lifted it off, moving her back.

"A spider cannot be an imposter, if it is really a spider," Crayken said as he glared at the creature. "No spider is an enemy of another spider. It does not happen. We are not like humans," the king said and then continued on hurriedly. "Forgive my bluntness, Chosen, but your kind does seem to war with itself quite often."

"I wish I could disagree with you," Kade said with a sigh. "But, you do speak the truth."

Kade glanced around at the spiders, and for the first time,

seemed to see them for the cohesive group they were. They really did work together. If only humans worked the same way. He was ashamed of his species. It was his kind that caused any problem that threatened this world and its inhabitants. He threw a glance at Doren. Even though the Master Chosen gave no outward indication of what he was thinking, Kade was sure Doren was running the same thoughts through his head.

There was a gasp from the spiders. Kade turned back to the crevice and flinched as the creature stood just inside the opening. It never took its eyes off him, even for an instant. Kade instinctually danced through the moves for the Blue Flame of the Divine as his clothes billowed and flowed. He held out the blue fire, ready for use. He could feel waves of fear coming off the creature as it took a quick step back.

"Why does it not attack?" Kade asked, not taking his eyes off the creature for more than an instant.

"It attacked several spiders when they realized it was an imposter," Crayken said as he eyed the creature cautiously.

"How many killed?" Kade said as he readied the fire.

"Actually...none," the king said thoughtfully.

"Kade," Darcienna said, worry in her voice. "It may have been sent to kill you."

"Then why has it not tried? It could not ask for a better time than now," Kade said as he studied it. He glanced at Darcienna. Her eyes continued to glow and then fade. What did that mean?

"We almost had it until it changed," Crayken said as he studied the creature. Kade's head whipped around so fast that the king flinched.

"Changed?" Kade snarled. "It changed?" he asked again, putting emphasis on the last word as the muscles in his forearm involuntarily flexed. He knew he should have picked up on this already when the creature was accused of being an imposter, but now that it was clear how it was trying to be an imposter, Kade was certain what was happening. He turned his eyes toward the creature and the Divine filled him to over flowing. The block was gone and he was pulsing with power as his rage flared. The fire vanished. NO! He would not give this creature the satisfaction of a quick death. This one he was going to tear limb from limb. This one was going to die while he watched the life being squeezed out of it. "You!" Kade spat, venom dripping from that single word.

"Kade?" Darcienna asked, but he was too far gone to hear anything she said.

Hate filled him. Blackness covered his heart. He took a step toward the creature and it shrank back further into the crevice. The fear was palpable now.

"Get out here!" Kade hissed, the muscles in his arms flexed so tightly that he shook. "Get out here now before I tear this wall down coming after you!" There was not a person or spider in the room that doubted that Kade would try to do exactly what he promised. The king and queen took a step back. They were not afraid of him...not exactly. But, they did not want to be too close in the event that this turned violent. With the way Kade was acting, and the look in his eye, there was a very good chance of blood being spilled very soon.

"Kade!" Darcienna said more insistently. He hesitated momentarily. "Kade!" she said as she laid a hand on his arm.

"What?" he snarled.

"Kade," she said more softly. It was barely enough to get him to forcefully tear his eyes off the crevice. He turned his dangerous glare on her. "You have to ask yourself why it is here," she said. The blackness receded slightly. "It did not kill," she said as she laid her other hand on his arm. He felt like iron in her grip. "I am not saying it should live, but...," she said and then hesitated until she was sure he was actually paying attention to her. "We should find out why it is here. Don't you think it could have gotten away if it wanted?" Kade turned and spat in disgust.

"Change now and get out here. This is the last time I will tell you," Kade commanded, and he meant it. The creature changed and stepped up to the entrance. Kade locked eyes with the man. It was the same man he had seen at the bar, talking with his father. Darcienna gasped audibly.

"Vell!" she exclaimed.

"I thought you died," Kade said with a snarl.

"I did almost die," Vell said as his voice shook. "I barely escaped through the hole in the ceiling. I hovered near death for days. If I did not know a form that has the ability to heal, I would have perished."

"Give me one reason why I should not tear you apart?" Kade hissed as he stepped forward to stand within arm's reach of the creature. He flexed, ready to attack if Vell attempted to change or retreat. His hands balled so tightly into fists that they ached. Kade glared daggers. Vell glanced at the exit for a fleeting moment as he quivered in fear.

"Please, hear me out," Vell pleaded. "Just please hear what I have to say," he begged. Kade got the impression that Vell was on the verge of falling to his knees.

"Choose your words carefully, changeling, or they may be your last," Kade warned menacingly.

He wanted nothing more than to rip the life right out of this creature for what it did to him and his family. He wanted it to suffer long and hard for what it did to Darcienna. It was all he could do to force himself to listen. Darcienna squeezed his arm, and his mind focused. She knew that if he decided to attack, there was nothing she could do to stop him. She only hoped that she could get out of the way in time.

"Speak!" Kade demanded.

"I came here to find you," Vell said, trying to muster the courage to talk with confidence and failed miserably. Darcienna gasped for the second time. Kade ignored her and continued to bore holes in the shapeshifter with his glare.

"And…why would you want to find me?" Kade asked, clenching his jaw as he struggled to keep from lashing out and ripping the spine from the creature. A small voice somewhere deep inside him warned of the danger of hate. He heard the warning and hated himself for hearing it. He wanted to kill this creature without giving it the chance to speak, but the voice inside him would not leave him alone, so he allowed Vell another moment of life...for now.

"I want to join you," Vell said as he glanced from Kade to Darcienna, then to Doren, only to come back to Kade again.

"You...want to...join me?" Kade asked incredulously. He was so shocked at what he heard that his jaw hit the floor. The anger was instantly replaced with shock and disbelief. Was it curiosity that made him want to hear more or was there something else to this? "You tried to kill me," Kade said in a growl, but his curiosity had a firm hold on him. "You were ready to turn me over to Morg." He watched Vell closely. The shapeshifter flinched hard at that one. "Give me one reason why I should not tear you apart," Kade demanded, feeling the rage threaten to return.

The creature's eyes fell to the ground as it wet its lips, trying to get the courage to continue. This once arrogant, fearsome creature was reduced to begging, and Kade could not decide if he was disgusted or felt pity. Something about this reminded him of another situation. After a moment, it came to him. The veteran fighter, who he had killed in revenge, flashed through his mind. The fighter was helpless, full of fear, and Kade had destroyed him. A pang of guilt stabbed at him. The anger was receding again, but he was still cautious. He glanced at Darcienna and froze. Her eyes were almost back to normal with the faintest pulsing still showing. The more Vell spoke, the less her eyes warned of danger. He was telling the truth, Kade realized in amazement.

"Why would you want to help me?" Kade asked as he narrowed his eyes, watching for any signs of deception.

"Because...you are my only hope," Vell said as he glanced up and then back to Kade.

The Apprentice Chosen actually felt sorry for this...thing.

He waited for Vell to explain. Silence was a tool that Zayle had used on him many times. Kade recalled how he used to spill his guts, trying to tell the Master Chosen what he was looking for. He would always talk too much to the point of babbling until Zayle was satisfied with what he heard. Now, it was his turn to use the same technique on Vell. The shapeshifter started to fidget. Kade smiled to himself.

"Morg tried to kill me," Vell said in a rush. And there it was; the reason why he was here. Morg wanted him dead and Vell thought Kade could keep him alive.

"I should toss you out," Kade said in disgust.

"Please. I have nowhere else to go. My own people won't even accept me back," Vell pleaded as he glanced at the ceiling, looking for a way out. "They say that since you were able to beat me in battle, I am not worthy of leading. The one you let get away delighted in telling how you bested me so easily," Vell said, working his tongue as if he chewed on something that tasted rotten. "I told them of your immense power, but they did not care. I was exiled."

"How do I know that you will not try to kill me as soon as I turn my back?" Kade asked accusingly, as he locked eyes with the shapeshifter. Some of the fire returned. Vell glanced behind himself at the crevice and then turned to face Kade, once more. "Or maybe you will seize this opportunity to capture me and take me back to Morg so he will accept you back," he said as he advanced on Vell. The shapeshifter glanced back again, and this time, retreated a step. "Maybe capturing me will help reinstate you as the leader of your people," Kade said as he glanced at Darcienna. His breath caught in his throat. Her eyes were a steady blue. Not strong, but not faint.

"I will not serve someone who tries to kill me when I have been loyal!" Vell shot back with such vehemence that Kade stopped his pursuit.

But, why would her eyes be warning of danger, if Vell

wanted to serve me? Kade asked himself.

"If you will just give me a chance, I will prove that everything I am telling you is the truth," the shapeshifter said with such fierce determination that Kade actually paused.

Doren says he believes the shapeshifter, Rakna said in his head. Kade glanced at the queen. She gave a slight nod. He looked at Doren, who stood without moving as he regarded the shapeshifter thoughtfully. He almost looked as if he was amused with all this.

Kade felt his muscles relax. He took a deep breath and studied Vell for several long seconds, watching for anything that might be out of place. Kade even found himself hoping to see something, but there was nothing. Even that little voice inside his head did not speak of any danger.

But, why would Darcienna's eyes be warning of danger? he wondered again as he glanced at her once more.

"Do not every betray me, or I will find you, and you will rue the day we met," Kade vowed in an ominous tone. "Do I make myself clear?"

"Yes," Vell said firmly. "I will serve you with my life. You will not regret your decision," he said as he stood tall, squaring his shoulders and puffing out his chest. "I will serve as your personal guard and protector. I will stay close and keep you safe," he promised and then hesitated before continuing on. "If...you ever need it." Kade nodded once and turned to face the spiders.

There was an audible gasp from the clutch. They started to buzz furiously. Even though he could not understand the words spoken, he was certain they were warning him not to turn his back on the shapeshifter. Darcienna raised her hands casually, ready to bring her shield to life. Kade noticed the move and gave a slight shake of his head. She hesitated but did not drop her hands. He mentally sighed, not faulting her and turned back to the spiders. They were quickly working toward a frenzied level as their beloved second in command put himself in danger. Kade held up his hands for silence. The spiders fell deathly quiet, ready to hang on his every word. Kade let the quiet fill the room as his eyes scanned the clutch, looking for the elder spiders of the council. He found each and held their gaze for just a moment before moving onto the next.

"If you would please translate for me." Kade asked of the queen.

"I am ready," Rakna said.

Kade cleared his throat as he took a firm stance with his hands together behind his back. It was something he had seen Zayle do, and it always gave him the impression of someone who knew what they were talking about. Of course, Zayle always did know what he was talking about, but the image was there, regardless.

Kade had been around the spiders long enough to know that they expected him to give them another dead creature as a trophy. Another conquest for them to sing his praises. The spiders were already raising him to an exalted status with the telling of his victories. Of course, they tended to embellish a little too much. To listen to the clutch tell it, he single handedly destroyed half the Morphites by himself. That was just not possible. Or...was it? Regardless, if this kept up, he was certain that in just a year's time, this creature would have been the fiercest of monsters. They wanted its head.

"No one is to harm the shapeshifter," Kade said in what he hoped was a commanding and impressive voice. "He has sworn his life to me."

It was only a fraction of a second, and then the spiders erupted. The buzzing made his ears ring, but he showed no reaction. Kade turned his head back and forth as if to sweep the crowd with his eyes, but what he wanted to do was to look at the king, queen, Darcienna and Doren for their input. But, he could not look back. It would have been seen as a sign of weakness. NO. He needed the clutch to know this came from him. They were going to accept his decision. Several of the spiders started to approach angrily.

There was a gasp from the crowd and all eyes went over

Kade's head. It only took a moment for him to realize what had happened. He spun and attempted to glare at the shapeshifter but looked right into the chest of a creature he did not recognize. Its chest muscles heaved. The creature reeked of strength and power. As much as Kade did not want to admit it, it put a lump in his throat. This thing was dangerous. It was right on him, and he was never going to get through even one move before it had him. There was no way Darcienna was going to get her shield between them, either. Her glowing eyes flashed in his mind and he cursed himself for a fool.

Kade knew he had only three things that were going to save him: his strength, Doren's callings, and oddly enough, his confidence that he could handle this...somehow. In just a fraction of a second, he had seen that Doren still had his hands down at his side.

Well, I have two things, Kade thought quickly and prepared for battle as he flexed his muscles hard. He put on his fiercest scowl, and in his most commanding voice, hissed at Vell.

"Change!" Kade said with force. "Change back NOW!" he commanded as though he had nothing to fear. His heart pounded hard but the anger of the betrayal infuriated him. All he needed to do was get just a little room between him and this beast and he would turn it to ash where it stood.

"As you wish," Vell said, uncertainty in his voice. He melted back into the form of the man. "But, they are threatening you," he said, not taking his eyes off the advancing spiders. His form shimmered, threatening to change back into the beast.

"Do not change out of this form unless I allow it," Kade said, his tone giving no room for debate. Vell's form solidified.

Kade spun as the first spider got close enough to pounce. His mind, again, recalled how the queen had put one of her own on its back. He even recalled that he had killed a few of the spiders, and yet, she had put her own kind down. It was not that she was defending him, Kade realized, but that she was enforcing her rules.

He threw his hand into the air dramatically and light exploded to fill the room. The power filled him and he drank from it deeply. For a moment, he lost himself in its glory, and then his eyes stopped on the spider just in front of him. Kade stalked forward, his eyes never leaving his target.

So, this was the way it had to be, Kade thought as he closed in on the spider. Always showing them who is in charge. Always having to prove that he was willing to put them back in line. Yes, this was the way of the spiders.

Fine. I can prove to them that I am in charge, he thought as he propelled himself into the air with his all his strength. He landed on one knee with both hands on either side of the spiders head. It flinched and ducked, putting its chin to the ground. Kade's eyes came to within inches of the spider as he glared hard.

"I said he is NOT to be harmed," Kade hissed dangerously.

"But, he attacked us," another spider buzzed quietly. Rakna translated so smoothly with her mind that Kade forgot it was not the spider speaking.

"Did it kill any of you?" Kade asked. He thought back on the brute he was chest to face with and knew that Vell could have torn many of the spiders apart before being overrun. There was a loud buzzing of chatter between the spiders, but it did not take long for it to die down. The queen did not translate. Kade took that as a no. "You have to allow room for the possibility that it was defending itself. It came to see me, and even though it was a mistake, it felt that its best chance was to disguise itself as one of you until it could make contact with me," Kade said as he turned to look askance at Vell. The shapeshifter nodded firmly.

The spider started to edge back. Kade considered holding it in place, but his point was made. He allowed it to slide back to blend in with the crowd. If he had to pick it out of the clutch, he would have failed miserably. It did not matter.

"Does anyone else want to ignore my command?" Kade asked as he glared a challenge to any who would stand their ground.

104

His eyes sought out the eyes of the council and found nothing but approval. The elder spider that had stood against him previously, now had a look of respect. At least, Kade thought it was a look of respect. The spider's body language was still something he was working on.

"You have all seen him bow down before me and swear his loyalty," Kade said. "No one is to touch the creature or they will have to go through me, and…" Kade said as he turned to say the next part while looking Vell in the eyes. "If he betrays me, I will make a trophy of his head," he said firmly, wondering how the shapeshifter was going to react to his threat. "Is that clear?" He put heavy emphasis on each word.

Kade had proven he was in charge. The spiders, begrudgingly, backed off. Rakna and Crayken glided up to stand next to him. Kade felt the light touch of Darcienna's hand on his arm and reached over to cover it with his own.

"Is there a chance this is a trap?" Rachsin asked. Kade easily recognized the council spider.

"There is always a chance," Kade said as he glanced at Darcienna. Her eyes were still glowing. Kade tried to ignore it, but he could not. Nothing had presented itself…yet, but he knew it would be a mistake to forgo her warnings. He eyed the shapeshifter, again, but nothing in his gut warned him of danger. "We must always be cautious, but at the same time, we cannot ignore the fact that it could be useful," Kade said as he appealed to the old spider's wiser side. "The creature may have important information that could make the difference between winning this war," Kade said as he paused for emphasis, "or losing it," he finished.

"It did injure several of us," Rachsin said, but there was no strength to his words. Kade studied the spider for a moment as it lifted its chin, waiting for a reply. Kade gave a sly smile as he quickly realized what Rachsin was doing. He gave an ever so slight nod and Rachsin responded in kind.

105

"Yes, he did. And, I would have, also, to keep from being killed. He was defending himself," Kade said. Rachsin nodded as if analyzing the information. Several of the other spiders were watching Rachsin closely. "If he has important information that I can use, then I can accept his actions," he said as he looked at the old spider and continued on. It was clear what Rachsin was doing, and Kade could easily see why the king was so fond of him. "Would you have allowed him in or anywhere near me if you knew he was a shapeshifter?" Kade asked.

"Oh, clearly not. I would have chased him out myself," Rachsin buzzed confidently. Several spiders nodded their agreement and turned to watch Kade.

"Then, possibly the ends do justify the means," Kade said, nodding as though the spider had been the one that had worked the conversation around to this." The spiders turned to watch Rachsin.

"It would appear that way to me. At least, that is how I see it," Rachsin said and settled down. Kade had to fight to keep the grin from showing. Oh, how he did like this one.

"Then it is settled," Kade said. This seemed to quell any further turmoil.

Not one spider opposed or even showed any dissension at all. They settled down as they regarded the shapeshifter. Now, instead of being a fearsome creature that needed to be destroyed, it was a tool to be used in their fight against Morg. Many of the spiders even started to nod and buzz to the spider next to them. It spread around the room quickly.

"And, I am sure it is safe, now?" Rachsin asked. The old spider must have caught something said in the crowd.

"As safe as I am," Kade said and nodded his head for emphasis. "As you saw, I, myself, almost ended its life when I thought it was a threat," he said and then smiled as something occurred to him. "Do you still fear the dragon?" The room went still as the question hit home. "No, you do not. And now you have another that you have no need to fear."

"I agree with the Chosen," Crayken added.

"As do I," said the queen in all her regal glory. She was an impressive sight, her snow-white fur swaying with her every move. Kade was certain that she was fully aware of her appearance and had cultivated a way of moving that maximized its effect.

"It is plain for me to see that your decisions have merit," the old spider said as he gave a respectful bow of his head. "We shall trust your judgment, but know that if it is deceiving us," the spider said as it paused to look at Darcienna's glowing, blue eyes for several long seconds and then back to Kade. "It will die a horrible death," Rachsin finished with confidence born of years of experience. The warning was meant for Vell and Kade knew it. He felt respect for this spider grow.

If Rachsin was born twice his size and covered in black, flowing fur, he could easily have been a king himself, Kade thought.

"No you will not," Kade said, causing the spider to pause as it regarded him, "because the shapeshifter's head will already be on display for all to see." He held the spiders gaze. If spiders could smile, Rachsin would have been grinning. Kade could definitely feel a connection growing with this one.

The rest of the spiders relaxed completely and the tension in the room evaporated immediately. Kade felt himself relax, also. He turned toward Darcienna and studied her eyes again. They continued to glow softly but steadily. There were times when her warnings brought more questions than answers, and this was one of those times that the questions would go unanswered...for now. Until he knew why her eyes warned of danger, he was not going to be able to untie the knot in his stomach.

"I hope never to have your head as a trophy," Kade said as he reiterated his threat. "But, betray me one time, and I will end you." Vell seemed to be a mix of emotions. Kade was expecting the shapeshifter to grouse at the threat, but Vell's next words had him speechless.

"No one has ever defended me like that," Vell said in

confusion. "Not even my own kind would do that," he said as he grappled with the new concept of true trust and naked honesty. "We do not even trust our own kind," he said as he saw the look of shock in Kade's eyes. "We are, by nature and instinct, not trusted. Who can truly trust a shapeshifter? When I am not around, will your mind wonder if I am hiding in a corner or hanging in a web over your head?" Vell asked. Kade opened his mouth to answer but Vell cut him off. "No need to answer. Of course you can't trust me," he said but Kade held up a hand.

"The answer is yes. I can. But...only once. If you ever prove to me that my faith in you was misplaced, I will never trust you again, and if I do not kill you myself, I will most assuredly cast you out into a world where you will be alone once more," Kade said, guessing correctly that the latter threat was likely the one Vell would be concerned with the most.

"I can truly understand why Morg fears you so much," Vell said, his voice full of awe. "Now you will see what your trust has brought you," he said with a sly grin as he knelt down on one knee.

Kade glanced over at Darcienna and her eyes flashed danger. Kade was about to tell the shapeshifter to stand and that there was no need for the show of fealty when Vell launched into the air. Kade was caught off guard and stumbled backward. The shapeshifter became a blur as it twisted and contorted and then quickly expanded. Wings shot out and started to beat furiously. Vell's claws were like daggers and his teeth as sharp as razors. He screeched so loud that Rayden answered back with a roar that shook the ground. Kade could hear the dragon crash into the tree.

The Apprentice Chosen threw his hands out in front of himself and prepared to race through the moves for the Divine Fire Calling but held. He was not sure why, but...he held. Vell hovered for just a moment, and then with a screech that set Kade's ears to ringing and every nerve on fire, the shapeshifter shot up thirty feet, slamming into the rock celling. Rayden roared again, but this time, the sound echoed in the tree. Kade was afraid that the dragon was

108

trying to squeeze through the entrance.

Rayden, we are safe, Kade sent. *You need to go back out or you may bring this tree down on us. We are safe.* The link between them was filled with indecision. Kade sent the message again more forcefully, and the dragon backed out of the entrance. *I will be there shortly, when we get this sorted,* Kade sent, again trying to reassure his ever so protective dragon.

The spiders erupted into a fury of buzzing as they prepared to kill. Kade moved to stand under the shapeshifter and watched closely while the room continued to explode in panic. He ignored the clutch as he focused on Vell.

"Kade!" Darcienna shrieked. "What are you doing? Kill that thing!" she screamed as she jabbed a finger in the direction of Vell. She grabbed him by the arm as if to shake him from a dream.

"No," Kade said. Darcienna's shield sprang around them. "Drop it," Kade said. Darcienna looked at him as if he was a mad man. "Drop...it," he said firmly.

Darcienna froze, certain Kade had lost his mind. He placed his hand on her wrist and pulled her arm gently down to her side. The shield winked out. He turned and continued to watch the shapeshifter bounce off the ceiling and then the walls as it grappled with...something. The spiders buzzing reached a deafening crescendo.

"Silence!" Kade boomed as he rounded on the clutch. Rakna did not need to translate this. The king and queen moved a step closer to Kade, giving him their support while watching the clutch. This was enough to quell any arguments that might have started.

Kade was expecting to yell again, but to his surprise, the spiders quieted. That was not to say they calmed down, though. Their hearts beat wildly with the promise of battle. Kade turned and continued to watch Vell twist and contort in the air just over his head. Doren was watching the apprentice with searching eyes, but Kade ignored him, too.

"I hope you know what you are doing," Darcienna said as she turned her eyes up to watch.

Kade did not respond as he continued to observe the aerial display. He was not sure how this thing was able to stay airborne, but it did. It was not lost on him that he was the only one calm in the room. Even the king and queen had assumed a battle-ready pose.

The shapeshifter stopped its gyrating and slowly started to settle back toward the ground. Darcienna raised her hands, and Kade grabbed them without looking and pushed them back down once more. He gave her an extra squeeze that was meant to convey that she was not to try again. Everyone looked back and forth between Kade and Vell, waiting. The shapeshifter settled softly onto the ground and then bent to one knee. Vell shimmered back into his humanoid shape. He bowed his head and held out his hand to display what looked like a lizard about ten inches long.

"A shapeshifter," Vell said with his eyes still on the ground. The creature in his hands hung limp, no longer alive. "I believe it was one of Morg's spies." He raised his eyes and looked at it in disgust. "But, I know this one personally," he said as he squeezed the creature and crushed it. His lips pulled back with the effort and his half rotted teeth shown for all to see. If it was alive when Vell landed, it was definitely dead now. "This is the one that caused me to be cast out," he said as he opened his hand.

"One of Morg's spies?" Darcienna asked in shock.

"Yes," Vell said, disgust still in his voice. For a moment, Kade thought the shapeshifter was going to squeeze the lizard again. Kade took the shapeshifter spy into his hand and spun to face the crowd while throwing his hand high in the air for all to see. The creature was still warm to the touch and even had a decent amount of weight to it.

"A spy," Kade called out loudly for all to hear. "A shapeshifter caught by our new ally," he yelled as he pointed an open hand at Vell. Kade's chest was puffed out as he stood triumphantly.

The apprentice felt the small shape in his hands go soft as if it was starting to melt. He looked up at the creature in his outstretched hand and watched as it shimmered and then faded from site. He slowly dropped his hand to study the empty space that took the place of the shapeshifter. The spiders watched Kade in stunned silence. The apprentice turned and looked at Doren. The master Chosen was scratching his chin thoughtfully as he pondered what had just happened. Doren made eye contact with Kade and gave a slight smile of approval while nodding his head once. Kade turned his attention on Vell.

"You did well," Kade said, cautious not to put too much into his praise. He did not want to let Vell off too easy, but the right praise at the right time should help cement Vell's allegiance. Kade waited for a response, but Vell was searching for the right words to convey what he wanted to say. Finally, he spoke.

"Morg," Vell said with disgust, as if the word tasted rotten in his mouth, "always had nothing but harsh words for me. And you…have shown me mercy and now acceptance." There was more softness in his voice than Kade expected, but he brushed it off.

"Stand," Kade commanded.

Vell slowly rose to his feet while glancing around at the spiders. None moved as they studied him. Darcienna attempted to take a step back, but Kade held her still by putting his hand behind her back. She glanced at him for just a moment and then back to Vell. Kade looked at his still open hand that had previously held the lizard and then back to Vell. The shapeshifter shrugged easily and explained.

"It is what happens to my kind when we die. The best I can say is we are made of energy. It is why we can take on different shapes. When we die, the energy is released back to where it came from," Vell said as he studied Kade's open hand.

"You have no basic shape that you return to?" Kade asked in surprise.

111

"We do have a basic shape that we can return to, but it's not the same for every shapeshifter," Vell said matter-of-factly. Darcienna forgot all her fears as her curiosity took over.

"So, this is yours?" Darcienna asked as she looked Vell in the eyes. The shapeshifter sighed and shook his head.

"No, I must concentrate to hold this form. It is not my birth form," Vell said.

"Birth form?" Kade asked. "Then…what is your birth form?" he asked as he tilted his head while studying the shapeshifter.

Vell's shoulders slumped as he resigned to show them what they were asking. He shimmered and shrank into a stunningly beautiful girl that appeared to be around the age of twenty. She had gorgeous, curly, light-brown hair that hung down to her chest. Her eyes were a deep, solid brown. Her skin was smooth and the very image of health with just a hint of a color as if she were in the sun. Her lips were not full but perfect for adding to her attraction. She had a slight pout that made her even more attractive. She stood approximately five feet six inches tall and weighed around one hundred and thirty pounds. She was nicely proportioned with a perfect posture. There was not a man that would not stop to stare at her if she was to walk down the middle of town.

"This is my birth form," she said in defeat. "And, my name is Vendrall, but you may call me Ven," she said with her eyes on the ground.

Kade was speechless. He stood staring, stunned at what he was seeing. Oddly, even though he could see how incredibly beautiful she was, he felt none of the attraction a normal man might feel. Maybe it was that his heart belonged to Darcienna… who was driving her nails deep into his arm in an attempt to bring him out of his stunned state. Maybe the knowledge of her being a shapeshifter was something he could not get past, but it did not matter. He was smitten by another.

As he watched, her eyes slowly moved along the ground and

then up his body until they were locked with his. His eyes widened slightly as he looked into the very soul of this being. She was completely helpless and vulnerable. She was putting herself out there for him to see and placing her life in his hands. There was nothing of the fearsome creature that had previously stood before him. She bared her soul to him completely and openly. She was vulnerable in every sense of the word. He was stunned by what he was seeing and any malice he felt toward this creature was gone forever.

"This is my birth form," Ven said meekly in an innocent, sweet voice.

"Wow," Kade said, amazed at the difference between Vell and Ven. Darcienna's nails dug in hard. It was most definitely not the right thing for Kade to say, but he was a man and men did things without thinking. Ten years of virtually no interaction with the opposite sex was, also, clearly a factor in this blunder. He had a lot to learn.

Kade was afraid Darcienna might actually draw blood if this kept up. He grimaced and turned to look at her. "Jealous?" he whispered, half teasing, half irritation as he flexed his arm to withstand the next squeeze that was sure to come. "Oh, stop being foolish. My heart is already taken," he said with a reassuring smile. Her nails retracted.

"Do all of your kind appear as you do?" Doren asked as he glided up to examine Ven.

"No. Shapeshifters have no natural shape," Ven responded hesitantly.

Kade could see that she was uncomfortable with the questions, but there was no stopping now. They were all curious and hung on every word she spoke. Besides, the more information he had, the better he would be able to protect against another of her kind. Knowledge is power, Zayle used to preach. Kade agreed.

"No natural shape?" Darcienna asked, a bit more aggressive than was needed. Ven sighed. The secrets she was sharing were clearly not meant to be shared. But, she knew she was committed so she continued.

"When we are birthed, we do not specifically have a form that is ours. It is only when we take a shape using our abilities that we take our real birth form," Ven said as she took in a deep breath and let it out. Kade felt Darcienna tense as Ven's chest rose and fell with her breath. Although he did not feel the attraction, he could definitely see how other men would have forgotten their names at a breath like that.

"Stop," Kade growled with his teeth clenched, trying to not be too obvious. Darcienna huffed and then relaxed.

"The first biological life form we touch is what will forever be our birth form. We absorb a portion of the life force, and it is as simple as that," Ven explained.

"How do you procreate?" Doren asked, ever the searcher of knowledge. Kade shook his head at the bluntness, but nevertheless, listened curiously for the answer.

"We must find another of our kind with a basic form of the same species."

"You appear to be every bit as human as we are. Can you not…procreate with another human?" Doren asked. Kade knew this talk should be saved for another time, but again, found himself listening intently.

"No. It would form such defects that it would not survive," Ven said. Darcienna relaxed completely and even appeared very pleased with the answer. "That is not to say we cannot be intimate with humans," she said as she looked each of them in the eye. "Just that we cannot allow off spring to develop," she finished.

Darcienna squeezed again with a vengeance. *The perfect girl for the man who is scared witless of having children and committing to a relationship,* Darcienna thought scathingly. She turned to look at Kade and froze as he glared at her. Her grip softened….at least she tried to soften it.

"What prompted you to take the other form?" Doren asked.

"I need to keep from drawing attention to myself. I only take on my birth form when I need a more persuasive approach," Ven said with a glint in her eye. "As Vell, people don't see me or they try to avoid me. In this form, everyone sees me. We are shapeshifters. We deceive by nature. It is more important to not be seen than to be seen so I show people an old, unremarkable, but still formidable man," she said with a shrug of her shoulders.

"Now," Doren said as he put his thumb and first finger on his chin as he pondered his next query. "How did you know there was another shapeshifter here?" he asked casually but Kade could sense the depth of the question and watched Ven closely. He had to give Doren credit for this one.

"I...knew he was there," Ven said nervously. "I knew he followed me in. Some of our kind can sense when other shapeshifters are around. It is one of the reasons I was chosen to lead. I could find others of our species. He, on the other hand, could not. He always believed that since he could not, others were just as blind as he," Ven said with her very feminine voice. It was not seductive but it was definitely very female.

"So, you were waiting to see how we reacted to you? If things went bad, you would have done what?" Doren asked casually, but again, there was nothing casual about his probing.

"I would have fled. Surviving is a very useful skill that I have developed," Ven said quietly.

"Leaving us to be spied on by the shapeshifter, who would have reported back to Morg," Doren said as he cocked an eyebrow. Ven's nervousness grew.

"I was hoping Kade would accept me, and then I could prove my loyalties by showing him I could be useful," Ven said. "I did catch the spy, and I have sworn to give my life to keep him safe," she said pleadingly. Kade had had enough of watching her squirm. He was satisfied with her loyalties. As much as he did not like how things would have turned out had Ven fled, it did not work out that way, and that had to be enough.

"I believe you," Kade said firmly with a nod of his head. *Was I swayed because she was in female form?* he asked himself. *Would I have gone this easy if I were looking at Vell?* He gave Doren a look that said enough. Doren turned that same cocked eyebrow on him but Kade brushed it off. He went to turn toward the king when Darcienna spoke.

"Well, I think that you should change back to Vell," Darcienna said frostily. In seconds, Vell was, once again, standing there. Kade turned and looked at Darcienna while shaking his head. "What?" she asked challengingly.

"Forget it. Just, forget it," Kade said, exasperated.

If this kept up, he was going to have to do something to put a stop to it. A little jealously was a good thing, but this level was just too much. To keep the peace, Ven changing might be for the best, for now. It would not bode well for him if others were to suspect a more intimate relationship. And, her being in her female form would definitely give people reason to talk. That did not mean Darcienna had to act like he was going to run off with her at the first chance he got. Of course, having others believing he was with Ven would be a valid reason for her frustrations. He sighed aloud, dreading that he was going to have to deal with this for a long time. Setting the issue aside for the time being, he turned to face the royal couple.

"We need to have a meeting with the other kings and queens. We should see if the shapeshifter knows anything that will be of use," Kade said.

"We will meet at the great table shortly," Crayken said.

The king has a high level of respect for you, Kade, second king to our people, Rakna said in his mind. "He was very impressed with how you handled that," she hissed.

"Thank you," Kade said as he turned to face the queen. "The support from you and Crayken was critical. I may not have been able to get the spiders to listen to reason if it were not for you," he said as he smiled fondly at Rakna. The way her snow white fur

116

swayed with her movements caught his attention, and again, he appreciated the beauty of her. Seeing her made it difficult for him to recall a time when he did not like spiders.

"It is only proper," the queen responded. "They need many reminders," Rakna said and let it go at that.

"Nevertheless, I do appreciate it," Kade said as he turned to face Vell.

"So, you can warn us if any other shapeshifters are near?" Kade asked.

"If they are close, and I am not distracted, then I should be able to. It is not a complete certainty," Vell said. Kade pictured the shapeshifter in her female form and then looked at this ugly man. He was amazed at how he felt toward each one, as if they were two separate people. Yes, he had to be sure that he used sound judgment no matter which form she took.

She did try to kill me, he thought, but that did nothing for putting him on guard. Something about her female form brought out his protective nature. Ven could easily fend for herself, and yet, he felt the need to look after her.

He shook his head and turned to go when Doren caught his eye. He walked up to the Master Chosen, who appeared to be deep in thought, as he looked up at the ceiling where the two shapeshifters had fought. Kade cleared his throat and Doren casually regarded the apprentice as if he was seeing Kade for the first time.

"You knew Vell....Ven was no threat when she changed?" Kade asked, recalling Doren's lack of concern.

"I was confident that I had analyzed the situation correctly," Doren said a bit too smug for Kade's liking. He could have gotten the same type of response if he had asked if the sun was going to come up the next day.

"How?" Kade asked. Doren took on the air of someone drawing on infinite patience while being forced to deal with something that was extremely obvious.

"His eyes...her eyes," Doren said, correcting himself "were on the spiders. When they moved in, she changed. Her eyes never left the spiders. If she was a danger to you, then she would have been watching you," Doren said as if talking to someone who might struggle to grasp such a simple concept.

Kade felt his blood start to boil and had to take a deep breath to steady himself. Getting angry was not going to help. Besides, if he had eyes in the back of his head, he would have easily seen this, also. So, Doren gets no extra points for catching the obvious. He gave a tight lipped smile, and with a nod of his head to say he understood, turned back to Ven.

"Come with me," Kade said. "We have some things to discuss."

Kade turned and watched the spiders slowly dispersing. Several were still casting cautious glances at the shapeshifter, apparently still not trusting the creature. When the spiders saw Kade watching them, they would quickly avert their gaze.

As Kade started to move forward, he felt Ven touch him lightly on the arm, pulling him to a stop. He turned to see why and froze as he looked into her beautiful, brown eyes, again. He should have realized that she had returned to her birth form from the touch of her hand, but he missed it. He shook his head, not sure if he was going to be able to deal with such a radical change in how he felt toward each form.

Why am I so soft toward her in her female form? he asked himself. After a moment, it hit him. She had put herself in his hands completely and allowed herself to be vulnerable when she showed her true form. She might be a tough looking man in one shape, but who she really was came out when she looked at him with these eyes. And, the look she gave him was one of deep admiration. At least, that had to be part of it. Any hard feelings he had about her in the past were completely forgotten. Darcienna elbowed him so hard in the ribs he thought she might have cracked one.

"Darcienna," Kade growled. "Stop," he hissed. She shoved away from him so hard that he almost lost his balance. She turned and stalked off. Kade exhaled in exasperation. He went to call after her, but he knew her well enough to know that his words would have fallen on deaf ears.

"That is my fault," Ven said as she changed back to her male form.

"No. You should not have to be Vell if you don't want to be," Kade said as he tried to ignore the awkwardness of talking to the female, Ven, while staring at the male, Vell. "You had to be someone else for Morg, but that time is done. If you want to be Ven when you are with me and away from prying eyes, then be Ven. I will tell you when you need to be Vell," Kade said. "What did you stop me for?" he asked as he glanced down at the hand still on his arm.

"I just wanted to say...well...what you did back there. Those spiders. They were ready to kill me without hearing a word I had to say. But, you were willing to fight for me when I had tried to kill you. You had no reason to trust me," Ven said as she paused once more. She melted into her female form, and her eyes shown as though her emotions were going to have her in tears at any moment. "What I am trying to say is...I have never had anyone willing to stand up for me, ever. As I already said, even my own kind would rather see me fall than defend me. It is only out of a drive for the race to survive that they followed any leader at all. On an individual basis, they do not care. But...you cared," she said as her eyes moistened.

Kade felt compassion well up in him, and without thinking, he wrapped his arms around her and pulled her into a hug. She melted into his embrace, and he knew, at that moment, she was every bit a helpless young girl as any human. He just prayed that Darcienna did not see this and jump to the wrong conclusion. He glanced around the Great Hall and thought he saw a flash of green disappear through the door to the stairs. After several seconds,

119

Kade stepped back and gave her a reassuring smile.

"I will never betray you!" Ven said fiercely.

"Just remember that when the time comes for you to save my life," Kade said as he smiled again and turned to join the meeting.

Doren fell in step next to Kade. The Master Chosen watched the Apprentice as they walked. After just five steps, Kade stopped and turned to face him.

"What?" Kade asked a little testier that he should have.

"I was just thinking that you might have a better chance of surviving a battle with Morg than the battle you are soon to fight," Doren said as he turned to look at the exit. Kade let out a breath as his chin dropped to his chest. He wished he could argue this one, but it did not take a wise, old Chosen Master to know these were very true words. "When it comes to women..." Doren said as he slowly shook his head as if at a loss. For Doren to be at a loss for words was something Kade thought he would never see.

"Does it ever stop?" Kade asked. Doren leaned forward to look past him at the shapeshifter. After a moment of studying Ven, he stood back up and shook his head firmly one time as he pressed his lips together. The meaning was not lost on the apprentice. "I can only do my best," Kade said as he prepared to continue on his walk. Doren put a hand on his arm to hold him in place. When Kade looked at the Master Chosen once again, the hunger was back in his eyes.

"I think it would benefit us to know how your visit with the Ancients went," Doren said, trying to sound casual. He might as well have been a dragon looking down on a helpless boar. Kade recalled Zayle's warning about not trusting other Chosen and this time it rang like a bell that could be heard for miles. He tried to think quickly on how much he wanted to tell as Doren studied him closely. After a moment, he could see no reason to keep any of it from the man so he started to talk. Kade could not help but to notice the way Doren almost appeared to be salivating as if every word was more precious than the last.

"I did meet with two of the Ancients," Kade said as he watched the way Doren hungrily devoured everything said.

"And?" Doren asked a little impatiently. "Did they tell you of any other artifacts that we may use to counter the staff? Are there any other books of power that will help us in our fight?" he asked eagerly.

Help in our fight? Kade thought sarcastically. *The man is probably happy for this excuse to covet more power,* Kade thought in disgust.

"Well?" Doren asked, starting to become more impatient.

"They only told me that we must take the staff from Morg," Kade said, intentionally leaving out the part about the four metal books. Those books were not relevant for the current situation. Kade decided he would share that little piece of news at another time, if Doren needed to know. For now, only information that would help in their battle against Morg was all that the Master Chosen would need to hear.

"And?" Doren prompted, eager to learn something more.

"They said that we needed to take the staff. They said it would be best if we were to attempt this while he is at the mountain Drell." He watched as Doren almost appeared to be deflating like a balloon losing all its air. It was becoming all too clear to the overweight man that there was nothing new to be learned here. "They said it was imperative that the gate be kept safe or an evil on the other side could be loosed on the world. If Morg finds the arch, he could destroy the calling set within the arch."

"Why is this important?" Doren asked, the hunger in his eyes gone.

"They said that if the calling set within the arch is destroyed, the veil between worlds would be removed and anything on that side could cross over." Doren's eyes lost focus as his mind worked.

"Destroying the calling would set the dead free on the world?" Doren said as if shocked. "I thought the calling was in

121

place so we could communicate with the dead. And they say destroying it would cause a hole between worlds?" For just a moment, Kade thought he sensed doubt in the Master Chosen's tone. "If that is what they say, then it must be so," Doren said as he nodded his head. "Well, we must protect the arch at all cost. We would never want to lose access to the Ancients."

"We wouldn't," Kade agreed.

Maybe Doren did not learn anything on his previous trip to the cave, but losing the arch to Morg would mean he would never have a chance to ever learn anything ever again from the long dead Chosen. That was too much for him to take. Having access to the Ancients, even if it was through the apprentice, was something Doren was not about to let go just yet. Contact with the Ancients had the promise of great powers beyond his wildest dreams. Kade thought about Talos and Lokk and felt sorry for Doren. There was no way those two were going to easily give a man like this anything that was important. Doren was his own worst enemy and he did not even know it.

"We shall have to keep the arch safe at all cost," Doren said resolutely.

"I would agree. They said the same thing. It is important for us to be able to communicate. I sense there is much going on that we are unaware of," Kade said as the king got his attention. Kade nodded toward Crayken for Doren to see that they were being waited on. The Master Chosen immediately started walking to join the meeting.

Kade was relieved that the talk was over. If Doren knew of the metal books, he would be relentless in his pursuit of the hidden knowledge. It might be part of a set that went with the staff, but there was nothing saying that the callings in this book could not be cast as normal callings without the staff. This, alone, could be power beyond what was safe for any one man to hold. For a fraction of a second, Kade found himself wondering what he would do if he were to find all the books. Would he read through it, looking for something he wanted to learn? Would he destroy it as he suggested earlier? Before his mind could pursue this thinking too deeply, he heard the sound of a throat being cleared. His eyes focused on the group of spiders waiting on him. His mind dismissed the thoughts that were attempting to wake a hunger that all Chosen seemed to have. And with that, he joined the group.

"You are to sit on the King's left," Rakna said. "Darcienna is to sit next to you followed by Doren," Rakna said as she glanced around for Darcienna. "Ven is to stand at your back, if she is your chosen protector," Rakna finished. She seemed to be waiting for him to confirm the statement. Kade nodded and Rakna nodded back once. The grizzled form of Vell took his place behind Kade and folded his arms while looking around the room for anyone to challenge. There were five other royal couples settled around the table. One of the kings was black with one leg that was pure white. Another had the shape of a red diamond on its chest and still another had red bands around the joints of its front legs. The other two appeared to be similar to Crayken. The queens sitting next to their kings appeared as Rakna did but Kade could see the difference just by looking in their eyes.

"Darcienna should be back soon," Kade said.

It was as if saying her name caused her to appear. She stalked over to her seat without so much as a glance for Kade. He got up to pull her chair out for her but she ignored him completely and sat down while adjusting the chair herself. He glanced over at Doren who looked like he genuinely felt sorry for Kade. With a grimace and a slight shrug of his shoulders, Doren turned his attention to the king. Kade sighed to himself and took his seat.

"Fellow brethren, I have called this meeting to question our newest...ally," the king said with hesitation. The plans for the next few days may very well hinge on...her?" Crayken asked of Kade while looking at the male form standing behind him. Kade shook his head. It would do no good for someone to realize her true form was female. So, while in this form, Ven was referred to as she appeared. "The plans for the next few days may depend on what he has to say," Crayken said as he locked eyes with Kade. "Are you sure we can trust what he has to say?" he asked. He already knew the answer, but Kade was certain that this was for the benefit of the rest of those at the table.

"I would stake my life on it," Kade said firmly.

"You may very well be doing just that," Red Diamond said. His tone was one of caution. Kade nodded his understanding but still held his ground.

"Then we will get right to the heart of the matter," Crayken said as he turned to face Vell. "What information have you for us?"

"I can tell you that Morg will soon learn that what he seeks is close by. When his spy does not return, he will investigate. It won't take him long to realize. He has a sizable army ready to march at a moment's notice," Vell growled in his deep, manly voice.

A gasp when up from the spiders. The buzzing started around the table and then the spiders in the Great Hall started to join in. Although the main clutch of spiders was not allowed at the great table, it was not meant for them to be kept from hearing.

"Then was it wise to kill the spy?" White Leg asked.

"I was not aware of the spy until I was in the tree. By then, it was too late. It had to be eradicated. It knew too much to be allowed to live," Vell said firmly. "We must assume the worst. I believe that Morg may come with his forces by the following night. He is desperate to find what he seeks," Vell said.

"Then we will be here to meet him!" Red Diamond said as he pounded the table for emphasis.

Kade and Doren exchanged grim looks but quickly hid them before anyone could take their eyes off the king that had pounded the table. Kade stopped as he noticed the queen studying him. Not all had missed the look on his face. Doren cleared his throat lightly. Kade glanced over as the Master Chosen tilted his head ever so slightly toward Kade and then nodded toward the other spiders. The apprentice took that as a prompt to take a turn at speaking. He stood and all eyes swung to him. The place grew so quiet that he would have sworn it was empty.

"We have a plan," Kade said. Not a spider moved. "We must take the staff from Morg," Kade said. Several kings looked at him in disbelief.

"And, how would you accomplish such a dangerous task?" one of the kings shot back.

"I am going to go to him in the mountain of Drell. He will never expect it. If I can catch him off guard, we can win the war without the life of one spider being lost," Kade said confidently. Even kings needed to see that the one who leads them, leads with complete confidence. At least, he needed them to believe he had complete confidence.

"Your words do ring of wisdom," Crayken said. Several of the kings nodded in agreement. It was risky. It was extremely risky, but it was also a plan, where before, they had none.

"I can only take a few spiders with me. Too many will call attention to us, and we cannot take that risk," Kade said.

"Then you plan on leaving your dragon behind? You will not get there in time," another king said.

"I can take Rayden with me. I have the ability to render him unseen and unheard. But, I cannot do that for an entire army. It would be too disorganized. Besides, I need you to keep watch over the tunnel. If he comes, we must be ready to defend it," Kade said, knowing that the spiders would not fare well if this came to pass.

"Then, you shall take my queen with you so we may stay in contact," Crayken said. Rakna never wavered for a moment. Kade was sure she would have pressed to be included if that was not already part of the plan.

"I believe I know a way into the mountain," Vell said. Everyone froze. Not all who sat around the table had a protector, but those protectors that were present stared in open shock and dismay that Vell had spoken without being invited. It was one thing to answer a question, but to openly interject while the kings and queens were talking was clearly something not done. Every eye turned on him.

"Your protector speaks without being invited," White-leg chastised.

"I brought him, not only as protector, but also as a source of knowledge. I would ask that you allow him to join in the planning where he sees fit. I suspect you will not regret his involvement," Kade said. He fought to keep from glancing at Crayken as he did not want the king to feel as if he needed to come to the rescue.

"I do hope he proves his worth then," the king said as he waved a leg in the air as if to say, "Continue." Kade found himself irritated at the king's arrogance. He quickly reminded himself that this was their culture and he was still learning their ways. With a nod of his head, he said, "Thank you for your understanding." The king responded with a slight nod of his head and quickly turned his attention back to the shapeshifter.

"You may continue," Kade said to Vell.

"I am confident I can get us in undetected. I know that mountain well. I have been in and out of there for years."

"Excellent!" Crayken exclaimed with hope. Kade suspected that the king had spoken with enthusiasm to show Kade support for allowing this break in tradition. But, it had to be done. Vell was a source of information that was needed.

This was the first time Kade felt real hope and the possibility of success coming from the king. He, too, felt the thrill the more they planned. "Then it is decided. We shall prepare for battle in the event that Morg does find his way here," he said as he rose from the table. "You need to get some rest before you go. I will have someone show you to your new chambers," Crayken said as he buzzed at two spiders that quickly ran to the table. The queen got up and joined him along with the two guards. "Doren, may I speak with you to help in preparing?" Crayken asked of the Master Chosen.

"Of course," Doren said as he rose from his seat. He glanced at Kade as if considering something and then shrugged, letting it go. He turned and walked with the king.

Kade was grateful for the chance to be away from the Master Chosen. He was certain that Doren was going to question him for any small detail of his meeting with the Ancients that he may have missed. The more he thought about it, the more he knew he had to keep the metal books a secret unless it was absolutely necessary. Doren might be an ally now, and very well could become his new teacher, but Kade was not under the delusion that Doren would not also become…an…issue…was the best way he could think to put it. With a sigh, he let the entire line of thinking go and focused on the queen.

"My new room?" Kade asked.

Kade noticed Darcienna stalking alongside of him on his left with her arms crossed tightly. It was painfully obvious that she was not going to make this any easier than she had to. Ven walked on his right in her female form. Kade gave a mental sigh and hoped that Darcienna would be willing to talk to resolve this, but after another glance at both women, he had his doubts.

"Yes. The room you stayed in the first time is not befitting someone of your status. It would be shameful for us to allow you to stay in a room that did not match your rank. The guards will show you to your chamber," Rakna said as she gave several buzzed commands to the two spiders. They buzzed back and then turned to lead the way.

"Wait. I need to feed Rayden," Kade said as he turned for the exit. Rakna buzzed at the guards and then joined the king. "It won't take long," Kade said as he rushed up the stairs. Ven was close behind followed by the two guards. Kade was certain that when he was done with the dragon, they would know to take him to his new quarters. Darcienna stayed in the great hall.

Kade stepped outside and called to Rayden. The dragon eagerly responded to his friend's call. The link exploded with affection as Rayden sniffed him several times. *Odd,* Kade thought as he watched his dragon's new, curious habit. Kade tried to push the dragon's muzzle out of the way but Rayden was not to be denied. More out of curiosity than anything else, Kade let the dragon continue. *He should be used to these new clothes by now,* Kade thought. *Maybe he was just checking me over to make sure I was ok.* At least, that is what Kade thought he was doing. As the dragon took several long draws with its nose firmly pressed against Kade's chest, its hackles came up and its wings flared. There was a dangerous growl coming from deep within the dragon.

"Rayden, what are you doing?" Kade asked as he shoved the dragon's nose back. Rayden sniffed in the direction of Ven and his wings shot out, his lips pulling back violently as he readied for a strike. "No!" Kade screamed as he threw himself between the dragon and the shapeshifter. "She is safe," he said with his hands up in the air. Confusion assaulted him through the link. "No, Rayden! No! She is with us! Easy, Rayden, easy!" he said as he turned and pushed Ven back into the tree.

The dragon never took its eyes off the entrance. Rayden obviously remembered the scent of the shapeshifter, who had chained him to the ground. It would appear that not all were going to accept his new companion as readily as he had hoped, but...they had to. Ven might make the difference between success and failure. Rayden just had no choice, but Kade got a sick feeling that this might end in disaster...if he could not mollify his friend.

"I do not fault him," the female voice of Ven said from the entryway. "I would not trust me either."

"I know just how to distract him," Kade said as he called his first piece of meat. As he expected, the link filled with the craving for food, but the desire to rend and kill was still dominant. He tossed the morsel in the air and the dragon caught it in its mouth but did not swallow or even chew. The rumble from deep within continued as its shoulders bunched. Kade got the feel that Rayden wanted to strike but the juices starting to run down his throat were getting the dragon's attention. Rayden's wings slowly retracted and then its jaws started to slowly grind up the meat. Kade gave a bit of a smile as he felt the dragon's stomach win it over.

He worked the Food Calling for as long as he could concentrate, grateful for the temporary reprieve. After almost twice the normal amount of food, he patted the dragon on the neck and then returned to the tree. *Hopefully the extra meat will take his mind off his desire to kill our best chance of defeating Morg,* Kade thought as he gave the dragon one last glance before disappearing into the tree. Ven was waiting patiently. It was not lost on Kade that his new ally was not very welcomed by his closest of friends and companions. With a sigh, Kade turned to follow the two guards.

Ven followed him back down to where Darcienna was waiting. She gave Ven an icy glare that could have frozen water solid. The shapeshifter gave no indication of seeing the dagger like glances. They made their way down the tunnel they had used previously to get to the spring. Before they turned the corner to the room with the pool, the guards stopped and motioned to their left. There, in the side of the tunnel, were two brand new doors imbedded into the rock. There were real brass hinges on two ornate doors. Each door had to weigh close to twice his weight as it was large enough to allow entry for someone twice his height. Kade pulled on one of the rings and the door swung open smoothly without making a sound. The inside was easily three times the size of the room they had stayed in previously.

Kade went in gaping as he slowly scanned the room, taking in the vastness of it. Darcienna was close behind. Ven hesitated, unsure if she was to follow until Darcienna turned and gave her a hard stare. The shapeshifter moved over to stand in front of the other door and turned to face out. Darcienna closed the door with considerably more force than was needed. Kade was sure the echo could be heard all the way down the hall and out the exit. He swallowed hard.

"I don't know what is going through your head, but she is a shapeshifter!" Darcienna said with such heat in her voice that Kade flinched. Her face was starting to flush.

"I know," Kade was able to get out before she cut him off.

"You cannot have anything with her," Darcienna said as she violently jabbed her finger at the door.

"I know," Kade said, but Darcienna continued on with fire in her voice, full of passion.

"As much as you might think she is beautiful and has all those curves, she cannot be with you," Darcienna said, showing no sign of slowing down.

"I know," Kade repeated, but again, she charged on.

"She will never love you! She is a shapeshifter!" Darcienna raged.

"I know," Kade said. By this time, he knew this was all he was going to get out and stopped so she could continue. He hoped she would get this out of her system sooner than later.

"And you could never love her!" Darcienna practically screamed as she furiously walked away from him.

"I know!" Kade said forcefully. Darcienna reacted as if this was the first time she had heard him talk. She marched at him with eyes blazing.

"And, how do you know?" Darcienna challenged.

"Because, she is not the one who has my heart," Kade shot back as he grabbed her and pulled her firmly into an embrace, pressing his lips to hers.

What better way to silence her than to cover her mouth with mine, he thought.

Darcienna fought him for several long moments. She even pounded on his arms with all her strength, but her lips never left his, even when he gave her enough room. She melted under his embrace. When he finally pulled back, the fire in her was completely gone. Her eyes were filled to the brim with tears. Kade pulled her to himself and hugged her tightly. She cried the cry of a broken heart. Kade did his best to calm her as he stroked her hair. He hated himself for causing her this kind of pain.

"Darcienna," Kade said with such passion that she paused and melted a little more. "You must know by now how I feel about you. Yes, I feel compassion for her, and yes, I do feel a bond already forming, but not in the way I feel with you. She is not you. You must not let that cloud your judgment," he said as he continued to stroke her hair.

"I thought you…when I saw you and her…" Darcienna said and then started to cry again.

"You were wrong," Kade said, backing up and placing a hand alongside her face as he looked deep into her eyes. She turned her cheek into that loving touch. He spoke gently but firmly. "I have what I want and I am not going to give it up," he said as he forced her to look at him. He needed her to see that what he said came from his heart.

"You better not," Darcienna said as a new stream of tears started down her cheek. Kade was not sure why, but he believed that these were the good kind of tears. He was only a guy, so what did he know? She reached her hand around behind his head, wrapped her fingers in his hair and pulled him into a deep, passionate kiss. After several long, heart pounding moments, she broke contact. Breathless, she pushed him to arm's length.

"You need rest," Darcienna said before the passion could build past her self-control.

"You may be right," Kade said as he regretfully let her go and walked over to fall heavily into the bed. He put his hand to his chest and felt his pounding heart. His self-control was completely and utterly shattered. He might be unfamiliar with how to interact with females, but his body needed no lessons. The hurricane of emotions slowly ebbed as his body returned, ever so slowly, back to normal. He spread his hands out to his side and noticed the plush feel of the bed.

It was the most luxurious, soft bed he had ever felt in his

life. It was as if it were made of the same stuff his clothes were but thicker and lots more of it. Kade slid toward the headboard and laid his head on the pillow. He motioned for Darcienna to join him as he patted the spot next to him. She hesitated momentarily as she studied him.

"It's safe," Kade said with a chuckle.

They laid in bed for quite some time, talking. Kade took that time to explain the game of The Taking in Plain Sight. She, of course, thought it was completely foolish that they did not just share their knowledge and said as much. Kade explained why it was like it was and even repeated some of what he had already said, but in the end, she still believed the ways of the Chosen to be devoid of sense. The conversation turned to more lighthearted topics and Kade started to drift off to sleep. She snuggled into his shoulder, afraid to move for fear of losing this moment. As she lay there looking at the door, she pretended that nothing existed beyond this room. For now, this was the extent of their world, and she was more than good with that.

The night was quiet as all activity died down. Darcienna laid there with her head on his chest, enjoying the sound of his heartbeat. She closed her eyes, listening, waiting for the next strong beat to hit. The room had a soft glow from the algae on a small spot here or a crevice over there. It was just enough to see the shadow slip into the room and glide toward them soundlessly. Darcienna barely saw it in time. She screamed and threw her hands up just as the black mass bounded at them.

CH5

"What?" Kade yelled as his hand shot out. The Divine raced through him, setting his nerves on fire. Light exploded into the room just as the black shape smoothly bounded off the shield to land cat-like next to the far wall. The sack of books it was dragging landed with a thud. Kade rubbed his eyes with his free hand and focused on the animal. "Chance?" Kade asked as he reached for Darcienna's arms and pulled them down. The shield faded.

The silky creature calmly got up, padded over to the bed and leapt up gracefully. Darcienna just stared, still trying to get her heart to slow. Kade knuckled his eyes and reached over, scratching behind Chance's ears. The animal leaned into his hand, enjoying the affection. After a few minutes of scratching Chance's head and back, Kade climbed out of bed. He picked up the sack of books and dropped them next to the bed.

Kade fell heavily to land next to Darcienna and turned to face her. Chance fidgeted and squirmed until he had himself pressed against Kade as tightly as possible behind his knees. As soon as the Mordra was content, he quickly slipped off to sleep. Darcienna propped herself up on her elbow and looked from the Mordra to Kade and then back to the door.

"I thought Ven was watching the door," Darcienna said suspiciously.

"I am sure there is a simple explanation," Kade said as he sighed and slowly climbed back out of bed. Chance opened his eyes and watched Kade walk to the door. After a moment, the silky creature got up, moved up to the pillow and then fell as if his legs had given out.

Kade lazily opened the door. Peeking into the hallway, Kade now saw that it was Vell standing guard. The shapeshifter was surprised to see Kade and showed as much in his questioning look. Kade gave him a lazy, tired smile as he glanced back at the animal covering his pillow, wishing it were him in the bed.

Turning and facing Vell, Kade said, "Darcienna was wondering...how the animal got in."

"I was informed that this creature belonged to you," Vell said hesitantly. "Was I mistaken to let it in?" Vell asked as he shimmered and changed form.

"No. You did the right thing," Kade said to Ven as those beautiful, brown eyes looked back at him.

It was obvious that she liked being herself while in his presence. Kade was very conscious of the fact that he had no shirt on when she was in this form but could have cared less if he was buck naked while she was in the form of Vell. He had to get this worked out in his head, or he was going to drive himself nuts. It was only a fluke that he even had pants on. He gave her a smile and slipped back into the room.

"Well?" Darcienna asked tersely.

"Well what?" Kade responded, sliding back into bed, eager to slip back into his dreams. Chance had moved to the middle of the bed and was waiting for Kade to get situated.

"How was Chance able to get in the room?" Darcienna

asked, tight lipped.

"She let him in," Kade said, feeling irritation of his own growing. "She was told that Chance belonged to me so she let him in," he said as he looked at her. "I am glad she did. He has my books," he said as he glanced over the side of the bed at the sack, conscious of the fact that he, once again, forgot about them.

"Oh," Darcienna said, all the heat gone from her voice.

"You need to get over this thing with Ven," Kade said firmly. He was not going to tolerate this kind of irrational behavior, and he meant to make sure she understood. "You know how I feel about you. That is clear for all to see. You are the one who lies here next to me," he said with conviction as he looked deep into her eyes. It was best to quell this before it got out of control. Darcienna squirmed slightly under that gaze. "She is not you. But, I have accepted her, and she is a part of our lives. You need to find a way to accept that. Sooner would be much better than later, but you must."

Darcienna deflated. She was like a flower wilting right before his eyes. Kade waited, giving her all the time she needed to work through this. Her eyes shifted back and forth occasionally as she considered the situation. It was the only evidence that she was even still paying attention.

"She just seems so attached to you," Darcienna finally said, her voice small and helpless. "I want that for me," she said, not able to bring herself to look him in the eye. "I can't help how I feel. It makes my stomach twist in knots."

Kade felt himself go soft inside. He put the crook of his finger under her chin and lifted her head gently until he was looking deep into her blue eyes. The anger he had seen earlier was nowhere to be found.

"I wish I had all the answers, but I don't. All I can do is tell you over and over how much I love you, and that she will never...," Kade was saying when she inhaled sharply.

Kade flinched and looked at her questioningly. Her eyes

135

went wide and tears started to well up. *Now what?* Kade asked himself, frustrated that she was upset again. He sat with his mouth gaping, completely at a loss as to what was wrong now. His ten years in seclusion were definitely working against him. *Women are so bloody confusing*, he thought, exasperated. It was so easy to say the wrong thing and not even know it.

Darcienna lunged at him. He was too slow to duck what was sure to be a stinging slap. He tensed, waiting with his eyes shut tight. Before he knew what was happening, she had her arms wrapped around his neck tightly and planted a kiss so passionately on his lips that he completely forgot what they were arguing about. From a slap to a kiss in no time flat. Crying and then kissing him was beyond his understanding, but he was not going to question it. He wrapped his arms around her and pulled her close. His muscles relaxed and his body molded with hers as the passion exploded. His logical mind shut down and his body took over. There was no stopping where this was going, and neither one tried.

Kade fell onto his back, sweat glistening off his chest. Darcienna's eyes were half closed, a slow smile spreading across her face. She was still breathing hard from the exertion, but she was more than ok with the workout. It took a solid ten minutes before her heart returned to normal. She gazed at the glowing algae on the ceiling as the pleasure of the last hour brought a smile to her face. Neither said a word as they relaxed more and more, letting the memory of their togetherness drift though their thoughts. He reached for her hand. She held on tightly for a second and then relaxed her grip but did not let go. They lay there for quite some time as the passion faded, their muscles turning to water.

"Where did that come from?" Kade asked while his eyes followed the pattern of lights on the ceiling. Darcienna did not answer. He wondered if he had said something wrong, but her grip had not changed. She was not digging her nails in so she could not be mad. Maybe she did not hear the question. Not letting go of her hand, he turned to ask her again and stopped. Her eyes were closed, and her breathing was deep. She wore the most peaceful smile he had ever seen on her. He lifted her hand to his mouth and kissed it as though it were one of the most precious things he had ever held. As carefully as possible, so as not to disturb her, he laid her hand on her stomach. He was too wide awake now for sleep and decided that a nice walk in the cool night air would be just what he needed.

Kade climbed out of bed and took his time dressing, making sure to keep quiet. He moved to the door and slipped into the hallway. As he slowly closed the door, Ven turned toward him, watching curiously.

"Is there a problem?" Ven asked.

"As a matter of fact, right now, everything could not be better," Kade said, the memory of his activities still fresh on his mind.

"Would you like me to accompany you?" Ven asked.

"No. You stay here and guard the door," Kade said as he turned to go.

"Are you sure?" Ven asked, a little more insistently. Something in her voice caught his attention and brought him to a stop. He turned back toward her, curious. "She does not really like me much, does she?" Ven asked. And then, Kade understood. Ven did not want to be at the mercy of Darcienna's wrath without Kade there to protect her. It was not as if Darcienna tried to hide her ire.

"She just does not share me very well," Kade said.

"I mean her no harm," Ven said innocently. Kade had no doubt that she spoke the truth.

"She will adjust," Kade said confidently with a smile. He considering giving her a reassuring hug and mussing her hair to lighten the mood, but with his luck, Darcienna would choose right then to walk out the door. He left it at just a smile and turned to walk down the tunnel for the exit.

He worked his way up the stairs and out into the night air. He was still overheated from his activity so the cool air actually felt good. No, not just good, but great. The dragon raised its head and looked over at him, happiness drifting through the link. Kade walked up and scratched under the dragon's jaw. Rayden radiated pleasure. Kade could not help but to smile.

"How is my friend doing?" Kade asked.

Rayden let out a deep rumble of pleasure as Kade found that one spot that made the dragon purr. Kade smiled as his friend stretched out his neck and twisted his head to the side. Rayden's eyes closed as he soaked up the affection. Kade stifled a laugh as he watched the dragon start to bob its head. He scratched until his fingers started to cramp and then patted his dragon to indicate the spoiling was over. He leaned against Rayden and looked up at the sky.

The stars were out by the thousands. Both moons were on the other side of the planet, leaving the stars to shine brightly. The world seemed peaceful and quiet. Kade put his back to the dragon and slid down. He pulled his knees to his chest and let the peacefulness of nature seep into his soul. The sounds of the night were calming and helped his mind slow. This was a welcomed change. He knew it was going to be short lived, but he enjoyed it, nevertheless.

"You are a better friend than I could have ever hoped for," Kade said as he laid his head back against the dragon, turned his head and looked into its eyes. "You have put your life on the line and saved me more times than I can count. I will always cherish you." Rayden shifted to curl around him.

"May I join you?" Darcienna asked, causing both dragon and man to jump.

"Blood and Ash, woman! Don't sneak up on us like that!" Kade exclaimed as he settled back against the dragon, his hand clenching his chest over his heart.

"Was that a yes?" Darcienna asked with a grin.

"Of course," Kade said, as he slid over a little. "I thought you were asleep," Kade said as she slid down next to him.

"I was until you got out of bed," Darcienna said as she

glanced sidelong at him. "It felt lonely without you in there so I got up and was going to join you. I saw you talking to Ven through the crack in the door and thought I would give you some time to chat with her," she said as she looked out over the open plains. Kade swallowed hard, feeling he had just barely dodged another disaster. He was very happy he passed on that hug. "I did lie back down after you walked out, but it was too quiet so I came to find you."

"And, you found me," Kade said as he placed his arm around her. She turned toward him, leaning into his embrace, pulled her knees up and let them fall over his legs while putting her hand on his chest.

"You don't have any regrets, do you?" Darcienna asked.

Kade was about to ask her what exactly she was talking about when his inner voice screamed at him. *She is a woman*, it reminded him. *If you ask that, she will assume that there is something that you do regret and she will have all kinds of suspicions that will take you a day, if not more, to recover from. Just assume it is about everything. Be smart here. There is only one safe answer.*

"No." He said casually. He was paying very close attention to her to make sure it was the right answer. So far, it seemed that it was. "Do you?" he asked.

"Of course not," Darcienna said with a smile. After a long pause, she looked up at him. "Did you expect something different?" she asked sweetly.

Kade felt alarm bells going off. He felt he was walking through a field riddled with callings. This was supposed to be relaxing, so why did it feel, as though at any moment, this could end in disaster. Maybe not saying anything was best. No. If he said nothing, she would assume the worst.

"What else would I expect?" Kade asked, proud that he had come up with a clever response that was going to keep him out of trouble.

"Why did you take so long to answer?" Darcienna asked

innocently as she looked him in the eye. "You…meant what you said…right?"

"Absolutely," Kade said with conviction. This was an easy one. Now, if he could only bloody well figure out what he had said that seemed to matter, he could work this out.

"Good," Darcienna said as she leaned into him again and took her hand from his chest to hug him around the waist. "I would not want you to say that if you did not mean it."

"I meant it or I would not have said it," Kade said, still feeling like sharks were circling his life raft.

"Say it again," Darcienna said with her head still against his chest. If Kade could see the look in her eye, he may have seen the mischievous glint, but unfortunately for him, he could not.

"I said a lot of things. I meant them if I said them," Kade said, wanting to end the conversation. Darcienna giggled just a little.

"You big ox. You don't even know what you said," Darcienna chided. Kade exhaled in exasperation.

"Woman, you have been toying with me this entire time, haven't you?" Kade asked in frustration but also in relief.

"Maybe just a little. I do enjoy seeing you squirm," Darcienna said and let out a laugh that made his heart sing, even though it was at his expense.

"Would you mind telling me what I said that seemed to be so bloody important?" Kade asked.

"You said…you love me," Darcienna said playfully, but there was a slight edge to it as she paid close attention to his response.

"Oh. I said that, eh?" Kade responded as he pretended to think. Darcienna sat up as she watched him. "When did I say that?" Kade asked, trying hard to keep the smile from his face.

"You really have to work on your lying skills if that is the best you can do," Darcienna said as the smile reached her eyes. She beamed with joy as she radiated love. Her laugh echoed across the

140

land. Kade felt happiness flood through him like the sun fills the land on a cloudless day.

"Am I that obvious?" Kade asked, joining her with laughter of his own. A smile spread across his face so open and honest that it touched her heart. Her tough Chosen warrior was putty in her hands, and she knew it.

"You tensed up solid as a rock when I asked," Darcienna said as she smiled and shrugged, giving away her secret. "You are a man. You say things without realizing what you say, but I knew you meant it," she finished with a gleam in her eye.

"Well, I will practice so I can be as good as you, then," Kade said as he trapped her arm around his waist and tickled her sides. She squirmed and laughed and he laughed right along with her. The dragon watched them with curiosity, but sensing nothing of danger in the link, it laid its head on the ground.

They played for a good few minutes until she put her hands up in surrender. They fell back against the ground, breathing just a little heavy as they stared up at the sky. Kade could barely make out the few clouds that had drifted in as the stars winked out only to return a moment later. The silence stretched on, and then suddenly, he recalled his meeting in the tunnel at the arch. Jorell.

"I have something to tell you. I have been waiting for the right time, and I guess this is as good a time as any," Kade said as he sat up and leaned over her, locking eyes with her. She raised her brow in curiosity and then sat up, sensing it was important.

"I saw Jorell," Kade said.

"I know," Darcienna said as she looked at him in confusion. "We buried her, Kade. Why would you tell me that?" The smile in her eyes melted away at the painful reminder.

"I mean, I saw her when I was in the tunnel," Kade said as he studied her face. Her eyes slowly opened wide as she stared at him.

"When you went through the arch?" Darcienna asked, almost in a whisper.

"I did not go through the arch. They came to me," Kade said as he reached out a hand to cover hers.

"She was there? She was in the room with us?" Darcienna asked, her eyes starting to moisten.

"Yes. Well…she was still in the arch, but yes, she was there."

"Could she see me?" Darcienna asked as her eyes started to spill over.

"She could," Kade said simply, his heart starting to ache.

"What did she say?" Darcienna asked as she wiped a tear from her cheek.

"She said, as long as I take care of you that you will take care of me."

"How did she…what did you tell her?" Darcienna asked as hundreds of questions raced through her mind.

"I did not need to tell her anything. She is very wise, Darcienna."

"Yes," she said as she smiled back at him. Kade reached over, and ever so gently, wiped the next tear away.

"Now, enough of this crying," he said as he leaned forward and put his forehead against hers.

"Is it possible for me to talk to her sometime?" Darcienna asked as another tear spilled over. Kade was expecting a little of this, but she was truly broken hearted, and this was hard for him to handle. The more she suffered, the more his hate for Morg grew. He put his arms around her and held her tightly, hoping to calm her suffering heart.

"We can talk about that later. For now, let's just…," Kade started to say but could not find the right words to finish what he wanted to say. He let out a sigh and just held her. She broke down as the floodgates within her opened wide. The wall she had erected around her heart crumbled to dust. She wept long and hard. She missed her teacher dearly and the pain was flowing through her heart like a torrent. Kade felt his eyes water as her pain filled him.

He was at a complete loss as to what he should do so he did nothing.

Darcienna leaned back and looked up into his eyes. Kade quickly went to turn his head to hide his emotions when she put her hand on his cheek and turned his face back. She reached up and wiped the tear away that was forming at the edge of his eye. She leaned up and kissed him deeply for several long seconds. Her kiss tasted slightly salty from the tears that had run along the edge of her mouth, but that did not take away from the love he felt in that embrace. She pulled back just far enough to look him in the eye.

"I love you," Darcienna whispered just barely loud enough for him to hear. He was not sure what he had done that deserved such a powerful declaration, but he was glad for it, nonetheless. *Maybe it was the hug*, he pondered. Maybe it was that he told her about Jorell. Maybe he would never know.

"I love you, too," Kade said and bent down to kiss her again. Darcienna leaned into him and he wrapped his arms around her.

"We have a long day ahead of us. We should get some rest," Kade said as he gently leaned her back. She nodded in agreement so he stood and offered her his hand. She curled her soft fingers into his and he pulled her to her feet.

"I think a good night's rest right about now sounds great," Darcienna said, exhaustion evident in her voice. She was mentally worn out and her red-rimmed eyes were proof of this.

Without saying another word, Kade took her gently by the hand and turned for the tree. Before he could reach the entrance, something came through the link from the dragon. Kade turned to study Rayden as he titled his head to the side, listening to the thoughts.

"You have got to be kidding," Kade said, just short of exasperation. The dragon was hungry...again!

"Rayden is dying of starvation," Kade said with sarcasm to Darcienna as he readied himself to cook. The dragon easily recognized that Kade was preparing to conjure food and jumped up, eager for the late night meal.

"Well, you better feed him before he wastes away," Darcienna said as she walked up to the bottomless pit and patted it on the side. The dragon spared her a quick glance but turned its eager gaze back to Kade.

"Yes, I can see he is on the verge of collapsing," Kade said playfully as he chuckled. "It just takes so long to feed him, and it never seems to be enough," he said as he planted his feet and tried to clear his mind. He was grateful that this calling was not too dangerous. Typically, the less moves in a calling, the less danger if something were to go wrong.

"You were trying to make a larger piece of meat before, weren't you?" Darcienna asked and then continued on without waiting for a response. "Why don't you work on that?"

"I guess I can give it a try, but I have my doubts," Kade said as he closed his eyes, preparing for the calling.

Kade opened his eyes and went through the moves while envisioning a piece of meat twice the size as normal. It materialized...but just barely. Kade could feel it threaten to fall apart just before it formed. Yes, that was his limit.

"That was better," Darcienna said with encouragement.

"But, that is the best I can do," Kade said, not very enthusiastic at all.

"Why are you not able to make it larger?"

"It is just...I can't seem to channel more of the Divine into the calling. It is like our previous efforts. I just can't get past the block."

"Maybe if you try different ways of calling on the Divine. How do you call on it when it has been more than normal?"

"I...have only been able to draw on more when I am angry," Kade said. "Doren says my gift is my ability to channel unlimited amounts of the Divine, but what good is it if I can only channel when I am so angry I can't think? And how can I be angry when I am making food?" Kade asked as he shook his head.

"There has to be a way. It can't be just when you are angry.

It just can't be or you would become too dangerous. No man can safely make decisions while angry; not and command such power as you can," Darcienna said, trying to be confident.

"I would hope you are right," Kade said, frustrated.

"Just keep trying. You have to be able to do this. I just feel I am right about this," Darcienna said, not willing to accept failure.

Kade cleared his head and felt for the Divine. He opened himself up, pulling on the ancient power with all his will. He completely shut out the world and focused on the flow within. He opened himself up, again, as he called on the meat, but...it failed to materialize. He tried to create a piece equal to the one he had conjured just moments before, but even that one fizzled and fell apart.

"It just...does not want to do as I say," Kade said with his eyes still closed.

He called on the Divine, again, but like the last time, the meat did not materialize. He huffed in exasperation. He took several steadying breaths and tried again. Again, failure.

If I could just repeat the calling like I did at first, that would be progress, he thought. His frustration grew and so did his anger. Darcienna watched, hoping to see the food materialize, but time after time, he failed. Even when he was angry, he failed.

"Do I truly need to be enraged to the point of no rational thinking?" Kade asked of no one in particular. "Blood and Ash!" he swore. "It just will not do as I say," he growled as he looked for something on which to vent his anger. "No matter how much I try to increase the flow, it just won't change," he said though clenched teeth.

"Maybe we should try again later. There has to be something we are missing. We will figure out what triggers your ability, but a break would do you good," Darcienna said with confidence. Kade wished he could join her in her optimism, but his gut said otherwise. The more he tried, the more doubt grew in his heart.

145

"Maybe later," Kade said as he looked into her tired eyes, letting the anger ebb away. Regretfully, he began making the normal size of meat. Ten pieces later, he decided it was enough. "I think we should get some rest," he said as he patted Rayden on the neck and turned for the tree.

They worked their way back through the Great Hall and down to their chamber. Kade paused, seeing Chance sitting just outside the door to their room. Something about the way the animal looked at him did not feel...well...not wrong but not the same. Darcienna saw Kade's look and cocked her head at him.

"Ven?" Kade asked of the creature as he narrowed his eyes.

The black, silky creature shifted and grew into the beautiful, young girl. Darcienna squeezed Kade's hand. He was not sure if it was for the tight fitting outfit that Ven was wearing or the fact that Darcienna had just been fooled by the shapeshifter. She gave Kade a warning glance with a tightlipped look of displeasure.

"Was I convincing?" Ven asked.

"For the most part," Kade said cautiously. Ven beamed at the praise. Kade looked at her, puzzled. It was not that strong a compliment but she reacted as if it were.

"It is difficult for us to emulate a shape perfectly the first time we try. It takes a lot of ability to be able to succeed on our first attempt," Ven said as she smiled. Pride was evident in her voice. This, obviously, meant something in the world of shapeshifters.

"Well, you did an admirable job," Kade said as he moved for the door. Ven glowed at the comment. "If you need to rest or sleep, you are welcome to," Kade added before going into the room.

"That won't be necessary. We don't need sleep," Ven said, still happy with her success.

"You don't ever get tired?" Kade asked, coming to a stop. Darcienna went into the room and tried to pull him after her. He turned his attention to Darcienna before Ven could answer. "I will be there in just a moment. Don't worry, I will not be long," Kade said as he gently disengaged his hand.

"I will be waiting," Darcienna said. She cast a suspicious glance at Ven before disappearing into the room.

"We don't get tired in your sense of the word. We do tire while trying to maintain certain shapes, but it is more a mental fatigue. I can hold a form for days and even weeks, but then I must either return to my birth form, or I must take a shape that takes little effort to hold," Ven said, pleased that Kade was taking an interest in her. "I like that you ask these questions," she said with a genuine smile that said she meant it.

"You don't mind me asking?" Kade asked, surprised.

He expected that she would not want to divulge her secrets, but surprisingly, she was eager to answer anything he asked. Ven was a marvel the more he got to know her. He was grateful for the chance to learn as much as possible about her and her kind. He glanced at the door, conscious of the fact that Darcienna was, most likely, becoming more heated by the moment and decided that he should wrap this up before he had another issue to deal with.

"I don't mind at all," Ven responded with a smile. "It feels…good to trust someone. I trust you, Kade," she said as her eyes lit up like those of an innocent child who knows no better. Kade's mind flashed back to the first time he met this shapeshifter in the bar and found himself shocked at such a profound transformation.

"Well, I should get some rest," Kade said, resisting the urge to ask question after question. He very much wanted to know how large of a creature she could emulate, or the most powerful shape she could take. Or even, a creature with the most interesting abilities, but he knew he was pushing it already. This was a conversation that could last for hours. He sighed as he glanced at the door, saving this talk for another time.

"Sleep well," Ven said as she stepped aside for him to enter the room.

With a good night to her, he walked through the door, hoping Darcienna had not become too restless. One glance at her,

147

and he realized he was too late. He stopped just inside the room. Darcienna was clearly unhappy with his delay as she gave him a look of displeasure. It was not quite a glare but it was not far from it. If she had not been exhausted, he was sure he would get more of a scolding. He mentally sighed and moved over to the bed.

"Darcienna," Kade said as he slid into bed. "You have to accept her. I do not want to have this talk every time I interact with her," he said gently.

"Kade, it's not that I don't like her. I don't trust her. Not like you do," Darcienna said as she glanced at the door. "It's just that I know she wants you for herself. Maybe not in the way that I do, but I can tell she likes your company. It just feels…uncomfortable. Others will see and think you have feelings for her. They most certainly will think that she has feelings for you," she said as she looked at the door again.

"I cannot control how others think, Darcienna," Kade said as he cast a glance at the door that Essence Guardian was still studying.

"Does she have to keep that form?" Darcienna asked as she turned back toward him. Her eyes were large and innocent. He found it almost impossible to be angry with her.

"Is it fair to ask her to be something other than who she is? What does that say to her? If she wanted to be Vell, then I would support that, but she wants to be who she is," Kade said as he shrugged his shoulder. "In a way, it is more honest."

"And you have no interest in her?" Darcienna asked.

Kade could tell the question was only meant to help reassure her, but it did not sit well with him that she even asked. He considered getting out of bed as his irritation rose. *Maybe I will sleep on the floor*, he thought as he cast a glance at the ground. *How many ways do I have to tell her? How many ways do I have to show her? Women can be so mentally exhausting*, he thought in exasperation.

"I am sorry," Darcienna said, sensing his irritation. "Kade, I am trying, but it is not easy for me. I don't like sharing you, and the fact that she is so beautiful makes it that much more difficult. I want people to know you are mine," she said as she caressed his face. Kade melted under that touch.

"I wish I knew the right thing to say, but I don't. I can only do what I think is best," Kade said as he laid back down.

He was starting to feel mentally exhausted. He was not sure if it was more about what was to come or because of the battles he had to fight right here. Darcienna laid down next to him and reached for his hand.

"I am sorry," Darcienna said, meaning it with her heart and soul. "I will do better."

"I am sure you will," Kade said as he smiled at her. He was not convinced she would be perfect but he was certain she was going to try.

They did not speak another word as each lay quietly, time slipping by. He let his mind wander as he contemplated the mystery of his abilities. *Why can I not get past the block within me? What is the problem?* he asked himself. *Maybe this is the way my ability works. Maybe I needed to be out of my mind with fury before I can call on my special gift.*

If he had let his rage make all his decisions, he would have killed Darcienna that day outside Doren's house. This put a knot in his stomach instantly. It was a memory he hated. She almost died at his hand because he was out of control with anger. Ven, also, would have been killed if he had given in to his rage. She may have deserved it, but seeing how things turned out, he knew it would have been the wrong thing to do.

There had to be something he could do. Darcienna believed he could overcome this and her sense of things, so far, had been pretty good. *Maybe she is right, but how do I get around this block?* he asked himself as his mind started to drift. He was barely aware of Darcienna snuggling up next to him and whispering in his ear as he sank deeper and deeper into the plush bed.

"Please don't hurt me again," Darcienna said, but Kade was starting to breathe deep. "I can only give you my heart so many times," she said and then let herself drift off to sleep.

Darcienna's dreams were not the soothing, sweet dreams of love but dreams of terror so profound that it shook her very soul. She had nightmare after nightmare, losing her one true love as his image floated through the arch. She woke up drenched in sweat. She was so petrified by what she saw in her dreams that even screaming was not possible. She could only recall one other time that she had had dreams so terrifying and vivid. When she was but a young girl of fourteen, she believed her dreams to be nothing more than night terrors. Now, she knew different. The dream she had six years previous was of her beloved master lying dead in a pool of blood. That very scene played out just days prior. Now, she was seeing Kade's death and her heart suffered dearly. *If this is another gift from Nature, then Nature has a very sick sense of humor*, she thought as her pulse continued to pound.

Maybe it was nothing more than a nightmare, she told herself desperately, but she knew she was only trying to deceive herself. *Maybe knowing what may come will give me a chance to change it, she told herself. I have to be able to save him. I will never again turn a blind eye to what fate threatens me with*, she thought with determination. *Maybe...maybe knowing what may come to pass gives me a chance to change it*, she considered. *This gift might turn out to be the most profound Nature's Gift after all*, she thought as she mentally apologized to Nature for her previous bad thoughts. If it helped her save the one she loved, then it would turn out to be her most precious gift after all.

Darcienna wrapped her arms tightly around Kade and laid her head on his chest, listening to his heartbeat. *I am not going to give him up without a fight*, she thought fiercely. The pound of his heart helped push the night terror away. Moment by moment her mind stopped reeling as she listened to the life still beating in his chest. He was alive, and she meant to keep it that way. She held on tightly, as if death might come that very night. The nightmares receded and were replaced by dreams of a future with children. She embraced the dream with all of her will and allowed it to build around her.

"Kade, wake up. It is time to prepare for your journey," Doren said as he leaned over the bed. The apprentice showed no signs of waking. "Kade," he repeated as he shook the sleeping form.

Kade lifted his head and struggled to open his eyes. After a moment, he let his head fall back onto the pillow and stretched. He knuckled the sleep from his eyes and then swung his legs over the edge of the bed.

"How long?" Kade asked as he stood.

"Almost ten hours," Doren said casually. "Come. It is time to prepare," he said, moving to stand by the door.

Kade reached over and shook Darcienna. She groaned and slowly forced her eyes open. She smiled and reached out a hand for him. He took it, expecting to pull her out of bed, but she pulled him down, instead. There was a fierce determination there that made Kade stop and study her. He opened his mouth to ask what had her so concerned, but the look faded. He put it off to waking up and smiled.

"Do we really have to get up?" Darcienna asked as she returned his smile. Kade glanced at Doren, and then with regret, nodded his head. The Master Chosen breathed a sigh as he stood, watching.

"I need time to get ready," Darcienna said as she ran her fingers through her hair. "Maybe a quick wash in the spring," she said as she looked around the room until her eyes found what she was searching for. She climbed out of bed and pick up a towel. "You coming?" she asked as she reached for the door.

"Why not," Kade said as he grabbed the last remaining towel.

"Apprentice," Doren said tersely. "Do not take too long," he

151

said and then disappeared out the door without waiting for a response. Kade rolled his eyes and did his best to keep his irritation in check but failed.

There was an outfit lying on the table that was identical to the one he was wearing. He roughly grabbed it and the green one meant for Darcienna and stormed out to follow her to the spring. Ven was close behind until Kade held up a hand for her to stop.

"Wait by the door," Kade said. Ven seemed ready to persist when he gave her a look that said it was not open for debate. Some of the harsh look was driven by his irritation with the Master Chosen, but he did not care. She moved back to the door.

Kade already regretted the cold water and he was not even in, yet. They bathed quickly and eagerly climbed out of the cold spring. He wondered if there was a way for him to heat the water as he dried off.

Maybe I will try heating a rock and dropping it in, he thought as he dressed in the new clothes. Maybe he would heat a rock that they could warm themselves by when they got out. It was all speculation meant for another time.

"That does feel better," Kade said as he rubbed the water out of his hair with his towel. The cold definitely got his blood pumping and helped his mind become more alert. He could almost say it was refreshing but not quite. It was just too darn cold.

"See? Nothing helps start the day right like a nice washing," Darcienna said as she squeezed the excess water out of her hair. She dried off and then slipped into the fresh, clean clothes.

"Kade," Doren said, making both of them jump. "They have food for you in the Great Hall," he said with all the patience in the world. Darcienna pulled her outfit tighter about herself and gave Kade an irritated look.

"Master Chosen," Kade said, anger flashing in his eyes at the invasion of their privacy. "A little discretion when we are bathing would be appreciated."

"I will see you in the Great Hall for food," Doren said

casually, ignoring the comment and turning to walk out of the room. Darcienna glared after him.

"Food is a good idea. And, I don't have to make it," Kade said, trying to lighten the mood but failed. Darcienna was still glaring after the Master Chosen. Kade felt his anger flare, knowing that the Master Chosen was not interested in what mattered to Kade or Darcienna. Rarely would Doren ever care for an apprentice's opinion.

Maybe Morg wants an apprentice, Kade thought sarcastically. *I am certain I would get more respect from him instead of this....* A decade of training to respect a Master Chosen would not allow him to finish the thought.

They left the spring and headed for their room. As they rounded the corner, Kade froze and Darcienna squeaked. His heart beat hard as he stared at the large creature standing in the tunnel. Before he could prepare a calling, he recognized it as the one he had seen the day before.

"Ven?" Kade asked as he tried to calm his pounding heart.

"Yes?" Ven responded.

"I did not expect that form," Kade said, trying to hide his shock.

"I can change back," Ven said and started to shift.

"No," Darcienna shot back so quickly that Kade flinched. "No," she said much calmer the second time. "That form is perfect."

"I shall keep it then," Ven said as the shape solidified. Kade gave Darcienna a flat look that warned her not to start. She pretended not to notice.

They dropped their towels in the room and worked their way to the Great Hall. He would have sworn that it was virtually empty, due to the lack of sound, but as he rounded the corner, he could see it was filled to overflowing with spiders. Every seat was taken as the spiders ate in silence. The room was large enough to fit close to five hundred spiders, if not more. The mood was somber. This was the day their second king was to go off to fight an overwhelming force, and they knew it. This was the day they could lose Kade, their champion and hero.

As the couple stepped into the room, every spider stopped what they were doing and turned to stare at him. Kade could not deny that the mood was heavy. He could have felt it even if his eyes were closed. He found the queen and locked eyes with her. After a moment, he continued, sweeping the crowd with his gaze. Kade took a deep breath and spoke, making sure his voice carried to every part of the room. He held his head high as he let the sound of his voice carry.

"This is not a day for us to dread but a day for us to celebrate as we make our stand and send a message that we will live in fear of no one," Kade said as he led Darcienna to the royal table and indicated for her to sit. The queen was up and translating smoothly as Kade spoke. "This is the day that we strike first," Kade said as he put strength into his voice and slammed his fist into his open palm, causing many spiders to jump. It was having its desired effect. The spiders started to perk up. "This is the day that we show Morg that he should be the one living in fear," Kade said, raising his voice. The spiders started to come alive. His words were stronger than any calling he could have ever used. "This is the day that we let it be known that we are the ones to be feared. We have overcome much and we will continue to overcome all who make the mistake of believing we are weak," Kade said as he called on the Great Divine and let light spring forth from his hands. Both hands were glowing as he purposefully strode amongst the spiders. It was an impressive sight and even Doren had an approving smile...along with hands that were in the shape of a bowl. The light was not enough to cause any to turn away, but it was definitely chasing away the shadows. "Today," Kade said as he raised a fist and let more light shine, "is the day we take the fight to him," he finished with such ferocity that a vein pulsed in his neck. The spiders erupted in a deafening buzz as the hall exploded into life.

"That was quite impressive," Rakna said as she took her place next to the king.

"Agreed," Crayken added.

"You have given them something to believe in," Doren said approvingly, as he studied the light still coming off the apprentice's hands. Kade recalled Doren's reaction the previous day when he had used light to sway the kings and queens. He saw how Doren was holding his hands and realized what was going on instantly. *One of these times the Master Chosen was going to figure it out,* Kade thought to himself, reminding himself to be cautious. Zayle's wise words about simple callings being just as important as any other callings drifted through his mind.

Maybe someday I will trade him this calling for one of his, Kade thought, not realizing that he was fully thinking like a Master Chosen. *Of course, as an apprentice, it would be expected for a Master Chosen to divulge callings to his student,* Kade thought in amusement.

Kade took the empty place next to the king, knowing it was meant for him and Darcienna took the one next to that. Kade wondered what Doren thought about having to be sat behind him and Darcienna as he took the place three down from the king. Regardless, he earned this, Doren did not.

Darcienna looked at him with pride, but there was no denying that there was fear there for him to see, also. Kade stopped, looking deep into her eyes and cocked his head as if to ask what was bothering her. The image of him floating through the arch sprang into her mind. She was certain that telling him of her vision would be a grave mistake. If she told him, he would question his every decision, and that would not do. Because of this, she knew it would be up to her to thwart fate and keep him from crossing over into the world of the dead. This was her secret and she was not going to burden him with it.

"I just worry," Darcienna said as she smiled reassuringly at him.

Kade nodded, satisfied with her answer. Had he watched her just a few more seconds, he would have seen fear dance through her eyes, and most assuredly, would have pressed her for more. He knew her well enough by now to know when she was holding something back. She swallowed hard and closed her eyes as she steadied her nerves. She opened them and flinched. He was locked onto her.

"Is there more?" Kade asked suspiciously as he studied her closely. Darcienna tried to hold her smile but it slipped. He could see the fear in her eyes.

Bloody ash and all curse the Divine! she thought as she tried her best to put on a brave face.

"Darcienna?" Kade pressed.

"I am afraid for your life. I don't want to lose you. Just promise me you will be careful," Darcienna said. *What I said was true,* she told herself. It was the only way she could keep the secret. She had to put some truth in it or he would see that there was more.

"You will be there to protect me. How can I not be safe?" Kade asked as he covered her hand with his.

"Yes, I will be," Darcienna said to fate as much as to him. "Yes, I will be there to keep you on this side!" she said with conviction.

Kade smiled at her determination, satisfied, and turned his attention to his plate of food that was set before him. The fruits, nuts and vegetables were a welcome change to the meat, cheese and bread. Not having to cook was a relief.

The room was full of animated gestures and loud, excited buzzing. Kade had his fill of food and leaned back, allowing the meal to settle. As he sat looking around the room, a spider raced in and came straight to the king and queen. It cast a quick glance at Kade and then moved to the other side of the king to include Kade in the conversation. He buzzed dramatically as he looked back and forth between the apprentice and the king as though Kade could understand.

156

The queen quickly translated as the spider rushed to give all the information. The more the spider spoke, the quieter the room became. By the time the spider finished, the room was deathly quiet with all eyes on the royal table. The spider withdrew while the king and queen talked in quick whispers.

"It would appear that things are not well," Doren said thoughtfully.

"Morg has scouts in the area," Kade said. "They are scouring the land as they move, searching. They are heading in the direction of the cave. The spider says they will be there soon," he said as he looked between Doren and Darcienna. The Master Chosen nodded thoughtfully as he clasped his hands together and placed his fists under his chin, giving off the air of someone who is about to solve a complicated puzzle. Darcienna pressed her lips together. Kade watched her as a fierce determination flashed through her eyes so strongly that he wondered what was going through her mind. He touched her hand and she jumped. Her eyes focused on him but the determination did not fade. He was about to ask what had her so tense when a voice directly behind him drew his attention.

"The spy from the previous day did not return," Ven said in her huge beastly form. That was all that she needed to say. Everyone understood.

"It would appear that things are progressing faster than we had hoped," Doren said as though they were discussing gardening techniques. His nonchalant attitude irked Kade.

"We either protect the cave, or we go after Morg, but we must decide," Crayken said.

"It is imperative that we protect the cave," Doren said with some intensity. "If they find the tunnel, Morg will not wait for us to come to him. He will come to us in force, and it may very well end badly," he said as he turned his attention on Kade. It was clear he was expecting Kade to continue on with what he was saying. Even though Doren made perfect sense, there was a smugness about the way he did what he did. It was as if he believed he was directing the conversation and Kade was no more than a puppet waiting for a cue. Kade sighed, not liking being manipulated. Doren very much enjoyed showing how smart he was and it was starting to grate on Kade. He knew Doren was correct in his thinking, but the Master Chosen enjoyed showing how brilliant he was just a little too much. Pompous, was the word that came to Kade's mind.

Why did it not bother me when Zayle showed his superiority? Kade asked himself. He knew the answer before he even finished the question. Zayle was not concerned with what others thought. He taught what he needed to teach without trying to impress. Zayle was not pompous. Zayle was just knowledge, power and an excellent teacher who cared more about his students than what his students might think of him. Kade smiled at the memory of his teacher and then returned his attention to the spiders.

"We need to know exactly how close they are to finding the tunnel. We must avoid engaging the enemy for as long as possible. It is important we see how they are scouting," Kade said as he stood.

"The queen shall join you while I lead the clutch to the caves," Crayken said.

"Let us scout ahead, and when we know more, we can formulate a plan," Kade said.

"I shall ready the clutch and we will await your command," Crayken said. Kade felt odd at the implication that he, a mere Apprentice Chosen, was to lead them all.

He stood and faced the spiders once again. This was the last pep talk he was going to give and it had better be the best of his life. Many of these spiders would never dine here again, and he was painfully aware of that fact. Darcienna gave him a slight nod of her head for encouragement.

"Today, we get our chance to rid this world of an evil that threatens all peaceful creatures. Today, you get to be the protectors of the world. Today, the world will know that you saved it from a torment so horrendous that peace would have never been a possibility ever again. I am honored to stand with you in this fight," Kade said loudly. The kings from all the clutches nodded their approval as he spoke. Kade's courage and conviction were contagious. The spiders knew that this was going to be a bloody war, and with Kade to lead the charge, they were ready for it. They started a chant that grew into a crescendo. Kade wanted to cover his ears but that would not be very kingly at all. He stepped onto the table as the buzzing echoed. "Today, I am proud to fight alongside each and everyone one of you!" he shouted, almost becoming hoarse. "Fight for your people!" he chanted as he pumped his fist in the air. "Fight for your family. Fight for your king and queen, but most importantly, fight to destroy this evil and make him regret ever setting foot in our land!" Kade thundered as he stomped hard on the table. To Kade's shock, the spiders responded in kind. They hit their tables as one and it echoed throughout the cave. They started pounding over and over, hitting harder with each strike. He expected tables to start splintering under the assault, but miraculously, they held. The booming picked up pace as they worked themselves into a frenzy. Kade feared if they became any more excited, they would race off to confront Morg without waiting for the order to attack.

He stepped down from the table and reached a hand out to Darcienna. She took it with a gleam in her eye. Doren nodded his approval. The smug self-satisfaction coming from the Master Chosen irritated Kade, but he nodded back, regardless. He should have liked the approval he was getting, but for some reason, he did not. He hated to think he was going to have to study under this Master Chosen, but he could not see that he had much of a choice. As an apprentice, he had to study under a master until he was assigned the rank of Adept. It was true that Doren could help him reach the next level, but studying under the Master Chosen as an apprentice just did not sit well with him. He mentally sighed and looked around the room as the spiders calmed.

"I leave you in the hands of your capable king. He will know the right time to bring the war to them," Kade said as he looked to Crayken. The spiders erupted again, eager for the bloodbath. By now, Kade was certain he could just throw his hands into the air and the spiders would go into a frenzy.

"We should be going," Doren said as if Kade needed prompting.

Kade tensed and glanced away so Doren would not see the look of pure irritation on his face. Darcienna wrapped both her hands around Kade's arm for support. He looked at her and she shook her head just barely enough for him to see. He knew she was right. Now was not the time to let personality clashes get in the way of what they must do.

Doren is correct, but wasn't I just saying that already? Kade thought as he headed for the exit.

The shapeshifter was close behind Kade and Darcienna as they exited the tree. Doren was next, followed by the queen. Kade mentally called out to the dragon. Rayden swooped in from out of the sky to land gracefully in front of the small group without the extra pumps of its wings. Kade expected the usual playfulness from the dragon, but even Rayden seemed to understand that things were about to get very dangerous. Kade opened his mind to the link and connected with his friend. Yes, even Rayden understood, but there was also an eagerness for battle. Rayden was all killing machine now and Divine help the creatures caught in his path.

"It is time for us to leave. We must go to the cave as quickly as possible. Morg's scouts are closing in on it, and we must stop them. We have to ride now," Kade said as he indicated for the dragon to kneel. Rayden was restless and huffed several times, resisting Kade's directions. "Rayden, we must go," he urged, but the dragon's agitation grew. Rayden eyed the hulking creature that was standing close to Kade. The dragon's lips quivered as the fangs flashed into view and its wings half opened as it readied to attack. Kade felt the dragon's desire to kill assail him through the link. It was overwhelming and made his head spin.

Is this what I am like when I thirst for revenge; not thinking or caring, only wanting to give in to the desire to kill? Kade asked himself as he struggled to communicate with the dragon. The shapeshifter was too valuable to leave behind, but Kade was not convinced that the dragon could be calmed. Hate came off Rayden in waves. For the first time that he could recall, Kade became angry at the dragon's stubbornness.

Enough! Kade communicated firmly to his friend. He sent the thought so hard through the link that the dragon winced. *I need the shapeshifter. You must not harm her!* Kade thought forcefully. The link was full of surprise and confusion. He turned to Ven quickly. "Change back to your birth form."

"I shall, but I fear your dragon is about to tear me apart," Ven said nervously as she glanced back and forth quickly between Rayden and Kade. "If you believe I am safe, I shall trust you and do as you say," Ven said. She hesitated, waiting for his reassurance. Kade glanced back at the dragon and then nodded his head to her. With that, she shimmered and changed into the beautiful form of Ven.

Yes, it is a female, Kade sent through the link. *This is her true form. Do not hurt her!* he thought firmly. Rayden edged closer, step by step, not taking his eyes off the shapeshifter. Ven fidgeted nervously as she glanced at Kade for reassurance.

"We do not have time for this," Doren said impatiently.

"We must make time for it. I need them both and they must work together," Kade said, trying his hardest not to glare at the Master Chosen. Doren gave an irritated huff and crossed his arms while giving Kade a stern look. The Apprentice Chosen ignored it and focused on Rayden as the dragon closed in on Ven.

"Easy, Rayden," Kade said, feeling anger and confusion through the connection. "Easy."

Rayden edged closer yet. His head was right next to Kade, still locked onto the shapeshifter. Kade looked at the massive jaws that were too large for him to reach around and prayed Rayden would listen. The dragon was now so close to the shapeshifter that if it decided to lunge, Ven would have been in trouble. Kade's palms became clammy under the stress.

"Rayden," Kade said firmly as he put his hands on the side of the dragon's head, ready to push it away. "Do...not...hurt...her!" he said, emphasizing each word. As he spoke the last word, the dragon's lips stopped quivering. Rayden's nose started to work furiously as he inhaled the shapeshifter's scent. His wings were still half extended as his nose touched Ven's chest. She gave a slight whine as fear gripped her heart. "Rayden," Kade warned again.

Dragons really hold grudges, Kade thought as he readied himself to dive at Ven. He was not strong enough to stop the dragon, but maybe he could get her out of the way if Rayden attacked. Kade flexed his muscles as he prepared to act. He looked at Rayden's wings and recalled the last time he saw the dragon in this position; it was when the dragon had torn into the first cat-like creature they had encountered.

"Kade," Darcienna said with deep concern in her voice. He wanted to look at her, but he could not chance taking his eyes off Ven for even a moment. His muscles started to ache.

"Rayden," Kade said as he put pressure on the dragon's head, trying to push it out of the way. It was like pushing against a boulder. The dragon gave no sign of moving, and Kade knew it was going nowhere until it wanted.

"Kade," Doren said in that tone a master uses with an apprentice. "We do NOT have time for this. Leave the shapeshifter behind and let's go now!" Doren commanded.

Out of his peripheral, Kade saw flowing black fur approach the Master Chosen and knew that the king had interceded on his behalf. He made it a point to thank the king profusely for his timing. He decided to try another approach. Stroking the dragon gently on the jaw, Kade spoke softly.

"Rayden, I need you to forgive her. Just as I saved your life, she may save mine," Kade said, sending the words through the link along with speaking them aloud. "You must respect my wishes," he said as he moved next to the shapeshifter. "She is with us now."

Rayden moved ever so slightly as he studied the shapeshifter for several long seconds. Kade could feel the hate melting away. Rayden turned his attention to Kade and his wings slowly folded tightly to his body. The dragon let out its breath. Kade's eyes widened as he realized that Rayden had dragon's fire ready to envelop the shapeshifter.

I could not have saved her, Kade thought as he felt his heart pound. He closed his eyes, took a deep breath and then let it out unsteadily. Ven smiled her thanks but her lips quivered with the effort. She had been scared to the core of her being.

"I am happy my trust was not misplaced," Ven said innocently. If only she knew how unsure Kade was.

"You did the right thing," Darcienna said as she let her hands fall to her side. "We may need her," she said as she spared a glance for the shapeshifter.

"Would your shield have stopped the dragon's fire in time?" Kade asked as his nerves calmed. He dried his hands on his pants.

"Who says I was going to use my shield?" Darcienna asked pointedly.

"Let's get going," Kade said as he gave her a knowing look. Darcienna rolled her eyes and turned for the dragon.

Rayden quickly dropped to his knees and held still for the riders to mount. Darcienna was first, followed by the Master Chosen and then the queen climbed up the dragon's tail to settle behind Doren. Rayden shuddered as usual. There was no getting used to it for the dragon. Kade vaulted off the dragon's knee to land right in front of Darcienna. Rayden's wings came out and he was ready to pump when Kade had him hold.

"What form would be best for you?" Kade asked the shapeshifter.

"How about this one?" Ven asked as she changed to a monkey and swung up to hang around his neck. Kade could feel irritation through the link, and then just as quickly, it was gone.

"That should work. Hold on tight," Kade said as he put an arm around the monkey and held her close. Darcienna tensed. He ignored her nonverbal protest. "I am going to make us unheard and unseen," he said to the dragon as much as to the other passengers.

The king was standing next to the dragon as the clutch poured out of the tree in waves. It was a never ending flood of spiders as they exited and climbed the tree. Many came out to surround the dragon and see their queen off. Kade was amazed that this many spiders had even fit in the tree. True, the Great Hall could fit five hundred or more, but where did the rest come from? There had to be close to a thousand. The more spiders poured out of the tree, the more confident he felt that they had a chance to win this war. Those poisonous fangs were not to be ignored.

Kade closed his eyes and focused on the callings he needed. He opened his eyes and performed the Transparency Calling flawlessly. There was an audible buzzing from the spiders as the dragon and its riders faded from view. Kade could not help but to grin to himself, considering how their disappearance must have looked to the clutch. He readied himself for the Silence Calling and hesitated.

"Be ready. We will know how to proceed shortly," Kade said to the king and then performed the calling.

Rayden opened his wings, but there were too many spiders around for him to get into the air. He nudged the spiders out of the way as he headed toward the open plain. When he had a clear path ahead of himself, he took several powerful lunges and then launched into the air. Kade had to hold on tightly as his head threatened to rock back from the force of the thrust. If it was this difficult for him, then how Doren stayed on was beyond his understanding.

"Thank you," Doren said.

"You are welcome," Rakna responded.

"That was close," Doren said, his voice slightly unsteady. Before the apprentice could ask what he was missing, the Master Chosen's words made it clear what had happened. "Your webbing held me in place nicely." As much as Kade found the Master Chosen grating on his nerves, he would have regretted it deeply if anything were to happen to him.

"Maybe a harness to help for travel," Kade offered.

"That would be most optimal," Doren said, regaining much of his composure.

The dragon pumped hard until they gained enough altitude to see almost all the way to the cave. The mountain came at them quickly. As they approached their destination, Kade looked down at the ground, and for a moment, noticed that it appeared to be moving. The more he focused on it, the more he was able to make out what he was seeing.

"Master Chosen!" Kade yelled over the noise of the wind. "Look at the ground!"

"My eyes are not as sharp as they once were. What are you seeing?" Doren asked.

"Darcienna? Rakna?" Kade asked as the shapes started to become more distinguishable.

I see, Rakna said in his mind. Darcienna squeezed him hard as her eyes widened. Kade turned to look at her, forgetting that she was unseeable. Regardless, it was obvious she was seeing the same thing as he through eyes he was sure were glowing. *They appear to be giant ants,* the queen said in his mind. *They are, at best, minutes away from discovering the cave,* the queen warned as they swooped in toward their destination.

"Rayden, you must not disturb the ground. Find a patch of grass. We cannot allow ourselves to be detected. Rakna, warn the spiders not to attack. Under no circumstance are they to attack unless we give the order. Any spiders not already in the cave are to take to the trees and stay hidden, no matter what," Kade said, feeling panic start to build.

If those ants found the tunnel, it would have disastrous consequences. They were crawling all over everything. They were covering the mountain as a blanket covers a bed. There was not one spot that was being left unchecked.

"The spiders are hidden in the cave, but if those ants find the cave, they will find the clutch," Rakna hissed.

"Then we have to stop that from happening," Kade said as the dragon touched down.

The closest ant was a mere one hundred yards from the tunnel and closing in as it walked on the side of the mountain. The ants were being methodical as they covered every inch of ground. It was inevitable that they were going to discover the tunnel if something was not done.

"To the cave! Hurry!" Kade said as he quickly found Darcienna's hand and pulled her along. "Rayden, back into the air and stay there until I call," Kade commanded. He felt the beating of wings as the dragon leapt into the air.

The closest ant was now just fifty yards. More ants were beginning to fill the area. Doren ordered them into the opening as he readied himself to cast his calling. Kade hesitated, certain he knew what calling Doren was going to use.

"I will stay with you in case you need me," Kade said as he stopped outside the entrance. Doren did not answer. Kade could feel the Divine building and then the cave disappeared to be covered by what looked like mountainside.

"In!" Doren commanded. Kade felt the ground vibrate slightly and knew that Doren had entered the cave. Kade stood watching as the ant moved closer and closer to the entrance. He knew he should have done as the Master Chosen ordered, but he could not take his eyes off that one ant. He held his breath and took a step back. The ant continued to search the ground for any sign of the hidden treasure as it moved closer and closer, its head swinging back and forth as it searched. Kade felt his chest ache as his heart beat like a drum.

"Kade," Darcienna called, but he continued to watch the ant move closer by the second.

Twenty yards, Kade thought as he mentally measured the distance. It made a zigzag pattern along the mountainside as it continued in its methodical search. Its antenna quivered every few seconds. It was about five feet long and had eyes that bulged out like a fly. It stood two feet off the ground and its body undulated on five pod-like shapes as if it were a snake. Its legs ended in points that were sharp as daggers. Above all else, Kade noticed the mandibles that were over a foot long and sharp as razors. They flexed open and closed every few seconds as the creature prepared them for use. He was certain that those weapons could tear his arm off with virtually no effort if it got the chance. He glanced around and saw an army of ants scouring the area, but it was this one he was locked onto that was his concern.

Ten yards Kade thought, as he swallowed hard. He could hear a slight hum now every time its antenna quivered. It hit him that this was their way of communicating. He glanced at the cave and then back at the ant as it moved closer, yet. It stopped and its head moved back and forth rapidly as if catching a scent.

"Kade!" Doren said forcefully, anger in his voice. The apprentice, barely breathing, ignored the command as he focused on the ant.

It moved closer to the edge of the cave. Kade carefully approached, making sure not to disturb the ground. Just one yard from the edge of the cave and one yard from Kade, it stopped to crane its neck in his direction. Its antenna quivered and the hum could easily be heard now. He could feel the vibration in his teeth as the ant continued to communicate. Its head swam back and forth as it tested the air for the presence it sensed. After just a moment, it moved forward…and then…disappeared around the corner and into the cave.

CH6

Kade felt the shapeshifter climb to his shoulder and launch through the air as it propelled itself through the illusion. He lunged through the opening at almost the same time. As he passed through the entrance, he saw the ant hanging in midair for just a fraction of a second and then its head was torn from its body.

"Kade, quickly, remove the protective callings," Ven said in her giant-form voice.

The callings from the group vanished just as the ant was falling to the ground. There, stood another ant just like the one on the ground. It was unnerving, but Kade knew what had happened. The ant's antenna quivered, but in this form, there was no way for them to understand what she was trying to say. Ven turned and raced out through the illusion just in time to intercept several other ants that were headed in their direction. Her antenna quivered rapidly and then the other ants turned away and continued their search elsewhere.

"That was close," Doren said.

Kade cast a glance at Darcienna, but quickly looked away. He thought about pointing out that contrary to what she had argued, Ven had proven herself useful but decided not to make the point. It was too late. Darcienna caught the look.

"Yes, she did help," Darcienna said, begrudgingly.

"I was not going to say anything," Kade added. "But, yes she did," he finished.

Kade turned and realized for the first time that there were spiders completely covering the walls, ceiling and floor. It was a sea of spiders. One of them buzzed to the queen dramatically. Kade thought he could just start to make out the difference in tones. It was not a good buzzing.

"A spider got too close to the arch, and something came out of it. Shortly after, the spider started to attack the others. They had to kill it," the queen said, anger in her voice. "This is unacceptable. Spiders do not attack other spiders, Kade. We threaten to use force, as the leaders of our kind, but it is extremely rare that we ever have to follow through on that threat," Rakna said, highly agitated. "What came through was evil. We should consider destroying this thing," she added in great distress.

"We need this as much as Morg does. We must make sure all spiders stay away from the arch. I am sorry, Rakna, but we cannot destroy it. Not yet," Kade said as he waited to see if Doren had any input. The Master Chosen stood by silently, but Kade knew his mind was working.

"Kade," Darcienna said from the entrance. "The ants are moving on. What do we do now?"

"We must go to Morg," Doren said firmly.

"Once we are sure the ants are gone," Kade said and then turned toward Doren for the next part, "And...Ven is back. Only then shall we go. I am going to recast the protection callings." And

169

with that, the group disappeared once again.

It was not lost on any of them why Kade had spoken as he did. If the Apprentice Chosen could have seen the Master Chosen, he would have seen the fire that was building in Doren's eyes as he attempted to control his anger. Kade could tell that Doren was furious from the gasp he let out. It almost sounded like he had been hit in the gut. Did he push too far? Was the Master Chosen going to explode in rage? Even though Doren could not see, Kade winced. He looked toward the entrance, hoping Ven would not take too long.

"Kade," Doren said in a tone that made him cringe. "We are going to have a very firm talk, when we have time. You forget your place," he said, all civility gone. For him to vent so strongly in front of the others was an obvious indication of just how angry he was. "You are an apprentice, and if you want to continue on the path of the Chosen, you will respect our ways. While you are an apprentice, you will do as you are instructed." Although his words definitely indicated his displeasure, it was how he emphasized certain words as he spoke them that really hit hard. Darcienna inhaled sharply at the strong rebuke.

Kade cringed. He was grateful for the transparency calling. It would buy him the precious few moments he needed before deciding how to deal with this. He was not sure if he should stand his ground, or give in. He was still an apprentice, and Doren was correct that as an apprentice, he was bound to submit to the Master Chosen but to be handicapped by tradition and custom at this moment was debilitating. He believed that with all that had transpired, Doren was not going to pull rank, but there it was. Not only did he need to deal with Morg and the monsters, but he had to deal with Doren, also? He shook his head in anger and ground his teeth. Doren was waiting for a response and Kade's mind was blank. He just could not submit at this time. Not yet.

"Kade...," Doren said in an ominous tone, but before he could say much more, Ven rushed into the cave.

"Kade!" Ven exclaimed in near panic as she changed form. "His army is only hours behind. It's massive. They come. There are many individual creatures that would rival even the dragon."

"Then we need to go now," Kade said, recovering from the verbal assault that Doren was preparing. "All out and onto the dragon," Kade commanded as he exited the cave. "Follow my voice. I cannot take the chance that we might be seen. We will have to mount the dragon as we are," he said while reaching out, hoping to find Darcienna.

"I must stay here to ensure that the arch stays safe," Doren said. "Leave the Transparency Calling but let the Silence Calling go, Kade." I will work with the king when he arrives.

"Be careful," Kade said to Doren as he drew the power from the Silence Calling.

"Kade, you have the ability to stop him. I can only delay him. You must stop him or we are all lost. Go," Doren said. "If you fail, I will destroy the arch...if I am able."

Rayden, come. We need to go quickly, Kade sent. *Come to the entrance, but try to keep from disturbing the ground. We must not be seen.*

Kade expected a roar, but there was nothing. Rayden was definitely in stealth mode. His roar would have been unheard by the ants due to the Silence Calling, but Kade was grateful for not having to clear his ringing ears after one of those blasts.

"Stay by the entrance until the dragon lands," Kade said as he turned. His breath was caught in his throat as he realized Ven was still visible. He lunged at her, throwing her back through the illusion. He stood and quickly cast both the Transparency Calling and then the Silence Calling. She winked out of sight, but not before he could move to grab her arm. "Change for the ride," he commanded.

"Head west," Ven said. "The mountain Drell should be about three hours away on the dragon," she said and then shifted. She melted in his hands and then swung up to cling to his neck in

171

her monkey form.

"Rayden," Kade called just as he heard the flapping of wings. The dragon lowered to the ground, causing dust to rise into the air. It could not be helped. Hopefully, any ants still in the distance would only see this as a small dust storm. Kade could feel a gentle thud as the dragon touched down. "Everyone mount," he said as he worked his way forward with his hands out.

It was a little disorganized, at first, but they were able find their places without too much of a delay. Ven hugged Kade tightly and laid her head against his neck as she prepared for the launch. Kade put a hand on her back and could not shake the feeling that she enjoyed being held. He was still certain she did not mean it in the sense that Darcienna did when she had her arms around him, but nevertheless, it was something to consider.

"Here we go," Kade said, giving everyone a chance to prepare for the launch.

After a moment, he gave the dragon the mental command to take to the air. Rayden turned, made several powerful lunges and then leapt. The wings came out and pumped hard as the dragon's head and tail bobbed with each powerful thrust. Darcienna had her arms wrapped tightly around Kade's midsection. It took the wind out of him until she was able to relax her grip. Kade gave a grunt and then resituated himself.

"Rakna," Kade called over the wind, "tell the king that he must get to the cave now. By the time he gets there, the ants should be gone. He will need to hold the cave at all cost," he said as his eyes scanned the horizon. "Let him know that Doren will be there waiting for him."

Kade gave the dragon the mental command to head west. Rayden banked sharply and then leveled off, continuing to pump hard to gain altitude. Kade's stomach lurched. One of these times he was going to lose his meal, but fortunately, it was not going to be this time.

Rayden continued to climb until the trees looked like small

bushes. As Kade scanned the horizon, a movement caught his eye. The ground appeared to be shifting. He paused, trying to make out the shapes that covered the landscape. He leaned forward slightly as he forced his eyes to focus.

"Kade?" Darcienna asked, feeling him tense. "What is it?"

"Do you see?" Kade asked, a sense of helplessness threatening to crush his hopes. "Do you see?" he repeated in awe. Darcienna gasped. "Rakna?" Kade called over the wind.

Kade! She said in his mind so strongly that he winced. *There are so many!* It was like a dagger of thought in his mind. This was the first time he had felt true fear from the queen.

"There are thousands," Kade said in a whisper too quietly to be heard. The wind took his voice away. He swallowed hard and took in a deep breath. "There are thousands," he yelled.

How can we hope to survive? the queen asked in his mind. It was not quite desperation, but it was not far off. *The spiders cannot defeat this army. There are many creatures large enough to wipe out a good portion of the clutch by themselves,* she thought in despair.

"Did the clutch make it to the cave yet?" Kade called to the queen.

They have just arrived, the queen sent.

"Advise the king to let Doren know so he can prepare. The Master Chosen is going to be pushed to his very limits. I just hope he has callings that can hold them off," Kade said to the queen. After a moment, Rakna responded.

Doren says our only hope is to break the link.

"What link?" Kade yelled back.

Doren says they are all controlled by Morg through a calling. That is the only reason so many answer to him. If you can take the staff, you can break the link. If the link if broken, they will, most likely, disperse and go back to where they came from. Break...the...link. Kade recalled the giant Alluvium that was under Morg's control and knew what Doren was trying to explain.

Kade turned to face forward as they crossed over the leading edge of the army. Several turned their attention to the sky as if sensing the presence passing overhead. They paused only momentarily and then continued on with their slow march toward the cave. All riders watched in awe at the army that passed below.

"Warn the king," Kade called back to the white spider.

"There is only one way they are going to survive," Darcienna called to Kade. The Apprentice Chosen cringed.

"I am aware," Kade called back. "We will prevail," he said, putting as much strength in his words as he could. If any doubted what he said, they kept it to themselves.

Kade felt Ven push from him and turn to sit on the dragon. Her form shifted and began to grow. It took only a moment for her to solidify into her birth form. Kade moved his hands to make sure they were not in the wrong places. Ven caught his hand at her waist as he was sliding it back and held it in place.

"I need to be in this form to talk. Please keep me from falling," Ven said. Kade was certain that she meant what she said, but there was no way he was going to convince Darcienna that it was purely innocent. He was grateful that none could see. "That is the mountain we are headed for," Ven said. Kade felt her shift as she pointed. Off in the distance was a mountain that rose so high that a good portion of it was shrouded in clouds. "We still need to climb. The entrance is much higher, yet," Ven added. Kade sent the information to Rayden and the dragon put everything it had into climbing.

Rayden continued to pump his wings hard, struggling to gain altitude. Kade could feel exhaustion though the link. Without being able to glide, the dragon was going to wear out quickly. Kade prayed to the Divine for the dragon to be able to hold out long enough to reach the mountain.

He felt a knot in his stomach as the mountain continued to grow. It was immense, easily dwarfing any other in all directions for as far as the eye could see. It was where the fate of this world

174

was going to be decided.

"Around the back is a way in that is rarely used," Ven said over her shoulder. "But, we will need to climb much higher than this, Kade."

Rayden, we need to climb, Kade sent the dragon. Rayden pumped his wings and struggled to go higher but to no avail. The dragon had reached its limit as it put everything it had into just maintaining the current altitude. Rayden was breathing hard and had no choice but to level off. This was the best he was going to do. Unfortunately, the rest had to be on foot. The air was just too thin for the dragon to continue on as it labored to breathe.

The mountain rose miles into the air. Kade started to believe that as much as half of the mountain was shrouded in clouds. The dragon started to glide, trying to gain as much rest as possible as they approached their destination, but unfortunately, while gliding, the dragon was losing altitude. Rayden was breathing hard as they circled the mountain, looking for a place to land. He could feel the dragon's suffering through the link and did his best to help with his healings. It had marginal effect at best. Sore muscles were not damaged muscles so his calling was virtually useless.

"There," Ven said as the trees gave way to an opening.

Rayden glided toward the spot and was doing everything possible to keep from falling out of the sky due to exhaustion. The dragon touched down and collapsed onto its chin as it slid to a stop. It was breathing heavy as sweat glistening off its hide. Its landing was anything but smooth as the riders were roughly thrown forward. Ven clung to Kade, trying to keep from being pitched over the dragon's head. Kade fell forward, pinning her to the dragon, causing her to exhale loudly as the wind was knocked out of her.

"The dragon may be done," Darcienna said, her voice strained.

"Kade!" Rakna said as she tried to control the terror that threatened to overwhelm her. "The king says the army is almost upon them. We must do something or the clutch will be wiped out.

Hurry, Chosen, hurry!"

"We have too far to go on foot," Ven said. "We need Rayden to get us to the top. The clutch will be destroyed and the tunnel found if we continue on foot. I am sorry, Kade, but we still need the dragon."

"Can't you change into a dragon or something that can carry us the rest of the way?" Darcienna asked. Kade gave her a look, not liking the tone in her voice, but nonetheless, quickly glanced back at Ven for her response.

"I cannot change into such a large form. I am one of the strongest of our kind, and yet, that form is too large for me to take. I am sorry but the dragon is our only hope."

"I know one way that may work," Kade said as he let the Transparency Calling go while keeping the Silence Calling intact. "I take it that we will not be seen?" he asked Ven as she came into view. He chastised himself for not asking before releasing the calling but his mind was spinning as he struggled to keep from joining Rakna in her panic.

"Yes. This area is not watched. Morg does not expect an attack so he takes no care to guard this section of the mountain. He will, most likely, be focusing on his army," Ven said.

"Then this should make the difference," Kade said as he readied himself for the calling.

Kade hesitated only a moment and then performed the calling. The piece of meat materialized. The dragon's nose began to twitch instantly. Kade waved the food in front of the dragon, and he could see its throat starting to work.

"Let me try," Darcienna said as she placed her hands on the dragon's side and closed her eyes in concentration. Kade could see the muscles in her forearms start to twitch rapidly as she sent her healing into the dragon.

Rayden breathed in deeply and started to salivate as his nose followed the meat. His breathing eased as Darcienna clenched her teeth in concentration. She gasped and stumbled back as if she were being repelled. Kade caught her with his free hand before she could fell.

"He is too large for me to do much more," she said as she fought to regain her breath. This clearly took a lot out of her.

Rayden rose as his energy quickly returned. Kade tossed the meat up and the dragon caught it in its mouth. He chewed for the second time that Kade could recall and then swallowed.

"With your healing and my food, he should recover quickly," he said as he continued to call on the meat.

Rayden was eagerly eyeing the food. Kade tossed it into the air and the dragon quickly snapped it up. Kade closed his eyes and focused on removing the internal block. He did not have time to stand here making food over and over. He ground his teeth, and with all his focus, he called on the meat. Once again, it failed to materialize. Kade felt rage explode in him. Not only did he have to face fearsome creatures, the most dangerous man in the world and an over bearing, pompous Master Chosen, but now he was his own enemy? Something in him was not letting him use his gift and it pushed him over the edge. Exasperation and rage crashed through him like a dam breaking.

"I said, COME!" Kade demanded with a scream as he worked the Food Calling.

Rage clouded his mind but determination to conquer this internal enemy drove him on. Meat the size of a cow fell through his hands and hit the ground with a thud. Breathing heavily, he barely had enough sense to look from face to face. All were watching him wide eyed with caution. Was there fear, also?

"Kade," Darcienna said gently as she laid a hand on his arm. "Kade," she said again, calling him back to himself.

"Kade, we still have a ways to go. If Rayden can carry us, he can get us the rest of the way up the mountain. It won't be easy, but I am sure he can get us to the entrance," Ven said, imploring the Apprentice Chosen to think.

"Kade!" Rakna said. "They have engaged the army."

177

This last was enough to stem the tide of rage and return Kade to his rightful mind. He turned as the dragon consumed the meat with a vengeance. Kade felt his breathing returning to normal. He took a deep breath and let it out, and with that, the Divine and anger disappeared.

"Rayden, we must be going," Kade said to the dragon. He was trying to give his precious friend enough time to eat, but the clutch depended on him moving now. It could be just moments before the spiders were wiped out. Without being there to see, he just did not know.

Rayden violently tore out several large chunks of meat and then laid down, allowing the passengers to mount. He chewed eagerly as the passengers scrambled onto his back. Ven changed to her monkey form and gladly clung to Kade's neck. Darcienna eyed the shapeshifter suspiciously as she settled into her spot.

"We are ready," Kade said, feeling the adrenalin start to pump through his veins. *Rayden, we must hurry. Climb my friend, climb!* Kade sent, feeling panic for the queen as he gave the dragon the mental command to go.

Rayden turned and lunged up the mountainside. Ven clung to Kade's neck and held on tightly. Darcienna also clung to Kade as the grade of the mountain was steep. Ven was right; to walk this may have taken a day, but the dragon was going to make it in no time at all. Now, if they could only hang on as the dragon surged up the mountain.

"Kade, the king says Doren has laid many traps and is holding them off, but he also warns that it will not work for long," Rakna said, trying to be strong.

"We are doing our best," Kade said, feeling the queen's urgency.

Kade mentally urged the dragon to greater speeds. They moved through the lower level of clouds and felt the chill of the air as the moisture cooled their skin. Rayden labored but showed no signs of slowing. He struggled up the mountain until they came out through the top of the clouds. The bright sun made them all flinch and cover their eyes.

Ven shifted and then changed shape into her birth form. Before Kade could pull his hand away, she held it to her side once more. Kade was certain that Ven enjoyed the feeling of being close with him. He could not bring himself to look at Darcienna. This was definitely going to get more complicated if he could not sort this out.

There are much more important things than this drama, Kade thought angrily.

"The entrance is just ahead," Ven said as she pointed. "There," she said. The dragon came to a stop at Kade's urging. The opening was much more massive than it looked to be at first. It was large enough to allow the dragon entry. Kade directed Rayden into the tunnel.

"The king says that they have diverted the largest mass of the army by drawing them off, but there are still some heading toward the cave. We have suffered casualties, but it is minimal," Rakna said as the dragon entered the tunnel. "But, they cannot keep this up for long."

"We must hold out hope," Kade said as he lifted Ven easily and let her slide down the side of the dragon.

Kade swung his leg over Rayden's neck and then slid down with his backside to the dragon. He needed to walk to loosen his muscles and the ceiling was too low for them to continue to ride. His stomach twisted into a knot. Fear tore at him with every step he took. The memory of Morg making him dance to his every whim made his heart pound. He was breaking out in a cold sweat. Darcienna grabbed his hand. After a moment, she pulled him to a stop and turned on him, looking deep into his eyes.

"Kade, are you okay?" Darcienna asked with concern. He swallowed the lump in his throat and forced his mind to think. They needed to have faith in him. He could not afford for them to see him acting like a coward or being indecisive.

"Yes," Kade said as he forced his voice to be calm and commanding. "It is just a little warm," he said as he continued to walk, pulling her along.

Fear of failing the spiders assailed him. Fear of becoming a puppet for all to see made his heart pound. Fear of having to watch as Morg did what he wanted with Darcienna made his panic grow by the second. Fear of failing to enact revenge for what Morg had done to his family was more than he could take. Waves of doubt spread through his body the further they went.

"The king says the army is closing in on the cave. There are too many for them to hold much longer," Rakna said. "The king says the Master Chosen has created spiders that are keeping the attackers busy but it is not enough." Kade hit on an idea that was close to genius.

"Tell the king to have Doren make the enemy appear like the spiders so they will fight amongst themselves." The queen was silent for several long moments.

"Doren says the idea is brilliant," Rakna relayed.

"Ven, can I use light without being detected?" Kade asked, forcing his voice to stay calm. The further they moved from the entrance, the darker it became.

"Yes," Ven said in her large beast form. "We will not be detected for some time," she said as a distant laughter drifted up the tunnel. Kade gave Darcienna a passing look. She did not say a word. "This was originally meant to be an escape route, but in time, Morg has become complacent, not believing he needed it," she said, stopping beside him. "We will not be detected."

"I will risk a small light," Kade said as he drew on the Divine. "It would do no good to get this far only to fall and break a leg."

Kade considered the light for a moment, and just like the tunnel with the arch, let it go only to replace it with the brilliant Blue Fire of the Divine. He felt much safer with a way to defend himself, if the need arose. Not that it would do much good against

180

the shield Morg was able to call on, but it did help his confidence to have a calling ready.

"Kade! I thought you said Morg might be able to detect when you use strong callings," Darcienna said.

Just then, Morg's laughter cut off sharply. Everyone froze, listening intently, afraid. Kade could feel every beat of his heart as he held his breath, waiting for any sound. His chest burned as his ears strained. And then, the mocking laughter continued. They all let out the breath they were holding.

"The king says they have distracted the army and have taken down several of the larger beasts," Rakna said. As way of confirmation, Morg started to rant and vent his anger at the setback. "They are holding...for now," she added.

"What do you mean you are fighting amongst yourselves?" Morg screamed in anger. "Fight the spiders. It should not be that difficult to recognize what a spider looks like you fool!"

Even though they were still a long ways off, they could just make out what Morg was saying as his screams echoed off the walls. Kade smiled to himself as he imagined the chaos that the illusion must be causing. It was a small reprieve and he was going to take full advantage of it. He picked up his speed as they walked.

Kade felt his confidence grow ever so slightly with every step he took. He glanced around at his small party and sized everyone up. The dragon was no small matter, but one blast from that staff could bring it to a quick end. The shapeshifter had enough guile to cause Morg serious issues, but could it get through the shield if Morg activated it? He could only hope that Morg did not live in such fear that the shield was always up. Darcienna could protect them...for a short time. And the queen was only there to help communicate. The more he thought on it, the more his confidence waned. If he could just get that bloody staff, he could end this easily.

Kade stopped and considered using the Transparency Calling but feared they would stumble into each other. For now, he decided it was best to leave the calling off until they were closer. *Was this just an excuse to delay the inevitable?* he asked himself. He shook his head and continued walking.

They moved along with trepidation as they slid deeper and deeper into the mountain. The light from the entrance was gone long ago. Without Kade's fire, they would be cast in complete darkness. The eerie blue glow caused Kade to see shadows from combatants that were not there. Every time he turned a corner, he was afraid he was going to see Morg's smiling face only to be followed by the feeling of being ensnared. He reached up to feel his amulet and was relieved that it was cool to the touch. The amulet was cloaking the Fire Calling as he hoped.

No sooner had he dropped the amulet to his chest when it heated up to the point of almost burning him. *Morg is trying to find me,* Kade thought. The Evil Chosen let out a scream of rage and then the amulet cooled.

The tunnel started to lighten enough for Kade to see the ground in front of himself so he let the blue flame fade away. Morg's voice was getting louder the more they progressed. Kade's stomach twisted into an even tighter knot as the moment approached for him to finally end this, or fail every living thing on the planet. It occurred to him that it was not just every living thing but everything that had passed, also. This was too important. Too much depended on him. The responsibility was crushing. He swallowed hard, as he forced one foot in front of the other.

"Stay to the left," Ven said, startling him. "There are several traps on the right."

Kade closed his eyes and performed the Reveal Calling. Sure enough, there were several traps along that side of the tunnel. Had they blindly walked into those, it would have been enough to bring their hopes of ending Morg's reign to a crashing halt. Kade could feel sweat running down his back.

"Thank you," Kade said to Ven. She smiled with pleasure at the praise. It was odd seeing her smile while in the beast form she currently held. That smile would have sent someone screaming if they did not know better.

They continued on. The light was getting brighter and the laughter was getting louder with each step. Morg went silent and the amulet heated up again. Kade leaned forward, letting it hang from his neck. A moment later, Morg let out a string of curses and the amulet cooled down once more.

"Where are you my little nuisance?" Morg asked, every word dripping with sarcasm. "You are not smart enough to just go bury your head in the sand until I am ready to collect you."

Darcienna squeezed Kade's hand. He realized fury was rising in him at a dangerous rate and took a deep breath to calm himself. *When did the fear leave me?* he asked himself as he unclenched his jaw and forced his mind to think. His hands were clenched into tight fists, and his elbows were slightly bent as if ready to fall into a fighting stance. Now was not the time to act irrationally. If he was to succeed, he needed to do it while thinking.

"There is one more trap just ahead," Ven said as she pointed to the ground. "That is the last one, and then we will be in his main chamber," Ven said in a hushed voice, afraid of speaking too loudly, even though she knew their sounds were masked by the calling.

Kade closed his eyes and saw that there was, indeed, a Detection Calling spanning the entire tunnel. It was too far for them to jump. Kade studied the ground as he moved carefully, trying to formulate a plan.

"Ven, is there a chance you could take a form that he trusts and take the staff?" Kade asked, hoping for an easy solution.

"He trusts no one," Ven said as she gave a sarcastic laugh. "He is suspicious of all and would rather kill anything that got too close before asking why they were there. No. I would have no chance. Besides, he does not allow anyone in this room."

"Then we will find another way," Kade said as he studied the ground.

"What is it you see?" Rakna asked.

"There is a Detection Calling that goes for about fifteen feet and spans the tunnel. We have no choice but to find a way over," Kade said.

Rakna moved up next to Kade, studying the floor and then the walls. She moved over to the side of the tunnel and surprised Kade with what she did next. She put one leg up on the wall and then the next until she was up at the top of the tunnel. Kade had never seen her off the ground like this, but he should have realized that it was possible. She was, after all, a spider.

"The dragon will need to stay," she hissed quietly. "But the rest can cross with my help," the queen said as she lowered a web that drifted on the light current of air that wafted through the tunnel.

Kade took it in his hand and expected it to break apart at the gentlest touch, but it held. Still expecting it to break, he pulled hard, but again, it held. Unfortunately, it showed signs of cutting into his hand. He thought about it for just a moment when another idea came to him. He tied a loop at the end and stepped into it with his boot. The queen lifted him off the ground while he wrapped his arms around the light webbing. It was obvious she was straining as she cautiously lifted one leg, preparing to walk along the ceiling. She quickly put it back on the ceiling and gasped.

"I am not able to lift you without falling. I fear this is not going to work," Rakna said as she worked her way back down the wall.

"Let me help," Ven said as she approached Rakna and held up her hand, preparing to touch her. Rakna took a step back as she eyed Ven suspiciously.

"Ven?" Kade asked.

"I need to touch her," Ven said, confused at the queen's reaction.

"Why?" Darcienna asked. Kade did not like the suspicion in her voice and showed his displeasure by the glare he gave her.

"I can change into a spider but that does not mean I am a spider. I will no more be able to climb the walls than you can," Ven said as she answered Darcienna's question while looking at Kade. "But, if I can take in just a small amount of her life force, I can become just like her with all of her abilities. Do you see the difference?"

"Will it hurt her in any way?" Darcienna asked, trying to keep the accusation out of her voice.

"She will not feel a thing," Ven replied.

"I find this acceptable," Rakna said as she moved forward into Ven's outstretched hand. The shapeshifter let her hand settle onto the queen as her fingers sank deep into her plush fur. Ven closed her eyes and a smile slowly crept across her face. It almost appeared as if the shapeshifter was experiencing pleasure as she soaked up the queen's essence. She took her hand away and changed into a beautiful, white spider.

Kade walked between the two and looked back and forth, amazed at his inability to recognize the true queen. Ven spoke, but it was with Rakna's voice. It was eerie, and he had to be honest with himself; it was a bit unsettling.

"This should work," Ven hissed as she smoothly worked her way up the wall to hang from the ceiling.

"I believe it just might," Rakna hissed as she moved up the same side, avoiding the traps along the opposite wall.

After learning how it was done, Ven let out her web, as did Rakna. Kade made a loop from both webs and stepped into it. Rakna lifted a leg and moved forward. Ven followed her lead and mimicked her actions. Soon, they had a system where the queen would take a step and then the shapeshifter would take a step. It was slow going but it appeared as though this was going to work. Kade looked up at the two snow-white spiders and marveled as the queens worked their way across.

"Let me know when we are far enough," Rakna called down to him.

"That should be good enough," Kade said.

She gently lowered him to the ground and gave a grunt when

185

the weight no longer threatened to pull her off the ceiling. The two spiders quickly skittered across the rock to Darcienna. She looked at each spider, trying to figure out which was the shapeshifter, but quickly gave up, realizing that there was no way to tell. With a sigh, she stepped into the loop from each spider and was soon lifted off the ground. Rakna and Ven were grateful for the weight difference between the man they had just carried and the woman who now hung down below them. This was clear as both spiders moved along at a quick pace without waiting for the other to get set.

It was not long before Darcienna was standing next to Kade. Ven changed into some sort of insect and easily flitted over to land on Kade's shoulder. Darcienna watched, waiting for Ven to change back into the beast, but the shapeshifter was content to stay in the form she was in. Kade glared hard at Darcienna, not believing he was going to have to deal with this. Darcienna saw the look on Kade's face and quickly raised her hands in surrender.

Rayden, you must stay there until I call. It is critical that you do not try to follow until I send for you, Kade thought as he locked eyes with the dragon. Kade could feel the dragon's protest through the link. He explained as best he could, but in the end, he had to settle for promising to let Rayden join the fight when it was time.

"They have found the cave. The clutch is divided. The king and a large group are trying to draw the army away but something keeps them focused on the cave. It will only be…," the queen was saying when she paused, listening to the far off voice. "The king says the Master Chosen is unable to hold the Illusion Calling any longer." As if to confirm what Rakna had just said, Morg let out a scream at his army.

"Ignore them!" Morg raged. "They are protecting that cave for a reason. Kill them all and get in that cave! Kill them or I will make you suffer!"

"Kade," Rakna said in panic. She did not try to hide her fear. Kade could feel his heart start to pound hard.

"I am going to cloak us," Kade said as he planted his feet, feeling the queen's panic becoming contagious. He spun through the moves for the Transparency Calling and everyone faded from view.

"Kade!" Rakna said again more insistently. She was losing her composure as the realization of her clutch being destroyed threatened to overwhelm her.

"I understand," Kade said. "Have faith." It was all he could think to say as he fought to keep from rushing to his death. The clutch was in dire trouble, but if he did not do this right, they were all finished.

Something had to be done and it had to be done now. Kade looked at the next bend in the tunnel and saw light dancing on the walls as a flame from the chamber shown directly on it. Morg's voice was clear, as if he was standing just a short stride away. The four of them crept down the tunnel to the next bend and stopped. Morg was pacing at the far side of the room by a pool of water that had a scene dancing on the surface. He screamed at the image and then raised the staff with both hands held high over his head and slammed it into the pool as if to crush something. Water splashed in all directions.

The pool of water was in a rock formation that was six feet across and came up to Morg's waist. It almost reminded Kade of the well back where he had grown up except the walls of this well were much thicker and there was no bucket. The outside of the well was made of large rocks the size of a man's head. The pool was no more than two feet deep. The water flashed colors and lights as an image played out. Kade wanted desperately to see what the image displayed, but from where he stood, that was not going to happen. Morg leaned over and peered closely into the water as the ripples settled down into images once again. The evil Chosen stood as the muscles in his jaw flexed.

"Where are you?" Morg raged as he held the staff in front of himself and closed his eyes. Kade clenched his teeth hard as he did

187

his best to ignore the scalding hot medallion on his chest. "WHERE ARE YOU?" Morg screamed loudly as he shook. His face contorted into one of hate, rage and insanity. He let out a yell as he turned toward the tunnel where the infiltrators hid. After just five steps, he turned and raced back to the edge of the pool to peer at the scene once more.

Morg paced wildly about, not straying far from the pool of water. Again, he walked toward the tunnel where the small group was hiding but never even considered looking in. It was clear that he was very used to the tunnel being empty. Morg had become complacent as his eyes passed over the area where the tunnel was as if it were not even there.

Kade tried to calm his heart, but it was racing. The combination of fear, anger and the anticipation of confronting Morg made it hard for Kade to think. Just one look at the Chosen carrying that dreaded staff brought back the memory of the immense weight that had crushed the life out of him back in Doren's secret study. Kade struggled to formulate a plan. Anything. He was hoping a solution would present itself by now, but he was still at a loss.

The room was not small by any means as it reached approximately two hundred feet across, if not a little more. The ceiling rose nearly fifty feet into the air with a small opening at the top for light to come in or smoke to escape. The walls were of solid rock with torches every ten feet or so until they got to the back of the room where there were none. Even if Morg were to look around the room, he would not see someone standing in the tunnel unless he looked directly at them trying to see them. There was a large bed with pillows and blankets so rich looking that any king would have been envious. The bedposts were jeweled and sparkled as the light from the fire danced off them. Directly in the middle of the room was an opening in the floor that was ten feet wide and went all the way to the base of the mountain. There was a bookcase that was large enough to hold hundreds of books, if not a thousand. There were books strewn all across the floor as if someone had discarded them after not finding what was being searched for.

The darkness was a blessing as Kade, ever so slowly, leaned around the corner. He moved like a cat, afraid that Morg may see or sense him, even with the callings active. He closed his eyes and checked the area for traps but found none. He took a deep breath to steady his nerves and pursed his lips as he let the air out. His eyes focused on the staff that was so close, and yet, so far away.

Kade watched, hoping that Morg might lay the ancient artifact down for just a moment, but it became clear that he slept with it in an iron grip. That staff might as well have been an extension of his body with how tightly he held it. No, this was not going to be as easy as he hoped. But, he still had the element of surprise on his side.

"Kade, Doren is trying a different tact but he is almost too exhausted to keep this up. He says you must do something soon or they will be lost. They are holding at the cave but it won't be for long," Rakna hissed quietly.

"What is that?" Morg asked as he gripped the staff and closed his eyes. "The Divine being used? There is another? It is too weak. No! Not the one I seek. WHERE ARE YOU?" Morg Raged again.

He gripped the staff in both hands and held it out in front of himself as if he was about to drive a pole into the ground. Kade gasped as the medallion scalded his skin. He leaned forward to let it hang away from his body. The slight scent of burnt hair and skin wafted up to him. He clenched his teeth until the pain subsided.

"Kade?" Darcienna asked, hearing the hiss of air being drawn in through clenched teeth.

"I am...okay. He keeps searching for me, and when he does, it heats the medallion. I suspect that being so close has something to do with it," Kade whispered.

"Get in that cave and kill everything!" Morg screamed, almost hoarse. "What do you mean the spiders changed to earth creatures? They are still spiders you imbecile. A Chosen in the cave is casting an Illusion Calling," he said as his grip on the staff tightened. His knuckles turned white as he listened to the distant communication. "Yes, I am sure. Either they die or you die!"

The king says they are truly fighting amongst themselves now. That is not the Master Chosen's doing, Rakna said in Kade's head.

"Then we have caught a break. It gives us just a little breathing room," Kade said, grateful.

"What are you planning?" Darcienna asked. Rakna edged just a little closer and Kade could feel Ven looking at him from his shoulder.

What am I going to do? Kade asked himself.

"I am going to walk right up and take the staff," he said. No one responded. Kade felt his stomach drop. "He can't see us or hear us. How can that go wrong?"

"Kade, I am not sure about that," Darcienna said, her voice full of doubt. "I just don't think it is going to be that easy."

"If any of you have a better idea, please let me know. I am very willing to try anything," Kade said, doing his best to sound confident.

He was met with silence. Kade felt a light breeze blowing through the chamber and down the tunnel. He closed his eyes to calm his nerves as he prepared to draw on the Divine. The connection with the dragon clicked into place and Kade felt the eager scaled warrior yearning to join them. Rayden misunderstood what the link was for and readied to charge down the tunnel.

NO! Kade thought in panic. Morg's head snapped around to look in all directions at once. The evil Chosen held completely still, not breathing as he listened for what had gotten his attention. Kade felt the dragon stop. *Hold still,* Kade sent strongly. He was holding his breath while he watched Morg. The man was studying the dark tunnel when something in the water caught his attention. He did a double take and immediately forgot about anything other than the scene playing out before him. His lip curled and his face reddened.

"How can you be so disorganized?" Morg yelled as he smashed the water with his staff, not just once, but three times in rapid succession. He clenched both fists as he screamed his rage at the small pond. "Pull back and organize your troops." Kade was hoping he would drop of a heart attack.

The Apprentice Chosen stood watching, trying to find any other solution to the problem, but nothing better than walking right up and snatching the staff from the man's hands presented itself. Morg began to smile and then laughed as he watched the scene. It was unnerving to see him go from such intense rage to laughter so quickly. Kade recalled how he and Morg had had, what appeared to be, a very civil chat in Doren's library.

"Much better. Yes, much better," Morg said with pleasure as he watched the scene closely.

"Kade, they have figured out what was happening and are now organizing again. They have renewed their attack and broken through our ranks. They are closing in on the tunnel. The king says they need you now. Kade...," Rakna almost pleaded.

"We can't do anything from...," Kade was starting to say in despair when he paused. "Wait. We can help. We can get Morg to stop them," Kade said excitedly. "Quickly, tell the king to tell Doren to make an image of Morg. He will know what to do from there," Kade said hopefully. This had to buy them time.

The queen was silent for several long moments as she relayed the message. Morg paced around the pool several times and then crossed the room to the hole in the ground. He leaned over and looked down, looking for something. Kade was shocked at what happened next.

"We will find that which we seek, shortly," Morg said. It was not only what he said that had Kade surprised, but that he said it in a completely subservient manner. If Morg was acting subservient, then who was he talking to?

A deep voice that caused a vibration to run through the entire mountain reverberated in Kade's bones. As the voice spoke, a hot wind traveled up the hole and brushed past the hidden group. Kade shivered. If he was not scared already, he was frightened to the point of paralysis now.

"YOU SHALL NOT FAIL OR YOU WILL SUFFER OUR WRATH!" the voice warned. "YOUR ARMY IS FALLING THROUGH TO THIS SIDE IN DROVES!" the voice said harshly.

"Soon, we will have the Chosen that you seek. And also, there is another. I sense someone else using the Divine," Morg said, hopeful that the news would placate the voice.

"DO NOT FAIL," the voice responded.

"Kade," Rakna hissed so quietly that he could barely hear her. He wanted to remind her that they were under the Silence Calling, but he knew it would do no good. Even he did not want to speak louder than he had to. "Crayken says it is working. He says he has them fighting amongst themselves again."

Morg glanced at the water, and before he could turn his attention back to the pit, he raced over to the pool and stared in confusion. His face started to redden as he clenched his jaw tightly. He screamed into the scene.

"What...are...you...doing? No, I did not tell you to attack the earth creatures again! No, I am not hovering over you. Attack the spiders and get in that cave NOW!" Morg bellowed.

"We are out of time," Kade said as he stood. "Ven, Rakna, Darcienna, stay here," he said as he readied to make his move. Ven, still in the form of an insect, flew off his shoulder and landed on a wall nearby.

"The bloody afterlife I will," Darcienna said as she stood with him. "If ever there is a time you will need me, it is going to be now. Do what you must, but don't even try to leave me behind again," she said and she meant it. The image of him floating in the arch blazoned in her mind.

Without arguing, Kade moved as smoothly as possible while he worked his way across the chamber. Morg showed no indication that he knew anyone was closing in on him. He was so focused on the scene unfolding in the water that Kade thought he might have been able to walk up on him uncloaked.

With every step he took, his heart beat harder. He felt as if the pounding in his ears alone was going to give him away. He wiped his clammy hands on his pants, making sure they were as dry as possible for when he snatched the staff away. He was now only fifteen feet from the Master Chosen as he wrinkled his nose. It was obvious that Morg had not bathed for days. Kade tried to calm his breathing. Darcienna had her hand on his arm as he continued to close the distance.

"You must stay here," Kade barely whispered. "Do not argue. I need room to move once I have the staff," he said firmly. Darcienna let go of his arm in acknowledgement.

Kade, lifting his foot ever so slowly, and focusing to keep his balance, moved another step closer. And yet, another step, as Morg circled the pool of water. Kade could almost see the scene dancing on the surface. Morg circled the pond again, putting himself just barely out of Kade's reach.

"Get in there now!" Morg demanded.

Kade clenched and unclenched his fist, readying himself to lunge for the staff. He got the eerie feeling that he was being watched and quickly searched the room. There was nothing. At least, there was nothing he could see.

Just nerves, he though as he refocused his attention on the man with the staff. He turned his body sideways, ready to lunge. Before he could strike, Morg ran to the other side of the pool of water to stare at another part of the scene. The evil Chosen threw his head back and laughed a raucous laugh of victory. Kade took another step and saw the cave being overrun in the scene playing out in the well. There was no more delaying the inevitable. He had to take the staff now. There was no other choice. He dried his hands one last time and lunged for the ancient artifact. Just when he was about to close his hands on the wood, he felt as if he had rammed his hand into a rock wall. For a moment, Kade was sure he had broken a few of his fingers.

"What?" Morg said in surprise as he brought the staff around to his chest. He held it in both hands as if to block with it and protect it at the same time. "Intruders? Where?" Morg asked of an unseen entity.

"He has the shield," Kade yelled. He ran back toward the tunnel and almost knocked Darcienna over as he reached for her to drag her along. As soon as they made it to the entrance, Kade threw Darcienna into the tunnel, and then in one smooth motion, spun to face Morg. He reached for the rage, but all he found was fear. He was soon to be a puppet, and worse, he was going to be at the mercy of whatever it was that even Morg feared. His mind raced as he desperately tried to come up with a plan. He knew that he could not breach the shield, but with no other plan to fall back on, he prepared to bring his most powerful calling to life. The panic he felt was overwhelming.

"Kade," Rakna hissed in alarm. "They have entered the cave!"

Something sliced through the air right next to Kade's head so close that he flinched and ducked. Somehow, they were being detected and something was coming after them. Kade forced his fear down and reached for the Divine. He had to try something so he readied the one Divine calling he knew well.

Kade spun through the moves and then attacked, sending a brilliant flash of lightning, racing across the room. It slammed into the evil Chosen, causing the shield to shimmer. For a moment, Kade thought it might have bent slightly, but then it was back in place. Was there a limit to how much assault it could take? For an instant, Kade wondered if it had a weakness similar to Darcienna's. Not dwelling on the thought, but not forgetting it either, he quickly performed the Divine Fire Calling. It hit the shield and enveloped the man. Kade held desperately onto hope that the fire was doing damage, but deep down, he knew that it was not going to be that easy. The blue flame slowly dwindled and then died out. Morg stood casually as if he found this amusing.   Kade watched in disbelief. His arms felt like lead as he stood, waiting…for anything. He was out of ideas.

"My turn, puppet," Morg said as he let out a devious laugh that shook Kade to the very core of his being.

Kade had no doubt that Morg knew who it was that had attacked him. The apprentice could already feel the ache of his muscles, expecting the power to ensnare him shortly. If he could not figure something out in the next few moments, everything would be lost. Morg's face contorted into one of fury and insanity as he raised the staff, aiming it directly at the young attacker. Kade dove out of the way as the wall directly behind him exploded into rock chips. He felt blood on the back of his arm and neck.

"Rakna, climb the walls!" Kade screamed as he struggled to his feet.

Before Kade could make another move, a roar so loud echoed through the mountain that even Morg paused. Any sane person would have considered running, but Morg was not a normal, sane person. But, it was not the roar that the evil Chosen heard, as the Silence Calling was still active, but the shaking of the ground as the dragon exploded into action and raced through the tunnel. Rayden charged, activating Morg's Detection Calling. The evil Chosen grinned as though this were amusing and turned to face the challenge.

"The dragon comes!" Kade screamed, afraid that Darcienna, Ven or the spider-queen may be trampled. Kade sensed that the dragon was in a killing frenzy. It knew that its friend's life was in peril, and it was not going to be denied its turn in this fight.

Darcienna tripped over him just as the dragon burst out of the tunnel and made a full run at Morg. Kade tried to formulate a warning about the hole in the middle of the chamber, but his mind was nowhere near fast enough to catch up to the speed of the dragon. Rayden leapt, cleared the hole and crashed into Morg. The dragon clawed wildly at the man. The shield not only deflected

Divine Power, but it kept Morg safe from talons and teeth, also. The dragon was still able to knock the man and shield around considerably. Morg was lying on his back with the dragon putting all of its considerable weight on the shield as it viciously attacked over and over. The shield compressed greatly but not enough to kill.

"I have to get to Morg while he is distracted," Kade yelled to Darcienna, dislodging her hands.

Kade started forward when something slammed into him from behind, sending him sprawling. He tasted fresh blood from the split in his lip. He was on all fours as he struggled to get back to his feet when he felt a crushing blow delivered to his side. It lifted him into the air and sent him crashing onto his back. The world spun and his Transparency Calling slipped. Darcienna faded into view several feet away as she hugged the wall. Kade realized what had happened, grabbed what was left of the calling and forced it back into place. The calling around the queen held but the rest of them, including the dragon, were now visible.

"Kade!" Darcienna screamed as he materialized. Her arms rose in a flash, but just before her shield could materialize, something slammed into his other side, cracking two of his ribs. Kade doubled over and then the shield was in place. His mind reeled in pain.

Kade crawled over to Darcienna, afraid she was next as her shield was only around him. Her protective barrier dropped momentarily and then returned instantly to cover them both. An unseen force hit the shield and then rebounded off.

Kade was struggling to breathe through the pain. One of the ribs felt as if it may have punctured a lung. He needed healing but he knew that it was not going to happen while she held the shield in place.

The pain brought tears to his eyes as he struggled to focus on the dragon and Morg. He feared for his friend. If Rayden could not do damage soon, Morg was going to use his staff and, most likely, kill the dragon. Kade was struggling to his feet when his worst fear was realized. Morg got the staff between himself and the dragon and the ancient artifact jumped. Rayden was propelled across the room, slamming violently into the wall. The dragon let out a roar of pain and quickly scrambled back to his feet, lunging at man and shield once more. Morg aimed the staff but Rayden was ready and slid to the side in a snake like move. He launched at Morg but the evil Chosen was not to be taken so easily. Morg aimed the staff again and Rayden was caught in mid leap, slamming him violently into the wall once more. Kade cringed as he felt the impact from across the room. He desperately wanted to help his friend but it was all he could do to think clearly enough to save himself, much less anyone else.

"So, you came to me, my little puppet," Morg said in a taunt as he turned his attention back toward the Apprentice Chosen. Rayden was not moving. Kade was not even sure if the dragon was still breathing. He felt helpless as he struggled to stand. Morg reached up with the back of his hand and wiped the blood from his mouth. "Oh, I am going to enjoy this," he said as he hit the shield with a blast that caused Darcienna to cry out. "Wait until you see what I do with her," Morg sneered as he hit the shield again. Darcienna cried out once more. It was only a matter of time. Each attack might as well have been a direct assault on her with how she reacted. "I wonder how many of those you can take, my little beauty," Morg said and then laughed at his own joke. He aimed the staff at her and it jumped again.

Darcienna clenched her jaw hard as she squeezed her eyes closed tightly in determination and focus. The shield shimmered but then reformed. Morg walked slowly toward the couple. Again, he sent the Divine at the barrier, and this time, the shield took a considerably longer time to rematerialize. Morg smiled. He was next to the barrier now, looking in at the couple just a few strides away. It was as if he was looking at two helpless animals caught in a trap. Morg raised the staff and gripped it tightly in both hands, and then, brought it down to crash into the shield. Darcienna gasped.

"Kade," Darcienna hissed through clenched teeth. "That staff hits hard. It's…as if he is…swinging a house at me," she said with her eyes still closed. "It's not a…normal staff."

"This is quite indestructible," Morg said, overhearing Darcienna as he hefted the staff. "This thing is a weapon itself," he said as he opened his hands and then curled his fingers around the wood once more.

Morg grinned as he shifted his grip on the ancient artifact. His face contorted in rage as he raised the staff high over his head with both hands, his knuckles turning white with effort as he gripped it tightly. His back arched as he readied himself to put every bit of strength into this next swing. The muscled in his neck and shoulders bunched and a vein in his forehead bulged. His face turned red as his lips twisted into a snarl. This was going to hurt. Morg shifted as he swung the staff with all his might. It started on its way down for a crushing blow when suddenly, it stopped and jerked violently up toward the ceiling. Morg's eyes came open in shock and dismay. The staff had slipped almost completely out of his grasp before he was able to grip it tightly, barely catching the end of it. He was lifted slightly off the ground as he held onto his most prized possession. Terror shown in his eyes for just a moment, and then he recovered. He looked up with hate and the staff jumped. Rakna let out a shriek of pain. Morg and the staff fell back to the ground to land in a heap. He held the staff to his chest in a slightly hunched manner as he glared around the room, looking for the unseen attacker.

"You have many friends, it would appear," Morg said as his eyes searched the ceiling.

Kade flinched when a black flying creature almost identical to the leader of the morphites faded into view. Now, he understood how he was seen, even with his Transparency Calling active. It was the one creature that could see others who were cloaked. The creature oriented on the queen and readied for a strike. Kade flexed his muscles, desperate to try anything, but before he could move, he watched as another flying creature formed directly below the black beast. It leapt into the air and collided with the creature. Ven grabbed on tightly and then shifted again. Now, there were two identical black creatures. One vanished as the two combatants fought for life and death. The other one phased in and out as it struggled to learn a new ability. Morg raised the staff and readied to fire when Ven disappeared from sight.

Kade, the white spider said in his mind. *I...am...too badly hurt...to help.*

Two black creatures popped into view momentarily once more, each raking the other with dagger like talons. Kade said a silent prayer for Ven as he refocused on the spider-queen. He only hoped she could escape with her life.

Get safe, Kade thought to her. *Do not put yourself at risk any further. You have done all you can do. If we fail here, leave. Your clutch needs you.* There was no answer. Was she ok? Kade feared the worst, but he did not have time to figure out the answer. Morg was standing straight again, and that meant he had his confidence back. They were soon to be the target of his rage once more.

Morg turned slowly back to the two trapped people. Kade's mind raced as he tried to find a solution to this problem but failed. Darcienna was on the verge of collapse. He could not see a way that was going to get them out of this situation safely. Morg raised the staff and swung it at the shield. Darcienna fell to her knees as her Deflection Casting took the hit and then popped from view. Morg cocked his head to the side as if amused and just watched. She gritted her teeth and held her hands over her head as if she held the weight of the world in them. She was shaking as she exerted all her strength. To Kade's shock and awe, the shield slowly faded back into view. Morg grinned and raised the staff, swinging it again. Darcienna exhaled as though she had been hit in the gut, and the shield was gone.

"Let her go, and I will do what you want," Kade said in desperation. The dragon was on the verge of death, if not dead already, and Darcienna was helplessly down on all fours, panting from the exertion. He could only hope to salvage their lives by offering his.

"Now, you and I know that you would never do what I want willingly. But, then again, you are going to do what I want anyway, aren't you?" Morg asked as he took a step closer. He stopped as the two invisible combatants fighting furiously crashed into the bed and tore one of the posts off. He waited for the noise to reduce to a level that allowed him to talk casually again. "And, as for you," Morg said as he brought his right hand up across his body to his left shoulder. "I don't appreciate you interfering," he said as he clenched his jaw and then threw his body into a swing, hitting Darcienna across the face with the back of his hand. "You have caused me enough trouble," he finished. Darcienna went sprawling toward the pit. Kade gasped as she slid to a stop at the edge with her arms dangling over the side.

"No!" Kade screamed and then lunged for the big man. Morg whirled the staff like it was a perfectly balanced baton. He brought it crashing down on Kade's head with a loud crack. The world spun and Kade stumbled, falling to his knees. He lost all focus as blackness clouded his vision. He rocked forward and then his face was against the dirt. He was on the verge of being out completely when he saw Darcienna's finger flinch. He focused on that one move and was able to hang on…just barely.

"That was pretty stupid, don't you think?" Morg asked, gloating. "This what you were trying for?" he taunted as he took several steps forward triumphantly to stand directly in front of Kade. Morg let the butt-end of the staff plunk down right in front of Kade's face. "You got close. Very close, but you should have known you were destined to fail. Now, it is my turn to do as I wish," he said as he eyed the still form of Darcienna. He turned toward her, leaned down and grabbed her by an ankle. She groaned and tried to grab onto something groggily as he dragged her away. "She will make a nice addition to my play things," he said and laughed again. There was no question in Kade's mind what the man meant as he looked at the beautiful girl.

Darcienna reached out to Kade as she was being dragged away. She grabbed his foot but Morg yanked her hand free. He waggled a finger at her.

"Oh no you don't. I know you can heal, and it would do us no good to have you doing that, now," Morg said as he dragged her a bit further.

The despair Kade was feeling gave way and rage built in him like the deadliest of storms. Hate filled him and the blackest of black consumed his heart. A surge of energy helped clear his head and everything came back into focus. He got up on all fours as the adrenalin flooded through his body. He ground his teeth as he fought to ignore the agony from his side. He felt a profound hate more than he had ever felt in his life. He wanted to deliver the land of the dead another body and it was the man walking away with his back to him that was his target. Kade put one foot down and then pushed off as he struggled to stand. The world rocked slightly, but only briefly, and then it stabilized.

Kade took a breath and straightened his back as he let his hands fall to his side. The raging torrent of power helped numb the pain. His desire to kill was overwhelming. The block was gone and the Divine wildly raced through him. He ignored the blood that trickled down his forehead. He ignored the pain in his side. He ignored the throbbing on the back of his head where Morg had crushed him with the staff. There was only one thing he wanted, and he wanted it so bad he was willing to give his life for it. He took as deep a breath as he dared and then started to flow through the moves for the calling. The power paid close attention to his commands, eager to be used. Kade grinned evilly as he threw his arm forward, demanding the Divine to do his bidding. Lightning exploded from him and crashed into the shield. The mountain rocked from the impact. The explosion caused dust and rocks to fall into the chamber. Morg stumbled as he was propelled forward from the blast. He let go of Darcienna as he struggled to catch his balance. The shield buckled considerably as colors swirled through it and then reformed. Morg spun, and for just a fraction of a second, there was fear in his eyes, and then it was gone to be replaced by pure rage.

"You dare?" Morg screamed at him, his face turning crimson.

"FINISH HIM," a voice said, reverberating from the opening in the floor.

Morg raised the staff and aimed it at Kade. The Apprentice Chosen fought to think as the power raged in him. If Morg fired that shot, he was done. He had to force his mind to work through the anger that had him firmly in its grip. From deep inside, he heard a voice that whispered…every so quietly…an idea. It was a simple idea. He listened hard to his inner voice and then smiled. Morg was just a hairs-breath away from firing when he saw the smile and hesitated. He narrowed his eyes as he studied the beaten man. The Apprentice Chosen started to laugh. Morg clenched his teeth and raised the staff just a little more, preparing to unleash, but once again, he held. Kade spoke just one word. But, that one word caused Morg to freeze and his face to turn white.

"Mutt," Kade said. Morg stood in stunned disbelief. It was only a moment and then his face turned red with fury.

"You dare?" Morg screamed and his knuckles turned white as he clenched the staff.

"Do as you are told," Kade said as he continued to laugh. His side was hurting furiously with each laugh but he continued. "Obey, hound," he taunted.

"FINISH HIM!" the voice raged. The mountain shook. "DO AS YOU ARE TOLD!" the voice screamed in fury.

"Yes," Kade said, using the voice's own words against it.

"Do as you are told. Mind your master," he said, putting emphasis on the last word and then continued to laugh.

"Silence!" Morg yelled at Kade. But, something about the way Morg glanced at the pit made Kade think it might have been meant for the voice in the mountain.

"NOW! SEND HIM TO US, NOW!" the voice commanded.

"Yes. Cast your calling and prove that you are, indeed, their faithful dog," Kade taunted.

Morg shook with fury as he looked from Kade to the pit and then back to Kade again. The staff lowered just slightly. The Apprentice Chosen smiled as he planned his next move. It was a one way trip down this path, but at least he was going to end Morg's evil plans forever…he hoped.

There was a crash along the far side of the room and Ven faded into view in her birth form, lying on the ground, gasping. Injuries covered her entire body. There was so much blood. Yes, his plan was the right one. She was worth it. Darcienna was worth it. The dragon and Rakna were worth it. All those that had faith in him were worth it.

The black creature she had been fighting faded into view. It gasped, trying to breathe as its life in the form of tar-like blood came in spurts out of the deep wound in its neck. Ven found Kade's eyes and smiled weakly.

The Apprentice Chosen let all rational thought go as he focused on the last calling he was ever to cast. He let his chin fall to his chest as he closed his eyes. He immersed himself in the Divine and drew on it deeply. His gift was awakened fully now. He was drunk with power as it raged through him. It filled every fiber of his being and continued. He reveled in his gift and knew true power as it filled him to overflowing and then some. He threw his head back and laughed deep and long. His heart beat wildly as the power consumed his soul and mind.

The staff faltered even more. Morg misunderstood the

reason for the laughter and spun toward the pit. He was enraged and the weakness in his personality took over.

"FINISH HIM NOW!" the voice commanded again and again.

"I am not your dog to command!" Morg screamed.

Kade planted his feet and took a deep breath, knowing it was time. He clenched his jaw against the distant pain and performed the first move to the calling and then flowed into the next. He twisted and felt a tear inside as a broken rib caused internal damage. He clenched his teeth hard and ignored the injury as he continued on. Revenge was his painkiller and he filled himself with it. Morg screamed into the pit and the voice raged back. Kade completed the third move. Darcienna got up on all fours and crawled inch by inch back toward Kade. The forth move was smooth, as was the fifth. Morg shook with rage as he aimed the ancient staff at the pit and threatened to fire. Had Morg not been out of his mind with rage, he may have heard the warning from the voice.

"HE DRAWS DEEPLY ON THE DIVINE. FINISH HIM NOW!" the voice screamed. There was a sense of panic in the voice but Morg continued to rant without hearing a word.

Kade flowed into the sixth move. The seventh move was easy and then the eighth. Darcienna crawled a little closer. The ninth move flowed smoothly. Kade kept his eyes on his target as he felt the power raging through him. It had to be done. It was his only hope. Now, the tenth move and he drew the Divine into the calling. He opened himself up fully and filled the calling, and then filled it more. He felt sweat run down his back as he performed the eleventh move. Now the twelfth move and the air surrounding him came alive. Kade gritted his teeth hard as he brought his arm forward and then...held. The power swirled though him and built moment by moment. The pain grew as the Divine started to look for a way out. Kade shook with the effort. So much power coursing through him was too much to take. His teeth cracked as he clenched his jaw hard. His arm was almost extended and his hand started to open.

Just...a...little...more, Kade thought as his mind screamed in pain. A roaring so loud filled his ears that the screaming sound of Morg's voice faded out. It was like standing next to a waterfall as the deafening sound drowned out everything. Kade had to focus hard as his vision started to fade. He narrowed his eyes, forcing Morg to come back into view. His skin broke out in vicious burn spots and smoke wafted off his entire body. Welts from the heat broke out all over, and yet, he held. Tears leaked out of the corners of his eyes, and yet,...he held. Every muscle in his body shook with the immense effort, and still,...he held. This was his only chance and he had to make sure it was perfect.

"MORG, YOU WILL DO AS YOU ARE TOLD. IF YOU FAIL, WE WILL MAKE YOU SUFFER FOR AN ETERNITY!" the voice screamed.

This last threat caused Morg to hesitate. But, it was not the threat from the voice that caused Morg to spin. It was the scream from Darcienna as she looked upon the man she loved. It was not just the smoke that was wafting up from almost every part of his body that made her cry out. It was not even the smell of burning hair or the open soars that were rapidly forming all over his skin that scared her to the very core of her being. It was not the milky white eyes she looked into as he shook that made her heart feel as though it were being ripped out and crushed. It was knowing that he was sacrificing himself. The man she loved more than life itself was going to die.

Morg's eyes flew wide as he flinched hard at what he saw. He raised the staff quickly and performed the Slave Calling. Just as Kade was casting, he felt the power descend on him, ensnaring him in its web. He groaned loudly, the Divine racing through him as it continued to build. His vision faded as his eyes turned pure white. He knew he had only moments left, and then he would be done. He had to force the Divine to bend to his will for just a few more moments. The power flashed in his mind's eye so bright that he screamed in pain but there was no getting away from it. It flashed again, threatening to explode. Kade let out a continuous groan as he shook. His skin started to blacken in patches as he struggled desperately. He was being cooked from the inside out. He held on, furiously trying to control the Divine that was consuming him by the second.

Darcienna lunged, clamping her hands around his ankles and held on for dear life. She opened herself up and threw every bit of her remaining life-force into healing. The dismal amount was enough to cause the white in his eyes to recede slightly. A hint of brown showed through. Morg came back into focus. Kade concentrated every ounce of his will into opening his hand and extending his arm just a fraction more. Morg shook with the effort of holding him. Sweat was forming on his brow as he strained against the apprentice's will. It was as if the very source of the Divine itself were within Kade, and it was almost too much for Morg to control…almost, but Kade was held fast, unable to move. A few more moments was all Morg would need. Just then, a black shape glided into the room from the tunnel. The evil Chosen glanced past Kade at the silky, black creature that was preening itself as if it had not a worry in the world. It was only a mere moment, but it was enough. The slight loss of focus on Morg's part was all Kade needed. His arm straightened ever so slowly, and then his hand opened. An explosion so loud erupted from Kade that it could be heard for miles. The entire mountain jumped from the peak to the very core. The blinding flash ripped over the ground to explode violently into Morg. The evil Chosen's eyes bulged as the blast sent him flying across the room like a leaf caught in a tornado. He slammed into the far wall with a bone-crushing impact. The shield contorted, flashed briefly and then was gone. Morg hit the ground, and the staff flew wide. Kade collapsed to his hands and knees and then fell over. Darcienna fell onto her back with a gasp, her eyes glazing over.

Morg had a gash along his forehead and his nose was

already starting to swell as blood ran freely, smearing his face. He had landed with one arm out to his side with his other twisted behind his back. Whether it was broken or not was unclear. He was still breathing but it was obvious that he was not going to recover soon as the lump continued to grow on the side of his head.

So close, and yet, so far. Kade thought. In the shape he was in, there was no way to recover the staff. He lay on his side, helpless, unable to move. As he watched, the most powerful weapon in existence eerily started to slide across the floor a few feet at a time. Kade peered through half lidded eyes at the object that seemed to have a life of its own. Little by little, it moved closer and closer.

Kade desperately wanted to move for the staff, but his muscles were done. He had moments at best. The staff lifted only slightly and then landed in his hand. The instant it touched his skin, he felt a power so limitless that he knew he could do anything…except…cheat death. It was as if he was connected to the Divine without having to call on it. He took a breath and hoped beyond hope that the staff was imbued with the only calling that was going to save his life. He called on the Healing Calling and sent it into Darcienna. His breathing turned shallow and he became light headed. It was hard to formulate thoughts. Darcienna sighed. Hearing her voice, his vision cleared for just a moment and he performed the calling again. The color returned to her face and her eyes fluttered open.

She was worth it, Kade thought as his mind sank into the abyss. *They were all worth it,* he thought as a single tear seeped out of the corner of his eye. His breathing slowed and his eyes glazed over. He felt his body take a shuddering breath. He smiled at the relief as the pain melted away. And then…the staff rolled from his hand.

CH7

Zayle started to fade into view. The Master was shaking his head and looking over his shoulder as if he were being pursued. Zayle's mouth was moving as if he were talking, but Kade could not make out a single word. He could almost hear what the Master Chosen was saying when he felt something tugging at him.

Kade could hear a familiar female voice screaming his name, commanding him to do something. No. It was denying him something. It was not letting him go. The pain in his body returned with a vengeance and Zayle faded from view. Kade groaned loudly as he exhaled through clenched teeth. Darcienna was shaking as she held his head in her hands. Kade looked into her tear streaked face as she pleaded for him to return. She begged and commanded and bargained for his life; anything to bring him back.

"Kade," the queen hissed weakly.

"Rakna," Kade tried to say but his charred lips would not form the words.

"Kade," Darcienna gasped in immense relief as she placed

her hands on his head. He wet his lips and felt them soften enough for him to talk.

"Rakna," Kade said, knowing how the staff had worked its way to him. He let the Transparency Calling go and Rakna faded into view just a few feet away. She was badly injured. Two legs on one side and one leg on the other were bent or broken. Kade reached for the staff, and after calling on the healing, sent the Divine into her. She groaned loudly as the legs bent straight again, and then, she sighed in relief as the healing took effect. He performed the calling, once more, and then turned the healing on Darcienna.

"Get to the dragon and Ven," Kade said.

He tried his best to prepare for the pain. Kade knew that this was going to hurt beyond describing when she took her hands off him. He had no choice. He had to let her save them. It had to be done. No amount of preparing was going to ready him for how bad it was, though. He screamed, tears leaking from his eyes as he bit down hard against the torment that filled his mind. He was only able to stop screaming because he ran out of breath. He inhaled and held it just so he would not hear himself scream. He cracked open an eye and saw Darcienna hesitate, torn with indecision.

"Go!" Kade yelled and then clenched his jaw tightly once more.

Darcienna quickly raced for Ven and fell down hard on her knees, landing next to the shapeshifter. She starting working the healing, but Ven was close to death. *NO!* Kade thought as he watched. His heart started to ache. He looked over at the dragon and knew he still had work to do. He drew on the Divine to help numb the pain. It helped…just barely. He forced himself to roll onto his knees. The skin on his hands cracked along the blackened flesh and bled instantly. It made the ground slippery as he struggled to stand. The fingers on his right hand were virtually useless. His clothes were soaked with blood from open sores. He kept his eyes on the dragon to keep his mind focused. Maybe, just maybe, it would be enough to keep him on his feet. He did not even have enough strength to lift the staff. He dragged it behind himself as he forced his feet to take one step and then the next.

Darcienna turned and watched with a broken heart as the man she loved struggled to get to his precious companion. It crushed her to think how he would feel if the dragon was no longer living. She wanted to call out to him, but she knew it would do no good, and Ven's life hung in the balance

Kade stumbled and his hand sank into plush, white fur. The queen moved close to his side. He leaned on her and clenched his jaw as he lifted his foot and put it down again, moving closer to the dragon with each step. He got a sick feeling in his stomach as he closed in on his friend. Finally, after what felt like forever, Kade collapsed against Rayden's side and closed his eyes. He laid the staff against the dragon and performed the Healing Calling over and over with virtually no more than a second between healings. The power flowed through him without needing to be called.

The staff was dangerous. Even though the pain clouded his mind, Kade could see how the ancient artifact could make a man feel powerful and lose perspective. "Power corrupts," Zayle used to say, and this was more power than anyone should have. For now, it was his, and he was going to use it to save his friend.

Rayden let out a deep sigh as the healing did its work. Kade opened his eyes to see a large, golden disc not more than a few feet away from his face. The dragon inhaled Kade's scent and worry flooded the link that was now alive and strong. A keening sound came from deep within the dragon. Kade wanted to reassure his friend that he was ok, but he was afraid that he would not be able to keep from crying out in pain if he tried to talk. He was also afraid that it might be a lie.

"Ven," Kade hissed through a clenched jaw. It was all he could say.

"Lie across my back, Chosen," the queen hissed.

Kade forced himself to stand and let out a gasp when he

steadied himself against the dragon. He left a bloody handprint on Rayden's side as he pushed off. It took all his focus and concentration to get his legs to work enough for him to keep his balance. What should have been easy was now almost impossible. He stood and then fell across the queen's back. She almost collapsed to the ground with the weight but then stood.

"Kade," Darcienna called out. "I am losing her," she said, sincere sadness in her voice. She was on the verge of tears.

"Hurry," Kade hissed out through his clenched teeth. "Hurry!"

The queen situated Kade on her back and then crossed quickly to Darcienna. Kade rolled off Rakna's back and hit the ground with a thud. He ground his teeth as he held out his burnt hand and did his best to grip Ven's arm. It felt lifeless, but then, with the charred blackened flesh, almost anything was going to feel lifeless.

The Divine flowed through the staff and Kade sent a steady stream of healing into Ven. It was almost like watching an empty sack fill with air. Her life force grew quickly and steadily. In mere moments, her eyes fluttered open to stare at him. She gasped in panic as she took in Kade's injuries. The room was starting to spin as the pain threatened to overwhelm him.

"Darcienna," Kade pleaded through a clenched jaw.

He did not feel her place her hands on his arm, but the cooling sensation as the pain melted away was a profound relief. Kade let his head fall back on the ground as Darcienna pushed her healing into him. He exhaled deeply and felt every muscle in his body melt under her touch. He reached a hand over and placed it on her knee. He connected with the staff and healed her as she healed him. She gasped. Kade looked up at her and saw a look of wonder on her face.

"I can't explain why, but I can cycle the healing back to you," Darcienna said as she watched the burnt, blackened flesh on his arm start to fade and be replaced by new, pink skin. "Kade, I could not heal you this quickly on my own. I could not even get close. I would need hours of rest to recharge my ability and days to heal this much damage. I can't explain it, but I am grateful, regardless," she said as she brushed away the dead skin from his arm. Kade closed his eyes and focused on sending massive amounts of healing to Darcienna as fast as possible. His breathing became easier by the second. The open sores closed up and the throbbing throughout his body eased. Kade pulled himself to a sitting position as his body continued to mend. He closed his eyes as the rest of the pain melted away and immersed himself in the relief. He opened his eyes and got to his feet, flexing his muscles to loosen any remaining tension. His skin felt numb and there was a tingling sensation running through his body, but other than that, he was healed.

There was a low groan from by the wall. Kade and Darcienna looked at each other and then over to the broken body lying on the floor. Kade gripped the staff and considered finishing the man with a vengeance, but Darcienna put a gentle hand on his arm.

"He deserves it," Kade said with a growl. He considered ripping his arm free and blasting the man over and over again. He pictured himself pummeling Morg brutally until the evil Chosen was no longer recognizable. He wanted to call on a continuous stream of Divine Fire and listen to Morg scream.

"There has been enough of that," Darcienna said soothingly, feeling his muscles in his arm taught as iron. With regret, Kade relaxed his grip on the staff and turned to the queen.

"Rakna, can you secure him with your webbing?" Kade asked.

"It would be my pleasure, Chosen," the white queen said as she skittered over to the body.

She held Morg and turned him over and over as she spun a web, uncaring about his injuries. She dropped him to the floor with a thud and dragged him behind her. As she was working her way back, she stumbled hard as if she had been struck. Her front legs buckled. She tried to speak but nothing came out. It was as if she had the wind knocked out of her. Kade looked at her in confusion. He was ready to send Morg to his death, suspecting that he was the source of the queen's suffering, but the evil Chosen was still unconscious. Kade's grip on the staff tightened as he quickly scanned the area, but nothing seemed to be moving. He looked back at the queen and then over to Darcienna. Rakna struggled to stand and swayed as if the world were spinning beneath her. Kade raced to her side and caught her before she could collapse again.

"Chosen," the white queen said, her voice heavy with despair. "The king... The link between us...," she started to say but could not finish the words.

Rakna did her best to regain her composure, but she was crushed. Kade and Darcienna exchanged a glance. "The last he sent was that half of Morg's army had been destroyed. Most of those that remained stopped and just left, but there are still many fighting," she said, trying to be brave.

"She thinks the king has passed," Darcienna whispered quietly.

"I won't accept that until we know for certain," Kade said as he knelt down to look the queen in the eye. "Is there a chance that the king just cannot communicate? Maybe he is unconscious?" he asked gently.

"The connection is severed, Chosen. I fear the worst," Rakna hissed.

There was a slow rumble that started deep within the mountain. Kade cocked his head as he listened. Something was coming and it continued to approach by the second.

Kade got to his feet and winced at the soreness that was still in his muscles. If this was the worst of it, then he considered himself blessed by the Divine. He turned and looked at the hole in the ground as the distant rumble continued.

"SEND HIM TO US," the voice in the pit said in a whisper.

"HE FAILED US. GIVE HIM TO US."

Kade looked at the body wrapped in webbing and then turned toward Darcienna. She was standing next to Rakna with her hand on the queen's back, trying to console her, but it did not appear to be doing much good. Rakna was devastated. With the link between her and the king gone, the queen was struggling to maintain a semblance of composure.

"Why? Why would I do anything you say?" Kade asked with a sneer as he walked to the edge of the pit.

"BECAUSE HE DESERVES IT. HE TRIED TO KILL YOU. DO YOU NOT WANT REVENGE?" the voice asked ominously. It sounded as if it belonged to a hundred-foot tall giant.

Kade stared into the pit and hated the way he felt. He did want revenge. He craved to make Morg suffer but…for a reason he could not explain…something was stopping him. He looked deep within his heart and soul, trying to find any reason not to hand this evil man over to death but failed.

Turning, Kade walked over to Morg and studied him for a long time. Darcienna saw the struggle within him and called out his name. He stood as if not hearing. Darcienna walked over and laid a gentle hand on his arm. He slowly turned toward her, and even though his eyes were looking at her, his mind was still on the man lying in webbing on the ground. After a moment, she came into focus.

"Why should I not send him down that pit? Why?" Kade asked, anger in his voice. Why not make him suffer?" he asked as he turned to glare at Morg with pure hatred in his heart.

"Kade," Darcienna said gently as she put a hand on his chin and turned him back to face her. "Because it's wrong. You have to ask yourself if it benefits us to end his life."

"It will make me feel better," Kade growled as he turned once more to glare at the Chosen.

"Will it really?" Darcienna asked, turning him back to face her once more. She looked deep in his eyes. He hated that she was

214

right. Killing Morg would do nothing to change the way he felt. He had beaten the man and that should be good enough. Sending him to his death would not make anything better, but still.... Kade turned to the queen.

"Surely you would agree that he should die?" Kade asked Rakna, some of the fire gone from his voice. The queen climbed out of her despair to look at him. By way of answer, she grabbed the webbing that was hanging off Morg and dragged him over to Rayden where she firmly affixed him to the dragon's back. Rayden tensed as the queen worked.

"A decision to take a life should never be made from an emotional standpoint," Rakna said, but her tone was one of confliction. Kade could sense that she wanted Morg to suffer just as the evil Chosen had made others suffer. Kade was also certain that she wished he would have perished in the battle. But, regretfully, seeing as he did not, they were obligated to deal with things as they were, without taking a life if possible. She would never admit this, but it was clear, nonetheless.

Kade clenched and unclenched his fists over and over as he felt the urge to kill still coursing through his veins. Oh how he craved to see the life spill from this man. He exhaled in exasperation and turned on the pit.

"You cannot have him!" Kade said firmly.

He wanted nothing more than to shove this man screaming over the edge to suffer at the hands of the voice. He knew Morg would be treated to incredible agony, and something in him wanted that desperately, but as the anger drained from him, he understood more and more that it was wrong to give in to the voice. No, he was not going to give them what they badly wanted.

"GIVE HIM TO US! WE WILL NOT BE DENIED! GIVE HIM TO US SO WE CAN PUNISH HIM AS HE DESERVES! GIVE HIM TO US NOWWWWWW!" the voice echoed through the mountain. The ground shook with the fury.

"No," was Kade's simple reply.

"THEN WE SHALL TAKE HIM AND THE REST OF YOU, TOO!" the voice boomed and the ground continued to shake.

Kade looked into the hole and saw something forming in the blackness deep in the mountain. At first, it was just a faint, red spot barely showing through the darkness. Kade felt a waft of heat gently blowing in his face as he narrowed his eyes, trying to make out what he was seeing. The faint redness turned into glowing red crimson as it came rushing up the hole. The heat it pushed with it became hotter by the moment. Kade's eyes widened in panic as he watched the molten lava rush to fill the pit. It was only moments away from making it to the top.

"RUN!" Kade screamed as he raced over to Darcienna, grabbed her by the hand and almost yanked her off her feet as he sprinted for the tunnel.

Rakna left her despair behind and ran for the exit. There was a steady flow of heat pouring into the room, increasing the temperature quickly. Kade raced by the bookshelf, and for just a split second, regretted leaving behind what had to be an immense amount of knowledge. Doren would, most likely, die trying to scoop up as many of the books as possible, but he was not Doren. The books were only a momentary thought, and then, he was back to racing for his life.

Kade rounded the corner with Darcienna close behind as he pulled her along. A wash of heat hit him. He glanced over his shoulder and saw red dancing on the wall.

"Kade, it is coming too fast!" Darcienna screamed.

"We must mount. It is our only chance!" Kade yelled, fear of being boiled in the lava filling him. "Rayden, down so we may ride," he commanded.

Rayden skidded to a stop and dropped to the ground. Rakna skittered up the dragon's tail while Kade grabbed Darcienna and threw her up onto the dragon's back. If he used any more strength, he would have slammed her into the ceiling. He vaulted up just as the monkey form of Ven swung up to hang around his neck. He held the staff between his arm and body as he used his hands to grip the dragon.

"Go Rayden, GO!" Kade yelled.

Lava splashed against the wall as it rounded the corner and started down the tunnel. The mountain shook and rumbled as if it were alive. The voice in the pit continued to scream in fury as its prey raced for their lives.

Dust started to sift down from the ceiling as the tunnel threatened to collapse. The dragon stayed low so as not to scrape its passengers along the ceiling. Unable to stand, Rayden struggled forward, but it was still considerably faster than being on foot. Kade and Darcienna ducked low, but even with that, they feared injury. Kade could feel the brush of the ceiling on his hunched shoulders as he hugged the dragon. Darcienna had to lean slightly to keep from hitting the rocks that were jutting downward.

Rayden rounded the next corner and raced headlong into a trap. Kade flinched as the calling on the side of the tunnel went off. A boulder half the size of Rayden hit the ground and rolled to block the passageway. Rayden slithered by but not before the boulder caught his tail. He let out a roar of pain as he was jerked to a stop, unable to pull free. The riders lurched forward, almost pitching over the dragon's head. Rayden roared in pain and fury as he pulled, but the boulder had him trapped. Lava was starting to seep around the edges of the rock. The heat was intense and started to eat through the boulder. Rayden let out a roar of pain as the lava started to boil his tail.

"Hold on Rayden. This may hurt, but if we want to live, it has to be done," Kade yelled as he swung the staff around.

An explosion rocked the tunnel as lightning slammed into the boulder where it had the dragon pinned. Rayden cried out. Kade hit the boulder again and it split, freeing the dragon's burnt tail and the lava at the same time. Rayden lunged forward. Kade cringed as he saw the blackened tail. He called on the healing and sent a continuous steam into the dragon. The silver flesh spread over the tail quickly, leaving no trace of the burn.

The roof grew higher, giving Rayden the much needed room to stand and run instead of the half-run, half-crawl. He still needed to keep low, but now he was able to stretch his legs and put some speed into it. Kade felt a blast of heat against his back. He turned just in time to see the lava filling the tunnel fast as the boulder gave way.

"Darcienna!" Kade screamed as he pointed.

She turned and threw up her hand just as the lava was closing on the dragon. The shield phased in and out as the molten rock pounded it brutally. As exhausted as Darcienna was, the fact that she was able to call on her shield at all was a blessing and the Apprentice Chosen knew it.

Kade swung around to search for the opening. There! Straight ahead, just seconds away, was escape. He spun and saw Darcienna's shoulders shaking as the shield gave way. He recalled her saying something about it being difficult to hold the shield while moving and mentally thanked her for this much.

Rayden stretched forward as far as he could and planted his front feet as he readied himself to launch. Kade gripped the ridges tightly, waiting for the powerful burst that he knew was coming. Next, Rayden brought his hind legs as far forward past his front legs as he could and then dug in. His muscles exploded, propelling himself with every bit of strength he had. They shot out of the cave. Its four legs trailed behind as its streamlined form shot through the air. The dragon's wings gave a sharp pop as they expanded to catch the air.

"Bank hard right!" Kade screamed. The dragon reacted immediately and the lava shot by, barely missing the dragon.

As if staying on after that last burst was not difficult enough, Rayden turned so tightly that Darcienna lost her grip and slid off. She let out a shrill scream of terror. Kade's reflexes took over and his hand shot out to grab her by the foot just as she was falling away... and missed. Ven leapt off Kade's shoulder and dove for

218

Darcienna as she plummeted. The shapeshifter changed into the flying creature Kade had seen back in the spider's lair as she fell. As soon as she finished the change, she folded her wings and her legs tightly to her body and descended like an arrow slicing through the air. As Ven closed in on the falling woman, her talons extended to grab Darcienna by the shoulders and her wings came open. She struggled to level off but was unable to fully extend her wings as the weight was too much. The best she could do was to slow their fall in hopes that the dragon could reach them in time.

Rayden did not need to be told what to do as he folded his wings and dove. Kade felt his stomach float up into his throat as he gripped the dragon tightly to keep from joining Darcienna in her fall. They were catching up quickly but Kade feared he would not get to them before they entered the clouds. Just as the clouds came racing at them, he reached a hand out and clamped it tightly around her wrist. Kade gripped the dragon's ridges for leverage and grunted as he pulled Darcienna back onto the dragon. He felt the familiar small hands of the small monkey on his shoulder as it swung around to cling to him. He hugged it tightly, vowing to repay Ven for all she had done.

With a bit of maneuvering, Darcienna found her seat and latched onto Kade so tightly that he found it difficult to breath. The staff shifted dangerously just as they came out the bottom of the clouds. Kade shoved it back up into his armpit and clamped his arm down hard. He glanced at the ground and imagined the staff spinning away toward it. He became dizzy at the thought. Then, the image of Darcienna falling away flashed through his mind and he almost got sick.

Rayden banked again, but this time, he was much gentler as they descended. Kade pried Darcienna's hands loose and turned to check on her. She was ghostly white and there was a profound fear in her eyes.

"Kade," she said, forcing her throat to unclench. "That was too close," she said, latching on tightly around his waist again. She was on the verge of crying but was doing her best to stay in control.

Chosen, we must get back. I fear that even with what we have done, the clutch may still be destroyed. Is there a way for that staff to help us return home quicker? Rakna asked in his mind.

"I have one thing I can try," Kade yelled back as he searched his memory, his heart still pounding. If the staff worked the way it was supposed to, and he remembered the calling as well as he hoped, then they had a chance. "I am going to try to transport us there...if this staff is imbued with the calling." Darcienna let out a slight whimper just barely loud enough for Kade to hear. "We have to try," Kade said over his shoulder. Darcienna could only nod her head. She desperately wanted to have her feet planted firmly on the ground.

In his mind, Kade pictured the page with the Transport Calling on it. He visualized the symbol that was at the top of the page and wondered if it was somewhere on the staff. He knew the word in the ancient language that was needed and he also recalled the simple instructions:

Visualize firmly in your mind the destination. Complete the moves for the calling and then intone the ancient word for travel.

Kade readied himself. It felt odd and extremely uncomfortable to use this powerful of a calling with only the staff. He was scared to death. For ten years, he was taught to fear callings of this magnitude. There were more moves to this calling than any other he had ever performed. But mostly, it just did not feel right to cast this without performing the motions to activate it.

"Hold on," Kade yelled as he held the staff out.

Kade pictured the symbol from the calling, unsure if this was needed, and then visualized the cave. When he was sure he had his destination firmly etched in his mind, he gripped the staff tightly and intoned the word. The staff came alive as Divine Power surged through it and out into the world. The staff vibrated so strongly that Kade found it almost too difficult to keep a tight grip on the artifact. Everything spun wildly. Kade could not tell if he was falling or still on the dragon. Darcienna screamed. Ven latched on so tightly that Kade felt his breathing cut off.

There was a pounding so intense in Kade's head that his stomach clenched tightly. The world stopped spinning as a tree just outside the cave came into focus. Kade could not keep his balance and fell to the ground. His stomach heaved hard and emptied itself. There was nothing to empty, and yet, it tried over and over again as it clenched as hard as a rock. Kade struggled in agony to get in a breath between heaves. Darcienna hit the ground next to him and suffered the same fate. Rayden struggled to stand as he shook his head violently from side to side, trying to escape the misery.

Kade cracked open an eye and reached for the staff. He put his hand on the ancient wood and then rolled onto his back as he put his other hand on Darcienna. He focused as best he could and called on the healing. He had no way of knowing if the casting had worked. He turned his head and retched so hard that he could not even tell if the Divine had done his bidding. His mind spun and the heavy thrum made it difficult for him to open his eyes. And then…all of a sudden…it was gone. Kade inhaled as if he had been held under water for what felt like hours. His lungs burned. After just a moment, he looked up to see Darcienna sitting over him with her hands wrapped around his head. She still had sick on her chin. She wiped her lips with the back of her hand and fell onto her haunches. The queen did not appear to be affected as she quickly climbed the tree to be with her clutch.

Kade steadied his breathing and struggled to his feet. Ven was rapidly shifting through different shapes. Kade quickly reached for her body, that seemed to be ethereal, and sent waves of healing into her, also. The shapes she took slowed and then stopped. She was lying in her birth form, panting heavily. It took her a moment, but she struggled to her feet. With several more healings, she completely recovered and looked around, readying herself for battle. She leapt into the air and changed into the formidable flying black creature. With an ear splitting screech, she blinked from sight and dove at victim after victim.

Next, he turned and caught up to the dragon. He had to duck its wild motions as Rayden swung his head violently back and forth. It was not lost on Kade that he could be knocked out or even killed if he was too careless. Rayden was out of his mind as he thrashed about, trying to get away from the torment inside his head. Kade tried to connect with the dragon in an attempt to communicate, but nausea flooded the link, making his stomach heave. He quickly slammed the link closed just as his stomach was threatening to empty again. Kade waited until Rayden paused, and then he lunged, making contact. He opened himself to the power of the staff and let the healing flood into the dragon. Rayden slowed and then collapsed, panting hard with his tongue lolling out of his mouth. Kade continued to let a steady stream of healing infuse the dragon.

"By the great Nature's Gift, I do not EVER want to travel like that EVER again!" Darcienna vowed vehemently. Kade wiped his mouth and spat out a string of curses that made her eyes grow wide. With that, she knew he shared her dislike for that form of travel.

Kade heard the sound of another getting sick and turned to see Morg suffering the same fate. He firmed his resolve not to help the man, expecting Darcienna to show compassion. He turned, ready to stand his ground and locked eyes with her. Darcienna was watching the evil Chosen with her eyes narrowed in thought. After several long moment of contemplation, she turned her attention to Kade. With the slightest of movement, she shook her head. Kade's eyes came open wide in shock.

"This is all his fault," Darcienna said as she swept the area with her arms. "He can deal with it," she said by way of an explanation. Kade grinned and loved her even more for sharing his lust for revenge. He knew it was wrong, but he did not care. Morg should be grateful that he was going to live.

A buzzing worked its way into his mind. His vision cleared more and more and then the scene around them came into focus.

There were bodies strewn for as far as he could see. Many were spiders but most appeared to be creatures that he did not even know existed. There were reptile species and bird-like creatures. There were two dead grimalkin closer to the cave, but there was one still very much alive. It was half inside the cave, struggling furiously to get in at something. Occasionally, it would jump back quickly only to lunge in again.

"Kade," Rakna hissed in panic.

"I have this," Kade said as he stood and turned on the creature. Before he could bring the staff to bear down on its target, Rayden sent a thought so strong through the link that Kade flinched. It translated into one simple word and it took no effort to decipher. MINE!

Rayden leapt to his feet and tore after the creature, sending dirt spraying high into the air as its claws fought for purchase. If only the grimalkin knew what was coming for it, it may have had a chance to run for its life. Kade watched as the dragon and its one lone, trussed-up passenger took off to do battle. He shook his head at the poor creature that had no clue how bad it was going to suffer. He also knew he should do something about Morg, but he just could not get himself to care.

Morg caused this, so he gets to see it up close, Kade thought. Maybe he would survive, maybe he would not. At least he was not actively trying to kill the man, even though he was not actively trying to save him. *Was there a difference?* he asked himself. He did not get to answer that thought.

There was a battle raging around him and it was his turn to unleash death on those that dared attack his clutch. The buzzing that he had heard in his head formed into sounds that he recognized. The trees erupted into a cacophony that almost drowned out any other sound. The spiders were growing into a frenzy as they looked down on the battle field. News of Kade's arrival spread quickly. Their hero and savior had appeared from out of nowhere to pull them from defeat and bring them victory.

223

Darcienna's shield popped into existence right before Kade's eyes. He turned to see an earth creature swing something heavy at them. The shield took one hit and was gone. Darcienna was in no shape to keep this up but she had made the difference. She was exhausted, but Kade was another story. He grinned eagerly. It might even be accurate to say he grinned evilly.

"You are going up into the tree where it is safe," Kade said as he put his hands on her hips and propelled her up into the tree. She landed with an "Umph" on a branch and latched on.

Kade quickly back peddled to avoid the next attack and tripped over a root. He fell and then rolled just as the creature's club slammed into the spot he was just occupying. He came up with the piece of wood in his hand and blocked the next swing. The ancient artifact showed no signs of breaking and Kade easily had the strength to absorb the hit. That was it. That was the best chance this creature had of prevailing, and now, it was his turn. His blood boiled as he spun in a circle and swung the staff with all his might. The creature shattered, breaking in two. The staff hardly slowed as it passed through the Alluvium. Had the creature taken on the rock form it was capable of, it may have survived, but it had not reacted quickly enough to Kade's counterattack.

"So, it does hit as hard as a house," Kade said as he spared a glance for Darcienna. He spun to face the bulk of the army and let his hate explode. "You will all die!" Kade screamed, eager to kill as he raised the staff and let lightning after lightning explode into the air. The first several bolts were just to get their attention. He wanted them to see who was going to end their miserable lives. The next were to maim, kill and destroy. Blood flew everywhere as he alternated between calling on the Divine and flat out crushing skulls with the deadly piece of wood. Kade preferred crushing skulls so he could physically feel the life being ended through the staff. He was careful not to hurt the dragon, Ven, Doren, if he still lived, or any spiders, but beyond that, anything that moved died.

Kade was soaked with blood of many different colors. The

224

lizard's blood was blue, while the bird-like creatures was red. The earth creatures had dark, brown blood that was like mud. It did not matter. They were going to die, whatever the color. The ground was going to flow with it. The staff was coated with the liquid life force, but Kade continued to swing.

The spiders renewed their attack. For any creature that got too close to a tree, it would be quickly ensnared and lifted into the branches. Shortly after, it would fall to the ground, dead. The trees were alive with spiders. Every tree in the area had spiders. Kade instantly understood why his clutch was still in this fight. The spiders on the ground would engage and then back up to the tree as if they were cornered. Their clutch mates would then pull them up. It was simple and effective. But, even with this clever ploy, had Kade not returned, they would have been beaten. But, he did return, and the spider's morale shot through the roof as they fought with a vengeance. Their savior was there and this alone was enough to erase any fear as they fully engaged the enemy.

Kade stopped for a moment, panting hard. There was nothing but dead creatures surrounding him. Some were smoking from the lightning but most were in pieces with crushed skulls. When Kade wanted to see them suffer, he would call on the Blue Fire of the Divine and let them burn to death. He basked in their screams as they died in droves. He was pure rage as hate filled him.

Kade turned to see the dragon flanking the grimalkin, lunging in and back out again. The creature was struggling to turn with its opponent. Its hind end was smoking and its right, back leg struggled to work. It cried out pitifully but there was nothing close enough to come to its rescue. At least...nothing that Kade saw.

The body of Morg was hanging off the dragon's back now as the cocoon swung wildly. Kade watched in horror as a massive creature emerged from around the mountain. It oriented on his dragon and charged. Kade screamed a warning through the link. Rayden leapt out of reach of the grimalkin as he whirled to meet the new challenge.

225

"Kade!" Darcienna yelled as she pointed at the huge beast bearing down on Rayden. "Another dragon!"

Kade's eyes went wide with panic and his heart raced out of control. He quickly raised the Ancient staff, and just as he was sending a blast at the massive, green and black dragon, Rayden leapt in the way. The bolt was already firing. Kade twisted slightly and the blast sizzled through the air just over both dragons' heads.

Rayden and the new dragon that was half again as large came together and tangled. Kade could not get a shot off as the dragons spun. He feared for his friend. He expected, at any moment, that the larger dragon would tear into Rayden easily, but it did not happen. They spun around each other in some sort of dance, but neither attacked. After four or five rotations, the giant dragon started to back away as Rayden pursued. Rayden was furious. Kade could feel the rage through the link. Never before had he felt this much anger from his dragon. Rayden was directing the fury at the larger dragon, who was looking left and right for escape. Kade glanced at Darcienna who appeared to be just as mystified.

"Kade?" Darcienna asked, still trying to make heads or tails of the situation.

The apprentice just shrugged his shoulders and stared in awe. Darcienna's shield popped into existence right in front of his face, startling him. He jumped back and then turned to see a creature backing away quickly. It turned to run. The shield disappeared and Kade raised the staff and fired. He did not care if it was retreating. He would not have cared if it was down on its knees begging for its life. Enough was enough. If they wanted to continue to attack him after knowing who he was and what he could do, then so be it. He felt no remorse as the fire enveloped its target. They tried to take his life and that meant they forfeit theirs. He was sure Darcienna was going to have a chat with him about not killing when it was running, but the time for being compassionate was past. The creature screamed in agony.

Kade dispatched several more creatures that were not smart

226

enough to run for their lives. Morg's army was thinning by the moment. The spiders from the trees descended like death from above. There were only a scattering of creatures now. The spiders hunted then quickly, driving them to the ground and filling them with venom.

Several spiders ran up to Rayden, happy to see the dragon. The larger dragon flared its wings and prepared to attack. Rayden placed himself between the spiders and the larger dragon, snapping at the green with a crashing of teeth. It shook its head as it looked between the spiders and Rayden. The beautiful, silver dragon circled the larger dragon once more while the green tried to retreat. Rayden gave a continual stream of guttural grunts, growls and hisses. The green became agitated as it fought to understand what was happening. Rayden gave several more vehement guttural sounds and then returned to Kade's side. The green slowly turned and looked at the grimalkin. Green looked back at Rayden one more time and shot back in the language of dragons. Rayden took a couple of steps toward Green, responding to it, and then the large dragon rounded on the grimalkin with a vengeance.

Rayden turned his back on the green dragon and trotted toward Kade with Morg hanging sideways off his back. The webbing was coming loose. The grimalkin wailed in fear as the green and black dragon started to stalk it. Rayden and the grimalkin might be an even match but this was obviously not. Even the grimalkin knew this was the end for it as it tried to turn and run for its life. The green dragon leapt into the air with a mighty roar, its wings expanding to blot out the sun, and then it came down on the grimalkin's back with its claws extended, driving it into the ground. The cat-like creature turned, desperately fighting for its life, but the dragon drove its teeth deep into the grimalkin's throat and tore. And with that, it was over before it even began.

"It is about time you made yourself useful," the dry voice of Doren said from the direction of the cave.

Kade slowly turned to see Doren walking toward them.

There was blood down the front of his clothes and his left arm hung limp at his side with an ugly gash that ran from his shoulder to his elbow. Kade ran up to Doren and let a flood of healing fill the Chosen. Doren closed his eyes and soaked up the relief as the pain evaporated. Every wound closed up instantly and Doren gave a deep sigh of relief. He opened his eyes and locked onto the staff. Before he could demand that the apprentice hand it over, Kade spoke quickly.

"We should seek the Ancients' wisdom on what to do next," Kade said as he turned away from Doren.

The Master Chosen grunted but did not pursue the matter further. Kade was certain that the only reason Doren let it go was because the Master Chosen expected to have the staff shortly. Kade walked up to the tree with Doren close behind. He leaned the staff against his shoulder and held his hands up toward Darcienna. She hesitated a moment and then slid off the branch to be caught in his arms. The staff started to fall but Kade grabbed it. Although he did not see it, he was certain that Doren had started to move.

The Master Chosen saw Morg hanging off the side of the dragon and grunted again. Kade was not sure if it was in contempt for the injured man all trussed up in webbing, or for Kade's careless manner in which he treated the evil Chosen. Either way, he just did not care.

Kade walked up to Rayden and patted him on the side as he approached Morg. Doren fallowed closely. The evil Chosen had sick covering his face. Kade grinned, feeling not even one bit of sympathy. He glanced at Doren and did a double take as the Master Chosen glared hard at him.

"You find this amusing?" Doren asked dryly.

"And I am supposed to feel sympathy?" Kade growled, pushing his luck.

Darcienna walked up and put her hands around Kade's arm. Her nails dug in hard. Kade cast a glance at her, wondering what he might have done wrong and flinched. She had daggers in her eyes as she glared death at the Master Chosen. Kade realized that she was digging in her nails in an attempt to control her temper, but it was failing miserably. He cringed, seeing another verbal lashing coming for Doren. He may be powerless as an apprentice but she was Darcienna and nothing got in her way, if it knew what was good for it.

"He may have committed evil acts, but he is a Master Chosen," Doren said much more civilly. "He will have to atone for his crimes," he said as he kept from making eye contact with Darcienna. His arrogance was still there, but he made sure not to direct any of it at Kade as he spoke. "Remove him from the dragon."

Kade tried to pull the webbing free and failed. It was firmly affixed to the dragon's side. Doren barely hid an eager grin as Kade grabbed just a small strand with one hand, and with considerable effort, was able to break it. Kade turned toward the white queen who had just joined them.

"Can you free him from the dragon?" Kade asked.

"It will be no difficulty at all," Rakna said as she bit down on the webbing. It easily parted. The grin faded from Doren's eyes.

Morg was awake and glaring at any and all who dared look at him. He stopped looking around and his eyes affixed to the one thing he desired more than life itself. Kade did not need to see to know the man was locked onto the staff. His expression was of longing and desire. This staff was everything to the Chosen. Kade felt a slight twinge of pity for Morg and hated himself for it. The evil man deserved nothing but torture for the suffering he had caused.

"It will do you no good to hold onto the hate," Doren said as he saw the look in Kade's eyes.

"So many have died at his hands," Kade shot back.

"Yes," Doren said. He offered no more.

Before Kade could say another word, Darcienna turned pale and closed her eyes. She turned and got sick again. Kade put his hand on her, but before he could call on the healing, she pushed him away and stood up.

"Darcienna?" Kade asked.

"I don't know," Darcienna said as she wiped her mouth with her sleeve. "Maybe I am still not fully recovered from that travel," she said as she shook her head. The color returned to her cheeks.

The green dragon finished tearing the grimalkin to shreds and cautiously approached the group. All turned to see the massive dragon as it slowly slid closer. If Kade did not know better, he would have thought that the dragon was stalking them. But, after seeing the interaction between Rayden and the green, it was clear that it was just approaching with uncertainty.

Rayden turned and trotted over to the dragon. They exchanged several hisses and guttural sounds and then Rayden returned to Kade's side. The green edged closer, clearly not comfortable and stopped almost a hundred feet away. Kade stared in awe. Two dragons in one month and both of them were right here.

Kade glanced at the tunnel as he considered his next move when he got the light touch on his mind that he was all too familiar with. He looked at Rayden and rolled his eyes. He was shocked that the dragon wanted food at that moment. It was even fair to say he was speechless as he shook his head in wonder. But, Rayden had earned his right to make this small request after all he had done.

Kade was readying himself to call on the food when he remembered the staff. *Would it have this symbol carved into it?* he asked himself. Kade grinned and closed his eyes. Sure enough, the food materialized instantly. Kade smiled from ear to ear. *No more cooking,* he thought with immense relief.

Rayden eagerly snapped up the steaming, hot meat. Kade smiled, visualizing a massive chunk of food. The Divine fizzled and was gone. Shocked, Kade closed his eyes and called on the Divine only to find that he was still unable to draw on the vast, unlimited amount. *Fine,* he thought to himself as he conjured piece after piece of meat in rapid succession. It was a much appreciated improvement compared with how he used to cook. Kade had well over twenty pieces of meat lying in a pile within seconds. Rayden was drooling, eagerness flooding the link. Kade stepped back and nodded his head. It was more the mental command to eat than the nod, but it still looked impressive to any who watched.

The green looked on curiously as its nose worked rapidly, inhaling the scent. Kade watched as it started to drool. He created a piece of meat and tossed it to the dragon. It flinched back and let the food fall to the ground. Cautiously, it put its muzzle close to the tasty morsel and inhaled the scent. It gingerly picked it up in its teeth as it watched Kade, uncertainty in its eyes. It chewed the food slowly, tasting the flavor and then swallowed. Kade grinned as he called another piece of meat into existence. He tossed it, and again, the dragon let it hit the ground. But this time, it did not take long for Green to pick it up and chew several times before swallowing.

Kade found himself enjoying this, especially since he was not worried about this dragon eating him. Well...he believed it would not eat him, but the way Rayden was acting.... He had to remind himself that this dragon was wild, but with his dragon close by and the staff in his hands, he did feel considerably safer than he would have otherwise. He called on another piece of meat and tossed it in the air. The green caught it, held it in its mouth for a moment and then hungrily swallowed it. Kade called another piece and tossed it, but this time, he tossed and it landed short. The green took a step closer, picked up the meat and swallowed, barely chewing. Kade called another and tossed it even closer. The green took another step and snapped up the meat. Kade called another one and held it out.

"Kade," Darcienna hissed. "That's enough. You don't know what it will do," she said as she eyed the dragon cautiously. It reeked of power. Its presence was overwhelming as it loomed over them. Bats started to flutter in her stomach.

"She speaks wise words, Apprentice," Doren added, but the

way he said it was…not convincing. It was almost as if he had ulterior motives for being okay with this foolishness.

Kade could not resist as he extended the food. The dragon's nose worked furiously. It took a step as it waited for Kade to toss the meat. The apprentice held it out with no intentions of throwing. The dragon took another hesitant step as it eyed the tasty morsel. Rayden stopped chewing. The beautiful, silver dragon was ahead and to Kade's right with just a few pieces of meat left. Its back had been to the green as the large dragon approached, but now, Rayden turned to watch the massive killing machine intently. Kade held out his hand as far as he could without taking a step. The dragon stretched its neck, but it was not close enough. It took another step as it stretched toward the food. Rayden turned to stone as every muscle in his body tensed. He eyed the green hard, the food in his mouth all but forgotten. The dragon stretched even more. It almost appeared that if it leaned any further forward than it was, it would topple from being overbalanced.

"Kade," Darcienna hissed in warning.

The apprentice grinned to himself as he continued to hold onto the meat. The green huffed and pulled its head back, but its eyes never left the food. It moved closer and then stretched its neck out once more. Its wings unfurled slightly and quivered. Kade was certain it was an instinctual habit for dragons when they readied themselves for action. He was betting that it was an action that would not end with him losing a hand, but…it would be a lie to say he was not at least a little nervous. He held the meat by the very end, and the dragon, once again, reached out inch by inch as it closed on the food. The chunk of meat was just short of two feet long, so Kade knew this was a bad idea, but he just could not help himself. If that green lunged, it could take his entire arm off with just one snap.

"Apprentice, you have had your fun. Now feed it and let it go," Doren said as the Master Chosen stepped back from the massive form that was casting a shadow so large that it covered

232

them all. This time, the master sounded like he meant it.

Kade heard the stern words given by Doren, but again, just could not resist. Morg grinned, hoping the unheeded warnings would prove to be a disaster. The green stretched closer, yet. Rayden flexed his leg muscles, and his wings fluttered slightly. The closer the green got, the more Rayden's lips started to twitch. The silver dragon slowly edged toward the green as it inched closer to the meat. Rayden let out a deep rumble as he continued to close in on the green, but the massive dragon seemed to not hear the threat as it put its nose on the meat. It inhaled rapidly and then its lips started working as it tried to take the food. Kade loosened his grip. The green pulled the piece of meat into its mouth and backed up rapidly. It swallowed while barely chewing.

Rayden turned toward Kade and butted him with his head. Kade fell on his back side hard and was only barely able to keep hold of the staff. Doren eyed the ancient wood eagerly and seemed disappointed when Kade kept his grip. He was almost able to hide the hunger. Almost. Morg took everything in and let out a laugh as if he had heard a joke that no one else had been privy to.

"Even Rayden thinks that was stupid," Darcienna said, scolding him.

"You worry too much," Kade said, but he could not hide the grin.

"You laugh now, but someday you are going to do something that is going to get you killed," Darcienna said with fire in her eyes. "Besides, do we want two dragons around?"

Kade's laughter slowly died down as he considered her question. Two dragons would be amazing, but he was not sure if he wanted two. However, it would be very amusing to see the look on his parents' face if he came back with both of them. The size of this one was impressive. Kade stopped as he noticed Rayden staring at him.

"No one will ever replace you," Kade said as he got to his feet, wrapped his arms around the dragon's head and squeezed.

Rayden enjoyed this immensely, and Kade could feel proof of this with a deep rumble that vibrated up his arms.

"Master Chosen," Rakna hissed. She took a moment to compose herself.

Kade and Darcienna became somber as they realized that the issue of the king was still unanswered. Kade felt a stab of guilt for his playfulness. His mood turned serious as he locked eyes with Darcienna. It dawned on both of them that he had not seen the king. Neither needed to voice the deep fear they felt.

"Rakna," Doren said gently. "He fought bravely, giving his life for the clutch and for the cause," the Master Chosen said with deep respect. "If not for him, we would have been lost. He is a hero to be proud of."

"We knew the risks when we entered this, and we believed the cause was just," Rakna hissed, trying to stay composed. "There will be time for mourning later." The despair of a crushed heart was plain for all to see.

Kade marveled at her strength. He glanced at Darcienna, not able to fathom losing her and then back to the queen. He did not feel half the being he believed her to be. The loss he knew she was feeling had to be overwhelming, and yet, she stood proud. He glanced around and noticed that there were a multitude of spiders surrounding them and knew why she had to put on such a strong appearance.

His eyes opened wide as the realization of his new status with the spiders dawned on him. *This could not be happening,* he thought. He did not know what to do as he watched the spiders place their heads against the ground in homage to him. They gave the green dragon a wide birth but filtered in and out of Rayden's legs as if he were not even there. Rayden craned his neck to peer at the clutch as they continually flowed in and out from beneath him.

The green flexed his wings as he glared at the spiders. Rayden huffed a serious warning and the green settled down. Going from enemy to neutral was clearly a challenge. To call them allies was too big a leap for the green.

The queen looked at Kade as the spiders crowded around. There were close to a thousand still alive. Kade slowly looked from face to face as they looked back at him, waiting. Darcienna was watching him, curious. Even Doren was watching him thoughtfully, patiently. Kade slowly turned and surveyed the area as the spiders settled down. They watched their new king and their cherished queen, waiting for their leaders to lead.

Kade directed the silver dragon to lie down and then climbed onto its back. The green watched in confusion as Rayden allowed the man to stand on his back. Kade could feel amusement through the link as Rayden eyed the green. The large dragon continued to back up, trying to stay clear of any spiders as they filtered in. It was not going to trust these poisonous beings anytime soon.

Kade took a deep breath and felt his emotions start to grow. He glanced at the queen, and with just a look, she seemed to convey what was expected of him. Showing weakness through emotions was not one of the luxuries he had. He did his best to emulate the queen's strength of character. After pausing for several long moments, he collected his thoughts and then started.

"We have lost a great king today," Kade said loudly and firmly but without yelling. He was doing his best to project his voice without looking like he was putting effort into it. "Without him, this world would have been in grave peril," Kade said while holding the staff as though it were a scepter and sticking his chest out with his shoulders squared. "Many of you mourn the loss of Crayken and rightfully so," he said as he swept the crowd with his gaze. "But, instead of mourning this great loss, I say we celebrate the victory that he has given his life to bring to us," he continued with enthusiasm as he raised the staff for emphasis. "Not only do we celebrate his victory, but from this day forth, I decree that this day shall be deemed a day of celebration in his honor," Kade yelled and the spiders cheered. "This celebration is a tribute to one of the greatest kings to ever lead this clutch, and he will never be forgotten. Raise your voices with me in honor as we rejoice in Crayken's victory," he yelled dramatically as he thrust the staff high into the air and sent a blast of lightning skyward.

The explosion shocked the spiders but only for a moment. The words along with the Divine Power were all it took to send the spiders into a frenzy of buzzing as they cheered their hero and their fallen king. Kade was going to do everything in his power to ensure that Crayken's name would live on forever. He waited until the cheering quieted.

"We have work to do. We must bury those that have given their lives for this noble cause. Then, we prepare for a feast in Crayken's name," Kade said.

They cheered again. Several long moments later, the cheering ceased as all eyes turned to him once more. Kade stood, staring out over the spiders. None moved to collect the dead as he had instructed. Kade glanced down at Darcienna and then the queen. Her voice echoed in his head.

They wait for you to descend from the dragon's back. It is considered disrespectful for them to move while you may have more to say.

Kade jumped down and found himself face to face with Morg. He sneered at the fallen Chosen. Morg grinned back. Kade gripped the staff and envisioned crushing the man's skull with it.

"Go ahead," Morg said, taunting him. "Kill me so I do not have to listen to your drivel any longer," he said with contempt. "Besides, it won't be long until he tries to take the staff," Morg said as his eyes darted toward Doren. He let out a knowing laugh as his eyes shifted back to Kade.

The Apprentice Chosen tightened his grip on the most powerful weapon he was to ever hold. His muscles flexed as he fought to control his emotions. Hate filled him. His mind clouded as his desire to end this man's life grew.

So Morg thinks this is the easy way out? Kade thought malevolently. *Let's see how bad he wants it.*

"Then I shall send you to those who wait for you," Kade barked as he raised the staff high over his head in one swift motion.

"Kade, no!" Darcienna yelled, but Kade showed no signs of hearing her words.

Hate filled him and the block melted away. The Divine raged in him, but it would not be the power he would be using to end this man's life. Morg clenched his teeth as he held his ground, but there was no mistaking the fear behind the false front.

A tick developed in Morg's right eye as the evil Chosen watched the staff, waiting for it to descend. Kade let the man suffer for several long seconds as he held the most powerful weapon in the world over his head. The air was thick with tension as all looked on, waiting for the execution that seemed imminent. There were several sighs of relief as he relaxed and slowly brought the staff down to his side. Morg let out the breath he was holding and would have collapsed to the ground if not for the webbing that was providing support.

"Remember this the next time you decide to speak your mind so freely," Kade said as he stepped up to glare directly into Morg's eyes. "I will send you to them and you will know suffering greater than anything you could ever imagine. Do…you…understand…me?" Kade asked dangerously.

Morg's lips formed a tight line as he desperately tried to stand his ground in defiance. Sweat was beading on his forehead but his composure was slowly slipping under Kade's hard stare. Morg swallowed hard.

Kade clenched his teeth as he spun on his heels and marched away. While still encased in the webbing, Morg sank to his knees and his eyes fell to the ground. He was a broken man through and through. For just a second, Kade thought the evil Chosen was on the verge of tears. Kade felt a momentary sense of compassion and then the image of his parents on the towers sprang into his mind. The compassion evaporated as quickly as it had come. Kade had no doubt that if the man was to get his hands on the staff once more, he would quickly return to the evil Chosen he was.

"You were not planning on killing him, where you?" Darcienna asked. Kade stood, looking at her without saying a word as he clenched his jaw in anger. He turned and started walking away without saying a word. "You were just trying to scare him, right?" she asked, as crease lines of concern formed in her forehead. She had to walk quickly to keep up with him.

"Would it be so bad?" Kade asked as he rounded on her. She flinched hard and staggered backward, her eyes coming open wide at the sudden reaction. He cast a glance back at the man still on his knees. Even though they had already had this conversation, all the evil deeds Morg had done sprang into his mind, feeding his desire to kill. "Would not the world be a better place without him in it?" he asked heatedly as he resisted the desire to send a blast of lightning to end this miserable man's existence.

"What would it serve to take his life?" Rakna hissed as she stepped up to the couple. "Kade. You must show that you do not rule with your emotions or you run the risk of losing the respect of the clutch," she said as she indicated the many spiders close by. "If you kill this man while he is helpless, you will appear as a tyrant. You must think when making decisions this critical," she implored him. "It is your decision, but you must consider every decision you make, or it could have disastrous consequences."

Kade paused and turned slowly to see that many spiders were, indeed, watching the scene. He clenched his jaw as he pressed his lips into a thin line. He took a deep breath in through his nose and then out again through his nose, still not able to unclench his jaw. He found it almost impossible to let his hate go. It was not anger or rage that he felt but a pure hate for the man. After a moment, and with considerable effort, he let the fury go. The queen was right. With that, the Divine melted away.

"Your words are wise, Rakna. I shall need your council or I fear I shall stumble along blindly," Kade said as he tried his best to speak calmly. "I have much to learn," he said humbly, feeling embarrassed at his rashness. In a flash, the image of the helpless, old man in Arden popped into his mind. His head whipped around to look at Morg. Kade's eyes lost their focus as his mind worked. After a moment, he took another deep breath and let it out once again, nodding to himself.

"And, I shall do my best to guide you," the queen said humbly.

"Kade?" Darcienna asked hesitantly. He looked at her with curiosity. She rarely used that quiet tone.

"Yes?" Kade asked as he turned and gently took her hand, all the anger gone from his voice.

"Would it be possible?" she asked as she cast a glance at the cave and then paused to collect herself. Kade waited patiently for her to finish the question while she formulated her thoughts. He could feel the emotions in her growing by the moment. "Would it be possible...for me to see Jorell?" Darcienna asked. She smiled up at him but the tears forming in her eyes betrayed her true feelings. Kade knew that the wall she had worked so hard to keep around her heart was starting to crumble.

"I would not know. I can attempt to contact Zayle and ask. There may be a way," Kade said gently as he leaned down to look her in the eye. Darcienna swallowed gently and nodded her head, unable to speak. "I need to talk with him anyway," Kade said as he turned to face the queen.

"Would you please keep an eye on him while we go into the cave?" Kade asked, indicating Morg.

"You are sure he is not a danger?" the queen hissed.

"He is almost as helpless as a baby," Doren said, "even if he were free," he added. Clearly, Doren knew something they did not. He waited for them to ask so he could impress them with his knowledge. Kade decided not to play the game. Doren could show how smart he was another time.

"You will have Rayden to help," Kade said as he patted the dragon on the side.

"Then we shall keep watch over him," Rakna hissed.

"Rayden, keep an eye on Morg. We are going into the cave," Kade said. Rayden acknowledged by way of turning to face the evil Chosen and lying down to stare at him. Morg tried to find some of his lost bravado and failed. With the dagger-long teeth flashing into view, the man would have to be a complete and utter fool not to be afraid. Morg was definitely not going to be a problem while they were away.

"Let's go," Kade said.

Doren was close behind as they walked into the cave. No one talked as they worked their way down the tunnel. Kade brought his light up and the darkness fled. As they got closer to the arch, Kade could see a soft glow emanating from the walls. He smiled, recognizing the plant-like material from the spiders cave. They stopped in front of the arch. Darcienna was fidgeting as she stared hard into the darkness, trying to find the image of her teacher. Doren was suspiciously quiet. Kade turned to study the Master Chosen, expecting some input from him, but the man stood, waiting. The apprentice turned his back on Doren and studied the staff. His eyes shifted toward the Master Chosen, but he did not actually turn to look at him. His grip tightened on the powerful artifact. Kade glanced at Darcienna as an idea came to him.

"I am going to try to make contact with Zayle," Kade said. Doren gave the slightest hint of a smile and then it was gone. "So I would like you to use your shield to ensure nothing can get to me," he said as he let his eyes flit toward Doren and then back again.

"I will keep you safe," Darcienna said as she nodded her head in understanding.

"I can keep you safe," Doren said as he stepped close. "There is no need for her to drain her already weakened abilities."

Kade flexed his fingers and then wrapped them tightly around the wood. He could feel the Divine flowing into him as he feigned his lack of understanding for Doren's motives. His mind struggled with how to proceed. If he refused, it would surely be considered an insult. Doren gave the slightest hint of a smile as he looked on confidently, waiting. Kade was sure that, at any moment, Doren was going to pull rank and demand to stand by his apprentice. Or, maybe he would just cut to the chase and demand Kade hand over the staff. His mind whirled as he frantically searched for an answer to this dilemma. There was no way out, with the exception of flat out refusing to capitulate.

"Thank you so much for your consideration," Darcienna said as she put a hand on Doren's chest and pushed him back. "You are too kind," she finished as she turned and casually, but quickly, raised her shield around herself and Kade.

Doren opened his mouth to protest but Darcienna was a bit too quick for him. He eyed the staff and his smile turned to a scowl. He locked eyes with her.

"Just make this quick," Doren said flatly.

"It will be," Kade said as he laid down in the spot he had used previously, letting the light fade from his hand. He gave Darcienna a serious, hard look to which she nodded once.

Doren looked on intently, turning his head ever so slightly as he stared at the staff. Darcienna could see the hunger as his fingers worked, eager to feel that power. She envisioned another Morg and put a little more strength into her shield. She was still weak, as she had not been able to meditate yet, but they had no choice. The shield was mostly just for show. She knew she was not strong enough to withstand more than the lightest hit. Hopefully, it would serve its purpose.

Kade closed his eyes and called on the Divine. The power flowed through him easily. He grabbed on and was quickly pulled out of his body. He turned slowly in the air and studied Doren for several seconds. The small voice deep down inside warned him to be cautious.

"My Grandson," a familiar voice said to him. Kade turned and could not help but to smile broadly as Zayle stepped through the blackness. But, he was not alone. Jorell stepped out, also, and looked upon him wisely.

"Grandfather," Kade said happily. "Jorell," he continued, smiling broadly as he cast a glance at Darcienna.

Zayle came through and wrapped Kade in a tight hug. If he did not know better, Kade would have thought that his grandfather was on the verge of tears. After several long moments, Zayle grabbed Kade by the arms and pushed him back just a little. He glanced over Kade's shoulder and then quickly back to Kade.

"Okay, here is what you must do," Zayle said as he lifted a finger to point at nothing. "You must see this symbol," he said as he drew an image in the air. Kade was stunned to see Zayle using the Divine. The faint outline of the power hung there. "Picture this and then repeat this word as you work the calling," Zayle said as he cast a quick glance past Kade. He smiled briefly as if something funny occurred to him.

"What calling?" Kade asked, completely at a loss as to what Zayle was planning.

"Just do as I say, and you will understand. Picture this calling," Zayle said as he traced the symbol over and over to keep it from fading.

"Okay, I think I have it," Kade said cautiously, still confused.

"Now repeat this word," Zayle said as he spoke in the ancient language. It was familiar to Kade, but he could not place it. He repeated the word over and over until Zayle nodded in satisfaction. "Now, when you use this calling, direct the Divine here," Zayle said as he indicated the spot on which they stood. "Hurry, quickly, go and do as I said. Picture the symbol, say the word and direct the Divine here."

"Okay, give me a second," Kade said as he turned back for his body.

For a moment, Kade froze. Doren was right next to the shield with his hand on it. Darcienna was smiling but the smile was forced. Her arm shook slightly. Doren turned his head this way and that way as he studied her. There was a look in his eye that Kade did not like. He quickly slid back into his body. His grip on the staff tightened until his knuckled turned white.

"Apprentice," Doren started to say.

Kade knew that the Master Chosen could not contain himself any longer. Doren craved the ancient staff so badly he could taste it. Kade's eyes widened as it hit him what the ancient word meant that Zayle had given him to say. He grinned and spun as he raised the staff. He envisioned the symbol and then drew in the Divine. Doren growled. Kade aimed the Divine at the place Zayle had indicated and then said the word "empower" in the ancient language.

"Nicely done," Zayle said as he slowly took form along with Darcienna's beloved teacher, Jorell. Doren flinched and took a step back with his mouth gaping open. He gasped, shocked at what he was seeing. The surprised look on his face quickly turned to frustration and then exasperation.

"Jorell," Darcienna blurted out in surprise. "Teacher," she said, her voice full of emotion. "Teacher," she said again as the tears started to flow.

"My precious student," Jorell said as she stepped up and wrapped her arms around the young Essence Guardian. Darcienna's eyes went wide at the unexpected contact. Her mind reeled. It only took a second and then she wrapped her arms around her cherished teacher, as if how tightly she held on decided whether Jorell was going to stay or go.

"Darcienna," Jorell said gently, pushing back just slightly. The young girl loosened her grip just a little but not enough to put any space between them. She had her head on her teacher's shoulder as she cried tears of joy and sadness. "I am here my child. I am here," she soothed as she stroked her student's hair.

Doren recovered and gave Zayle a flat stare. His eyes went to the staff and then back to Zayle. Kade's old teacher stared back and gave a confident, knowing smile, and with that smile, he shook his head slowly back and forth. Doren tried to hide his anger and his contempt, but he failed miserably. His eyes turned to fire as he glared from apprentice to master and back again.

"By my right as Master Chosen, I am demanding that the staff be turned over!" Doren said as he started forward with his hand out, all pretenses gone. "As he is still an apprentice, and me a master, I have the right."

"I would agree," Zayle said casually.

Kade's head whipped around in shock to stare at his one true master. He wanted to plead with Zayle, but he held his tongue. He knew, from ten years of training, not to question his teacher's judgment. For a moment, his pulse raced wildly, and then, the confidence in his master helped quell his pounding heart. What he was planning was beyond Kade's understanding.

"Good," Doren said in victory as his eyes hungrily devoured the ornate piece of wood. He started forward again when Zayle continued.

"But," Zayle said casually as he put his hands behind his back, bent slightly at the waist and made a show of looking around the room, "I see no apprentices," he said easily. It only took a moment for Kade to realize where Zayle was going with this. Now, his heart raced for a good reason. Doren froze. His eyes locked with Zayle and the fire returned with a vengeance. Zayle continued as if not seeing Doren's rage. "You are very aware of the fact that any Adept who acquires knowledge or artifacts has no obligation to turn over either," Zayle said ever so wisely, an eyebrow cocked.

"He is an apprentice," Doren stated flatly. "He may not have to turn over his books of knowledge, but the artifact is not protected by our laws."

"He WAS an apprentice," Zayle said.

"He needs to be endorsed by at least two Master Chosen to receive a new rank," Doren said. He smiled, smugness coming off him in waves. Zayle sighed. "And as I see it, he has much to learn," he added as the color in his cheeks returned to normal.

"I believe he has easily proven he has the skill and knowledge to continue on his journey toward being a master," Zayle said. He feigned exasperation for this imagined loss and let his shoulders slump. Doren smiled as his hand came up again, preparing to reach for the staff.

"I would endorse the raising of Kade, son of Garig and Judith, Grandson of the Master Zayle, to the new rank of apprentice," Talos said as he stepped out from the arch. Kade recognized him as one of the Chosen he had seen previously.

"As do I," Lokk said as he stepped to the other side of Zayle. "You have displayed skills beyond that of an apprentice. It would be unjust to hold you at your current rank when you have done so much, for so many. Every Chosen, present or past, is in your debt. From this day forward, you are Adept Chosen Kade."

Doren's hand started to sink as he stared from Ancient to Ancient. It was one thing to banter with Zayle, whom he considered his equal, but to argue with an Ancient... Doren's eyes went to the staff and he appeared to be on the verge of getting sick as his face turned ashen.

"But, does it not have to be a living master?" Doren asked pitifully, making one last desperate plea.

"Master Doren," Talos said as he stepped up to face the man. "Do you really believe that Kade does not deserve to be risen?" he asked critically, his commanding voice resonating. He did not blink as his eyes bore into Doren. His presence was overpowering.

"I...," Doren said but then stopped. He visibly wilted under the scrutiny. "I... endorse Kade, grandson of the Master Zayle, be raised to the rank of Adept," he said as his eyes looked at the staff one last time and then his hand fell to his side.

"Very well," the Ancient said as he turned to face Kade. "Seeing as there are none who oppose your new rank, you are now known as Adept Chosen Kade.

"And...if any were to oppose?" Doren asked weakly.

"Then we would have to convene a panel of at least three

Master Chosen to consider the reasons for not raising the apprentice," Lokk said.

Doren's eyes went from each Master Chosen as if he were counting. His shoulders slumped in resignation. He turned to face Kade and held out his hand.

"Congratulations Adept," Doren said.

"Thank you, Master Chosen," Kade said as he switched the staff to his other hand and reached out to the Master Chosen. He held the staff away just a little as they shook. He did not expect the Chosen would try such an audacious move, but then again, he did not want to take a chance. Doren turned and walked from the tunnel. He was so crushed by this defeat that he completely lost the fact that he was finally speaking with the very beings he had been trying to find for decades.

"Now that that is done," Zayle said as he stepped up and wrapped his arms around his Adept and hugged him tightly. "I love you Grandson. I was very worried when you started to cross. It is a fortunate thing that you have a good woman at your side," Zayle said as he turned to look Darcienna in the eye. He gave her a smile and nodded his thanks. Darcienna smiled back.

The two Ancients turned and faded into the darkness of the arch. Zayle moved back but stayed on this side. He stopped and looked deep into Kade's eyes. All compassion and love faded from Zayle's eyes to be replaced with a deadly, serious look. Kade could feel that something very important was going to happen. The Adept Chosen feared he was not going to like what was coming.

"You must hand over the staff," Zayle said. It was not a command but a statement of fact.

"But, you said that as Adept, it is mine," Kade said as his hands clenched tightly around the wood. His palms instantly started to sweat.

"I did," Zayle said, understanding the struggle that ensued within Kade. "As one who knows what will happen with so much power, I am asking you to hand the staff over."

Kade looked at the ancient piece of wood and felt his stomach twist into a knot. *What is this hesitation? Why is this so hard?* he asked himself. He found that he could not get his arm to extend. *Should I not be able to just hand it over?* He wanted to, but his arm just would not rise. He swallowed hard as his eyes locked onto the staff. His breathing deepened a little as he noticed every little twist in the wood. He took in every symbol and found he recognized very few of them. *What abilities might I have if I was to unlock those symbols?* he asked himself. He struggled to tear his eyes off the powerful artifact. He tried to look at Zayle, but he knew that when he made eye contact with his master again, it would have to be with an answer. His palms continued to sweat as his mind worked furiously. *Why is this so incredibly difficult?* he asked himself over and over. Zayle waited patiently.

Kade realized that Jorell and Darcienna were not talking anymore and glanced sidelong at them. They were both watching him intently. There was more going on here than he realized, but right now, he could only think of the staff. He felt the Divine flow into him as he struggled. It swirled in him, ready for him to mold it, as if it sensed he might need it. He tried to lift his arm, but there it stayed, at his side, tightly gripping the staff. Kade swallowed hard, again. He tore his eyes from the powerful weapon, but they would not move off Zayle's boots. The war that raged in him was fiercer than any he could have ever imagined.

The staff has so much power. I can defeat any enemy and keep the world safe, he thought. But, he knew he was only making excuses. His mind would rationalize anything to keep the staff. But...

Kade took a deep breath and looked Zayle in the eyes. The war continued to rage inside. The staff was still in his hand until he turned it over. He could decide to change his mind at any time. He was told the staff was his. He would not be breaking any rules if he kept it. His mind fought furiously, struggling to find a way...and then, Kade took a step forward and held the staff out. He struggled

247

to get his hand to relax its grip. At that moment, he understood Morg's loss.

"Power corrupts," Kade said as his stomach twisted into a knot so tight it hurt. "I understand," he said as he forced his fingers to uncurl from around the wood. His connection with the staff vanished. Kade gasped, and for just a split second, he wanted to lunge for the power once more. He felt empty. He craved to feel the Divine that was always coursing through the wood. It was as if the staff called to him...but... he forced his hand to drop to his side...or tried to.

"I will keep your staff safe," Zayle said as he stepped back. Hearing Zayle refer to it as "his staff" helped, but he found it almost impossible to tear his eyes off it. "You will have need of it again, but you must always remember...power corrupts. You must choose wisely when you use it," Zayle said as he let the butt end of the staff hit the ground. If Zayle knew he would have need of it again, there must be more to tell.

"What can you see of my future?" Kade asked, forcing his mind to think of anything other than the powerful artifact. It was virtually impossible as he yearned to feel the wood in his grasp again. He felt as if he could get sick and hated himself for it. He let his hand slowly drop to his side, and inside, he hurt.

"I can't see that much because there are too many variables. There is one thing I can tell you that is good, though," Zayle said with a grin. "You will enjoy your family."

"Yes," Kade said, taking a deep breath and letting it out. "I am very much looking forward to seeing my family," he said, a smile creeping across his face. His breathing was starting to return to normal. He had not realized that his breathing had become so forced.

Zayle glanced at Darcienna and smiled. Kade looked over and saw Darcienna with a confused look that matched the one on his own face. He looked back and cocked his head as if to ask, "what," but Zayle was onto the next subject.

"You have one more task to perform," Zayle said. Kade cringed. "You must perform the Chosen's rights for Valdry. Although we have yet to find him, it is our understanding that he has passed."

"He had no apprentice?" Kade asked, relieved that the task appeared to be an easy one.

"No. Not all masters take apprentices."

"Master...Grandfather, if he is not on your side, is there a chance he still lives?"

"It is possible," Zayle said as he considered the thought. "You must make sure one way or the other. If he is no longer alive, you must perform the Chosen's last rights," Zayle said and then his eyes went distant as a thought occurred to him. He spun through the moves for the Divine Fire Calling and his eyes turned pitch black. He studied the scene only he could see for several long seconds, intently searching, for what, Kade could not tell. After a moment, the flames drifted away and his eyes returned to normal. "Something blocks my visions. There is a power here that has been working against me for decades. I believed that once you learned who hunted the Chosen, it would end, but it appears to be intensifying. Caution my Grandson. If something seeks to block my vision of Valdry, he may yet be useful. Learn what you can of his fate."

"I shall take care of that shortly," Kade said as he glanced at Darcienna.

"Good," Zayle said as he turned to Jorell. "We must go. We have to plan. With this," Zayle said as he hefted the staff, "we will be able to make a better stand." Jorell nodded in agreement.

"I love you, Grandson," Zayle said as he slowly stepped backward into the arch, not taking his eyes off Kade.

"I love you too, Grandfather," Kade said, conflicting emotions swirling within him.

"I am very proud of you," Jorell said as she placed her hand on Darcienna's cheek. "You have done better than I could ever have hoped. Nature may bestow another gift on you soon, as you have proven to be responsible with the gifts you have," she said. Her hands dropped to Darcienna's waist and slid around toward the front while she talked, as if she were going to gently push her away.

Darcienna was speechless. Jorell smiled as she stepped back from her student. She turned and looked at the arch over her shoulder as if it were calling to her. After a moments consideration, she turned back to look deep into Darcienna's eyes. She smiled fondly on her student.

"It is time for me to return. We will talk again. Just know I am safe," she said as she gave Darcienna one last hug and then stepped back to the edge of the arch.

"I miss you," was all Darcienna could say.

"I miss you, too. Keep him safe," Jorell said as she cast a glance at Kade. "Even if it is from himself," she chided. The sadness Darcienna felt lifted slightly at her teacher's joke. She gave a chirp of a laugh. "And you take care of her," Jorell said to him as her smile waivered slightly. Kade got the feeling there was more in that warning than she was letting on. He opened his mouth to ask what it could be when Jorell held up a hand, forestalling any more questions. "Soon, Kade, soon enough you will understand."

As she stepped back, her smile faltered. Kade stopped as his mind captured the look on her face. It was worry that he saw in her eyes. *But, why worry?* he thought to himself as he glanced at Darcienna. *What did she not tell us?* he pondered as he turned slowly to see Darcienna staring after her teacher. He glanced back, eager to see his grandfather one last time, but the arch was empty. The vision of Jorell floated back into his mind.

CH8

"Thank you, Kade," Darcienna said as she wrapped her arms around him and hugged him tightly.

Had she seen the look in his eye, she would have been concerned and most likely would have forced him to confess his worries, but she didn't. His head was on her shoulder as he studied the arch. He replayed in his mind the last few seconds as Jorell faded from view. He was certain there was concern there.

Darcienna stepped back, and Kade hoped she would not see the worry. She smiled broadly as she turned to look at the arch one last time. Kade was deeply relieved. He did not want to upset her when she had finally found peace. This was her time to be happy. With all that she has gone through, he was not about to ruin it with what had to be just an overactive imagination.

The two walked up the tunnel without saying a word. Each was in their own thoughts as they pondered their recent interactions.

He replayed Zayle's words over and over in his head, and his chest swelled by the moment.

Adept, he thought to himself as the worry melted from his heart. I have to be the first Adept in decades. He could not remove the smile from his face as he exited the cave.

Kade looked around and flinched as a large, winged, black creature popped into existence as it flew directly at him. Spiders everywhere started to buzz wildly. His heart pounded hard several times as Ven shifted in the air, changing into the form of a monkey and then dove for him. The shapeshifter grabbed him around the neck as it landed squarely on his shoulder. Kade stumbled momentarily before getting his balance.

"Hello to you too, Ven," Kade said as he gave her a pat on the back with one hand and placed the other over his chest, feeling his pounding heart.

Kade turned to see Morg still trussed up tightly with no sign of his previous arrogance. Doren was studying the evil Chosen thoughtfully with his chin in his hand. For just a second, Kade felt a twinge of sympathy for Doren.

How can I blame him for wanting what I also found almost impossible to let go? Doren did play a huge role in helping us win the war. He took a breath, knowing he might regret this and then asked his question.

"So, how did you know that Morg would not be a threat?" Doren's mood improved slightly as he puffed out his chest. Kade could swear his head swelled as he watched.

"Would you mind releasing our prisoner?" Doren asked of Rakna. The white queen glanced at Kade. Before he could answer, Doren prompted her again. Kade took an uneasy breath and then shrugged his shoulders.

"As you wish," Rakna said as she easily bit through the webbing.

Morg stretched for several long moments as he worked the kinks out of his muscles. He kept his eyes hidden as a smile crept across his face. Kade got a sick feeling in his stomach as he took a step back. The Adept could feel Morg drawing deeply on the Divine, but for some reason that he could not fathom, Doren just stood and calmly stared at the man.

"Now you will pay!" Morg screamed as he spun into action. His arms flew out and then…he froze.

Doren smiled that smug smile of superiority as he feigned indifference. Morg stood for a very long time, unmoving. Kade felt his heart pounding like mad and realized he was holding the Blue Flame of the Divine in his hand. He looked from Doren to Morg and then back to Doren again, trying desperately to figure out what was going on.

Had Doren cast some sort of calling? Kade asked himself. No. He had not moved one inch. Doren turned casually to look at Kade with that condescending look and said, "He knows no callings. How can he? He has become so dependent on the staff that he has forgotten all that he has learned. He is as dangerous as any normal man, but no more. The only callings he will ever learn, from this point on, are the callings I let him learn," Doren said as he cocked an eyebrow at the man. Now, Morg had another crushing revelation bestowed upon him. He could feel the Divine, and yet, could not use it. This grown man sank to the ground as his knees buckled.

"You…intend on teaching him?" Kade asked incredulously, the blue flame fading away.

"I do not know what I plan on doing with him, but you can rest assured that he is no longer a threat. As soon as the staff was taken away, he had nothing to covet. We are no longer his enemy. And if we are, he will find his way to the other side quickly," Doren said in that elitist way of acting that only he had mastered. Morg's head came up quickly. "If he were a smart man," Doren said as he lorded himself over the broken Chosen, "he would know his best chance to escape the torture that awaits him is to work with us."

Kade shook his head. Never did he ever consider that this

man would be allowed to do anything other than suffer for what he has done. Kade just could not wrap his head around this new revelation. He wanted no part of it.

"Is that wise?" Rakna hissed, clearly displeased with Doren's plans.

"A dead man cannot atone for his sins. He must put right that which he has made wrong. He has decades of work to do. Morg was once a brilliant man, but he lost his way. He is still a Chosen," Doren said as he sighed.

Ven slid through his arms and shifted into her birth form at the same time. Kade took his hands off her waist and stepped back. He stopped and watched as she studied the man. For reasons he could not explain, he waited for her to speak, curious what she may say.

"He would not show you the same mercy, would he?" Ven growled.

"Might you have books of knowledge, somewhere?" Doren asked, heading this off before it could get to far. He appeared casual as he asked the question, but Kade knew there was nothing casual about the way he listened for the answer. Morg stood weakly as he took an unsteady breath.

"All gone. Burned up," he said as he cast a glance at Kade. Doren made a quick fist and then let it go.

"It was all destroyed when we escaped from the mountain," Kade said.

Doren closed his eyes and tilted his head back, giving off the air that to deal with such inferior people was torture. Kade rolled his eyes, looked at Darcienna and mouthed the words, "Kill me." Her hand shot to her mouth to stifle the laugh, but before it got there, she let out a squeak. Doren eyed them suspiciously.

"I think we should get back to the Great Hall," Kade said, changing the subject.

"Yes," Darcienna said as she turned and pulled him away.

Kade stopped as his eyes came open wide. There, not more

than a hundred yards away, was Rayden...lying next to the green. *They were getting to know each other quickly,* Kade thought.

"Rayden, we need to get back to the Great Hall," Kade yelled to his friend.

The dragon lazily got up, trotted over to Kade and laid down. The green followed but kept its distance from people and spiders alike. It appeared that Rayden was the only one it trusted.

"Kade, what about Morg?" Darcienna asked as they approached the dragon. Kade paused to look back at Doren and Morg.

"He is no longer our concern. If Doren wants to deal with him, then leave him," Kade said as he turned to his dragon. "Let's go."

"How is he going to get back to the Great Hall?" Darcienna asked as she glanced back at the two Master Chosen.

"We shall be coming with you," Doren said. Kade froze. He turned slowly to stare at Doren.

"Rakna, could you please secure Morg once again and then help him onto the dragon," Kade said firmly.

Doren might be the Master, but if he wanted a ride back to the Great Hall on his dragon, it was going to be under his rules. Doren sighed loudly, raised his finger in the air and spun it in three or four circles before letting it fall to his side. What that meant was beyond Kade's understanding, but he knew he did not like it. He turned back to Darcienna and she winced, feeling his frustration with the Master Chosen.

Rakna was more than happy to wrap Morg in her webbing once again, and she was none too gentle about it, either. It might have been a touch too tight, but Rakna was not about to loosen it. Ven eagerly changed to her monkey form and swung up to hang around Kade's neck. The Adept casually wrapped his arms around her without realizing that it had become a habit that took no thought. Darcienna glared at Ven but did not say a word.

The small group mounted and soon found themselves

soaring into the air. Kade looked back and saw the green close behind. He tapped Darcienna on the knee and motioned to the massive, flying beast. She turned and looked at it in surprise.

"You are the one who fed him," Darcienna said accusingly.

"By the great Divine," Kade said, as he thought about how much cooking he was going to have to do. He flexed his hand around the staff that was no longer there. He firmly resolved to figure out how to remove the block so he did not have to suffer through so much cooking. He glanced back at the green and wondered how much it would take to keep that one fed. Yes, he was definitely going to figure out how to remove the bock, even if it killed him.

They landed at the huge tree that the spiders called home. Each rider dismounted and worked their way into the Great Hall, looking forward to the feast. Kade and Darcienna continued through the expansive cavern and down the tunnel to their room. The Adept walked in and fell onto the bed as he let his mind slow. The room was quiet with the only sound being the babble of the spring just down the hall and around the corner.

Kade and Darcienna laid arm and arm for a while as they talked about the task of performing the last rights for Valdry or learning what had become of him. Kade was not particularly comfortable with going to the Master Chosen's home, but it had to be done. He was just going to have to be smart about it and watch for any traps.

Besides, there may be some books of knowledge there, he told himself. He froze, realizing he was thinking just like Doren. No, this would not do. He was not going to be hungry for knowledge to the point that it was all he thought about.

Look what happened to Morg with all the power he had, Kade thought critically. *No, there was more to life than the search for knowledge and power.*

After both felt they had had enough time to unwind, they got up, surveyed each other, seeming to notice how dirty they were for the first time and glanced around the room, hoping for a new set of clothes. Sure enough, there in the corner on a mat were freshly made outfits. They both picked up their shirts with matching pants and made their way to the spring, eager to be clean. Kade stopped as he studied the water, dreading the cold.

"Just get in," Darcienna said as her clothes started to hit the floor.

"Fine," Kade said, but it was clear he was not pleased. He was in and out of the water quickly.

The rest of the night was uneventful as they enjoyed the meal and the friendly interaction with the clutch. The other kings and queens had returned to their own trees with their own clutches. The night was relaxing, for the most part, with the exception of watching the queen suffer through her sorrow.

"Rakna is still upset with the loss of the king," Darcienna said as she urged Kade in her direction. The two approached the queen as she sat in her chair with the king's empty chair next to her.

"Can we help?" Darcienna asked gently.

"I do miss Crayken dearly," Rakna hissed softly as she looked at the throne to her left. "But...there is more. The link remains open. I will not be able to stop other kings from sensing me and coming," the queen said sadly. "Maybe our custom should be observed," she said with sincerity.

Darcienna gasped. She looked at Kade and tilted her head in the queen's direction, prompting him to say or do something to help. Kade racked his brain, trying to figure out a solution to this and failed. A sound off to his right caught his attention. He turned, and there sat Morg surrounded by six spiders. He was staring at the ground, his shoulders slumped. Kade glared, but Morg did not notice.

"Bond with her," Morg said again, almost too quietly to hear.

Darcienna turned to stare at Morg, gaping like a fish. She slowly closed her mouth and turned to look at Kade. The Adept

257

was just as shocked, but the glare faded from his eyes as he turned to look at the queen.

"How?" Darcienna asked as she took a step toward the man. Morg breathed in and then raised his head to make eye contact with her. He was still a broken man with no spark.

"He can bond with her and close the link," Morg said, still deeply depressed from his crushing defeat. No one spoke for a long time. Morg took another breath and then continued. "I was trapped in that bloody mountain for decades," he said as he attempted to cast a glare at Doren, but failed, empty of emotion. "I had plenty of time to do a lot of reading. One of the books I read was about the spiders. Forgive me," Morg said to the queen, "but it is how I knew that killing the king would destroy the clutch. I learned that in a book. I also learned that all she needs to do is bond again, and the link will close," he said as he turned his attention back to Darcienna.

"You are mad!" Kade said as he turned his back on Morg's babble and faced the queen.

"What are you talking about?" Darcienna asked as she started down the steps toward Morg. The Master Chosen sighed. Doren appeared, as if out of thin air, and stood off to the side, listening. Kade turned, irritated at Darcienna for even talking to the man. Kade's forgiveness was not going to come easy.

"Use the Divine and force the connection," Morg said simply.

"What does the Divine have to do with it?" Kade asked, contempt heavy in his voice. Morg flinched from the heat in his words.

"She uses the Divine but only in a very limited sense," Morg continued. Doren edged closer, curious. "How do you think she communicates with you?" Morg asked, amusement in his voice.

"The same as she does with anyone else," Kade said, hating himself for being drawn into this. He desperately did not want to accept any help from Morg, but he was not willing to let the queen suffer if there was a way for him to help her.

"Not so," Morg said as he eyed the queen. Kade gasped in exasperation. Morg locked eyes with Darcienna. "Does she speak to you in your mind?"

"Kade was right. This is a waste of time," Darcienna said as she turned to ascend the steps. "Speak in my mind? Bah," she said as she stopped next to Kade. She glanced at him and then did a double take. "What?" she asked.

"You have not heard her speak in your mind?" Kade asked and then turned to look at the queen.

"Kade?" Darcienna asked, confused. "I do hear her speak but...I hear it. Are you saying...?" she asked and then paused. Kade turned to look at Morg and then to the queen.

"Rakna. You have not spoken to Darcienna with your mind?" Kade asked as he tried to grasp what was happening.

"No, Chosen. Only with you and Doren. I can communicate with...him...if I choose," Rakna said as she cast a glance at Morg. "She is not one with the Divine so I must speak words for her to hear me." Kade's jaw hung open as he looked from the queen to Darcienna and then to Morg.

"It never occurred to me," Kade said in wonder. "I just assumed..." Kade took a moment to let this sink in and then clenched his jaw as he turned toward Morg. He hated that he had to ask, but if it meant helping the queen.... "How?"

"Force the link. It will be very painful for her, but it has been done with other queens in the past. Rarely is a king strong enough to actually make the connection, so the queen is usually put to death, but it is just the use of the Divine. If you force the link, it should work," Morg added.

"I believe I understand," Doren said as he stepped up. "When the queen makes contact, reach back through the link into her mind. You need to be filled with the Divine," Doren said as he cast a glance at Morg. Morg nodded in agreement.

"If it will help, then I am willing to try," Kade said. "Shall we try now?"

"Yes," Rakna hissed. All eyes turned on her.

"You would not prefer some time to prepare?" Darcienna asked, her voice full of compassion.

"It is best for the clutch if this were performed as soon as possible," Rakna hissed.

Kade felt her connect with him as she had done many times before. He closed his eyes and found that there was, indeed, a pathway back to her mind. He called on the Divine and started down the path, but before he could move halfway to the queen, he found so much resistance that he had to stop. He gasped and his eyes flew open.

"Did it work?" Darcienna asked quickly.

"No," Kade said as he steadied his breathing. He felt like he had been swimming up river against the current for hours.

"Kade," Doren said as he tilted his head back thoughtfully. "This may be why kings no longer try to bond with a queen that has been previously bonded," he said nonchalantly.

"Maybe if you focus and draw on more of the Divine?" Darcienna asked. Kade looked at her and she nodded her encouragement. He nodded once, took a deep breath and let it out.

"Let's try again," Kade said to the queen. She made contact almost immediately. Kade called on the Divine and started down the path once again. He opened himself up, trying to call on the unlimited supply of the Divine, but the block just did not want to budge. Kade struggled to the halfway point once more and found himself pushing against a current that was just too strong. He gasped and doubled over as he put his hands on his knees, breathing hard.

"Thank you for trying," the queen said, and the link was gone.

"Again," Kade growled as he forced himself to stand. The queen stood watching, unsure. "Again!" he said firmly. Rakna was uncertain if this was a command from the king or Kade being stubborn, but she did not resist.

"As you wish," Rakna said.

Kade closed his eyes and pulled at the Divine with all his might. He raced up the path, but there was still the resistance, and he was barely half way. He ground his teeth hard as he fought the tide. Inch by inch he struggled, but he hardly made any headway. He gasped again and fell to his knees. His muscles ached, as did his mind. His breathing was ragged. All eyes were on him, waiting for him to admit defeat.

"Again!" Kade said with heat in his words.

"Kade," Darcienna said as she got down on her knees next to him. "Maybe this was a bad idea. Maybe later when you have your strength back," she said, but one look in his eyes, and she knew it was useless to try to stop him.

"Again!" Kade commanded. There was no doubt that the king was speaking. Rakna made the connection easily enough, and Kade ground his teeth so hard that he was sure to crack them. Rage exploded in him. He hated the block and its ability to thwart him over and over. He wanted to crush it, and with that, he gripped the Divine as though it were the fiercest of creatures and turned it on the block. It shattered. The Divine filled him to overflowing. He grabbed ahold of it and slammed it into place as he forced his way against the current. The further he got, the stronger the current, and yet, he continued.

He could sense his goal was close as he clenched his fists into tight balls and shook under the effort. Closer yet. He could see thousands of rays of light coming off the queen in all directions.

This has to be what calls out to other kings, Kade thought as he steeled his will.

The current was pounding him, and yet, he continued to match it with even more Divine Power as he pushed on. His goal was now just out of reach...barely. The current was thunderous as he struggled. Just one more last step and he would be there, but he felt himself slip.

NO! he raged. He took a deep breath and called on even

261

more of the Divine. He put his head down, lunging against the current with everything, and then...the link snapped into place. In the blink of an eye, all rays of light swung together to lock onto Kade. The current disappeared completely, as if it never was. The queen wailed loudly; a sound that Kade had never heard before.

He fell onto his back, gasping. He gulped air hungrily as he struggled to breathe. His lungs were on fire, as if he had been under water for hours. The world was fading as blackness clouded his vision. After just a moment, he heard Darcienna's voice and felt her hands wrapped around his head. His vision cleared, and he looked up into her eyes.

"That's enough!" Darcienna said fiercely. "You almost passed out. You did your best now stop!"

"Kade," Ven said with worry. She had returned to her birth form and was wearing one of her form fitting outfits again. "You push yourself too far."

Doren was watching with deep curiosity. He had none of the concern that Darcienna or Ven had. It was only the quest for knowledge that had him involved. Kade closed his eyes and saw the link so strongly that he would have sworn there was a bright, blazing trail that should have easily been seen by the naked eye. But, when he opened his eyes, it was not there. He could feel the queen's emotions, and if he listened closely enough, could even hear her thoughts.

"You are right," Kade said as he struggled to stand on wobbly legs and moved over to the queen. "I am done trying," he said as he grinned weakly.

"I am guessing it worked," Doren said thoughtfully as he tilted his head this way and that way. Darcienna's head snapped back around to lock eyes with Kade. He smiled and nodded once.

"My king," Rakna said weakly, but Kade quickly cut her off and helped steady her.

"Please, just Kade for now. It is too soon," the Adept said as he felt his heart slowing.

"Kade," Rakna said. He could feel the relief through the link. "Thank you. You continue to save me over and over. I will never be able to repay you."

"Keep the arch safe, and that is payment enough," Kade said as he eyed the way to the bed chamber. Darcienna saw where he was looking and nodded in agreement. "We need some rest," Kade said as he turned to go. He was mentally and physically wore out.

He considered thanking Morg but he just could not bring himself to show that man gratitude. His mind recalled, very vividly, how Morg had used the staff to crush the life out of him. With a glance at the Chosen still sitting slumped over, he turned with Darcienna holding onto his arm and worked his way to his room. With a smile for Ven as she stood guard at the door, he and Darcienna slipped into their chamber.

It should have been a night of peacefulness as they stood victorious against their foes, but it was anything but. That night they both tossed and turned as nightmares assailed them over and over again. In one dream, Kade died violently as lightning exploded from every pore of his body. In another dream, Darcienna watched as Morg crushed the life out of the man she loved. The shield phased in and out around their bed throughout the night as she saved him over and over again. It would be a night of restless sleep.

CH9

Kade awoke to the sounds of life throughout the Great Hall. Neither he nor Darcienna felt very rested as they climbed out of bed. She ran her fingers through her hair as she attempted to make herself more presentable while Kade just mussed his hair and called it good. Darcienna rolled her eyes and pushed his hands away from his head while she did her best to flatten some of the more wild tufts. She shrugged her shoulders as if in defeat. Kade grinned in amusement as he turned and walked out the door with Darcienna close behind. Ven fell in behind the couple as they walked.

Kade and Darcienna entered the Great Hall. Ven had changed in to her beast form, which Kade was grateful for. Doren and Morg were talking quietly in a corner. Well…it was more like Doren was doing all the talking, and Morg was doing all the listening. The beaten Chosen was still an empty shell of what he used to be, but he was looking better, even if just slightly.

Doren turned to watch as Kade and Darcienna entered the room. Several spiders skittered over to usher the two to a table that was set with so much food it would be impossible for them to eat even half of it. Kade knuckled his eyes to rub the final bit of sleep out and then lazily sat. Darcienna followed suit.

"We will be going to Valdry's home to perform the last rights," Kade said to Doren. "Then, most likely, returning to my parents' place in the country."

"I shall wait here until you are finished with Valdry," Doren said casually.

"And then?" Kade asked, feeling his appetite fading.

"And then go with you to meet your parents, of course," Doren said plainly. "I should know where to go in the event that I need to find you."

Kade turned cold. The very idea that Doren would even consider letting Morg anywhere near his parents almost pushed him over the edge. He turned his eyes on Morg and glared, his appetite gone instantly. Doren sighed as he caught the look.

"Morg will be staying here under the watchful eyes of the spiders," Doren said. Morg gave no reaction. Somewhat mollified, Kade gave Darcienna a look that very plainly said, "I am not pleased."

"We shall be back soon…as long as we do not parish from any traps," Kade said, still unhappy with the situation. He shook his head and refocused on his task. *If Valdry has as many traps as Zayle…,* Kade thought as he recalled the demon from the book. He left the thought unfinished.

Doren stopped what he was doing as something occurred to him and opened his mouth to speak, but Kade spoke first. "We are going alone," Kade said firmly, easily anticipating Doren's motives for wanting to join them. He was surprised it took Doren this long to wonder what secrets Valdry might have. The Master Chosen let his shoulders sag momentarily and then turned back to continue his talk with Morg. *It was good not being an apprentice,* Kade thought.

But, he still knew that he had to be cautious with how he interacted with the Master Chosen. There were still lines that should not be crossed as an Adept.

After eating very little, the couple left the tree and stopped as they took in the sight of both dragons. Rayden flooded the link with joy at seeing his friend. The green stood and watched warily, as the couple started toward them. The familiar feeling of hunger assailed him through the link. Kade smiled, sure that his feedings were going to be much more acceptable. He had not tried his gift since the previous night, but he was certain there was a change.

Kade planted his feet and squared his shoulders. He could not keep the grin from spreading as he prepared to call on his special gift that was unique to just him. He reached for the Divine and found…that the block was gone. He opened himself up and felt connected to the world. The power was exhilarating.

No one can stand in my way, he thought as he drank in the feeling. He realized where his thoughts were going and felt bats in his stomach. The world spun momentarily as his eyes flew open. *Power corrupts,* he reminded himself as he tried to erase the thought from his mind. *I am not going to turn into Morg,* he told himself vehemently. Darcienna saw the look in Kade's eyes and tilted her head at his as if to ask, "What?"

"Just hoping this works," Kade said. Darcienna smiled. Kade felt a twinge of guilt for lying to her, but if she knew what just went through his mind, a seed of doubt about his humanity may begin to grow.

Kade closed his eyes and started through the moves. He pictured a large, steaming chunk of meat and felt it fall through his hands to hit the ground with a thud. Darcienna clapped her hands excitedly and ran up to wrap her arms around his neck. He smiled broadly as he returned the hug.

How could a man not love a woman who is so supportive? Kade thought as he looked deeply into her eyes. His heart filled with the image of her.

266

"What?" Darcienna asked with a gleam in her eye. She was still beaming.

"I was just thinking how much I love you," Kade said as he felt his heart swell. "Even to say I love you does not do justice for what my heart feels."

His brief, romantic moment was interrupted as a burning craving for the food blazed through the link. Kade looked up and saw that the dragon's eyes were locked onto the meat. The green was also staring eagerly but still stood its distance.

"Well," Kade said as he smiled at Rayden. "Eat," he said as he indicated the meat. Rayden practically pounced on the food, as if it were about to escape, and tore into it. He ripped huge chunks off and chewed eagerly, enjoying the large mouthfuls. The silver dragon closed its eyes and savored the taste as the juices slid down its throat in large quantities. The link was filled with pure pleasure. Kade could not help but to laugh deeply as he watched his dragon enjoying its morning meal.

The smell filled the air so much so that Doren and his new apprentice came out of the tree. As much as they tried to feign uncaring, it was clear that the smell of the fresh cooked meat was making their stomachs rumble. *Sometimes, the simplest callings are the most powerful*, Kade thought with a grin. *Two Chosen Masters at the mercy of an Adept.*

"Stay here," Kade said to Ven as he pointed at the spot where she was standing.

The green looked between the food, Rayden and Kade as it fidgeted eagerly. Its nose worked furiously as it started to salivate. It edged closer and then quickly retreated, still not trusting the man. Kade smiled and marched straight at the green. The massive dragon watched intently as Kade approached. Its nostrils flared and it huffed, but Kade continued to walk without any signs of slowing. Rayden stopped chewing, and Kade could feel irritation flood the link. Kade smiled and let out a laugh as he cast a glance at his friend.

"You worry too much," Kade said as he confidently continued toward the green. The dragon's wings twitched as Kade closed the distance.

"Kade," Darcienna said, irritation showing in her voice.

The Adept continued on, pretending not to hear. Darcienna gave a huff as she ran to his side. She flexed her fingers and rubbed her palms on her pants. Kade glanced at her and could not help but to laugh again.

"You are not funny," she said in all seriousness. This, of course, caused him to laugh even more. She glared at him but then turned her focus on the massive dragon.

Green's lips twitched as Kade approached. Rayden grabbed the huge chunk of meat in his mouth and quickly bounded after Kade, who was almost to the green. The monstrous dragon backed up as its muscles flexed. Kade stopped and closed his eyes.

Maybe it was good Darcienna came, Kade thought. He did not realize how unpleasant it would be to shut his eyes while this close to such a deadly creature. But, even still, he would not have changed what he did.

Kade reached for the Divine and could not help but to enjoy the feeling as it filled his mind and soul…but not his heart. That belonged to Darcienna. *Maybe that would be enough to keep me on the right path,* Kade thought, and then, he was on to making the meat. It hit the ground with a thud. Some of the juice from the meat splattered against his legs. Kade opened his eyes and watched as the dragon locked onto the food. Kade backed up slowly, step by step as he watched the green.

Rayden plopped his meat down next to this freshly prepared food and continued to tear it apart. Kade turned and smiled at him as he continued to move back. The irritation that was previously in the link was gone, replaced with contentment.

The green crouched to the ground as if it were stalking the meat. It flinched back slightly, causing Kade to let out a burst of laughter. This incredibly deadly creature was not crouching to hunt but crouching to flee if the meat so much as twitched.

Fear of the unknown, Kade thought. Rayden stopped chewing as a piece of meat hung from his mouth and turned to watch the green. The silver dragon made a guttural sound around the food. The green glanced at Rayden and then move up to the meat. It sniffed rapidly and then a tongue came out to taste it. Satisfied, it took a small bite, but Kade could see it was only moments before it would be tearing hungrily into the food.

"We can let them eat, and then we will go," Kade said as he walked back to the tree.

"You know that was not very smart," Darcienna said but there was no strength to her words.

"Nothing as intelligent as a dragon bites the hand that feeds it," Kade said as he glanced over his shoulder. "Especially dragons who love to eat," he said as he chuckled.

"I see the dragons are well fed," Doren said as he stood with his arms behind his back.

It appeared that not all were content with just fruits and vegetables. Kade knew the feeling as neither he nor Darcienna ate much themselves. Kade stopped and made a piece of meat. He handed it to Doren and paused, not allowing himself to even so much as to glance at Morg. He clenched his jaw and closed his eyes. He made another piece, but this one was not quite as large. He opened his eyes and handed this one to Doren, also. Kade could not watch as Doren turned and handed the smaller piece to Morg. As humbled as Morg was, Kade still could not find compassion in his heart for the man. It was going to take a lot to convince him that the man he knew deep, down inside, was no longer there. He ignored the men and turned to watch the dragon. Both Master Chosen moved over and sat with their backs to the tree as they ate.

"Do you know where Valdry's place is?" Darcienna asked.

"I do. His name was in the black book, so I should have no problem finding it," Kade said as he felt the muscles in his back slowly unknot.

"Good," Darcienna said and then turned to look at him. "Now, how about making me some of that?" she asked casually.

"I am such an ox," Kade said as he instantly forgot about everything to focus on her. "I am so sorry. I did not even think to ask," he said as he quickly conjured the food. He handed it to her and smiled as she sank her teeth in and took a bite.

It did look good, he thought as he conjured a piece for himself. Kade and Darcienna moved to the opposite side of the tree from the masters and sat with their backs against the tree.

There wasn't a person or animal that did not find immense pleasure in Kade's cooking. No one spoke as they devoured the tasty, mouthwatering food. Well...no one but Doren. The Master Chosen appeared to love to hear himself talk. After finishing their food, Doren and Morg made their way into the tree. Doren was lecturing at great lengths and Morg was trudging behind with his head down.

Serves him right, Kade thought, but he could not help but to feel just a little pity for Morg. *The threat of having to listen to Doren's prattle alone would be enough to keep me from turning into an evil Chosen,* he thought.

Kade waited for Rayden to finish his food and then called to him. The dragon trotted over and laid down. He and Darcienna mounted. Before he could give Rayden the signal to go, Ven changed into her monkey form and swung up to hang on Kade's neck. He put his hand on her back and held her in place. Darcienna tensed just slightly and then relaxed.

"Hold on," Kade said as he gripped the dragon's ridges tightly.

Be safe, Rakna said in his mind so clear that it was as if she were standing right next to him. Kade flinched, not yet accustomed to this close contact. But, it was something he had to get used to. Never again was he going to be alone. He never fathomed it would be a spider queen that would keep him company, but it was not as bad as he might have feared. As a matter of fact, he found it surprisingly pleasant.

The dragon turned and then turned back as if missing the direction it wanted to go. Kade and Darcienna shifted rapidly, and Kade almost lost his balance. His eyes half-lidded in suspicion as he felt amusement drift through the link.

Keep it up, Kade thought to himself as he started to plot his revenge. *Just keep it up.* And with that, they launched into the air. The green was close on their tail but soon moved up to fly just off Rayden's right wing. Kade looked over to see the green eyeing him and Darcienna. Again, there was amusement coming through the link from Rayden. This time, Kade smiled along.

Several hours later they landed outside an elaborate home that rivaled Doren's. Kade thought back on the shack he used to live in and wondered, for just a moment, why? As soon as he asked himself the question, he had the answer. Zayle wanted to keep him safe, and the best way to do that was to make sure that they were not noticed. Elaborate mansions had a way of drawing attention sooner or later.

Ven leapt into the air, and before she landed, had transformed into the beast. She hit the ground hard with a heavy thud. Kade smiled, grateful for another set of eyes. He stood surveying the house and the countryside. It was quiet with only the sound of the wind. He could not figure out if it was calming or eerie. With a shrug, he turned for the house.

Kade walked to the mansion and closed his eyes. The Reveal Calling showed nothing. He walked in the door that was just barely hanging on its hinges. The place was a disaster. Kade got the feeling that it was not a battle that caused this damage but the ravings of a mad man destroying just to destroy. Curiously, there was no blood or bodies anywhere, and there were no callings active set as traps…that Kade could see. This made him nervous. It made him very nervous.

Kade worked his way through the house to the den. He closed his eyes and used the Reveal Calling. There was just a slight haze hanging in the air. Kade studied it closely. It appeared to be like a very thin mist. He opened his eyes and could not shake the feeling of being watched. He prepared to enter the room when a flash of black caught his attention out of the corner of his eye. He turned his head, expecting to see Chance. There was nothing. He turned back to walk into the room when he flinched as an insect almost two inches long buzzed right by his ear and flew through the doorway. Kade watched as its wings stopped their frantic motion and slowed to barely moving. Then, just several feet into the room, they stopped completely. He turned to look down the hall again, as he thought of his silky, black friend. He shook it off and turned back to the bug that was suspended in flight. By all laws of nature, it should have fallen to the floor, and yet, it stayed up as if it were floating. Darcienna walked up and put her hand on his shoulder as she readied to brush past, but Kade's arm shot out to bar the way.

"What?" Darcienna asked, confused.

"Look," Kade said as he pointed to the insect. Darcienna leaned forward just slightly as she focused on the bug.

"What is it doing?" she asked as she tilted her head. "It's...stuck."

"Yes," Kade said as he studied the chamber. As he was examining the room, he froze, making eye contact with an old man sitting in a plush, high-backed, winged chair. The man appeared to be very much alive. There was some sort of disturbance in the air half way between the door and the man.

"Kade," Darcienna said, as she looked from the man back to the Adept.

"I know," Kade said as he studied the disturbance in the air and then the man again.

Kade turned and searched the hallway for anything lying loose. His eyes fell on a broken vase that had been shattered against a wall. He bent and picked up a large piece. He turned and tossed it into the room. It quickly stopped in midflight as if something had caught it and were holding it motionless.

"Is he still alive?" Darcienna asked in awe.

"Not if that gets to him," Kade said as he pointed to the disturbance. He knew what it was instantly, and everything made sense. Time in this room was frozen. Morg had tried to get to Valdry but the Master Chosen was able to escape by either stopping time or slowing it so much that it was not perceptible.

"He was trying to trap Morg with this," Kade said as he recalled how Doren had laid a trap of his own. Now he understood why there were no callings set as traps throughout the house. Valdry wanted Morg to find him. Another plan that had been carefully crafted that ended in failure.

"What can we do?"

"For now...nothing," Kade said as he marveled at the deviousness of the trap. The man had a definite look of calm, calculating intelligence. It was eerie looking into his eyes. But, when Kade moved from left to right, the eyes did not move with him. "He is safe...for now," Kade said as he turned to look at Darcienna. "But, no one must know. I trust no one but Zayle. When we visit the arch again, I will figure out what can be done. Maybe with the staff I can save him," Kade said as his hands clenched around the non-existent, ancient piece of wood. He felt a warm flush run up his back and bats fluttered in his stomach for just a moment.

"So we do nothing?" Darcienna asked incredulously. "Maybe Doren can help," Darcienna said as she stared helplessly at the man.

"NO!" Kade barked so strongly that Darcienna flinched. "Doren...thirsts for knowledge first above all else," Kade said firmly as he recalled how Doren had tried to get his hands on the staff. Kade's eyes shifted to the bookshelf and then back to Darcienna. "No. If all else fails, then we bring him into it, but for now, Valdry is safe," Kade said as he turned her toward him. "This location is secure enough that it won't be found by accident, and anything that gets in that room will not be able to get to him," he said and then turned his attention back to the Master Chosen. "It is impossible for anything to get to him unless he allows it."

Satisfied that they had learned what they needed, the two quickly left the house, eager to be on their way. Ven was close behind in her female shape. She had shifted into her birth form sometime during their walk through the house. *Seeing as it was safe, why not?* Kade asked himself.

The Adept helped Darcienna onto the dragon and then leapt up himself. Ven changed into her monkey form and swung up to hang on him. Kade gave one glance over his shoulder at the grand home and then signaled Rayden to take to the air. The silver and green dragons took their time as they flew back to the tree. Kade was eager to see his parents again, but he was also grateful for not having to race off to save the world.

"How did it go?" Doren asked as Kade was jumping down from the dragon.

"As well as expected. As a matter of fact, it was better than I expected," Kade said.

"Find anything?" Doren asked as he scanned Kade for any hidden books.

"Nothing. It would take an eternity to find anything in there," Kade said as he headed for the Great Hall. Morg gave a smirk. Kade glared daggers at him and the smirk melted away. Kade mouthed, "Not a word," just as Doren was turning around. He paused as he looked from Morg to Kade and then cocked an eyebrow.

"The Adept cannot stand to have me around. If I were him, I would feel the same way. As a matter of fact," Morg said as he cast a glance at Kade, "I would have killed me already," he said, his eyes dropping back to the ground. With a last sneer, Kade ushered Darcienna toward the tree. When they were far enough from the two Chosen Masters, Darcienna whispered to Kade.

"What do you make of that?"

"He would have told Doren already if he was going to,"

Kade said roughly. He was not about to give Morg any leeway whatsoever.

When Kade entered the Great Hall, he was shocked to see that it was filled from wall to wall with spiders. There were even some hanging on the ceiling. It was obvious that they were here to see him off. He was their king and they were his clutch now, but they had to be his clutch at a distance. He just could not stay here, but still, it was not going to be easy to leave them behind.

Kade gave a heartfelt speech to the spiders and they cheered him on. Darcienna moved back while the queen took her place at his side. Ven was always just behind, keeping watch over him. It was more difficult to say goodbye than Kade expected, but alas, he found himself outside and ready to go. He knew that if he did not leave soon, he would arrive at his parents' well after dark.

"Doren, are you sure it is safe to leave him here alone?" Kade asked skeptically.

"He is no danger beyond what a normal man can do," Doren said patiently. "You will be in constant contact with the queen, so we will know if he misbehaves. And besides," he said in his superior way of talking. "If he does not behave, he will never learn another calling again," the Master Chosen said as he leveled his gaze at Morg. The evil Master Chosen wilted right before Kade's eyes.

"It is on you if something goes wrong," Kade said roughly. Doren turned cold and gave him a glare that froze him to the spot. "My apologies," Kade said meekly. Yes, there was still a line he had to be aware of. "He is dangerous, and I am not about ready to trust him as far as I can throw him, Master Chosen Doren," Kade said, using the full title to mollify him. It helped considerably. "You have no idea what that man did to me or my family," he added, gaining much of his conviction back.

"Kade, if you prefer me to stay," Doren said.

"No," Kade said, holding up his hand in surrender. "I am certain my parents would love to meet you, and my mother can cook like no other, "he said resignedly.

"Then let us get underway," Doren said with a smile. Kade paused, not recalling ever seeing a smile on the man's face.

"I hope I don't regret this," Kade whispered into Darcienna's ear. She shrugged her shoulders, but it was obvious she shared his concerns.

"Keep a close eye on him," Kade said to Rakna. *And use whatever force you must,* Kade sent through the link. He marveled at how crisp and clear the communication was when contacting the queen with his mind.

"As you wish," Rakna hissed eagerly.

Six spiders dropped from the tree instantly to surround Morg. They bared their venom coated fangs, each one appearing eager to sink them deep into the man's flesh. Kade felt immensely better immediately. He gave Morg a smile. The man shrugged easily as if it was nothing to concern him. Kade truly got the feeling that these six spiders, each of which could bring down a grown man without hardly any effort, really did not bother him. Regardless, it was peace of mind for himself.

"Let's go," Kade said as he turned toward the silver dragon.

"Give me a moment," Rakna said as she quickly climbed onto Rayden's back. The dragon shivered and eyed Rakna as she worked webbing at the base of the dragon's wings. *He will feel none of this,* she said with her mind as she continued to spin her web until she had a type of sling for Doren to lean back into. The Master Chosen smiled gratefully as he recognized what the queen was building. She continued to weave as she worked her way forward. Rakna stopped and buzzed at several spiders in the tree. They dropped down and joined her. It was all Rayden could do to hold still while the spiders worked on him.

Kade watched in wonder and awe as a basic saddle with comfortable padding took shape. He grinned as he watched Rayden grow stiff as the spiders worked their way around him. His smile broadened as he plotted a little revenge for his friend.

"I am sure Rayden would not mind a few more spiders helping," Kade said innocently. Rayden flinched as several more spiders dropped down to start crawling all over the dragon, spinning their web. Kade laughed out loud as the dragon swung its head around to glare at him. Kade raised his brows and feigned innocence.

"Not very nice," Darcienna whispered.

"He deserves it," Kade said as he patted the dragon affectionately on the neck. "Thank you, my friend," he said as he eyed the rigging. He was eager to test out the new setup. Rayden settled down and allowed the spiders to finish, but he never fully relaxed.

"That harness should keep you safe," Rakna hissed. "We cannot take a chance with our king's life," she finished.

"You will take care of the clutch while I am away," Kade said as he affectionately put his hand on her shoulder. "Use your judgment and do what you feel is best. You have my full support," he said with a smile. The link between them hummed with genuine affection.

Having this connection with Rakna was not a bad thing at all, Kade thought. He smiled and turned toward the dragon.

"Time to go?" Darcienna asked as she inspected the rigging.

"Time to go," he affirmed as he readied to mount.

Kade gently helped Doren climb up into his seat. The backrest flowed in the wind but held firmly when Doren leaned into it. Kade knew it would hold no matter the amount of weight put against it. Next, he helped Darcienna up and then climbed on himself. The padding was a relief compared to the firm ridges of the dragon's spine. He reached down and picked up a pair of straps that ran to the dragon's chest to connect with the harness. Having these to hold onto was going to make things much more secure feeling. He leaned left and right, putting his booted feet into makeshift stirrups. He smiled as he looked over the setup. He leaned back just as Ven leapt up to land in his lap. He put his hand on her back and held her firmly, ready for the dragon's launch.

"I think it's time we test this out," Kade said as he gave Rayden the mental command to go. He gave a huge wave to the spiders just as the dragon turned and launched into the air. It pumped its wings hard and gained altitude quickly.

Kade looked back and was not surprised to see the green close by. He smiled to himself, eager to see the shocked look on his parents' face when he landed with another dragon. Rayden was impressive as it was, but this massive dragon was going to have their jaws on the ground.

They casually flew, enjoying the sun on their faces and the calm of the quietness. Only the sound of the wind could be heard. Occasionally one of the dragons would grunt or communicate back and forth but no other sound reached them.

They stopped once to rest and stretch their legs. They even enjoyed Kade's fine cooking. Doren would not admit how much he was impressed with the food, but Kade could see the pleasure on his face as he bit into the cheese, or when he chewed the freshly baked bread. The Master Chosen was definitely a lover of good food and it showed in the size of his waist. Kade even fed both dragons but made sure not to over feed Rayden as he was sure the dragon would eat until its stomach burst. It was not long before they were in the air and chatting calmly. They continued like this for the rest of the flight. A short time later, they glided in to land in front of the cabin.

"This is my parents' place," Kade called back to Doren as he leapt to the ground.

Darcienna swung her legs over and slid down on her belly while holding onto the rigging. Ven changed into her birth form and stepped up close to Kade. Darcienna glared at Ven as she moved to stand on Kade's right side.

Garig came out holding a club in his hands, ready to bash in skulls until he saw the silver dragon. He grinned hard as his eyes locked onto his son. Judeen came out close behind with a crying child in her arms. She was doing her best to console him, but the boy continued to wail.

Darcienna smiled broadly as she raced up to take Marcole in her arms. She walked back down the steps to stand next to Kade as she bounced the boy and whispered to him, trying to get him to calm. Marcole leaned toward Kade and put his arms out. Darcienna looked at the boy in confusion and then handed him over. The child quickly calmed down as he tightly wrapped his arms around Kade's neck, refusing to let go anytime soon. Kade glanced from Darcienna to the boy and then back again. Instead of being upset, as Kade expected, she smiled and patted her child on the back.

"Are you going to introduce me, or do I need to instruct you on better manners?" Doren asked dryly. Kade looked at Darcienna and rolled his eyes.

"Mother, Father, I would like to introduce the Master Chosen, Doren. He was instrumental in our fight against Morg," Kade said as he held a hand out to indicate the Chosen. Doren gave a slight bow with his head. "And these are my parents, Judeen and Garig. And this is Dran, the one with the knife." As if to make the introduction more dramatic, Dran whisked his knife out, flipped it around daftly and then slammed it back into the sheath.

"Master Doren, you are welcome in our home," Judeen said as she stepped off the porch.

"Yes, welcome to our home," Garig said with a slight bit of mistrust or possibly dislike, as he walked down the steps to stand with his wife. "I am sure you have much to tell," he said excitedly to Kade while cautiously looking at the only other Master Chosen he had ever met besides Zayle. Kade was relieved beyond describing that his father showed none of the previous apprehension toward him.

"We do, Father. Wait until you hear what I have to tell you," Kade said, eager to expound on their adventures and happy his father was genuinely making him feel welcome.

Kade turned to face his mother and saw a flat, very

displeased look on her face. She locked eyes with him to make sure she had his attention and then shifted her gaze to the very beautiful girl standing close to him. Kade realized what was going on and quickly whispered to Ven.

"Change form."

She did as was instructed. Judeen's hand shot up to cover a gasp as Garig gripped the club tightly. Dran froze for barely an instant before the knife sprang from its sheath, singing as the steel rang out with the promise of death. Kade's eyes went wide as he quickly glanced to his left and saw Vell. He did a double take and then stepped in front of her, cringing, expecting to feel the thunk of Dran's knife at any second. The memory of Man-boy flashed through his mind. Darcienna also screamed as her arms came up in a flash. The shield came to life.

"No!" Kade yelled as he raised his hands. "No. She is with me!" he said frantically. "Do not hurt her!" he said as their jaws hit the ground.

No one moved for several long seconds. Dran still held the blade over his head, his muscles twitching, eager to let the deadly blade fly. Judeen had climbed the steps to stand on the porch. Garig glared hard at the shapeshifter, his shoulders hunched, ready for battle.

"She will not hurt you," Kade said, and with that, all eyes looked at him in confusion. Dran slowly lowered his arm and Garig glanced back and forth between Vell and Kade. Judeen continued to stare in horror.

"She?" Dran asked.

"Yes. Her name is Ven," Kade said as he whispered for her to change back into her birth form. "This is who she really is," he said as he moved just slightly over so they could get a better look at her. Kade reached for Darcienna's arms and pulled them down, causing the shield to fade. He saw the disapproving look on his mother's face and glanced over to see Ven in one of her form fitting outfits. He cringed, wanting to hit himself in the forehead with his palm.

I just can't win, Kade thought to himself as he wilted under his mother glare. He was thinking it might have been better to leave her as Vell. "Mother," Kade said firmly, a slight edge to his voice. He reached over and took Darcienna's hand to make his point. Regardless, he knew he needed to have a talk with Ven about her choice of outfits.

"Yes. Very well then," Judeen said as she relaxed ever so slightly.

"I am ok with her," Dran said as he started to grin. "I mean…if Kade says she is ok, then, who am I to disagree?" he asked, not taking his eyes off the ever so beautiful, Ven. Kade glared hard and moved to stand back in front of her again.

"Dran, I really don't care for the arrangement you have with your wife," Judeen scolded. The knife wielding man casually shrugged his shoulders.

Kade recalled how quickly Darcienna had rushed to protect Ven and gave her a sly grin. Darcienna continued to stare straight ahead for several seconds until she could no longer pretend not to see his smile. She glared at him.

"I was only returning the favor," Darcienna said. "She did save my life," she said with a huff.

"Oh, just admit that you are okay with her."

"She has been useful," Darcienna said. Kade grinned once more and left it at that.

Before Kade could say another word, there was a loud groan from behind him as Rayden dropped to the ground. The dragon moaned pitifully as its eyes half closed. Kade could sense misery through the connection.

"What is wrong?" Kade asked as he walked up and looked Rayden in the eye. The dragon lay there, waiting for the misery to pass. Before he could say another word, Darcienna groaned and leaned into a bush. Kade looked back and forth between Darcienna and Rayden and then at Doren. "What is going on?" he asked, concern in his voice. "A calling?"

"Oh no. Nothing like that. It is only that of nature," Doren said as he studied the dragon.

Kade looked at the Master Chosen and then back to the dragon. Doren noticed Kade's confusion and took on the air of a teacher who calls on his infinite patience to teach a student who is slow on the uptake. As he spoke, he put just a bit of a pause between each word as if to make sure what he said was understood. Kade felt the temptation to fill with the Divine.

It would serve him right, Kade thought and then cut off his connection to the power.

"Your dragon is going to have a pup," Doren said as he ran his hands over the dragon's belly.

"How can Rayden have a pup. It's not possible for him to do that," Kade argued. Doren stopped rubbing the dragon's belly and turned to study Kade, uncertain if the Adept Chosen was serious or if he really did not understand. Kade felt exasperation as Doren continued to force himself to be patient. The condescending attitude was almost too much to bear.

"Yes SHE can," Doren said as he grinned. Kade just stared with his mouth gaping like a fish. "Rayden is a female," Doren said, enjoying Kade's surprise just a little too much.

Kade's mind raced and then everything made sense. When Rayden realized that Ven was a female, she was not as angry. He had felt her relax, but it just did not stand out enough to get his attention at the time. It was when he thought back on Rayden's interaction with the green that it became obvious. The dragons were not fighting when they first met. Rayden was giving the green a thorough dressing down. The green and Rayden were not circling each other. It was Rayden who was circling the green as she gave him the tongue lashing of his life. And, when the green tried to back down, she stalked him as he struggled to find escape. It all made sense why a dragon that large would cringe in the presence of one considerably smaller. He glanced at Darcienna for just a moment and fully understood the green's plight.

"A female," Kade said, stunned. "I always thought…,"

"Well, you thought wrong," Doren said, cutting him off.

As if on cue, the green dropped in from out of the sky. Judeen and Garig called out a warning to Kade and Dran had his knife back out, ready to throw once more. Not that the green would have even noticed, but it was something Dran did out of instinct.

The green slowly moved closer to Rayden and inhaled her scent several times before settling in next to her. It was beginning to accept people, but nothing was going to come between the beautiful, silver dragon and itself. Kade looked at the green suspiciously as the pieces of the puzzle started to fall into place. Doren saw the look and grinned.

"Yes. Meet the father of the pup," Doren said.

Kade recalled when they had first come to the cabin. *The roar off in the distance,* Kade thought. *You did not want to run off and play,* he thought as he looked deep into the golden eye. *You wanted to run off and…*

"So, you are going to have a pup, eh?" Kade asked, as he scratched Rayden's jaw. "This is definitely going to be interesting," he said as he cast a glance at the green. "And you better take good care of her," he said, scolding the larger dragon. The green watched him wearily but did not show any signs of understanding a word.

"You are going to have your hands full," Doren said as he chuckled. This was another first for Kade. He was starting to believe that Doren did not have the ability to laugh, until now. "A pup and two kids to raise is going to be quite a lot of work," the Chosen said as he walked up and patted Marcole on the head. The child seemed to scowl slightly. "Your boy does have your likeness," he said as he turned to walk toward the house.

"Oh, he is Darcienna's," Kade said, correcting the Master Chosen. Doren stopped and slowly turned as he narrowed his eyes and studied the boy. He tilted his head as if listening to something and then slowly approached the child. He closed his eyes and Kade could sense the Divine being drawn in. He then opened his eyes and went to place his hands over the boy. Kade turned away slightly, unsure of what the Chosen was doing.

"Hold still," Doren commanded.

Kade hesitated momentarily but then held. Doren placed his hand over the boys head without touching him. He then raised his hand to hold it over Kade's head. After a moment he turned and did the same thing over Darcienna's head. He grinned as he looked at Kade. Next, he looked at the boy one more time and then back at Kade, nodding. The Adept Chosen looked over at Darcienna and noticed she was fidgeting as she suddenly seemed very interested with something in the dirt.

"But...I don't have any children," Kade protested weakly.

"Hmmmmm. Well, according to my calling, both the born and unborn child are yours," Doren said as he studied Darcienna.

Kade gasped loudly at that one. The world was spinning wildly out of control. He put his hand on Rayden to steady himself, certain his knees were going to give out.

"Unborn child?" Kade choked.

He felt as if the wind had been knocked out of him. He turned to look at Darcienna, again, and froze as he watched as the red in her cheeks intensified. He struggled to find words, but his mind was reeling. He looked at his parents, but there was to be no help found there. They were standing, arm in arm as they grinned at him and gave each other knowing looks.

Kade felt as if he were caught in the middle of an avalanche. He gaped as he struggled to make sense of it all. After regaining just a bit of composure, he moved over to stand next to Darcienna.

"But how?" Kade asked quietly, even though all could still hear.

"Do you need that clarified for you, also?" Doren asked dryly.

"I will explain," Darcienna said, her cheeks glowing just a little more.

"I can't wait to hear this one," Kade said as he looked at Marcole again, as if he were seeing the boy for the first time. "How long have you known?" he asked as he craned his neck, trying to make eye contact with her.

"Since the day you first came to my cabin. I didn't recognize you until after you got cleaned up," Darcienna said as she cast a quick glance at his parents and then back to the ground. Kade recalled seeing that look of recognition in her eyes. It made sense. She HAD known all this time.

"It was you," Kade said, as he recalled a flash of memory from that night almost two years ago. "You were that beautiful girl I could not remember. Your hair was up, and you wore a dress, but it was you," Kade said as the memories fell into place. "But, wait," he said suspiciously as his eyes drifted down toward her stomach. How...?" Kade started to ask while indicating the baby on the way. "It has only been days." Kade cringed as he recalled his parents were hearing every word he was saying.

"I can explain that, too," Darcienna said as she took him by the hand and dragged him to the side of the house.

"It would appear that our young couple have much to discuss," Doren said, clearly amused by this.

"You snuck into my roommmpphh?" Kade started to say when his words were quickly muffled.

"Keep your voice down," Darcienna hissed, "or do I need to keep my hand where it is?"

The two whispered for several long minutes while Kade's parents, Dran, the shapeshifter and Doren waited patiently. There was a long stretch of silence, and then the couple came around the side of the house, hand-in-hand. Kade blushed furiously as all eyes watched them.

"Mom, Dad, meet Marcole, my son. And oh, by the way, I am going to have another baby boy in about eight months," Kade said, glancing at Darcienna and then back to his parents again.

"Or a girl," Darcienna corrected.

"Or a girl," Kade echoed.

His parents beamed with happiness and hugged them both, making it known that Darcienna was very welcome. She hugged them back and then returned to stand arm-in-arm with Kade. Dran was eagerly talking with Ven, again, as she stood in her birth form. Kade shook his head and reminded himself to give Dran a good thorough talking to. The Adept considered having her change into her beast form. The surprised look he pictured on Dran's face brought a smile to his lips. Yes, he would save that prank for later.

Judeen and Garig ushered the couple up the steps and toward the door. Doren followed close by, looking very forward to a good home-cooked meal and a comfortable bed. Kade smiled, seeing his suspicions validated for the Master Chosen's motivation for coming. As they started to enter the cabin, Darcienna stopped and motioned for Kade to continue.

"I will be in shortly," Darcienna said as she gave him a gentle push through the door.

"Don't be too long," Kade said as his father clapped him on the back and excitedly encouraged Kade to tell the story from the very start.

They entered the house, and just as Kade was passing his room, something caught his attention out of the corner of his eye. He took a step back and leaned around the corner to look into the room. He could not help but to laugh a genuine, deep laugh as he stared. There, lying on the bed, curled protectively around a sack of books, was Chance. The silky, black creature lifted its head lazily to peer at him for just a moment and then laid back down. Kade stopped laughing and smiled fondly at the creature. He stepped into the room and patted it affectionately on the head. It sat up, eagerly awaiting its reward for faithfully keeping his books safe. Kade gladly fed the creature and then walked out of the room to continue down the hall to the back of the cabin.

Darcienna watched as the family melted into the house. She tried to smile, but for the first time in days, the smile slipped. True, she was excited about the child, and happy that Kade finally knew the truth about Marcole, but that was not enough. She was also relieved more than words could describe that Morg was finally beaten, but none of that could help get rid of the dread she felt building in her heart as she looked off in the distance. She closed her eyes and saw the dream once more. It was so vivid that she shivered right down to her very soul. The scene of Kade drifting on the other side of the arch was so clear, it was as if she had seen it while awake. Her pulse raced as she studied the vision. No matter how much she tried to convince herself that it was nothing, she knew this was no ordinary dream. She could take it no longer as her eyes flew open. She took several deep breaths to steady her nerves. A single tear slipped down her cheek. She wiped it away furiously as she ground her teeth in defiance. She did her best to put the smile back on her face. It was a struggle, but for him, the man she loved, she had to. He had already gone through too much for her to burden him with this just yet. When the time was right, she would tell him. With one last glance over her shoulder in the direction of the arch, she turned and walked into the house.

THE DIVINE SERIES
CONTINUES

LOOK FOR THE
NEXT BOOK TO BE
RELEASED OCTOBER 27, 2014

ABOUT THE AUTHOR

Allen Johnston is a resident in Lansing, MI. His wife, Amber, keeps life fun and interesting for him. They share four children. He loves aviation and works as an Air Traffic Controller at the Capital City of Michigan. He lives by the motto that anything is possible. When considering learning to fly, he was told that it is not possible to achieve a pilot's license in less than a month by his supervisor, who was also an instructor pilot. Needless to say, he proved that the impossible was, indeed, possible.

Allen loves to interact with his readers. He encourages everyone to send him a message from his website, www.AllenJJohnston.com or go to his Facebook page and comment there.